FANTASTICAL

Discover other titles by Kristen Ashley at:
www.kristenashley.net

Commune with Kristen at:
www.facebook.com/kristenashleybooks
Twitter: KristenAshley68
Instagram: KristenAshleyBooks
Pinterest: kashley0155

FANTASTICAL

Kristen Ashley

First ebook edition: November 2011
Latest ebook edition: January 2016
First print edition: January 2016

ISBN-10: 0692619356

ISBN-13: 9780692619353

DEDICATION

~

This book is dedicated to the memory of Sarah
Ellene Glossop Mahan, my grandmother,
who would clean a cave because, she told me, only stupid people get bored.

That said, she'd have more fun dancing in the streets.
And she'd do that too.
Definitely.

1

Holy Crap

~

I heard birds.

They were singing. Not chirping. Singing. It wasn't birdsong. It was just plain old song but in chirps. It was hard to describe but there it was.

A lot of it.

It made me open my eyes.

Then I blinked and felt it. I was lying in a bed but not my bed. The mattress was strange, very soft, very plush. I wasn't on it. I was *in* it. It partially enveloped my body like a warm, comfortable, squashy cloud.

What on earth?

I stared at the sun-washed walls, felt the bed and heard the strange birdsong.

One thing I knew for certain. I was not home.

I shot straight to sitting in the bed and looked around the room.

I was in a four-poster bed, gossamer, pale-lilac curtains all around, a fluffy pale-lilac-covered duvet on top. The walls of the room were an even paler lilac and I looked around at the bizarre white furniture.

A big wardrobe with scrolled feet, the sides bowed in, the top an arch. It was bulky and yet delicate. A miracle of construction. There was no way that wardrobe could stand on those flimsy, curled feet, but it was.

Two tall dressers. One that zigged at the top, zagged in the middle and zigged again at the bottom. Another whose drawers went up like steps on one side, a different miracle of construction for it appeared to be teetering yet stood true.

Then there was a dressing table with a big oval mirror on the top and two smaller ones to its side. The dressing table was also delicate with curly whirls for legs, around the mirrors and carved into the three drawers down either side. It was covered in fragile, intricate glass bottles, all of them in various shades of purple.

"Holy crap, I'm dreaming," I whispered.

That had to be it. I was dreaming. Dreaming the most freaking real dream I had ever had in my life.

Suddenly, the door flew open.

I jumped and looked to my right to see a blonde woman dance into the room wearing an old-fashioned blinding-white nightgown, the voluminous kind that had a string at the neckline and gathers all around.

Yeesh, how did she get that nightgown so white? I was never good at keeping whites white. They always grayed out.

It had to be new.

Oh wait, this was a dream. Of course it would be that white.

"Cora!" she cried my name, whirling into the room. "Cora, Cora, Cora! Today is the best day *of my life*!"

She stopped at the foot of the bed, shoved a diaphanous curtain aside and smiled down at me while I stared up at her.

Whoa.

Seriously.

She was gorgeous. Bright-blue eyes. Thick blonde hair. Delicate features. Petite. A stunner.

"Can you believe it?" she asked then clapped her hands. "I'm getting married today!"

"Uh..." I started but she rocked swiftly up to her toes and then danced gracefully on them to one of the two sets of French doors that were on either side of the dressing table.

She flung them open, the birdsong stopped, she stepped out on a Juliet balcony and threw her arms up and out to the sides.

In position, she let out two beautiful, perfect notes in a gorgeous soprano. The birdsong started again, in earnest this time (and I thought it was earnest before) and I blinked through the sheer curtains as I saw a tiny colorful bird (and I knew there were colorful birds in the world but there weren't birds *that* colorful) alight on her outstretched hand.

She brought the bird to her face and the bird chirped gaily at her instead of flying away.

"I'm getting married to the man I love today, Aggie! Isn't that *marvelous?*" she told the bird.

The bird chirped happily at her and then pecked her nose. Not like a peck, more like a kiss.

She giggled and it, too, sounded like a happy song.

Whoa!

I blinked.

That was when I knew.

I was dreaming I was in one of those animated movies.

Wow.

Cool! What an awesome dream!

She turned and the bird hopped up to her shoulder and somehow kept its place as she danced on her toes back to the bed with more grace than any human I'd ever seen. Then again, seeing as she was part of a dream, she could be as graceful as any character in an animated movie that my mind could make up.

She threw the side curtains aside and ordered merrily, "Get up, silly! We have to get ready! So much to do, so much to do! Tra la! Tra la, la, la, la! Tra, la, la, *la*, *la*!"

She emitted the tra las in her gorgeous voice while whirling toward the door and the bird fluttered off her shoulder onto the bed as she did so. Then it hopped to me, looked in my eyes and chirped.

God, I swear I knew that the bird was saying, "Heya."

Holy crap.

"Heya," I whispered to the bird.

That was when I could swear the bird's eyes lit up with a smile.

Holy crap!

"Up, Cora, you can't be lazy today! I stayed with you to make certain you got up and got ready in plenty of time. As my matron of honor, you have to be nearly as beautiful as me!" the girl called from the door then threw her shining, golden-blonde mane back and laughed a sing-song laugh before she tipped her head back down and smiled a stunning smile at me. "Not that *that* will be hard, my exquisite sister."

She clapped her hands with delight again and exited the door, closing it behind her.

I stared at the door. Then I looked back down at the bird who was still looking up at me.

"This is a way cool dream," I told the bird and it tipped its head to the side like my words were confusing.

It took two hops so it was sitting on my thigh.

Awesome!

Then it said, "Chirp chirp," which I took to mean, "You aren't dreaming."

"I am so totally dreaming," I told the bird.

The bird replied, "Chirp, chirp, chirpity, chirp," which came to me as chirps but I knew meant, "No, really, this isn't a dream, Cora."

"It's a dream, bird. I know this first off because people don't talk to birds, or at least know what they're saying. Unless, of course, they're bonkers," I returned.

The bird tilted its head again and then chirped, "Chirp, chirp, chirp, chirp," (with a bunch more chirps) which meant, "Are you ill? Of course people talk to birds. And bunnies. And deer. And mice. And my name is Agglethorpe. You and everyone call me Aggie."

"There it is," I told the bird. "Your name is Agglethorpe. That's a perfectly ludicrous name that only could be given to a bird in a dream or a Disney movie."

That was when the bird hopped forward and pecked my hand, which kind of hurt, and then looked up at me and chirped what I took to mean, "My name isn't ludicrous! I know this because *you* gave it to me!"

But I was staring at my hand where the bird, or Aggie, had pecked.

That peck had kind of hurt.

What?

You weren't supposed to feel pain in dreams, were you?

At that point I heard a noise I'd never heard in real life before. The kind of noise you hear in movies when horse's hooves are beating on cobblestones or the members of Monty Python were cracking together coconuts. Aggie flew up and to the window to alight on the balustrade of the Juliet balcony.

It looked down then it started hopping up and down as it turned its head toward me and started chirping madly, telling me, "Come quick, Cora! Oh no! Come quick! Dashiell is here! With Orlando and..." the bird looked back down then urgently to me, chirping in a dire chirp (yes, seriously, a *dire* chirp), "*Noctorno!*"

Something about the bird's demeanor made me throw the covers back, struggle out of the bed (seriously, feather beds were awesome but hard as hell to get out of) and rush (not gracefully nor dancing on my toes, I was pretty certain) to the balcony as Aggie kept chirping at me.

"This can't be. Dashiell can't see Rosa! Not before the wedding! If he does..."

I made it to the balcony and looked down to see that indeed three horses were in the courtyard.

But I lost my sense of urgency when I saw the courtyard, its cobbles sun-warmed, gleaming clean and blond. It was flanked by fountains, their waters blinking brilliantly in the bright sunlight. There were also an abundance of flower beds of every shape and size, ditto with flower pots and hanging planters. There were flowers here, there and everywhere, willy-nilly, on the house, on the cobbles, in the lush, green lawns. The stone of the house itself was nearly covered either in flowering vines or jutting planters with bright petals and dripping greenery.

Wow.

Unbelievable.

It was so beautiful I couldn't breathe.

I looked up and out to see what surrounded the house.

To my right a tall mountain-like hill with a rushing fall of water that pooled in a glinting pond that fed in a thin stream to a river at the opposite side. To the front beyond the manicured lawn, a dark green, thriving forest as far as the eye could see. To the left, a winding river so clear you could see the rocks on its bed even from a distance.

God, my mind made up some seriously cool shit.

"*Cora!*" Aggie shrieked through a chirp.

I looked down at him, still slightly dazed from the spectacle before me.

"What?" I asked.

He twitched his bird head to the courtyard and I looked back down to see the three horses with the three riders again. They finally got my attention because they, too, looked magnificent. Just the horses were magnificent but the riders. Yowza. I couldn't see faces but those powerful thighs.

Um...*yum*!

I noted one horse was white, one was gray and one was black.

The white horse's rider was wearing a white hat with a fluffy scarlet feather flowing along its side and around its back. He was also wearing a scarlet vest over one of those shirts with puffy sleeves. His shirt was white. With this, he was wearing biscuit-colored breeches and dark-brown boots.

The gray horse's rider was wearing a gray hat with fluffy deep-blue feather flowing along its side and around its back. He was wearing a deep-blue vest over a dove-gray puffy-sleeved shirt, charcoal-gray breeches and matching boots.

The black horse's rider was wearing all black. Black hat. Black puffy shirt. Black boots. No vest. No feather.

Hmm.

Interesting.

I further noted the black rider had the most powerful thighs of the three.

Hmm.

Very interesting.

"Cora!" Aggie chirped.

"What?" I asked loudly and then I felt it.

Three sets of eyes on me.

I looked back down at the riders in the courtyard to see all three looking up at me.

Uh…*whoa*!

Holy…freaking…*crap*!

Those guys were *hot*!

The white-hatted guy was blond, blue-eyed and g-o-r-g-e-o-u-s, *gorgeous*. The gray-hatted guy had dark-brown hair with a hint of burnish, brown eyes and he was h-a-n-d-s-o-m-e, *handsome*.

And the black-hatted guy had black hair, longer than the other two, very tanned skin, much tanner than the other two (who were nicely tanned, might I add), his features were sharper, leaner, stronger but in all his darkness, clothes, skin, hair, he had light-blue eyes. Very light-blue eyes.

Oh, and he was h-a-w-t, *hawt*.

And the hottest thing about him was that he had a scar curving from his temple down his cheekbone.

Ultra hot.

Wow.

Yum!

How was it that I was thirty-two years old and I'd never had this good of a dream? It wasn't fair. This dream *rocked*!

"Heya," I called to the hot guys.

"Cora, the exquisite," the white-hatted guy called back, a blinding-white smile on his full lips, and I liked what he called me. It was freaking *awesome*.

"That's me, Cora the exquisite," I agreed, smiling back.

"Cora!" Aggie chirped desperately, hopping around frantically.

"*What?*" I snapped at Aggie then went on, "Quit chirping at me, you crazy bird. I'm talking to the hot guys."

"You're barely dressed," a hard, rough, deep, almost impossibly sexy voice came at me and I looked back down at the men. "Go inside, woman, for all the gods' sakes, and cover yourself."

It was the black-hatted man.

I looked down at myself to see I was wearing the same nightgown as the woman who had danced and tra la'ed through my room. It was the most material I'd worn to bed in my life. Hell, it was the most material I'd worn anywhere in my life.

My eyes went to the black-hatted man. "Dude, I've got about seven thousand yards of material on up here. I'm hardly barely dressed," I told him.

I watched his brows shoot together giving him a decidedly ominous (yet mesmerizing and definitely totally sexy) look and then his eyes left me and his head turned to look at the white-hatted guy who had also tipped his chin down and was looking back at him.

The gray-hatted guy was looking up at me.

"Are you well, Cora?" he called. "This is not a man named, 'Dude.' As you well know, this man is named Noctorno."

Oh dear. That wasn't a great name. Why couldn't he have been Dashiell? Dashiell was a cool name. You could shorten it to Dash, and Dash was a supercool name.

Oh well. It didn't matter. Usually with any good dream I had, I always woke up before the really good part. I just hoped I got to at least kiss one of them. I didn't care which. My first choice was Noctorno (regardless of his name). My second was the dark-brown-haired one mainly because I wasn't all that big on the white-hatted guy's use of red as an accent color.

"I'm perfectly fine," I answered. "Thanks for asking," I added as an afterthought because it was important to be polite, even in a dream.

The gray-hatted guy smiled a weirdly surprised smile but Noctorno spoke again.

"If you're well then you're well enough to walk into your room and don proper clothing," he informed me.

Dream or not, this dude was way too bossy.

And, might I add, a bit of a prude.

I put a hand on my hip and felt my eyes narrow. "What's your gig? It's not like I'm flashing you."

"Gig?" the gray-hatted guy asked the white-hatted guy.

The white-hatted guy shrugged and asked, "Flashing?"

Noctorno ignored both of them and growled, "Go inside and dress."

"Make me," I snapped back, bending over the balustrade.

Uh-oh.

Mistake.

I knew this because he scowled at me for approximately half a second then his lips curled into a supremely sexy, supremely scary, definitely wicked smile.

And, honest to God, dream or no, I felt that smile *all over*.

Yowza!

He straightened in his saddle like he was going to dismount his glossy, muscled black beast but he stopped when the white-hatted guy said in a low voice, "Tor."

Mm.

That was better. Noctorno was not a good name. But I could work with Tor.

At this point two things happened.

Aggie flitted up into my line of sight and chirped loudly at me, "*Cora!*"

And the second was the door was flung open in the room behind me and the blonde woman came rushing into the room, shouting excitedly, "Is that Dash?"

See!

Totally told you that you could shorten his name to Dash and it would be cool.

"No!" I heard a male shout from below and I looked down in confusion to see the men wheeling their horses around with what appeared to be sudden urgency. "Don't let her see me, Cora!"

It was the white-hatted man. I knew when he continued talking.

"Don't!" Aggie chirped, flying around my body in agitation. "Don't let her see him!"

"Dash!" the blonde woman yelled from inside the room. She was run-dancing to the door.

"Holy crap, what's going—?" I started.

"*Hee-yah!*" Noctorno barked, slapping his hand hard on the white horse's rump. So hard, the sound of the crack of it hurt *my* behind and the white horse took off running.

"Gods! Don't let her—!" This was the voice of the gray-hatted man.

But it came the second the blonde woman reached the balcony and shouted, "Dash! My love!"

"*No!*" the white-hatted man's horse had started galloping away but he swung it around, shouting deep and imperative and started galloping back.

But I was only paying scant attention.

That was because the minute the blonde hit the balcony and shouted her words, everything changed.

Just like that.

Snap.

One second, the flowers were bright, the sun was shining, the day was beautiful.

The very next second, the skies were dark and a pall was cast on the house, the flowers, the mountain-hill, the forest and the river. All that was once vibrant and breathtaking was now shrouded in darkness and gray.

And what made matters worse was that in the very instant the darkness fell, thunder rent the air so loud and eerie I—who had never in my life been frightened of thunder—was instantly terrified (the immediate change of my surroundings helped). Lightning cracked through the sky, multiple flashes coming so fast it was like a strobe.

"Holy crap," I whispered. "What on earth?"

"Cora," the blonde whispered. "What on earth?"

Trust me to have a cool dream turn to complete shit.

"Tor, Orlando…*go*!" I heard and looked down as the blonde's arms wrapped around me and the wind came up, whipping our hair and our nightgowns so violently, the material of our gowns snapped and cracked, biting into my skin where it hit.

Yes, *biting*.

And that was kind of painful too.

What...on...*earth?*

I held on to the blonde and looked down to see the gray and black horses were riderless and the white-hatted guy, who lost his fancy hat in the wind (by the way), was dismounting.

"Cora! Get her away from the window. Close it tight! Hurry!" he shouted up to us before he darted into the house.

"Now, Cora!" Aggie chirped before his little body was swept away by the power of the wind.

"Aggie!" I yelled, reaching out to him as his little body reeled away. As I watched him go, I knew at once there was no hope to save Aggie so I had to save the blonde. "Come on! Get inside!" I shouted over the wind and thunder, the strobes of lightning flashing eerie on her hair and skin. "Hurry!" I yelled, pushing her inside. "Now!"

I shoved her inside and was stepping over the threshold at the same time reaching for the French doors when I heard it. Over all the noise of the sudden storm, I heard a cackle. An evil, bone-chilling cackle.

I turned and looked over my shoulder into the air outside the balcony, and at what I saw I screamed bloody murder at the top of my lungs.

2
Love Match

~

We were racing through the forest, me and Noctorno on his velvet black steed.

And I knew I was not dreaming.

I knew this because I could *feel* the horse's power pounding beneath me. I could *feel* Noctorno's strong arm clamped around my waist. I could *feel* the heat and solidness of his body. I could *feel* the branches whipping at my face, my hair, my body. I *could* feel the driving, relentless rain beating into my flesh.

I could also hear the ongoing thunder, see the continued lightning, hear the horse's hooves thudding against the forest floor.

And none of this was pleasant.

And all of it was lasting a long, long time.

I didn't know where I was. I had no idea how I'd gotten here. I just knew I was there.

This was not a dream. This was real.

And it was a nightmare.

Lastly, I was fah-ree-king *terrified*.

"*Duck!*" Noctorno barked in my ear but he didn't give me the chance to duck. His muscular chest pressed into my back, pushing me down, and I heard a branch whip over our heads.

He lifted up, taking me with him but I closed my eyes.

And I saw that…that…*thing* sweeping away the blonde again.

I opened my eyes and bit my lip hard in an attempt not to cry.

One of those things almost got me. If Noctorno hadn't made it to the bedroom and caught me about the waist, pulling me back at the same time yanking a blade out of his belt and slashing at it causing blue sparks to fly out of it rather than blood, I would be gone like the blonde.

Gone over the side of the balustrade even though the gray-hatted man (otherwise known as Orlando) tried to hold on to her as Noctorno was busy struggling against my attacker.

But she didn't fall to the cobbles. She flew through the air, held by one of those *things*.

And then she disappeared.

Poof!

The white-hatted man, the man known as Dashiell, was too late and he stood on the balcony and shouted his heart-wrenching fury, but Noctorno didn't watch. He battled the monster that had hold of me until it yelped and slithered away so fast it was almost like it wasn't ever there.

"Safety!" Orlando had shouted at Noctorno, already running out of the room, pulling Dashiell with him. "Get her to safety. The curse is upon us and no matter how you feel about her, Tor, they want her too!"

"Gods, man, I *know*!" Noctorno shouted back and carried me bodily out of the room after them, down the hall, down the stairs and out the front door where he threw me up on his horse, swung up behind me and away we went.

But I couldn't think of that. It was too horrific. It was too frightening.

I had to concentrate on not crying, not trembling even though I was wet through and only wearing that damned thin nightgown. I had to try and figure out how one night I went to bed in my not-very-fabulous apartment after a day of my not-very-fabulous life only to wake up in another *fucking* world!

I mean, I was an administrative assistant! How did I end up on a horse, in a forest, in a hellacious thunderstorm with a man wearing breeches, for God's sake?

As I struggled with these thoughts, the horse drove ever onward and we rode silently through the forest as the rain pummeled our skin.

Abruptly Noctorno turned the animal and we started climbing the mountain-hill. Except here it was less of a hill and more of a mountain. The terrain was part scrub, part trees and part rock. We climbed and climbed, the horse laboring with the effort and our weight but it seemed to know where it was going.

Then suddenly, we were in a big cave.

And just as suddenly, Noctorno was off his horse and his huge hands were at my waist and he was yanking me down.

Yes, *yanking* me down. He didn't take any care at all, and I yelped in surprise and pain as the cold stiffness of my limbs uncurled and my bare feet hit the shards of stone that was the cave floor.

Once I was down, he grabbed on to my upper arms and shook me.

Shook me!

My head snapped back and forth and everything!

"*What are you doing?*" I screeched, grabbing on to his (steely, might I add) biceps to try to get him to stop and to try to hold myself steady.

He stopped shaking me and his dark face came to within an inch of mine.

"How could you be such a fool?" he barked and I shrunk away from the fury in his voice and on his face.

"Wh-what?"

"You knew she wasn't supposed to see him on her wedding day," he clipped, his strong fingers still gripping me tightly.

"How's she supposed to marry him if she doesn't see—?" I started.

"*Prior!*" he spat on another shake.

"Stop shaking me!" I yelled and he did, only to get in my face again.

"You knew it'd bring on the curse," he growled. "You knew and you just stood there—"

I interrupted him with, "I didn't know!" and his scowl grew more ferocious. "I didn't!" I yelled. "I'm an administrative assistant! I don't know anything."

His brows knitted dangerously over narrowed eyes. "You knew, Cora, you *knew*."

"I didn't!" I snapped. "And anyway, if he wasn't supposed to see her, why did you all come riding up all fancied up in feathers and shit on the wedding day? *That* wasn't too smart."

"She wasn't supposed to be there, you know that," he fired back.

I blinked. "She wasn't?"

"No," he gritted between his teeth, releasing me, and I stumbled back and hit his horse who moved slightly into me like it wanted to break my fall. And if that was what it wanted, the horse got it for I didn't fall. "She was to sleep at your parents' and *we* were there to get your lazy arse out of bed. *Rosa* was not supposed to be *at your home*."

Hmm.

I wasn't really fond of being known as lazy in this world. Sure, I could procrastinate with the best of them but I wouldn't describe myself as lazy.

"But—" I began.

"And if she *was* there, which *you* knew she was, *you* should have kept her from seeing Dash. But you didn't. You just stood there, gabbing at us like a fool. You didn't warn us she was there and when she arrived, you let her see him. *You* know the curse. *She* did not."

That sounded ridiculous.

"Why did I know and she didn't? That's ridiculous," I informed him.

He glared at me a moment before he asked quietly, "What's the matter with you? Have you gone mad?"

"I don't think so," I replied because I wasn't certain. Everything around me felt mad but I didn't feel mad.

Then again, I'd never been mad. How would I know?

Something about him changed and I watched it with fascination. He wasn't any less scary; he was only a different kind.

"We're not a love match, we both know this, but I would never have suspected you'd do that to your sister," he said softly.

"We...we..." I couldn't finish.

A love match? What was he talking about?

"You care for her, deeply, or so I thought. And if you didn't care about her," his face got hard, "we both know you care for Dash."

Uh. *What?*

He kept talking. "Your feelings for them, my feelings for them, *that* was why we wed in the first place."

Uh. *What?*

"Wed?" I whispered.

He glowered at me then warned, "Don't try me, Cora."

"We're...we're...you and me...we're...*married?*"

He leaned his face into mine again and growled, "Don't try me, Cora."

Holy crap!

I was married to this guy?

"So...uh, where were you last night?" I asked what I thought was a pertinent question, considering he was my husband and I woke up alone, and his face got even harder.

"You're trying me," he stated.

Oh dear. I was trying him.

Damn.

I studied him. He was a big guy. Very big. Very tall. Very broad. He wore black. All black. He had a scar. His horse was enormous and powerful. He carried a knife on his belt. He scared me just the way he could look at me and he had no problem with shaking me so my head snapped around.

I was thinking I didn't want to mess with this guy.

I was also thinking that maybe I shouldn't tell him that I was actually not his wife but a single girl who worked for an ad agency and lived in Seattle. I was thinking that wouldn't go down too well.

The problem was, I was in a fantasyland, he was the only human being around me, I needed him to talk to me. I needed him to get where I was coming from, which was definitely not here, and I didn't know what to tell him.

What I did know was that it appeared he didn't like me too much and so I figured my best bet was not telling him anything at all.

Which meant I was screwed.

Damn!

"I-I think I need a minute to, uh...get my head straight," I told him the God's honest truth.

We were just inside the mouth of the cave and the storm and trees outside meant the light coming in was dim. But I saw his hard, glittering, dark eyes examine me, traveling down my body. They stopped midway and his jaw clenched.

I looked down to see the thin material of the nightgown, no matter that there was a lot of it, had gone see-through. I was, luckily, wearing a pair of what looked like loose, white shorts, but up top there was nothing left to the imagination.

Double damn!

I grabbed fistfuls of the material in both hands, pulled it around my breasts and looked back at his face to see his eyes shoot to mine.

"Uh—" I started but stopped when he took a step forward while dipping his shoulder. Then that shoulder was in my stomach and I was up. I grabbed on to his shirt at the back and shouted, "What are you doing?"

"Quiet," he commanded.

I yanked on his shirt and kicked my feet. "Put me down!" I yelled, panicked and wondering what he was going to do next but thinking I wasn't going to like it.

I wasn't wrong.

I felt the crack of his hand on my ass. It sounded nearly as loud as when he slapped the rump of Dashiell's horse but since he did it to me, it hurt...a *lot*.

"Quiet," he growled but I had already quieted.

He hit me. He hit me, he yanked me off his horse, he shook me, he ordered me around, he called me lazy, and I will repeat, he hit me. So hard it hurt. A lot.

I didn't like this guy. Not at all.

I felt the stinging in my nostrils that heralded tears.

Oh man, I needed to get home.

3

Pure You

~

He walked me deeper into the cave, not far but where he took me was damper and darker.

Then he bent at the waist to drop me and my hands automatically circled his neck because I didn't want to go down hard on the shards of stone and he'd drop me hard, I knew it.

Surprisingly, I needn't have done this for his arms curved around my thighs and waist to lighten the fall and what he put me on was soft.

"You've gained weight," he grunted as he was straightening away from me.

Great. Just great. In this world I was fat. Marvelous.

"I've got to see to Salem, get wood, find food. I'll be back," he informed me then with no further ado, he turned and left.

I lay on whatever I was on and looked at the dim opening to the space that he'd disappeared through. I heard the horse heave a mighty, shuddering breath through his horse lips and decided that was his greeting to his master.

My mind was blank. So blank, I had not one thought by the time he came back. I heard what sounded like wood crashing to the cave floor then he left again without looking at me. He came back three more times and there were three more wood-crashing noises. Then he moved around, I heard more wood banging together, saw the strike of rock against rock and there was a weak fire. He moved to the wall of the cave, pulled something down and went back to the fire. I watched him light a torch then take it back to the wall and affix it to something. He did this four more times and the torches, with the fire, meant the space was better lit. It wasn't exactly blazing light you could read by but at least you could see.

And I saw that I was on hides, lots of them. That was when I realized I was trembling violently. I rolled, pulled a hide out, saw that under the top, dark hide there was a bed of what looked like fluffy, cream sheepskins. I crawled in and pulled the top hide over me and up high, wrapping its heavy weight clumsily around me as best I could.

When my eyes went back to him, I saw he was standing with hands on hips, watching me and he didn't look any happier than he had before. In fact, he looked downright peeved and maybe a bit disgusted.

I pressed my lips together because he freaked me right the hell out.

"Now, food," he grunted. "If you have it in you, don't let the fire go out. Keep feeding it. This would, of course, require you to move. Try it, you might not find it that hard."

Again with the lazy comments. What a jerk.

He turned, went to the mouth of the space, unhooked something I hadn't noticed before and another heavy, wide hide fell into place behind him, covering the opening to the space and closing me in as I heard his muted boots hit the loose stone outside indicating he was walking away.

I took in a shaky breath and pulled my wet hair out of my face.

"Okay, okay…think," I whispered as I looked around and tried to control my shivers.

The space was small. There looked to be a makeshift table with stuff on it against the wall. There was a pile of the wood he'd brought in on the floor next to the table (lots of wood, apparently he could carry a heavy load or there was some there before). There seemed to be what looked like weapons on the wall, two swords, some others that looked like long knives and other lethal-looking bits and pieces. There was a fire pit in the middle of the space and I tilted my head back to look up to the ceiling and saw a small, natural hole where the smoke could get through. I found this curious, seeing as no rain was coming in and I could still hear the distant thunder. But whatever.

When I got control of my shaking, I pushed the hides back and decided to explore. I noted the stone floor in this space was smooth, not the loose rock of the outer area. I went to the mouth of the space first and touched the hides. Cow,

I would guess. A bunch of them stitched together to make a panel wide enough to cover the opening.

After this, I went to the table and saw a pile of animal bones on the floor beside the table. Obviously, this space was well-utilized and although it was unhygienic, not discarding the bones, at least the pile indicated Noctorno was tidy.

The table had a bunch of stuff on top and a shelf under it. The stuff on top included a long-handled frying pan, what looked like a rough, rudimentary coffeepot or kettle, a tin (which I picked up, opened, sniffed and happily smelled the strong aroma of coffee grounds), a jug (upon sniffing, I noted was water), a bottle (sniff test, whisky), a cup, a bowl and a spoon, fork and knife.

The shelf under it held a bunch of iron rods, their use I didn't know.

I wandered around but except for the hides on the floor (which, upon closer inspection, I saw were also stitched together and the sheepskins were lying on a bed of long, dried grass which was another reason why the whole thing was so soft) there was nothing else to discover in the room.

I walked to the fire and stood beside it, as close as I dared, and held out my nightgown in an attempt to dry it.

"Right...now...what do I do?" I whispered, moving front to back, side to side by the fire shaking my nightgown and thinking.

I went to sleep at home. I woke up here.

Maybe I should go to sleep and I'd wake up at home.

The problem was, I was far from sleepy.

I'm getting married to the man I love today, Aggie! Isn't that marvelous?

Rosa's happy voice entered my head and I closed my eyes tight.

I'd fucked up. Big time. Of course, I had no way of knowing it. But those around me, including Noctorno, Orlando and her beloved Dashiell (not to mention Aggie, who I hoped was okay) didn't know that.

And now Rosa was gone. Disappeared with one of those *things*.

I shook my head, opened my eyes and walked to the wood. Grabbing a stick, I moved back to the fire pit and carefully placed the split log on it while talking to myself.

"Don't think of that. Don't think of Rosa, of Aggie, of Dashiell. Think of how to get home. Think of how to get the hell out of here."

I went back to the hides and tucked myself in, staring at the fire and thinking.

What could I have done? How did I get here?

I sifted through recent memories and all I knew about how this kind of shit happened in the movies.

I had not made a wish for a fairytale life from a weird fortune teller vending machine at a creepy magic store. In fact, I'd never been to a creepy magic store mainly because they were creepy.

I had not accidentally bumped into, therefore ticked off, anyone strange-looking, like a magician with white gloves and a top hat or a gypsy with long hair and flowing, jangly skirts.

I had not happened onto any object, say a magic vase or an enchanted crystal, and taken it home.

I had not sat by the light of a full moon on the banks of the Puget Sound and wished for a more exciting life surrounded by angry hot guys and birds that talked.

I hadn't done any of that.

So why was I here? This stuff didn't happen outside of the movies.

And yet it did because here I was, in a cave, in a nightshirt, with no shoes and a hot guy who apparently hated me, who I didn't like all that much either out finding us food.

Time wore on and I kept feeding the fire as I continued not to think of the sweet, singing Rosa being swept away, wondering if Aggie had been hurt, maimed or even worse while getting caught in that wind or contemplating why the Cora of this world married someone she clearly didn't get along with while harboring, it would seem, a crush on her sister's fiancé.

Instead, I wracked my brain to figure out what to do next.

Nothing came to me.

What I did notice was that the wood Noctorno brought in was very dry. It went up like tinder and to keep the fire going I was using a lot of it. Not to mention, he'd been gone a long time.

But the wood was dry. It was also split so someone had prepared it. So he hadn't gone out into the rain and gathered it. And he didn't have to go very far to get it so perhaps there was a stash somewhere. And if he was gone much longer, the supply he left me would be gone, the fire would go out and he'd get pissed.

I didn't like him pissed (which seemed to be his only emotion) so I didn't want to make him *more* pissed.

Therefore, since I needed something to do, and I didn't particularly relish freezing to death in this world (or any world for that matter), I decided to see if I could find the wood stash.

It wasn't hard. I pulled aside the hides, noticed the thunder and lightning were gone, as was the driving rain, but the day was still gray, dreary and a persistent drizzle was falling. The mouth of the cave was huge, the preliminary space, though, was wide but not vast. There were two hide-covered antechambers, the one I was in and another one I discovered that was full of split logs, kindling and more weapons—these, lances, knives, daggers, hatchets, hammers, clubs and a couple more swords.

Hmm.

Seeing as his cave was heavily armed, it seemed Noctorno earned that scar through his lifestyle.

Picking my way carefully on my bare feet, five times (with much smaller loads than Noctorno could bear) across the rough surface of the main space of the cave and back, I replenished the wood stock, threw a couple more logs on the fire and climbed back under the hides.

I barely got them settled over me when I heard the snort of a horse and hooves on the stones outside.

Noctorno was home.

Drat.

Not long after, the pelt at the opening was thrown back and Noctorno was there.

I looked at him. He looked at me.

Then he looked at the fire.

His head turned and he looked at the reloaded stash of wood.

His head swung back in my direction and he didn't try to hide his surprise.

Jeez, how lazy was I in this world? Only a moron, or someone really idle, would hang in a dark, damp, cold cave and not keep the fire burning.

Noctorno moved to the fire and I noticed he was carrying something over his shoulder. He swung it around and dropped two small, bloody, skinless carcasses that were hanging on a stick to the stone floor by the fire.

I stared at the carcasses.

Holy crap!

"Are those…*rabbits?*" I asked, sounding as aghast as I was.

He had been moving toward the table but stopped, his gaze sliced back to me and his lip curled.

"My deepest apologies, Cora. I didn't bag your favored venison," he stated sarcastically.

I stared at him in horror.

We were already having Thumper for lunch and he was apologizing that we weren't eating Bambi.

Ick!

I couldn't eat rabbit. And furthermore, I wasn't hungry. Not for rabbit, not for anything.

This was a first. I could always eat. But no way was I eating Thumper.

He continued to the table, grabbed the iron rods from the bottom shelf and moved back to the fire.

As for me, I decided not to share the state of my appetite seeing as he was wet, he looked (still) angry and he'd gone out to kill a couple furry critters so we wouldn't starve to death in a cave. Therefore, I figured I should keep my mouth shut on that score.

He set up the apparatus, which was essentially a rotisserie over the fire, and he set this up with the rabbit carcasses on it. Then he added more logs to the fire. He left and came back (three times) with even more logs to reload the pile.

I guessed this meant we were in it for the long haul.

When he was done with his chores, he crouched by the fire probably for the same reason I stood by it, in order to get warm and use it to dry his clothes.

What he didn't do was speak to me.

What he also didn't do was rotisserie the rabbits. He didn't turn the handle that was at one end of the iron rods at all. That meant one side would get roasted and the other wouldn't. Furthermore, even though they were rabbits, which freaked me out, all their juices were falling into the fire. If they were captured and used to baste the darned things, they would end up more succulent and flavorful.

I decided not to share this culinary expertise with him either.

Instead, I got out from under the hides, went to get the frying pan and then moved to the handle by the fire. I gathered as much of my nightgown as I could in my hand (which was a lot, seriously, there was a huge amount of material covering me), used it to shield my skin against the heat of the rod and squatted as ladylike as I could by the fire while using the handle and holding the pan under the rabbits to collect their juices.

I did this for a while feeling his eyes on me before he spoke.

"By the gods, what are you doing?"

I didn't look at him as I replied, "Rotisserie. You cook them like you were, one side will get charred, the other won't cook. And everyone knows you need to baste meat."

This was met with silence.

I kept turning, and when I gathered enough juices, I lifted the pan and poured them over the meat. Then I held the pan under again as I kept turning the handle.

Truth be told, the actions were tedious, the pan was heavy and my arms were beginning to ache. But at least I had something to do.

After a while, he called, "Cora."

"Yep," I answered, lifted the pan, basted the meat then returned it under the carcasses, all the while turning the handle.

"Cora," he repeated.

"I said, yep," I replied.

"Look at me, woman," he ordered.

I lifted my eyes to him. His face was blank but his eyes were alert and working and they were fastened on me.

"What are you doing?" he asked.

"I told you," I reminded him.

"What are you doing?" he repeated and I felt my brows draw together.

"Dude, I *told* you," I returned.

His face turned cold. "Do not call me this name," he commanded. "I do not like it."

I stared at him.

Then I sighed, looked back to the fire and muttered, "Whatever."

"Cora," he called again and my gaze cut back to his face.

"What?" I snapped.

"Explain yourself," he demanded.

"I already did."

"When did you learn this?" he growled, tipping his dark head to my movements.

Uh-oh.

Lazy Cora of this world clearly did not know how to baste nor would she trouble herself to do it.

Oh well. Never mind.

I shrugged and said, "I heard it somewhere, and if I have to eat rabbit, it might as well taste good."

He studied me then said quietly, "You are strange."

My hand on the handle stopped moving, I glared at him and bit out, "I'm not strange!"

His eyes moved over me and came back to mine before he kept speaking in a soft voice. "You are not you."

Hmm.

What did I do with this?

It was the perfect opener.

The problem was, I was guessing since he had lots of weapons, and none of them were guns, grenades or bazookas, he rode a horse and he didn't have a camp stove but an iron spit, that this world also didn't have movies. So he probably wouldn't respond positively to the fact that the me Cora of my world might have been (a guess) switched with the Cora of this world that he knew.

Then again, they had curses in this world that we didn't have in my world so maybe they had magic. Maybe he'd get it.

"Uh…" I started but couldn't think of what to say.

"It won't work," he told me and I blinked at him.

"What won't work?"

"This change," he stated.

Oh dear.

"Uh, Noc—"

"What you did was unforgiveable," he cut me off and I sucked in both lips and bit them at the harsh look on his face. "I will protect you, keep you safe from harm, keep you alive as I vowed to do as your husband and because your sister holds a place in my heart. But for no other reason. You cannot carry logs and cook meat and make me think you sweet. I know you. I know this is not you. What I also know is that the only energy you will expend is to connive and maneuver to take best care of yourself. Don't make the mistake of thinking me a fool."

I swallowed then began, "I—"

"Planned it from the beginning," he finished for me. "Hunting," he went on, "gave me time to think. You took me because you had no choice but also because you could not have Dash, but it meant you *could* have what I could give you, your home, your life lazy as you like it. But you schemed the whole time knowing that you couldn't have Dash but not wanting Rosa to have him either. So you got what you could from the arrangement but made sure your sister didn't get what she wanted most in this world."

Wow. That hurt.

And, obviously, it was totally untrue.

"That's not true," I whispered.

"I am no fool."

"It isn't true."

"It's pure you."

I held his eyes and he stared into mine, his handsome, scarred face a cold, blank mask.

There was no way I was going to convince him. Apparently, the Cora of this world wasn't all that great.

And I didn't like being her.

This whole thing sucked, like a lot, but now it sucked even more.

I broke eye contact, started turning the handle again and used the gathered juices to baste the rabbits.

I looked at him again when he rose.

"Call me when they're done," he ordered, turned on his boot, strode to the opening, shoved the hides aside and disappeared.

I stared back at the fire and I told myself it was the smoke that made my eyes wet.

But it wasn't.

4

Sleeping Arrangements

~

I ate Thumper.

What sucked was that Thumper didn't taste all that bad.

I ate him because I didn't want to suffer malnutrition before what I hoped fervently would be my happy ending and I was returned to my world.

When I used a knife from the wall to check the meat was done, I called Noctorno. He took the rabbits off the spit, carved them on the table and handed me the bowl full of meat. Then he watched as I ate my portion without a word (except to say, "Thanks," when he handed it to me which got me a heavy scowl indicting Cora of his world wasn't polite either) as he ate his portion, tearing it directly off the spit.

After all that, he disappeared again.

This meant I was left to my unpleasant thoughts and not much else. I'd get up every once in a while to feed the fire but other than that, I had nothing to do.

From the small opening in the ceiling, I could see night had fallen. There wasn't much light outside due to the bleak day but there was none at all when night fell.

I was staring at the opening, half-asleep and hoping when I woke up I'd be back in my bed in my apartment.

I didn't think much of my life before I left it.

Just two months ago I'd broken up with my boyfriend of four years, Brian, because he'd refused to take it to the next level, him telling me he was surprised there *was* a next level.

Why he thought we could date for the rest of our natural born lives was unknown to me. What stunk was, I loved him, I missed him and I wanted him back. He was fun. He was funny. He didn't scowl at me, call me lazy or accuse me of scheming. Sure, the truth was, he *was* lazy, case in point, him thinking that he didn't have to put more effort into a relationship beyond dating. But he was fun to be around, and furthermore, he'd been around for a while. I was used to him.

My job wasn't all that great either. I got paid well because I'd been there for ages but the air was rife with rumors of layoffs, the agency wasn't doing very well, and everyone knew that the people who got paid the most were the first to go. The economy wasn't booming, and even though I had good skills and my boss loved me so would give me a good reference, I'd been at the agency that long because the thing I hated most in the world was job hunting. So I avoided it at all costs even though I was in a nowhere job that didn't challenge me all that much.

And I'd decided just before I broke up with Brian that it was time to get on the property ladder. I was still in the one-bedroom apartment I'd moved into when I was twenty-three. It was dinky, the landlord refused to paint it (so I did, on my dime), the appliances were old, sucked and broke down a lot and my bathroom suite was mustard yellow. I wasn't big on change but I figured it was high time to move on. These plans were stalled firstly because Brian and I broke up and secondly because I wasn't sure I'd be employed for very much longer.

Even with all that, I wanted to go back. It was familiar. In my world, we had cell phones. In my world, we had plumbing. Okay, so the birds weren't as colorful and the landscape wasn't as splendiferous but that only was the case here when a curse hadn't settled on the land.

There were no curses in my world either. Another plus.

And I'd miss my folks. I was an only child (which, if Rosa was my sister here, and she seemed so sweet, it would have been awesome to get to know her better before she was swept away by malevolent creatures) but my parents were way cool. They were a little bizarre, seeing as they were screaming hippies (and I was so far from a hippie as to be not funny, how I sprang from their loins was anyone's guess) but they were awesome.

Not to mention my friends, who were also awesome. It didn't seem Cora of this world was very friendly. Though, Dash seemed to like her.

On this thought, I heard the hides being moved back and looked from the ceiling to the opening to see Noctorno arrive. I watched as he walked to the hides I was in. Then I watched as he lowered his big body to them and pulled off his boots. And I watched as he loosened the laces at his collar. I also watched as he lifted his arms and his long fingers curled into his shirt at the back between his shoulder blades. Finally, I watched him yank it off.

At that, my breath stuck in my lungs.

Holy crap, his back was out-freaking-standing! I didn't know a back had that many muscles. All of them defined, tight and hard.

Yowza!

On this thought, I saw them. Puckered scars. Three of them. One on his right shoulder blade. One along the right ribs of his back. The last along his waist.

This guy was either a regular at bar fights or he was a warrior.

I was guessing with his demeanor, both.

He stood, walked around and doused the torches. He dumped a couple of logs on the fire then I watched in the firelight as he walked back to me.

Whoa!

Freaking hell, his chest was even better (and more scarred).

He also had great chest hair, all dark and sexy. I was not into chest hair, or I wasn't until I saw his. It was not too little, not too much...it was *just right*.

Holy crap!

He bent low, threw back the hides and slid in beside me.

I shot to sitting, screeching, "*What are you doing?*"

"Preparing to sleep," he replied calmly.

"*Here?*" I asked shrilly.

"Yes," he answered, still calm.

"You can't sleep here," I informed him.

This was met with silence. He was on his back. I was on my booty with my torso twisted to look down at him and his eyes were on me.

Then he asked, "Where do you suggest I sleep?"

"I don't know," I replied. "Don't you have a bedroll or something?"

He got up on both elbows and returned, "No, I don't have a bedroll. I left this morning on the errand of getting my brother to a church and dragging your arse out of bed. I didn't come prepared to camp in the wilderness."

Hmm.

Of course he was right.

"Maybe you can take some hides and make a bed on the other side of the fire," I suggested.

"And maybe you can do that," he retorted. "I'm sleeping here."

He lay back down and yanked at the covers, which made me teeter as they pulled against me. I held firm and continued glaring at him.

"I'm not sleeping with you," I declared.

"As you know, I'm perfectly fine with that. The one time I took you to my bed, it was vastly unpleasant. I'm not yearning for another go."

I blinked and when I opened my eyes, I knew they were huge. "We've slept together?"

I knew this was likely a crazy question, seeing as we were married.

But still.

He got up on his elbows again and scowled at me, "Why do you persist in this foolishness?"

I didn't reply to his question, I was on a mission so I repeated, "We've slept together?"

He glared at me before he sighed and stated, "I'll play," on a mumble and continued, "We have, indeed, slept together. As you know, because you were bloody there, after our wedding we consummated the union. To say you were the worst I ever had would be to utter the definition of an understatement. You, Cora, are undoubtedly the worst *any* man could ever have."

Oh God.

He went on, "Then you spent the night in my bed. You snored," he paused before he carried on, "*Loudly*. Then you kept stealing the covers, moved around an inordinate amount and took up most of the bed. I endured it but never wished to repeat it. However, we're here. This is the only place to sleep. I'm sleeping here, with you, if I must. If you prefer to move across the way, be my guest."

Okay, there was a lot to consider there. First was the fact that he was my husband and he'd only had sex with me once, it didn't go well (to say the least) and he'd only slept with me in his bed once. Second was the fact that I was getting the sense we didn't live together which wasn't surprising to me since he was a jerk and he obviously didn't like the Cora of this world. Third was that Cora of this world was way not like me. I didn't snore and I slept like the dead, usually in a fetal position, waking up in the same spot as I fell asleep. Last was the fact that I didn't exactly know how to separate the hides so we both had our fair share considering they were stitched together.

It came to me.

"Okay, how about this," I started. "I take the sheepskins with me, you get the top hide and the grassy stuff."

"No, you want to move, you get the cowhide on top."

So that was cow.

Interesting.

"That isn't fair," I informed him. "The sheepskins are fluffier."

"I know," he replied.

Jerk!

"But you get the grassy stuff!" I snapped.

"I get that too."

I clenched my teeth. Noctorno was silent.

"You're a jerk!" I told him.

"Pardon?"

"A jerk!" I clipped, twisted further to him and jabbed a finger in his direction, "You! Jerk!"

"Jerk?" he asked.

"Argh!" I groaned, understanding they didn't have that term here and deciding against educating him. I made another decision and flopped on my back on the skins. "Fine, whatever, we'll sleep together. You just stick to your side and don't touch me."

"I'll stick to my side but you need to stick to yours."

"No problem," I hissed.

"Rubbish," he muttered.

"Whatever," I snapped, yanking the hides to my chin then turning to my side away from him and curling my knees into my belly.

"You kick me, steal the hides or snore, I'm moving you and the top hide across the way myself," he said to my back.

I closed my eyes and warned, "You touch me, I'll kick you so hard in the balls you'll kiss any hope of children good-bye."

"I did that a long time ago," he mumbled and I swiftly rolled to face him.

"Do you have to have the last word?" I snapped.

"Yes," he returned.

"Jerk," I gritted out.

"Cow," he returned.

Oh my God! He just called me a cow!

"I hate you," I spat.

"That feeling, my love, is mutual," he retorted.

"Ugh!" I grunted, glared into his face and rolled away from him again.

There was quiet as I watched the firelight dance on the cave wall in front of me.

Then he called, "Cora."

"What?" I snapped.

"You're welcome for dinner and saving your arse from the vickrants."

Vickrants?

What the hell were those?

Probably they were those *things*.

Shit.

He had gone out in a thunderstorm to get dinner and he had battled, rather mightily and with great skill and energy, that *thing* that had me, saving me from disappearing like poor Rosa.

Shit!

I gritted my teeth. I then sucked in breath through my nostrils.

Finally, I whispered, "Thank you, Noctorno, for dinner and saving me from the vickrants."

I didn't want to say it but that didn't mean it didn't have to be said.

"Bloody hell," he whispered back, his voice low and heavy with surprise.

Whatever.

I closed my eyes knowing I'd never get to sleep but hoping I did and when I woke up I would be at home.

5

TERMS

~

They had me.

The black, scaly claws were on me, grasping at me, their talons tearing at my nightgown while the thin, veined wings flapped sickeningly. It was pulling me away, pulling me over the balustrade behind Rosa and I could hear her shrill, terrified screams mingled with my own.

I jolted awake and bolted out from under the hides. Darting blindly, I ran into the cold, hard stone wall.

"Cora." I heard.

"Oh my God," I whispered, pressing myself to the hard stone.

I wasn't home. Why couldn't I have woken up at home?

I closed my eyes and felt the tears slide down my cheeks.

"Cora." I heard again and a warm hand was on the small of my back.

"They almost got me," I whispered.

"Cora."

"They got Rosa."

"Come back to bed."

"They took her."

"Cora, come back to bed."

"They flew away with her and then, *poof*, she was gone."

"You're trembling. Come back to bed."

"Just like that," I whispered, my nails clawing at the stone. "She was gone."

"Cora—"

Noctorno stopped speaking when my breath hitched loudly with a sob.

"Bloody hell," he muttered then he picked me up.

I slid my arms around his shoulders and shoved my face in his neck as he carried me back to the hides.

"I wanna go home," I snuffled into his neck.

"You can't," he told me as he went down to a knee and placed me on the hides. But I didn't let go of his neck, in fact I clutched him tighter.

"I don't like it here," I told him, my voice held tremors, the tears kept falling.

"Orlando will be working to—"

I cut him off by wailing, "I ate Thumper!"

I shoved my face further into his neck and arched into his body.

"Thumper?"

I yanked my face out of his neck and stared at him. "A furry bunny! I ate bunny! Bunnies are cute! You don't *eat* them!" I cried then pushed my face into his neck, tightened my arms around his shoulders and pressed my body to the solid heat of his.

"Bloody hell," he muttered, his arms sliding around me as he settled on his side in the hides, his body facing mine, mine pressed tight to his, his arms staying around me.

"I wanna go home."

"Let Orlando do his work."

"I don't like it here," I repeated.

"Cora, calm yourself," he ordered on a squeeze of his arms.

This was good advice and I tried. I took heavy, broken breaths and closed my eyes tight. It took a while, and along with the tears it exhausted me, so when my sobbing subsided I was tuckered out.

But I didn't let him go. He was real. He was warm. He was strong. He saved me from that *thing*. He fed me. He took me someplace safe, dry and warm(ish). He was a jerk, he hated me, but he was taking care of me. In this strange land, if I didn't have him, I would be royally screwed (more than I already was, that was).

"Thank you for taking care of me," I whispered, pushing closer to his body.

That body got tight.

"But I don't want to eat bunny anymore." I was still whispering.

"Fine, Cora, I'll not hunt *bunny* anymore," he sounded slightly amused, slightly surprised and slightly annoyed, a strange combination that worked for him. "Go to sleep," he said on another squeeze of his arms.

I pulled in another breath and sleep came closer.

Then I mumbled, "Pray God, those *things* don't harm her."

His body again got tight.

"Pray God," I repeated softly.

"Sleep," his voice rumbled the order.

"She tra la'ed and danced on her toes. Anyone who tra las and dances on their toes shouldn't be harmed, even by those *things*. No, *especially* by those *things*."

"Cora, what did I say?"

I fell silent.

On the edge of sleep, I whispered so low it was barely audible, "I hope Aggie's okay."

I felt his arms squeeze one last time before I was dead to the world.

I woke feeling *great*.

This feeling didn't last long because the next feeling that assaulted me was the knowledge that my body was wrapped around the long, hard one of Noctorno. He was on his back. I was nearly on top of him, my thigh thrown over both of his, my head on his chest, my arm tight around him.

To make matters worse, both his arms were around me too.

Holy crap.

My head came up but before I could move away I was imprisoned by his light-blue eyes.

"You didn't snore," his voice rumbled sleepily, and, might I add, sexily.

Uh-oh.

"Um—"

"Or move."

"Uh—"

"Or steal the covers."

I bit my lip.

"Gods, you *cuddled*," he muttered, his eyes narrowing dangerously.

Oh dear.

"I—" I started trying to pull away but his arms got tighter so I stopped mostly because his arms were really freaking strong and I had no choice.

"What's this now?" he murmured, his glittering, no longer sleepy eyes moving over my face.

"What?" I asked.

"Seduction?" he asked back.

Uh.

What?

Then it hit me.

"No!" I cried. "I—"

"I can't imagine you'd be very good at it," he remarked.

Oh Lord. I was seeing he was back to the jerk.

I tugged at his hold and put my hands to his chest to get better leverage.

This didn't work.

"Let me go."

"Though," he carried on, ignoring me, "you put your mind to something..." then he trailed off.

Oh God.

"Noctorno, let...me..." I shoved hard, "*go*!"

I got nowhere.

His eyes dropped to my mouth. "I've a mind to test your skills."

Uh-oh!

"Let me go!" I repeated.

He didn't let me go. His arms separated, one sliding up my back, the other one sliding low on my waist. The hand at my waist slanted down to my hip and his fingers pressed in.

"You feel better now that there's more to you. I like the curves. When you were skin and bones..." he trailed off again.

Great. Just my luck. He liked that I was fat in this world.

"I'm not going to say it again," I told him on another shove. "Let me go!"

His gaze moved back to mine. "Kiss me and I'll let you go."

My body went still.

Then I shouted, "No!"

"Can't even give your husband that," he muttered, his expression changing from speculative to daunting.

"Right. I can't. You're a jerk and I hate you, remember?" I snapped.

His arms tightened.

"I remember," he replied. "But that's not it. You can't do it."

"Can't do what?"

"Kiss me."

"I can kiss you. I just don't want to."

"I'll wager you can kiss me. What I mean is, you can't kiss me the way I'd like it."

It was my eyes that narrowed at that.

I really had no idea if I was a good kisser or not. Brian didn't seem to mind the way I kissed. In fact, all I had to do was kiss him, give him a good, long, wet one and he was all over me. Then again, he was a guy. Guys didn't need much and Brian needed less than most (in my, admittedly, not-so-vast experience).

"I could kiss you the way you'd like it but I'm not going to," I returned.

"Drivel," he muttered.

"I could!" I snapped.

"Not a prayer in this world," he retorted.

What a jerk!

"Why do you even want me to kiss you? You don't even like me." I reminded him.

"Because, my love, I'm a man and most of your soft body has been pressed to me all night, the rest of it wrapped around me. That happens to a man no matter whose body it is."

"Nice," I hissed. "Just the words any girl wants to hear."

"They're true."

"I'll give you that. Now let me go," I demanded.

He let me go and started to slide out from under me when I did it. I don't know why. Maybe because I was sick of having a bad rap due to the Cora of this world being a screaming bitch.

What matters was, I did.

And I shouldn't have.

I really shouldn't have.

I lifted a hand to his cheek, moved his head to facing me and I went in for the kill.

And I didn't start small. I pulled out all the stops and went all out. I pressed tight to him, my fingers slid into the thick, soft hair at the side of his head, I pressed my lips to his, opened my mouth over his and when his opened under mine, my tongue darted in, and Lordy, but he tasted *good*.

Sublime.

Yum!

That was when I *really* went all out, pushing close and giving it my all.

He took it and with a groan his arms closed around me. He rolled me to my back, his big body on mine and he took over.

Oh man, this was better. *Way* better.

He was a jerk, but damn the man could kiss.

My fingers slid through his hair to cup the back of his head and my other arm curved around his muscled back just as my leg forced its way out from under him and wrapped around his hip.

He tasted good, he felt good on me, his body so warm and solid and he could kiss.

Amazing.

He tore his mouth from mine and lifted his head an inch. I opened my eyes to see his glittering with a new light as they blazed into mine and I felt his heavy breath mingling with my own.

Jeez, he was hot and he was even hotter looking turned on.

"Gods," he murmured with feeling.

He had *that* right.

"Bloody hell," he went on.

He had that right too.

His gaze roamed my face and I wished they wouldn't mainly because I was hoping he'd kiss me again.

He didn't.

Instead, his eyes turned to stone and he whispered, "Conniver."

I blinked and my skin went cold.

"Cunning little schemer," he kept at it and for some reason I suddenly felt like crying.

"Get off me," I whispered.

"You'll do anything, won't you, Cora?" he asked.

"Please," I said softly. "Get off me."

"You'd given me that, even a hint of it on our wedding night, my love, I would have given you a better house."

Seeing as the house he gave me belonged in a fairytale, I couldn't imagine what would be better but I didn't share that mainly because I was concentrating on my stomach muscles contracting because it felt like he'd punched me in the gut.

I shoved at his shoulders, bucked and shrieked, "*Get the fuck off me, you asshole!*"

He shifted just enough for me to slide out from under him and gain my feet. I took several hasty steps away then whirled to face him, my mind searching for a stunning set down and finding nothing when I saw him on his side, the hides to his waist, up on a forearm, his magnificent chest on display, his black hair tousled from sleep and his eyes on me.

Damn, he was sexy as all hell and I wished he was ugly as well as a jerk.

"Have I mentioned I hated you this morning?" I asked spitefully.

He grinned.

Grinned!

Jerk!

"Actually, yes," he answered.

"Good, I don't want you to forget," I returned.

"Oh, I won't forget."

"Excellent."

"Though," he started, shoving the hides aside and moving lithely to his feet. "You don't want rabbit for your next meal, you pay the price."

Oh no.

This didn't sound good.

"What?" I asked.

"You don't like rabbit," he reminded me.

It wasn't that I didn't like it. It was that, even tasty, I couldn't stop myself from thinking it was gross because I liked bunnies.

"No," I said cautiously as he crossed his arms on his chest.

"You don't want rabbit, love, then you earn something you want."

This definitely didn't sound good.

"Perhaps you'll explain," I suggested, though truth be told, I didn't want him to explain.

He did as I suggested. "A kiss for a meal."

Uh-oh.

"I—"

"You want anything else, like clothes, you'll need to get creative."

Uh-oh!

"Noctorno—"

He leaned forward slightly but ominously. "I'm certain you can be creative, can't you, Cora?"

"I've decided I like eating bunny and my nightgown is perfectly fine, thank you," I snapped, wrapping my arms around my belly protectively.

"You'll need a bath. You like to bathe, I reckon."

Oh shit.

I did, indeed, like to bathe. Actually, I was hoping I wasn't already ripe.

"Noc—"

"You've earned breakfast with what you gave me on the hides. It was so good, love, you earned a trip to the river too. Anything else you want, you work for."

I unwrapped my arms from my belly and planted my hands on my hips, leaning forward slightly myself.

"How much more of a jerk can you be?" I asked.

"Why don't you see?" he returned.

"Ugh!" I grunted, my arms shooting straight down, my hands in fists, my head going back so I could stare in disgust at the ceiling. Then my chin tipped down sharply and I glared at him. "I hate you!" I yelled.

"You already told me that."

"Well, I hate you more than I hated you before."

"I don't really care."

"And I hated you a lot before," I informed him.

"I repeat, I don't really care."

"Well, you've made *that* clear," I snapped.

His head tilted to the side and he grinned.

"Is there something you need to do?" he asked.

"Plot your murder?" I replied.

His grin turned to a smile and it sucked that it was hot.

"Other than that."

Yes, there was something I needed to do and that something was go to the bathroom. Then bathe (in the river, for God's sake, yikes!). Then eat.

And I needed him for all those things, I was guessing. I mean, I could do the first and second myself but he had to protect me from vickrants or whatever else was out there while I did it.

I glared at him. He held my glare calmly.

I tore my eyes from his and asked myself out loud, "Why did I kiss this jerk? Why? Damn my pride! Damn it to *hell*!"

"I take it that means you agree to the terms of our continuing relationship," he remarked and my gaze cut back to him.

"Jerk!"

His eyebrows went up. "Are you saying you don't?"

"Go to hell!"

He shrugged and moved to his shirt. "You could, of course, go forth on your own. The vickrants will be hunting you or The Shrew may send toilroys."

He shook his head and I didn't like the idea of toilroys. Vickrants were bad enough. Furthermore, I didn't know who The Shrew was but any shrew, I knew, was bad news.

Damn.

He pulled his shirt on as I clipped out, "Fine."

He turned only his head to me.

"Fine?"

"*Fine!*" I snapped.

He grinned.

I glared.

He grabbed his boots and tugged them on.

When he straightened, he extended his arm to the hide-covered opening. "Fancy a bath?"

I growled under my breath and stomped to the hides.

From behind me I heard a manly chuckle.

Seriously, I freaking *hated* this world!

6

Written in the Sky

~

I had a plan.

It probably wasn't going to work but at least I had a plan.

See, Noctorno took me outside into the overcast day. He also took me somewhere secluded and gave me privacy while I attended to nature's call while I was in nature—not my favorite thing in this world or my own. In fact, I never did it in my own world but once and that was bad enough so I never did it again. But it was the call of nature and nature was my only choice so I answered the call.

Then he took me back to the cave, lifted me onto his horse, Salem (who seemed to snort his greeting at me though I couldn't sense this like I could sense what Aggie meant when he chirped, it was only the impression I got). He got on Salem behind me and we took what seemed to be a long ride to the river.

My bath wasn't all I'd hoped it would be seeing as he took off his boots and waded in with me, we both got in fully-clothed, we had no soap, and although the river was gorgeous (regardless of the gray day) and crystal clear, it was danged cold.

Sopping wet, we rode back, he stoked the fire while I sat by it, hugging my knees shivering then he informed me he'd be back and he took off.

That was when I decided on my plan. I sat there pulling my stiff fingers through my hair, detangling it and hopefully drying it as I alternately got up and fed fuel to the fire and decided what to do to get out of my latest dire predicament.

I was going to tell the truth.

He'd likely think I was mad but I didn't care.

I had to do *something*.

I heard hooves on stone and knew he was back.

I bit my lip and felt a thrill race up my spine. I didn't know if this thrill was fear or something else and I didn't think about it.

I had to concentrate on what I would say to get him to believe me.

The hides were swept back and he walked in looking great even though his shirt was wrinkled and his hair was mussed. Or, maybe it was *because* of the latter. He was also carrying two jugs hooked to just one finger with the rest of his fingers wrapped around a rough sack and another rough sack in his other hand. He dropped the sacks and put the jugs on the table.

Then he turned to me.

"I've returned," he announced the obvious, a smile playing at his gorgeous lips.

"Goodie," I muttered churlishly.

The smile grew full-fledged.

Ugh.

"Fresh milk," he said, tipping his head to the jugs. "And ale," he went on.

Yuck. I hated milk and beer. Still, it was something. Though, I wished I knew how to use that kettle contraption. I'd checked it out and it was beyond me. There was no filter. And even if I figured it out, there was no water. And I needed caffeine, stat.

"Right," I mumbled.

He lightly kicked one of the sacks with the toe of his boot. "Porridge oats, bread, butter, sugar and salt beef," he went on.

Now we were talking.

"Fabulous," I murmured.

He lightly toed the other sack. "Clothes for you. And shoes."

Oh dear.

I bit my lip.

He smiled again.

Oh shit.

"Now, love," he started walking toward me, "I hope you spent my time away thinking about how creative you can be."

Oh shit!

I started backing up.

"We need to talk," I informed him.

His head tipped to the side but he didn't stop moving. "Well, that's creative but not what I was thinking."

Oh *shit*!

My back hit stone so I lifted a hand, palm out.

"Noctorno," I whispered.

His chest came up against my hand and kept coming, pushing it back so it was caught between our bodies.

Yes, that was how close he was.

Yikes!

"Uh—"

"I warn you not to delay, Cora. I'm hungry and it'd be a shame, me eating in front of you," he advised.

I stared up at him and all I could see were his light-blue eyes. They were very blue and very clear. Like the sky on a sunny, cloudless day.

"Your eyes are like the sky on a sunny day," I blurted and his mouth twitched.

Oh God. Why did I say that?

But I knew I said it because he was that close and he was that hot. A hot guy that close would make you blurt anything, even if he was a jerk.

He pushed closer and I felt his heat hit more than my hand and let me tell you, his heat was *hot*.

Wow.

His head dipped so his face was close to mine.

"Sweet," he whispered in his deep voice.

Wow…and…*nice*.

"You're very hot," I told him.

"I can get hotter," he told me.

Yikes!

"Noctorno—"

"Whatever you do, I want you to do it with your mouth."

Oh dear.

"And tongue," he went on.

Oh man.

My fingers fisted in his shirt and I said quickly, "I'm not of this world."

He blinked and he did it slow.

Then he growled, "Pardon?"

"That's what we need to talk about."

He straightened to his full height, his head turned to the side, his jaw got hard and he muttered, "Gods."

"No, seriously," I said.

His head turned back to me. "Yes, I see. You've used your time thinking how creative you could be."

This wasn't starting great.

I persevered, mostly because I had no other choice.

"Okay," I began, moving up to my toes which did take me higher but even though I was relatively tall, he was far taller and I didn't even get close. "Listen to me, all right?"

"I told you, I'm hungry," he reminded me.

"I'll hurry but promise to listen, okay?"

He stared at me but said not a word. I took this as a yes.

"Right, okay. I'm not from here. I'm from somewhere else."

"And where are you from, Cora?" he asked with ill-concealed impatience.

"Uh...Earth?" I ventured.

His lips thinned before he told me, "I'm from Earth too."

Well, at least we resided on the same planet...*ish*. Good to know (kind of) I wasn't beamed to a different galaxy, just catapulted to a parallel world.

"Okay, that answers that but I'm from an alternate universe Earth where we have computers and smart phones and, uh...cable TV."

He scowled at me.

I kept at it.

"I'm an administrative assistant. I work at an ad agency. I live in an apartment. I'm single, as in, not married. I had a boyfriend, his name was Brian, but he wouldn't marry me so I had to cut my losses and break up with him before, you know, life passed me by."

He continued to scowl at me, but at the mention of Brian, I felt his body go still and I watched his face go hard.

These were ominous signs but I kept going.

"See, I went to sleep and then I woke up and I was here. I mean, I went to sleep at home, *my* home, where, you know, beds aren't made of feathers but of..." I didn't know what mattresses were made of but I was sensing his patience waning so I sallied forth, "Other stuff. And you don't understand birds and there are no curses. That was why I didn't know about the Rosa and Dash thing. See, we don't have curses, but even if we did, I wouldn't know about that curse because I'm not the Cora you know. I'm a different Cora, one who's fat but polite and doesn't snore and..."

He cut in with, "You aren't fat."

"You said I'd gained weight."

"You have. You've also grown your hair."

Now we were getting somewhere.

"See!" I exclaimed. "That right there proves I'm not the Cora you know."

"No, it proves that in the six months since I last saw you, you stopped watching every bloody morsel you put into your mouth and let your hair grow."

He hadn't seen me in six months?

"You haven't seen me in six months?" I asked.

"For the gods' sakes," he clipped.

"We're married!" I cried. "Why haven't you seen me in six months?"

"Because you hate me, Cora, and I'm not overly fond of you."

I latched on to that. "There you go. See, the Cora I am knows how to baste meat and isn't lazy. I'll admit, I'll drag my feet on stuff I don't want to do but eventually I'll do it. I'm polite and my parents and friends think I'm funny. I don't want to brag or anything, but I'm pretty cool to be around. If you give me a chance, I can show you I'm not the Cora you know."

"I'll wager you can. And I'll wager you'll stick with it every second of the day and live it with every breath you take. But all of it will be an act of pure deception."

Jeez, if he believed that then the Cora of this world must be a serious bitch.

"No one can do that," I said softly.

"You could," he returned. "You see, my love, a year and a half ago I bedded a woman so cold, it was a wonder my cock didn't splinter to shards when I drove it inside you."

I gasped at his words but he kept talking.

"And but hours ago, just your mouth was so warm it lit a fire inside me. If you could turn that around, you could do anything."

I flattened my hand on his chest, got higher up on my toes and said quietly, "But, don't you get it? That also proves I'm not the Cora you know."

"It, and this nonsense you're spouting, only proves how desperate you are to keep me on your good side so I'll keep you safe from Minerva and do it in the style which you undoubtedly require."

Minerva?

I didn't get the chance to ask.

He kept talking.

"But Dash believes your performance, Rosa adores you and therefore, out of respect for them, I'll keep you safe and fed but I'll damned well get what I can out of you in the process."

I fell back to the soles of my feet but kept my eyes to his, asking, "Why do you hate me so much?"

This was the wrong question. I knew it when the light of rage hit his eyes at the same time his face went stone cold.

"Why?" he whispered.

I knew he thought I shouldn't have to ask but I felt I should know what I was dealing with.

"Yes, why?"

"You dare ask?"

"Yes, Noctorno, seeing as I don't know you, I met you just yesterday, I dare ask," I stated cautiously.

"So this is your game now?"

"No, this is honesty," I told him honestly.

His hold on his temper slipped and his face got in mine where he clipped, "Sly cow."

Um...*ouch*.

"That's mean and it isn't true," I returned quietly.

He kept at me. "Black with trickery to your bloody soul."

"That isn't true either," I whispered.

He glowered at me and I did my best to brave it out. When I was about to give up, he gave in.

"This is the game you wish to play?"

"It isn't a game," I reminded him of something he refused to believe.

"This is the game you wish to play," he decided and I sighed.

I was right. He refused to believe, or likely Cora of this world was just that much of a bitch.

"Right," he went on. "Then you play your game, I play mine." That didn't sound too good, I braced and he kept talking which luckily meant he explained. "You're the other half to my soul."

I blinked before I whispered, "What?"

"You heard me."

"I'm the other half to your soul?"

"In all the kingdom, in our generation, there are only two men whose souls were split at birth, the other half put in their lifemates. Dash to Rosa and you to me. The she-god saw fit to award Dash all the sweetness of Rosa and for some bloody hideous reason she saw fit to saddle me with all the foulness of *you*."

I didn't know what to say to that. It wasn't nice but it also sounded like something the Cora of this world deserved so I didn't speak.

Noctorno did.

"For any other man but Dash or me, they could take anyone as bride. For him, it was only Rosa, the reason why *you* couldn't have him, not that he wanted you. To hold back the curse *you* started to unleash yesterday, and because we agreed to do it in order to give the others the happiness they deserve, you had to leave him to her and wed me. And for me, it was only you. I had no other choice."

Oh my God.

That was crazy.

"That's crazy!" I cried, pressing back into the wall.

"Bloody right it is," he agreed firmly.

I stared at him.

As crazy as this was, it was worse. Because he struck me as a man who liked choice. A man who would value, beyond anything, his free will. A man who'd fight and die for it and yet it had been taken away.

"Couldn't you, um...protest this decision?"

His brows shot up. "To the she-god?"

"Uh...yes?" I tried.

His brows descended and his eyes narrowed. "You *are* mad."

"I take it you don't question the gods," I muttered.

"No, Cora, even you wouldn't question the gods. Our fates were written in the sky the moment we were born."

Oh. Wow.

"Written in the sky?" I breathed.

"Me to you, you to me for all the kingdom to see."

Holy crap.

Something else occurred to me.

"Uh-oh," I whispered.

"Pardon?"

"Uh-oh," I repeated.

"Uh what?"

I guess they didn't have uh-oh here either.

I moved around that. "Noctorno, *I* am not the other half to your soul. The other Cora is."

"*Gods*," he hissed, losing patience.

"No!" I cried. "It's true. If you could get in trouble being with—"

I stopped speaking when he pressed closer.

"Excellent try, love, but it's not going to work."

"No, seriously—"

His hands spanned my hips and I quit talking.

"The she-god wrote that you're the other half to my soul, which meant I had to bind myself to you but it didn't mean I couldn't bed whoever I wanted and I do. So even if you aren't the Cora of my world, as you lie that you aren't, *none* of the gods would give a toss if I kiss you, touch you, taste you and drive into you, and they also wouldn't give a toss that I let you do the same to me. Except, obviously the last, so let's just say they won't mind if you ride me." His face dipped closer and he finished with, "*Hard*."

His words were coarse but even so I was stuck on something he said earlier and therefore asked with disbelief, "You've *cheated* on me?"

He grinned and his grin was wicked. "If you're not my wife, then no."

"You've cheated on me!" I cried.

"So you're my wife?"

"No!"

"Then no."

Ugh!

"Move away," I demanded, my hands going to his wrists and pushing.

"No. Now that I've put up with this rubbish, you earn your food and clothes, and I'm warning you, now I'm hungrier than I was before so I'll not tolerate any more of this absurdity."

"I'm not being absurd!" My voice was rising. "I'm telling you the truth!"

He kept my gaze even as he shook his head. "Make no mistake, Cora, I'll eat in front of you and you'll wear that nightgown until it falls off, if it comes to that."

"Fine!" I snapped. "Great!" I fairly shouted. "Do what you will. I'll not *earn* one more thing from *you*!"

He nodded his head once, muttered, "Your choice," let me go and moved away.

And that, apparently, was that.

Jerk!

I stood against the stone, realized I was breathing heavily and watched him go.

Well, that didn't work.

"You know what?" I asked him as he crouched by one of the sacks and started pulling stuff out. He turned his head to me and I kept going. "When your Cora comes back, and I hope to God she does, not only so I can go *home* but also so I can get away from *you*, you're going to feel just like the asshole, jerk, scumbag you are!"

He looked back into the sack, mumbling, "I'll take that chance."

Argh!

7

Only Stupid People Get Bored

~

I woke the next morning half on and totally wrapped around Noctorno again.

Great. Just great.

Why couldn't my unconscious self hate him as much as my conscious self, I ask you?

I rolled away, landing on my back, and he rolled with me, landing mostly on my body.

Fabulous.

I opened my eyes and looked into his.

Jeez, it totally sucked he was so freaking gorgeous.

"Good morning, love," he murmured.

I glared at him thinking there was not one damned thing good about it. First, I had a headache. Second, I was starving. Third, I needed a bath, with soap. Fourth, I was sick and damned tired of wearing this nightgown. Fifth, I was tired and damned sick of this cave. Sixth, I had to go to the bathroom and that meant he had to go with me which was humiliating. Seventh, he was there and I hated him no matter how gorgeous he was. And last, I was still not home.

Needless to say, yesterday did *not* go well. He took me to answer nature's call twice more and when I was back in the cave he left (taking the jugs and sacks with him, the king of all ultimate jerks) and came back after filling the one with water, which he informed me I could partake of at will. This was good for I could dehydrate faster than starve but it was bad because drinking water made nature call.

Other than that, he spent most of the day somewhere else (but close, I could hear him doing such things as murmuring to his horse, chopping wood, and what I guessed was sharpening weapons).

I spent most of the day alone, getting hungrier and hungrier by the minute, bored out of my skull at the same time scared beyond reason.

I wanted to go home.

"I need coffee," I informed him because I did. I knew my headache wasn't because I was hungry. I knew it was because my system desperately needed caffeine.

"Coffee sounds good," he whispered, his eyes moving to my mouth.

Oh God. Here we go.

All right.

Whatever!

"Okay, fine," I snapped. "What do I have to do for a cup of coffee?"

His eyes moved back to mine and they were smiling. "Why don't you do what you think a cup of coffee is worth, and when you're done, I'll tell you if you've earned it."

I glared at him a second, willing my eyes to annihilate him.

This didn't happen so I spat, "I hate you."

The smile didn't fade from his eyes when he replied, "I don't care."

What...

Eh...

Ver!

Oh well. Fuck it. A girl like me would do a lot for caffeine, and seeing as I was a girl like me, there it was.

Both my hands went to either side of his face, my foot went into the hides, I pushed off, rolling into him, taking him to his back with me on top and I kissed him, hard, open-mouthed, wet, long and hot.

God, oh God, oh *God* but I wished he didn't taste so *fucking* good.

When I was done, one of his arms was locked under my shoulder blades the other one was locked tight around my waist.

I lifted my head and said (unfortunately breathlessly, so good was that kiss), "Does that earn me coffee?"

"Sweets," he murmured, his rough voice rougher, his sexy eyes sexier and his arm moving from under my shoulder blades so that his fingers could slide up the back of my neck into my hair. "That was so bloody magnificent, you get coffee *and* porridge."

Yippee!

His arm around my waist moved so his hand cupped my ass and his head lifted so his face was in my neck.

"Fancy earning clothes?" he asked against my skin.

I shivered. His hand was so big, so warm, his grip so firm and his voice rumbling against my skin so hot my first shiver was followed by a full-on tremble.

Not to mention, I wanted *out, out, out* of this nightgown.

Shit.

"What do I have to do for clothes *and* a bath *with* soap?" I asked cautiously.

His head went back to the hides and his eyes caught mine.

"I have soap," he told me.

I felt my eyes grow wide. "You do?"

He nodded.

"Really?" I breathed.

He grinned. "Yes, Cora."

Oh man. He had soap. And I wanted to be clean from top to toe. I wanted it *bad*.

Shit!

I studied him as he patiently waited, his hands still warm on me.

Hmm.

"What do I have to do to get you not to be a jerk to me all day, from now to bedtime?" I asked.

His eyes warmed and let me tell you, they looked nice warm. So nice, my belly felt like keeping them company so it did, getting warm too. *Way* warm.

"That'll take some work," he whispered.

"If I, uh…do all the work now, will you, um…be nice all day?"

His hand at my ass squeezed. "You earn it, you'll get it."

I licked my lips.

Was I going to do this?

Shit.

Shit!

Shit!

I looked into his eyes, felt his hard body beneath mine then turned my face away, clenching my jaw and closing my eyes hard.

No.

No I wasn't going to do this.

No way.

He thought I was Cora of this world but I couldn't lose my hold on the fact that I was *not*. I didn't deserve this even though he genuinely and with reason believed I did.

I would not whore myself for soap and clothes and another human being nice to me.

I would *not*.

I turned back to him and whispered, "I think I'll make do with coffee and porridge."

Once I was finished speaking, I looked away and tried to slide off but his arms wrapped around me again, holding me where I was.

"Cora," he called but I stared at the hides to our sides.

"What?"

"Look at me."

"Just tell me what."

"Look at me," he repeated on an arm squeeze.

I looked at him and he had that blank look on his face with his eyes active again.

"I'll say this once and counsel you to take it to heart. You can play your game but you don't play me in mine."

"What?" I asked.

"Do not tease me."

Oh hell.

"I wasn't—"

"No excuses, no lies, just take that to heart. Am I understood?"

God, I couldn't win for losing.

"Understood," I whispered.

His arms loosened and I rolled away.

He rolled out of the hides.

I watched him walk to the table and thought, *I hate, hate, hate this fucking world and I hate, hate, hate Noctorno Whoever-he-is.*

And I hate, hate, hated them both so much, I felt the tears spring to my eyes. I rolled to face the wall and prayed I didn't make any noise with my crying as I listened to him stoking the fire.

Luckily, my prayer was answered.

"What are you doing?"

Noctorno was speaking from behind me.

I was at the mouth of the cave. The day had a hint of watery sunshine, which was an improvement, but nothing like the brilliant beauty of the fairytale world I woke up in two days ago and shattered because I inadvertently caused a curse to fall on the land.

I was also shaking out the bed hides.

"Cleaning," I answered, not turning to him and continuing awkwardly to shake the heavy, huge hide.

"Cleaning," he repeated after me.

"Yep," I said, giving up on shaking and decided to start beating it with my fist.

That worked. Dust flew out everywhere.

Brilliant.

"Why?" he asked.

"Why?" I asked back.

"Yes, why?"

"Because you're tidy with your bone remains but the rest of the place is filthy."

"Cora, it's a cave."

That made me turn to him.

"I know it's a cave, *Tor*."

I watched his mouth get tight.

Oh Lordy. For some reason, he was getting angry.

Jeez, with him it didn't take much and this time I didn't even know what I did. I could hardly be pissing him off by cleaning, could I?

Oh well, let him get angry. I was getting used to it.

I went back to beating.

I heard a clomp, clomp, clomp and then I felt the velvet of Salem's nose against my neck right before he blew.

It tickled so much, I giggled, dropped the hide and turned to him. His head jerked back and I lifted my hands to his nose and held gently.

"It's okay, boy," I cooed.

He snorted again.

"That's it." I kept cooing and started to stroke his muzzle.

He clomped a half a horse step closer.

"That's it, you beautiful beast," I whispered, still stroking.

He snorted his contentment.

I smiled at him.

"*Salem!*" Noctorno barked. Salem pulled his nose from my hands and looked down his massive body as my head turned to see the big guy standing, arms crossed on his chest, openly pissed. "Move away from, Cora," he ordered his mount.

Salem whinnied.

"Now, horse," Noctorno growled.

Salem blew breath through his horse lips and clomped away.

I glared at Noctorno. "Why'd you do that?"

"Do not think, woman, you can come between a man and his horse," Noctorno informed me.

"I wasn't trying to," I informed him right back, and I wasn't!

"Right," he muttered.

"Jeez!" I cried, throwing up my hands. "What is *with* you?"

"I warned you not to play me for a fool."

"Good God, man, I was just petting your horse!" I pointed out.

"You were playing your games," he returned.

"You know," I started, "this is getting old. The Cora of your world must be a huge freaking-ass bitch to make you think she'd use your fucking *horse* against you."

"There is nothing I'd put past you," he replied.

"Well, again, big guy, *I* am not *her* and I'm getting sick of you treating me like her."

"Then we share something because I'm getting sick of you pretending you *aren't* her."

I continued glaring at him and he withstood it.

Then I swung back to the hide, hefted it up and started beating at it again, hard, all the while muttering to myself, "I lived a good life. I was nice. If I saw someone drop a dollar, I'd pick it up and give it to them. If a beggar looked like a real, genuine, honest to God beggar, I'd give them change. If strangers walked by me and caught my eye, I'd smile and say hello. If my friends did stupid shit with guys, I kept my mouth shut and then let them cry on my shoulder when that stupid shit bit them in the ass at the same time I kept the mojitos flowing. Okay, so I didn't tell on Jenny Linklater when I saw her cheating on that test in sixth grade but *I* didn't cheat. I've *never* cheated. I've never done *anything* wrong enough to land me in this crazy, *freaking* world with a *lunatic* hot guy. What did I do to deserve this?"

Salem whinnied and I didn't know what that meant.

I looked at him. "I don't know what you mean but the way you said it, I agree."

He jerked his snout up.

"Damn straight," I muttered, gathered the hide to me and stomped through the loose stone back to the opening under the eyes of a glowering Noctorno and I did it only wincing a little at how much the stone hurt my feet.

When I got to my destination, I slapped the hides open and then for good measure I slapped them shut behind me thinking stupidly, *Take that, asshole.*

He wouldn't care if I slapped the hide closed but it made *me* feel better.

Hours later, the hides opened and Noctorno strode in.

I looked up from my sweeping and gave him a good glare.

Then I kept right on sweeping.

"Gods, what the bloody hell?" he muttered irately.

I ignored him and limped through my sweeping.

"Cora," he called.

I kept limping through my sweeping, seeing, belatedly, the error of my ways as I went about my business of the day.

I had—very stupidly—gathered all the bones in the dirty bowl, carried them to the mouth of the cave and tossed them as far away as I could throw them. I had also beat out the sheepskins as well as the cowhide. I had also trudged (again) through the sharp stone of the main cave, back and forth (four times), to replenish the wood supply. This meant my feet were raw on the bottoms but I was not, not, *not* going to be bored out of my mind like yesterday nor give myself the headspace to fret about my calamitous circumstances.

No I was not.

I didn't have any lemons to make lemonade but I was going to damn well do what I could with no lemons and no nothing.

So, when I saw the dried grass was filled with dead insects (ick), yes, you guessed it, I trudged right back through the cave (knowing big guy and his sweet horse watched me) back and forth, back and forth, yanking fresh, long blades of grass that grew close to the mouth of the cave and piling them up outside the antechamber we slept in.

Then I inspected the entirety of the cave and its cave chambers, found a long stick and enough pieces of twig to build my own freaking broom, which I did braiding the bristles at the top with a blade of grass and attaching it to the stick with more blades (this, by the way, was tedious and took a long time but, by God, I did it). And now I was sweeping out the old, dry, dead insect-ridden grass (as well as whatever else my admittedly not very great broom could pick up) even though my feet were killing me.

"Cora," he repeated when I didn't answer.

"Right here," I replied.

"Stop."

"No, I'm almost done."

"I said, stop."

"No," I kept sweeping the big pile toward the pelt curtain, "just a bit—" The broom was suddenly yanked clean out of my hands and my head snapped up to see Noctorno had it. "What are you—? *Oof!*"

Clatter went the broom as up I went on his shoulder again.

"Put me down!" I beat at his back with my fists.

He did, dropping me on the hides I'd bunched up in the corner to get them away from my sweeping. I barely got my body under control when his strong fingers closed around my ankle and he yanked it up.

"Hey!" I yelled as he bent low and to the side to inspect the bottom of my foot.

"Bloody...damned...*hell*!" he roared and I jerked my ankle from his hold partly because I didn't want my ankle in his hold and partly in a reaction to his scary roar.

"What—?" I started but stopped when he planted his hands at his hips and scowled at me so ferociously my breath caught.

Okay, now he wasn't just pissed, he was *pissed*.

"You've scraped the soles of your feet straight to hell," he gritted at me.

"I'm perfectly fine."

"Your feet are scraped to hell," he semi-repeated.

"Noctorno, I'm fine."

"What, by the gods, were you bloody thinking?" he demanded to know.

"I was cleaning."

"Yes, love, you were cleaning *a cave* which," he leaned into me, "by all that is natural, is *dirty*."

"But we're living here!" I sat up to lean into him. "So, being humans and with opposable thumbs and the ability to cogitate, means we can better our surroundings so *I'm doing that*."

"And injuring yourself in the ridiculous process," he shot back.

I felt my eyes narrow.

"It isn't *ridiculous*. There are dead *bugs* in the *grass* under the *bed* we sleep in! That is pure *ick*!" I shouted.

"If you weren't so bloody stubborn, you need clean rushes, you'd bloody well kiss me and I'd give you some bloody shoes!" he shouted back.

"I don't want to bloody kiss you!" I yelled.

"Then you should have sat on your arse and kept your feet healthy and clean!" he returned on his own yell.

"I did that yesterday and I can't do it again. It's boring and my mother told me only stupid people get bored and I'm...not...*stupid*," I fired back.

He leaned back and his brows knitted. "Your mother told you that?"

"Yes."

"Your mother didn't tell you that," he declared bizarrely decisively.

"Yes, Tor, she did."

"She did not."

"Yes! She did!"

"Bloody hell, woman, she's sweet as syrup and wouldn't harm a fly but Dara Goode isn't smart enough to *think* something like that much less enunciate it."

I scrambled to my feet, planted my hands at my own hips and snapped, "Are you calling my mother stupid?"

"Gods, Cora, she's beloved but she's not bright. It's not nice but it's well-known. Even you told me she's dull as a post," he retorted.

"I never said such a..."

Oh shit.

I never said such a thing because the Dara Goode in my world, my mother, was not dull as a post. Nowhere near it.

But the other Cora probably said that about her mother.

Blast!

"God!" I exclaimed, looking at the ceiling. "I hate the Cora of this world! She's an utter...*oof*!"

There I was again on his shoulder.

"Tor!" I shrieked, beating at his back and kicking out my legs. "Let me down."

"Quiet," he commanded, squatting to pick up one of the sacks.

"I said...let...me..."

Crack!

Another slap on the ass.

Serious *ouch*.

God, I *hated* it when he did that.

"You're having a bloody bath and you're putting on some bloody clean clothes and some damned, bloody shoes," he declared.

Oh.

Well then.

Okay.

He dumped me on Salem, swung up behind me, dug his heels in, barked, "*Hee-yah!*" and Salem burst out of the mouth of the cave.

I was on my belly but I carefully twisted and pulled myself to sitting even though my butt cheek still smarted from where he hit me and in this position he clearly felt the need to circle me with an arm and I knew this because he did exactly that.

I faced forward, ducked and swayed with him as the branches passed us and I couldn't stop the smile spreading on my face or the word from hitting my brain.

And that word was, *goodie*.

Okay, let me tell you this...

The clothes in this world *rocked*!

We were back in the cave. I'd bathed in the river (it was still cold but he had soap, the soap smelled like lavender and I'd cleaned myself with it from head to toe) and I had on clothes *and* slippers.

And what clothes.

They were straight from a renaissance festival but they kicked *ass*.

A silky, pale-pink, flowy top with gathers around the neckline and full flowing sleeves that gathered at the wrists. Also full, flowing skirts, these of a dusky purple with petticoats, these a lovely mint green and the bottoms were dripping with a same-color, glorious lace. To cinch in the flowy top, I was wearing a skin-tight vest, royal blue that hugged me at the midriff and shoved up my breasts over its top, somehow providing support at the same time looking way freaking cool. With the low-cut neckline of the shirt and the tight fit of the vest, I was displaying serious cleavage but from what I could tell, it...looked...*awesome*. There was also a braided belt in all the colors I was wearing that I tied to hang low on my waist.

And last, but not least, the underwear was d-i-v-i-n-e, *divine*. Silky, ivory shorts with delicate lace at the bottoms and matching camisole with lace at the bottom and bodice. These fit perfectly, clinging to the right places, tight to the right places looking crazy fabulous but comfortable as all get out.

And the capper was the shoes. Sweet little flat, no-heeled (but thick suede-soled) slippers made of purple satin. They were simple and comfortable at the same time they were fab...you...*las*.

I didn't know how I'd feel wearing something like this day in and day out. There was a lot of a fabric, the skirts were danged heavy and I didn't think it would be that great if it was hot or I had to do manual labor or something like that.

But right now, they were great. They felt strange on my body but they oddly fit perfectly, the colors were to die for and they were *not* that blasted nightgown (which I also, by the by, took the opportunity with the lavender soap to clean in the river).

For once in nearly three days I was content.

We'd come back. Tor had disappeared. I'd finished my sweeping, arranged the grass and hides and although I was starved, my body was tired, I was clean and I had on a killer outfit.

This would work for me for now. This was lemons and I was making some freaking tasty lemonade, let me tell you.

The hide was swept back at the opening but Noctorno didn't enter. He stood there holding the skins back and scowling at me.

"Yo," I greeted him with a smile.

He kept scowling at me.

Then he grunted, "Come."

I blinked before asking, "What?"

"We're going to dinner."

I blinked again and, get this, I felt my heart get light.

"What?" I breathed.

"I need a pulse and you need food. Come."

"A pulse?"

"The feel of the land, a sense of what's happening out there…the pulse. Now, come."

I shot to my feet, still smiling and agreed with an, "Okay."

He glowered at me as I walked (with only a slight limp, I had on my killer slippers but that didn't mean my feet weren't still raw) toward him.

The minute the pelts fell into place behind us, he swept me up in his arms and I let out a surprised girlie shriek before my arm automatically circled his shoulders.

"What on—?"

"Gods, Cora, just be quiet," he muttered on a sigh.

"Okeydokey," I muttered back.

If he wanted to carry me, so be it. I mean, the cave wasn't that big so he didn't have to carry me far.

And anyway, I was feeling good. I was clean, had on actual clothes and he was going to feed me without me having to kiss him (or alternate activities) to get it.

I was not going to argue.

He set me on Salem, swung into the saddle behind me, rounded me with an arm and dug his heels into the steed.

Salem bolted out of the cave.

The sun was setting and it was close to dark as we cantered down the mountain.

"Is this safe?" I asked.

"We'll soon find out," was Tor's not very reassuring response.

That shut me up.

But only for a while.

"This outfit kicks ass," I informed him and his arm tightened around my midriff in a weird way, like the movement was spontaneous and he didn't mean to do it.

Then he asked, "Pardon?"

"This outfit," I pointed to myself and twisted my neck to look back at him, "kicks *freaking* ass. I love it. It's awesome."

He looked down at my face as one of his thighs moved almost imperceptibly under my legs and Salem slowed.

"You like it?"

"No, Tor, I *love* it. The colors are beautiful and the shoes are totally fab... you...*las*."

"Gods," he whispered, his eyes moving over my face. "You like it."

"Okay, you can say I like it when I told you I love it. That's cool. Whatever," I replied and turned to face front again. "And thanks for the bath. That river is cold as Siberia but it feels nice being clean."

He made no response to this except his arm got tighter again. This time it felt like he meant to do it and it got so tight I slid the half an inch back so the side of my behind was snug in his crotch (because I was riding sidesaddle) and my back was tight to his front.

With no response from Tor, I kept blabbing as I watched the lush forest trees and beautiful stone of the mountain slide by.

"And I'm so glad to get out of that cave for dinner. I know you need to take the pulse but I'm glad you're taking me with you. That's very cool of you. Thanks."

Still no response but I felt his fingers open up at my side so they spanned my ribs then they flexed in.

"God!" I breathed, looking around. "This place is magnificent. Totally out of a movie. The colors are so...I don't know...*colorful*. The trees seem to have ten times as many leaves. The stone seems like it's almost *glossy*. It's bizarre but so stinking cool. I wish I had a camera and I could take pictures. No one at home would believe this."

Finally, he spoke. "Camera?"

I twisted to look at him again and nodded. "Yep, it's this gadget that's really small but it takes pictures. Do you have paintings here? Portraits? Landscapes?"

"Of course," he grunted, staring down at me.

"Well, a camera takes a portrait or a landscape by touching a button. You load it on your computer, print it out and *voilà*!" I threw out a hand. "You have your picture."

"That's mad," he muttered.

I grinned up at him. "I know but it's true."

"So my world is more colorful than your world?" he asked and my light heart lightened more.

Was I finally convincing him?

I nodded fervently. "Yes, totally. It's hard to explain but the birds are more vibrant. The flowers more dazzling. The river is cleaner than any river I've ever seen." I tilted my head to the side. "There's a lot of pollution in my world."

"Pollution?"

"People litter, big corporations dump waste. It's not good."

"Love, I don't know what the bloody hell you're talking about."

I looked into his sky-blue eyes and realized I was glad he didn't.

Then I said, "Well, I guess my world has a curse of sorts too but all of man caused it by getting rid of their rubbish, and we create a lot of rubbish and some of it is unnatural, in the rivers, the oceans, burying it under the fields."

"Why would they do that?"

I shrugged and turned forward.

"I don't know," I whispered. "Because we're stupid, short-sighted and greedy." I looked at the darkening landscape that was still verdant in comparison with my world even with the falling night. "I wonder," I went on in a whisper, "if my world looked like your world before we destroyed it."

"Maybe it did," he remarked.

"That would suck," I muttered.

"Suck?" he asked.

"It would be bad."

Silence then, "Yes, love, it would."

I fell silent and Salem trotted down the mountain, found a road and took it. Tor's leg moved under mine again and Salem speeded up to a gentle canter. At the same time I felt Tor's thumb start moving, up and down, stroking me at my side.

That felt nice.

Oh man.

"Tor?"

"Yes, Cora."

The trees rushed by, Salem took us around a curve and the road started to follow the river. The new moon shone on its translucent waters, my breath caught in my throat and I forgot what I was going to say.

"Cora?"

"What?"

"You called me, my love."

"Oh, right," I whispered and rested against him. "I forgot what I was going to say."

He rested his jaw against the side of my head.

"It'll come to you," he murmured.

"Okay," I replied on a whisper and relaxed completely against him.

His thumb stopped stroking but all his fingers tightened into the flesh at my side.

I sighed and gazed at the view.

8

Princess

~

"Holy crap! Look at that!" I cried and pointed straight ahead at the vision that lay before me.

A village at the base of the river. A quaint, adorable village with thatched roof, timbered buildings that hugged the riverside and crawled partially up the mountain, their windows lit warmly and—I leaned forward and peered ahead—an abundance of colorful lanterns hanging from the roof ends. There were short piers jutting into the river with small, charming wood boats attached to the piers that also sported lanterns.

It was unbelievable!

And as we got closer, it got more unbelievable for it, like my (or the other Cora's) house, was filled with flower beds, window boxes and planters burgeoning with thriving blooms *everywhere*. Not only that, there were glistening cobblestone streets and sparkling diamond-paned windows in the buildings.

"It's *gorgeous*," I breathed.

"It's a village, Cora," Tor informed me and I twisted quickly to look at him.

"No, honey, it's *gorgeous*," I whispered, watched him blink slowly again, then I turned back in order not to miss anything.

We made it to the edge of the village, and even though night had fallen, people were wandering the side of the road.

"Heya," I said on a smile when a man looked up at us and started.

"Well, uh…hullo there," he replied hesitantly as we trotted past.

"Cora," Tor said low.

"Yep," I replied then a woman lifted her head, looked at us and she started too but I caught her eyes and called, "Hello!" and capped it with a wave.

I turned, looked around Tor's body and kept waving until I saw her lift a hand and a tentative smile hit her face.

"I'm seeing we need to make a deal," he remarked.

I straightened and looked up at him. "A deal?"

"You need to be smart in the village. None of your games."

I stared at him and I felt my light heart drop a notch.

"My games?"

"You're Cora Hawthorne here."

"Who's that?" I asked.

"You," he answered.

"I'm Cora Goode," I told him.

"Yes, love, you were until you took my name."

Oh. Right.

And his last name was Hawthorne. Noctorno Hawthorne. All together that was a pretty badass name.

"So, what I'm saying is, you're Cora Goode Hawthorne here," he went on.

"Well, I'm kind of Cora Goode, um…Hawthorne everywhere."

"No," his face went ultra-serious, "you're *this* world's Cora Goode Hawthorne."

My heart started to feel heavy.

"What?" I whispered.

"I think you understand me."

"These people know me?"

"You're Cora Hawthorne," he explained without explaining.

"You mean," I moved closer to him and whispered, "they know I'm a bitch?"

"No," he answered.

Oh man!

My heart skipped.

"You mean they know I started the curse?" I breathed.

He sighed in a way that indicated he was seeking patience and he replied, "No, Cora. They know you're a Hawthorne."

He pulled back on the reins, Salem stopped but I felt my brows draw together.

"What does that mean?" I asked but he didn't answer.

He swung his leg around, dismounted with practiced ease then his hands spanned my waist and he pulled me down and set me between him and Salem.

Close between him and Salem.

He tipped his chin down, caught my eyes in the bright lights of the gaily lit lanterns and muttered, "Right, your game."

My previously light heart sunk like a rock.

I wasn't convincing him.

Damn.

"Tor," I whispered but said no more when his big hand came up and curled warm around my neck.

"It means, love, that you're mine and what's mine is part of me and I'm royalty."

My body jolted and my voice was a muted shriek when I cried, "*What?*"

"Quiet," he clipped, not releasing my eyes.

I got up to my toes and whispered, "You're royalty?"

"Yes."

"Royalty," I repeated, just to confirm.

"Yes," he forced out through his teeth.

"Honest to God, blue-blood royalty?" I kept at it, not taking it in.

His brows shot together as he replied, "Gods, woman, my blood's red just like yours."

"You know what I mean," I returned on a hiss, going further up on my toes and my fingers curling into his shirt to keep myself from toppling over at my precarious position and at the shock of his news.

"No, I don't."

Shit. They didn't have the term blue blood here either.

All right. Moving on.

"What are you? A baron? A duke?"

"A prince."

A prince!

"*What?*" I shouted.

His fingers at my neck squeezed and his face got to within an inch from mine. "Woman, *quiet*."

"What?" I whispered.

"Can we not do this?"

"You're a *prince?*"

He looked over my head. "I see we're going to do this."

I shook my head in shock and disbelief while chanting, "Oh my God, oh my God, oh my God," over and over again.

"Cora."

"Oh my God."

"Cora."

"Oh my *God!*"

"Cora," he clipped. "Stop saying that or I'll kiss you quiet."

I snapped my mouth shut.

"Get hold of yourself," he ordered.

I stared up at him.

Then I asked, "Your father is the king?"

"Yes, love, that's what being a prince means," he answered with waning patience.

"Holy crap," I whispered.

"Cora—"

"So, uh…where are you in line to the throne?"

"First."

"Holy crap!" My voice was rising again just as my body went solid and his fingers tightened at my neck.

"Cora, damn it to hell," he bit out.

I sucked in breath then I whispered, "First in line?"

"Yes," he gritted.

"Wow," I breathed.

"Are you done?" he asked.

"Do you have brothers or sisters?"

He glared at me.

Then he muttered, "I see you're not done."

I pulled the bunched fabric of his shirt in my fists back and then slammed them against his chest. "Tell me."

"Dash, the second son, Orlando, the third. *Now* are we done?"

"Those are your *brothers?*" I asked in shock.

"Yes."

"You look nothing alike."

"Three different mothers."

"Holy crap!" I cried.

"Woman," he clipped.

"Right, right." I glanced around to see eyes on us, a number of them. In fact, we were drawing a crowd. Then again, he was the future freaking king, for God's sake. "Sorry," I whispered when I looked back at him.

"Finished?" he asked.

"Um…for now," I answered.

He looked over my head again and muttered, "Gods, save me."

He let me go, grabbed my hand and guided me into a building with a wooded sign jutting out of it that had a painting of the very village we were in on it, over which it said, "The Riverside Rory."

I let him do this and let him seat us at a table by the window and kind of let the proprietress fawn over us and let him order for me and took a sip of the crisp, cool, pale amber fluid that was set before me (which tasted vaguely of apples and strongly of alcohol) and I did all of this without word because the only thought in my head was, *Whoa, I'm married to a prince.*

I snapped out of it when something hit me and I focused on him to see he was watching me. I leaned across the small clean wooden table toward him.

"Does this mean I'm a princess?" I asked.

He stared at me looking annoyed for a second then he sat back and sighed, "That's what usually happens when a woman marries a prince."

I sat back and looked dazedly out of the multi-diamond-paned, wavy-glassed window, mumbling, "Oh my God, I'm a princess."

"Gods, that you would have granted me this boon when she wed me and with it gave me one night of this hot, greedy tart rather than the cold, selfish fish you gave me," he muttered, my eyes moved to him and I saw he was speaking to the ceiling in audible prayer.

But his words penetrated so I leaned across the table again and asked, "What did you just say?"

His eyes cut to me. "You like being a princess?"

I sat back and threw out a hand. "Of course I do. That question is absurd. Any girl wants to be a princess. And in this world, I *am* one."

"Well, you are one but you aren't."

I blinked as my happy fairytale balloon deflated. "I am one but I'm not?"

"Love, you live in a house. It's a nice house but you live there because you choose to live there. You warmed my bed like you warm my hides, you'd live with me in my castle."

My eyes rounded and I breathed, "You have *a castle*?"

"Bloody hell, here we go again," he muttered, staring at my face.

The proprietress arrived with wide, shallow pewter bowls filled with divine-smelling, delicious-looking, steaming stew and a cutting board resting precariously on her forearm topped with a fluffy loaf a brown bread, a knife stuck in it and a small ramekin of creamy butter at the side.

And when she did, I looked up and informed her, jabbing my finger at Tor, "He owns a castle."

Her body jerked, her eyes shot to me then she dipped down in an awkward curtsy while still balancing the bowls and board.

"Yes, your grace," she muttered, her eyes moving to my shoulder.

"Isn't that cool?" I asked her and her eyes flitted to me then back to my shoulder.

"Cora," Tor warned in a low voice.

I turned to him and cried, "Well it is, Tor!"

"Gods," he muttered and I finally noticed the woman and her burden.

"Here," I reached out, "let me help you with that."

"Gods," Tor muttered again as I took a bowl from her and set it in front of Tor.

"My," she whispered and I looked up at her, smiled and divested her of the bread board.

"Heya," I belatedly greeted.

"Erm…your grace," she mumbled.

"This bread looks *fantastic*! And the stew smells *superb*!" I noted as I took the last bowl and put it in front of myself. "And what's this I'm drinking?"

"Cider," she whispered.

"It…is…" I leaned closer to her, "*awesome*!"

"Erm, I'm pleased you think so, your grace," she replied.

"I totally do!"

"We brew it from apples from our own orchards."

"Well then, you're clearly masters at it." She stared at me like I had three heads so I went on, exclaiming, "I can't *wait* to eat!"

"I hope you find it to your liking," she mumbled, her eyes slowly lighting as she looked at me.

"It can't *not* be. If it smells that good, I'm certain it tastes heavenly."

"We've had few complaints," she informed me, her voice getting stronger, her lips tipping up.

"I bet not," I replied and finally looked around to see the inside of the pub was as appealing as the outside. I looked back at her. "You have a lovely place here."

She bobbed again and pink came to her cheeks. "Thank you, your grace."

I looked back around, noted the pub was filling and my eyes went to her. "Sorry, I'm keeping you from your duties."

"It's my honor, your grace."

Wow.

I smiled at her.

"If you get a quiet moment, get yourself a drink and come sit with us," I invited.

"Bloody hell," Tor muttered under his breath.

"No funning?" the proprietress breathed, so shocked at my invitation, she didn't hear Tor.

I shot an irritated Tor a look then rearranged my face to smile at the woman. "No funning. I'm Cora," I extended my hand to her and she jumped back like it hissed and bared fangs. "It's okay," I encouraged her.

She studied me then timidly lifted her hand and her fingers closed around mine as I felt a murmur run through the crowd.

"Liza," she whispered as my fingers gave hers a friendly squeeze. "Liza Calhoon. My husband Rory and I own this pub."

"Lovely to meet you." I let her go and gestured to Noctorno. "My husband, *Prince* Noctorno."

Tor glowered at me but composed his features to a benign (but still gorgeous) smile when he turned and inclined his head to Liza.

She bobbed again, dipped her chin low, stayed bobbed down and muttered reverently, "Your grace."

"Rise," he murmured and she did.

Uh...*wow*!

"I'm honored, to be sure," she told him.

He inclined his head again.

She grinned at him then she grinned at me then she said, "Enjoy your meals."

"I'm sure we will!" I assured her.

Her grin turned into a smile and then she twirled and scurried excitedly away.

The minute she did, the crowd's low murmur rose and this was likely because the future king was in their midst but I didn't care. My mind was awhirl.

I was a princess. My husband lived in a castle. And there was a huge amount of food right in front of me.

All was right in my world.

I tucked in.

I wasn't wrong. The food was fan-freaking-tastic. I snarfed down a half dozen spoonfuls of scrumptious stew then stopped in order to cut into the bread.

"You want bread?" I asked Tor.

"Yes," he answered.

I sliced while asking, "Can I see your castle?"

"You've seen it."

I dipped out a huge wodge of butter and started spreading it before I looked at him. "Okay, then can I see it again?"

He eyed me.

Then he said, "We'd be safe there."

I stopped spreading butter and stared at him. "We would?"

"The Shrew cannot practice on sacred land. All royal land is sacred land."

Was he serious?

"Are you serious?"

He was chewing.

I waited for him to swallow before he said, "Yes."

I stared at him again, counted, got to two then exploded, "For God's sake, Tor! If we're safe in your blinkety-blank castle, why'd you take me to a cave?"

His eyes narrowed and he commanded, "Quiet."

"No," I shot back, dropping his bread and the knife. "I want to know."

"Lower your voice."

"Dude, you took me to *a cave*!"

His brows knitted ominously and he growled, "I told you, I do not like this name."

"I don't care!" I returned heatedly and, might I add, loudly.

Mistake.

Big one.

He rose from his seat and was around the table in a flash. Then I was out of my seat. Then I was in his arms. Then his hard mouth was on mine. Then his delicious tongue was doing equally delicious things *in* my mouth.

When my belly warmed, my bones turned to water, my nipples were tingling, a surge of wetness gathered between my legs and my arms curled around his neck and held on for dear life, he lifted his head and I gazed hazily up at him.

He held me plastered to his body and he didn't move back even an inch.

"When I say quiet, Cora, you be quiet," he said low. "You don't, I swear to the gods, I'll keep at you until you do and I don't care if that means I've got to throw your skirts up and take you on the bloody table. Am I understood?"

Oh dear.

"Yes," I whispered.

"You're a bloody princess," he clipped.

"Okay." I kept whispering.

"Act like one," he ordered.

I nodded though I wasn't certain what that entailed.

He glowered at me. I tried to look contrite.

He let me go and started to move around the table but as he did a wave of sound hit us. He moved back to me, his arm circled my waist protectively and we both looked at the wild, cheering like mad crowd.

"Hurrah!" someone cried.

"Long live Prince Noctorno!" someone else yelled.

"Behold, the black prince and his exquisite bride!" someone else shouted.

How. Totally. *Cool!*

"Hey, ya'll!" I shouted and waved.

At my greeting, the cheer rose so high it nearly took the roof off.

Cool!

I smiled. Tor's arm around my waist squeezed.

"Princess," he clipped into my ear.

Oh shit.

Right.

I stopped waving like a friendly person, closed my fingers, cupped my hand slightly and started waving like a royal person.

This had no effect on the crowd who kept shouting, clapping and stamping then someone yelled, "We love you, Princess Cora."

"Isn't that sweet?" I yelled back in the direction from where the words came even though I had no clue who said it.

"Deliver me." I heard Tor mutter from beside me and I looked to the side and up at him.

"What?" I asked.

"Just, gods, please sit down and eat," he replied.

"Sure," I said, smiled at the crowd, did the royal wave again then Tor let me go and we sat down.

The cheering kept going for a bit then subsided but only when Tor looked toward them, inclined his head but lifted a hand, palm up, and he pressed the air out. They took their royal command and cooled it.

Whoa. *Awesome.*

I got over my awe, finished with his bread then put it on the side of his bowl and started on mine.

"So," I began, "I need royal instruction. I'm not hip on this princess gig."

"Pardon?" he asked and I stopped slathering butter on my bread, dropped the knife to the board and brought the slice to my face.

"This princess gig. You'll need to explain," I told him and then took a bite of the bread.

It was chewy and full of flavor. Lush.

"Well, you can start with never asking the proprietress of a pub to drink with you," he stated.

I swallowed. "What? Why?"

"She's common," he informed me and my head jutted back with not-so-mild affront.

"So? So am I."

"You are not."

"I so am."

"Cora, your father is an Earl."

I was sipping at cider and I choked at this news. I managed not to spew it across the table at him and instead swallow it but my mirth was not spent. Not by a long shot. At the thought of my hippie dad being royalty in this world, well, I couldn't help it.

I lost it.

Totally.

I threw my head back, wrapped my arm around my middle and laughed myself silly.

"Cora," Tor called.

"Hang on," I choked between giggles, my other fist on the table was banging it repeatedly.

"Cora."

"Just a minute."

"Did you not understand me before?"

That sobered me. My mirth died away but my stomach still ached. I held on, chuckling and wiping tears from my eyes, then I looked at him.

The laughter ceased as I caught the look on his face.

He was not pissed, annoyed, irritated or impatient. He was staring at me like he'd never seen me before in his life. He was staring at me like a movie star would stare at his movie co-star when he saw her for the first time and was instantly intrigued by something that would mean he'd soon become lovestruck.

But Tor did it better because he was hotter by far than any movie star and he was real and sitting across a table from me.

Holy crap.

"I've never seen you laugh," he told me quietly.

"I do it often," I replied quietly.

"You should do it more."

"If you'd quit being a jerk, I would," I returned.

"That was worth not being a...*jerk*," he said the last word cautiously, like he was testing it out.

I liked that so I smiled at him.

He smiled back.

My skin tingled all over and I felt my lips part.

God, he was gorgeous.

He lifted his spoonful of stew and asked before putting it in his mouth, "Why were you laughing?"

"My dad's an Earl."

He chewed, swallowed and grinned. "That's amusing?"

"My dad's a hippie in my world."

Something shifted on his face, like a shutter closing but not completely. "A hippie?"

"A love child. A child of Mother Earth. He's kind of a loon. He's liberal. Like, *way* liberal. He smokes weed. He gets down to Grateful Dead albums. He wears tie-dye, kid you not, to this day, and he's fifty-five years old."

"Sweets, you know I only understood half of those words but I didn't understand the meaning of any of them."

I grinned at him, leaned my elbow on the table so I was closer to him and took a bite of bread. After I chewed, I swallowed but in that time, I hadn't come up with any answers.

"I haven't been in your world long enough to make a like comparison."

That shutter closed further, he looked to his stew and muttered, "Right."

"Tor?" I called. He took a spoonful of stew and looked at me while he chewed, brows up. "Is everything okay?" I went on.

He swallowed, then without hesitation he cut me to the quick and pulled the rug right out from under me, I landed flat on my back, winded and wounded.

"It would be, if this was Cora sitting across from me, having learned to be a decent person. It isn't because you're playing your bloody game, you're good at it and I'm annoyed that I'm half enjoying it."

Uh.

Wow.

Ouch.

"Tor—" I whispered.

"Cameras, pollution and hippies. Yes, love, you're good. I should just let go and allow myself to fully enjoy it. Hell, who knows how far you'll take it. You might eventually give me something I'll *really* enjoy, like a bloody heir."

I felt my breath stall and he went on.

"And you might play it so well, I'll enjoy creating that heir. But, gods curse me, I can't let myself enjoy it because I know it's all a game to get your way. And as hard as I try, I can't stop it from annoying the bloody hell out of me."

I felt tears sting my eyes because for once in this cursed (literally) world (at least since the very beginning with Rosa and Aggie) I was enjoying myself and he just reminded me that I could not and why.

To hide my tears, I looked away.

"Crocodile tears, even better," he muttered.

Great. They had the saying crocodile tears here. Perfect.

I sucked in breath through my nose, focused my attention on my stew and ate it.

It didn't taste as good as I remembered it being not five minutes ago.

I emptied my bowl and was picking at (but not eating) my bread when I plucked up the courage to call, "Tor?"

"Yes, love."

I took another breath and my eyes slid to him.

"Can I ask one thing without giving you a kiss for it?"

"You can ask it but that doesn't mean I'll give it."

Of course.

I nodded.

Then I asked it.

"Can you please not call me 'love' or 'my love' when you obviously hate me so much?"

It was small, I almost missed it, but I was pretty sure I saw him flinch.

"Cora—"

"Men call women who they care about that. My dad calls my mom that. He loves her. Deeply. He has for nearly four decades. Please don't sully that by using those words, words you don't mean, on me."

He held my eyes and I let him. Or, more accurately, I couldn't tear mine away.

Then he said quietly, "No."

I pulled in my top lip and bit it. I nodded before I looked out the window.

"I need to make some inquiries," he told my profile.

"Of course," I whispered to the window.

"Don't leave this table," he commanded.

"Right." I was still whispering.

I felt him move but didn't look. I soon felt his heat at my side.

"Cora."

I closed my eyes. Then I turned my head and tipped it way back to look up at him. When I did, his hand lifted to cup my cheek and he bent low and touched his mouth to mine.

I felt a tiny tear split through my heart.

When he lifted his head, he murmured, "For my people."

That loving gesture was for the crowd.

"Right," I whispered.

"Don't move from this table."

I nodded but made no further retort even though he was being bossy and repeating himself to boot. When I didn't speak, his eyes examined my face as his thumb tenderly swept my cheek.

That tear split deeper into my heart.

"Gods, I wish this was real," he muttered.

It is, you stupid man! my mind shrieked.

But my mouth didn't move.

"I'll be back," he stated.

"I'll be waiting."

His thumb swept back and his eyes held mine.

Then he let me go, straightened and he was gone.

9

I'll Hand You the World

~

I woke half on and totally wrapped around Tor again.

But I woke to the dark.

It was still night and the fire had gone out.

I slid away from him and out from under the covers. I then pulled on my flowy top that dropped all the way down to my upper thighs, covering my silky, lacy underthings. After that, I slipped on my satin slippers.

Then I went to spend time with a being that I was pretty certain actually liked me.

Walking on tiptoe and being careful to be quiet, I ducked under the pelt curtain and approached Salem.

"Hey, boy," I whispered as I got close.

He jerked his head up, greeting me but being quiet like he knew Tor was sleeping and he didn't want to wake him.

I got close and he let me curve an arm under his jaw and stroke the length of his nose.

"I'm not sure he's this kind of guy, so I'm not certain Tor has told you, but you should know from someone that you're unbelievably beautiful," I whispered.

He gave a gentle snort, nuzzling his nose closer to me, and I smiled.

I moved to his side, stroking him along the way and I leaned into him, snuggling his neck and stroking his chest. I could swear he took a teeny horse step sideways to get closer to me too.

I liked that.

"I want to go home," I whispered to him.

This got me a soft whinny.

"It's beautiful here but I don't like it."

A careful jerk of the head, done so as not to dislodge me.

"I *should* like it. I'm a princess married to a handsome prince and the rivers are clean and the horses are sweet…"

Another soft whinny and I smiled then sighed.

"But I wish I could get home," I said wistfully.

Another gentle snort to which I replied with another quiet sigh.

His head moved to the right and he took another teeny sideways horse step into me as I gave him a horse-hug and kept stroking his chest while looking out into the moonlight at the mouth of the cave.

Out of nowhere a steely arm closed around my ribs and another one closed around my upper chest as I felt a face bury itself in my neck.

Holy crap!

"Noctorno?" I whispered, let the horse go and my hands went up so my fingers could wrap around a hard forearm.

"Stroke me like that, I'll take you to a castle," he murmured into my neck.

I closed my eyes tight.

Jeez, how did he get across that stone without making that first freaking noise?

"Please, let me go."

His mouth moved up to my ear. "Let me stroke you, swear to the gods, sweets, you loosen up just a hint, I'll make you come so hard you'll think you've exploded."

Oh God.

I bet he could do that. He was a good kisser. If he was half as good with other things, I'd definitely think I'd exploded.

"Please," I whispered but his hand at my side drifted up and his thumb slid out and caressed the side of my breast.

Whoa.

This had to stop mainly because it felt so good.

Too good.

Fairytale good.

"Noctorno—"

His teeth nipped my ear and I shivered.

I liked that too, way better than Salem shuffling closer to me.

"You've been calling me Tor."

I had because he was becoming a Tor. But I had to remember he was Noctorno, always, always, *always*.

"I—"

I stopped talking when his arms squeezed and his tongue traced my ear. I stopped talking because my body trembled and heat rushed to very specific parts of me.

"Forget what I said in the village. I've changed my mind. Play this game, my love, I want you to," he murmured. "Let me take you to my castle where you can play it. Let me make you heavy with my heir and I'll treat you like a queen while you play it. You give me an heir, you can name your price. A bigger house, more land, jewels, whatever you want, by the gods, it'll be yours. Just open your legs, convince me you're enjoying it, settle a son on me, and before you leave, I'll hand you the world."

My body started trembling but for a totally different reason.

"Before I leave you'll hand me the world?" I asked quietly.

"Anything you want," he assured me, his arms getting tighter, his body pressing into mine.

"Leave you with my son."

"*My* son," he stressed.

"*Our* son," I corrected.

His teeth nipped my ear again and he whispered, "*My* son, Cora. My heir. My country's future king."

Dear God.

Was he serious?

For sanity's sake, I moved to another subject. "Convince you I'm enjoying it?"

"Yes."

"So I won't?"

"You let go, I'll make you enjoy it. That's a vow." His thumb moved in, stroking closer to my nipple and I bit my lip. "Let go, sweets," he coaxed into my ear.

"Let go so you can fuck me, get me pregnant and take my child?"

His head came up and he asked, "Fuck you?"

"Screw me. Boink me. Nail me. Tag my ass. You know, have sex with me. Sex with no meaning, no love, *fuck me*," I explained acidly.

He turned me in his arms to facing him and one hand sifted into my hair, clenching gently but making a statement nonetheless while his other arm caged me in.

"I take it...*in your world*...that's not a nice thing to say," he remarked.

"Nope," I agreed.

He was silent but he didn't let me go.

Finally he sighed and said, "You're clever, I'll give you that."

"So clever, you'd think I was from a different world," I noted sarcastically.

"Now, wouldn't go that far, love."

No, of course he wouldn't.

"Whatever," I muttered to his shoulder.

"I think you missed it, Cora."

"Missed what, Noctorno?"

I heard him pull a sharp breath in his nose then he stated, "The part where I gave you permission to play me."

"That'd be hard to do since I'm not a player."

I watched him tip his head back before he muttered, "Gods."

"Got that right," I muttered back.

He tipped his head down and his eyes locked on mine in the moonlight.

"You know, love, I go to bed and lay awake before sleep claims me wondering what it would be like to have the other half of my soul in Rosa."

Oh my God.

Ouch times, like, a *thousand*.

"I asked Dash how he felt," Noctorno continued. "He said the minute he met her, it was indescribable. The instant connection. The pull. Now it's constant. He can barely stand to be away from her and she feels it too. I know he's wounded, bleeding deep somewhere no one can see because he told me that being separated from her is like what he would imagine it felt like having a limb removed. You need it there. You can't live without it. When it's gone, the phantom of it remains and when you notice you don't have it close enough to touch, it drives you slightly mad. She can leave him for hours, days, even weeks but any longer, he starts dying inside. Minerva has her. She has her and while she does, my brother is dying inside."

God, that sounded beautiful. I wished I had that.

It also sounded awful.

Poor Dash. Poor Rosa.

"We should have that," he informed me.

"We don't," I informed him.

"Why?" he asked.

"I don't know." And I sure as heck didn't, except the part that I wasn't from this freaking world!

"I do," he replied.

Really? He did?

"You do?"

"Yes, Cora, I do."

"Then why don't we have it?"

"Because to have that pull you have to have a heart. You have to be able to fall in love. He fell in love with her the second he saw her and she the same. And, as you know, the minute my eyes hit you, I fell in love with you."

Whoa!

Wait.

What?

What, what, *what?*

Before I could verbalize my question, he kept speaking.

"But you didn't fall in love with me because you have no heart and then you proceeded to kill my love for you and twist it into something else entirely. And you keep doing it. Every bloody time I see you. Every time I speak to you. You twist it until there's nothing in it to recognize as anything even close to what it once was."

"You loved me?" I whispered, looking into his harsh, moonlit face.

"Don't," he clipped shortly.

"Are you saying you loved me?"

His arm got so tight I couldn't breathe and his hand in my hair twisted so it wasn't gentle anymore. Not even a little.

And as he did these things, he barked in my face, "*Don't!*"

"I—"

"Play your game but don't you ever, *ever*, Cora, play with that memory."

Oh.

My.

God.

He used to love me! And, obviously, he'd told me. And, just as obviously, I'd spurned that love.

Or, more aptly, the other me spurned his love.

Oh. My. *God!*

His arm gave me a shake. "Am I understood?"

"Tor—"

He lost it and I knew it when his hand twisted in my hair, I cried out at the pain and he roared, "*Am I understood?*"

"Yes!" I shouted.

At the same time I shouted, Salem threw his mighty head back and whinnied loud.

Noctorno's attention shot to his horse, his body went statue-still then he looked over my head to the mouth of the cave.

"Gods!" he yelled, let me go but grabbed my hand and dragged me behind him as he sprinted to the antechamber. He went so swiftly, I nearly stumbled twice on the way.

"Noctorno!" I cried and he yanked back the pelt and hauled me through so roughly and with such force, I went flying.

"Hurry, finish dressing," he ordered.

"What?" I asked, confused.

"*Dress!*" he thundered.

I jumped and ran to my clothes.

I was bending to snatch up my skirt when he commanded, "Meet me at Salem."

I looked up and saw him dragging a sword off the wall.

"Salem," I agreed, nabbed the skirt, tugged it on, grabbed the vest, shrugged it on then bent and snatched up my belt. I wrapped it around my waist on the run and saw that Noctorno had already disappeared.

I fled the space and saw him saddling Salem.

"In there," he jerked his head to the space where the wood was kept. "Arm yourself."

Arm myself?

I skidded to a halt three feet away from him.

"With what?" I asked stupidly.

"It doesn't matter," he answered curtly, cinching the strap under Salem's proud chest. "Just as long as it's sharp and you can wield it."

"Right," I whispered, ran to that space, snatched a lethal-looking knife off the wall and ran back out.

When I arrived, Salem was saddled, a sword in a scabbard at his left side. Noctorno put his hands to my waist, hefted me up, wasted no time swinging in behind me and this was good.

Really good.

For I learned what all the fuss was about.

Vickrants.

Everywhere.

Their near transparent wings flapping hideously, their claws reaching, their scaly skin glistening, they were filling the cave.

"*Hee-yah!*" Noctorno barked as he dug his heels in. Salem's mighty flanks bunched and we bolted out the mouth of the cave, vickrants following in a swarm. "Home, Salem," Noctorno yelled over the wind rushing in our ears and the branches slapping at our bodies, vickrants darting through the trees and making passes at us, so close I could feel their vile, cold, leathery wings and smell their stench.

Yikes. I forgot their stench.

Fetid. Hideous.

"Take the reins," Noctorno commanded, extending them to me.

"What?" I cried.

"Take the reins," he repeated.

"I don't know how to steer a horse!" I yelled.

"Take the bloody reins, Cora!"

I took the reins.

He immediately pulled the sword out of the scabbard and with one arm locked around me holding me tight to the safety of his body, the other one struck out with powerful swings and blue sparks and sharp hisses met his blows.

A smaller vickrant landed on Salem's neck, claws digging in. The horse screamed his fury but kept charging ever onward through the dangerous rock and scrub. Noctorno was busy swinging so I leaned forward with my knife, lifted it high and stabbed at the foul creature. Blue sparks flew back into my face, the thing shrieked and fell away.

Whoa.

I did it.

I *did* it!

So I decided to do it some more.

Okay, so I clearly wasn't as gifted with a knife as was evidenced by the practiced swings and thrusts that Noctorno performed with his sword but it didn't matter. When he was swinging right, I concentrated on anything that got close on the left. Same with his left, I went right. When he was circling his sword overhead, anything went.

The creatures shrieked, yelped, sparks flew and this happened not only from the shaft of Noctorno's sword but the sharp blade I carried.

Jeez, I was like a real warrior princess!

Totally cool!

The problem was, there were lots of them. As many fell back, there were more charging in. This lasted a long time. It lasted so long, Salem had made it down the mountain to the road. It lasted so long, it continued down the road. It lasted so long, Salem, Noctorno and I were breathing hard, sweating and, I couldn't speak for man or beast, but I was scared shitless.

They just wouldn't go away.

We finally hit a village, not the one we were in for dinner, a different one, just as picturesque but not on the river and it was asleep.

The horse's hooves clattered sharply against the cobbles and he raced us directly to the church at the other end of the village.

To the church then, no joke, straight up the church steps, then, still no joke, he reared back on his hind legs. Noctorno leaned deep into me, I reached out, dropping my knife and grabbing Salem's mane, the horse's powerful hooves beat down the door and he tore inside.

Yes, the horse tore inside a church.

The vickrants disappeared in an unholy (no pun intended), loud, ear-splitting screech of shrieks.

Salem stopped dead center of the church. Noctorno dismounted instantly and just as instantly dragged me off the back of the horse.

And suddenly his hands were on my biceps and he was shaking me.

Shaking me!

Again!

"Stop shaking me!" I shouted through my labored breathing.

"*What did you do?*" he barked, still shaking me.

Oh God.

Was he going to blame me for this too?

"Nothing," I answered.

"*What did you do?*" he thundered, still freaking shaking me.

I grabbed on to his arms and screamed, "*Nothing!*"

He stopped shaking me only to toss me away from him with such violence I went flying and stumbled into some pews, banging my thigh on the side of one so hard the pain beat in and radiated out instantaneously.

He advanced on me and I lifted a hand, palm out and cried, "Stay back!"

"Did you throw out the bones?" he asked, his voice quieter but no less scary.

"Wh-what?"

He lost it again.

"*Did you throw out the bloody bones, Cora?*" he raged.

I shook my head. "Yes, I...you mean when I tidied?"

"Gods!" he bellowed. "Do you *want* Minerva to find you?"

"No!" I yelled. "I don't know what you're talking about!"

He got close, my breath fled, and I shrunk away, cowering—stupid, stinking, weak *cowering*—away from his big, powerful body and his bigger, more powerful rage. I dimly heard Salem's hooves on the wood floor of the aisle and felt him get close to us but my concentration was on Noctorno and trying, and failing, to force air into my lungs.

"You know," he gritted between clenched teeth.

I sucked in breath, shook my head and whispered, "I keep telling you—"

He reached down and wrapped his fingers around my arm again, hauling me up and he gave me a shake that snapped my head back so hard, I saw stars.

Salem whinnied.

Noctorno's body went still and I heard him draw in a sharp, hissing breath through his teeth.

"Stop playing that damned, bloody game," he warned, his face close but I was still blinking away the bright lights in my eyes.

"I-I-I swear, God, I swear, *I'm not*."

He shoved me away again and the small of my back hit the sharp edge of the top of a pew. I whimpered but he strode away.

He stopped at the door and looked to his horse.

"Do not let her leave."

Salem snorted.

Noctorno turned and jogged down the steps, disappearing without looking back.

10

Minerva

~

"Get out of my way, Salem," I commanded.

The horse snorted and shuffled across the space at the front of the church, blocking the doors with his massive body.

"Get out of my way, Salem!" I shouted and the horse snorted again, his front legs buckled like he was going to go down on his knees then he reared up and snorted again.

"I'm leaving!" I announced.

Salem whinnied what sounded like frantically.

I planted my hands on my hips and looked the horse in his eyes.

"You saw him!"

He blew through his lips and his mighty head swung side to side.

"He shook me! He nearly snapped my goddamned head off!"

The horse moved closer to me and butted the side of my head with his nose.

I grabbed it and pulled it down to catch his eyes again.

"I don't care about Minerva," I told him, my voice suddenly low and trembling. "Right now, the devil I don't know is way, *way* better than the devil I do."

A soft, apologetic whinny.

I shook my head. "I have to get away from him. He's mean, he's bossy and he won't believe I am who I am."

He shoved his nostrils in my neck and blew.

I felt tears sting my eyes and wrapped my arms around the beast's neck.

"He hurt me," I whispered.

That got me another blow making his horse lips quiver.

"You have to let me go."

Salem was still.

Then he pulled his neck from my hold and twisted it to look down his body at the open church doors.

He looked back at me.

He shifted his big bulk so he was facing the doors and butted me with the side of the saddle.

Oh my God.

Was I reading him right?

"You...are you..." I paused then whispered, "Going with me?"

He threw his head back and whinnied then twisted it to look over his shoulder at me and jerked it up and down in an obvious affirmative.

"Are you serious?"

He whinnied a "someone's gotta keep you safe" whinny.

So...totally...*awesome*!

I surged up his body, threw my arms around his neck, gave him a huge hug and whispered, "Thank you."

Then I ran to the doors, snatched up the knife I dropped, shoved the hilt between my knees as I retied my belt tighter around my waist. I shoved the knife into my belt and approached the horse.

It took me three tries to heft myself into the saddle. I was not a seasoned rider, and mind you, I had ample fabric hindering me straddling a horse (so much for my kickass outfit, I had to get myself something that said "warrior princess"). Unfortunately, the minute I got up I realized the stirrups were way too low so I had to dismount, cinch them higher and do it again (this time it took four dratted tries).

But I got on that beautiful beast, touched my heels to his flanks and off we went, out the door and into the unknown.

I felt the bed depress, I opened my eyes in exhausted confusion, saw Noctorno sitting on the bed, his hips in the crook of my lap and he was leaning over my body with a hand that I guessed was in the bed behind my back.

Uh.

What?

What was he doing here?

My head shifted back on the pillow, my eyes darting to the nightstand.

"Looking for this?" I heard him ask.

I looked to him and saw his other hand raised, my knife dangling from his fingers by the tip of the blade.

Blast!

He flipped the knife up, losing hold on it but he caught it expertly by the hilt and he did this, no joke, without taking his eyes from me.

"You didn't think, did you, that my own damned horse was going to take you somewhere I couldn't find you?"

Salem, a traitor.

What a disappointment.

We'd ridden the rest of the night and all the next day, stopping only to bum water and, for my part, answer the call of nature. An hour or two after night fell we came upon this hunting lodge that Salem, in his Salem way, assured me was safe. He even reached out his powerful neck and pointed with his communicative muzzle to the window ledge that held the hidden key.

I thought he was my horse in shining coat.

Totally a disappointment.

Now, clearly, as the sun was shining, it was sometime the next day.

And I was back in the clutches of the evil, black Prince Noctorno.

Foiled.

"I own this hunting cottage. It's sacred ground. It's safe. My horse is no fool," Noctorno went on.

Great. Marvelous.

Or, more aptly put, phooey!

I carefully rolled to my back and just as carefully scooted up the bed until my back was pressed to the headboard. I pulled my knees up and circled my calves with my arms. I got in this protective position and held it all the while I kept wary eyes on him.

His eyes swept my truncated body and came back to mine.

They warmed and he started to lean in, murmuring, "Cora."

My hand shot up, palm out, and I whispered on a hiss, "Don't touch me."

His body stopped moving.

"Cora," he repeated on a whisper.

"Tell me about the bones," I demanded and watched his eyes flash. I dropped my hand and narrowed my own eyes at him. "I know you don't believe me and yadda, yadda, yadda. Humor me. Tell me about the *fucking* bones."

He studied me.

Then he stated, "They have my saliva on them."

"And?"

He studied me some more before he sighed and continued, "And, they can track me through my saliva. They can do it from miles away."

"So that's why you kept the bones in the cave," I surmised.

He nodded. "They had no clue it existed and I use it for hunting or for war. I'm always careful, out of habit, it's been ingrained in me since I was born. In ancient times, they could only track the females. They've adapted. Now they've learned also to track the mates. So, along with searching for you, they were searching for me. You threw out the bones, they found me, or since the remains of our rabbit meal were amongst them…us."

Hmm.

"And say, when we, uh…relieve ourselves. Can they track that?" I asked.

"That's acid so…no."

Interesting.

"Just saliva?"

"That and other bodily fluids."

"Like?"

"Blood. Semen. But not urine."

Yuck!

Time to move on before he went on.

"Okay, that's enough with the bodily fluids and other, um…bodily functions. Can they track scent? Hair?"

"Fluids only."

How weird.

So weird, my brows shot up. "Seriously?"

One side of his mouth twitched. "Seriously."

He looked hot with one side of his mouth twitching so I decided I was done. Therefore, I stated, "Thank you for the lesson. You can go now."

His eyes stayed glued to mine and I let them mostly because I had no choice. The guy had proven time and again he was freaking strong so I could never best him physically and wasn't going to try.

The bummer of this was, he didn't move.

He said quietly, "We must talk."

"Welp, Prince Noctorno, sorry to disappoint you but I am way, *so* done talking to you."

He shook his head.

"We must talk," he repeated.

"I have nothing to say and *you* have nothing to say I want to hear."

"We need to talk about what happened in the church."

My body went solid. "No, we absolutely, definitely, without a doubt, totally do not need to talk about what happened in the church."

"Cora—"

"Go away."

"Cora—"

"I said go away. I'm tired. My body's sore from riding all day. I need sleep before I'm on my way again..." I paused then finished, "*on foot*."

"Cora—"

"Don't worry, I won't bleed on anything. I, obviously, don't have any semen so we're good on that score and I promise to be careful with my saliva."

"Gods damn it, Cora."

"Seriously! Go!"

He didn't go.

Nope. He didn't.

What he *did* do was dart a hand out, wrap his fingers around my ankle and yank it out and straight down the bed. Unfortunately, as my body was attached to it, it too went down the bed. Then he shifted to lying and rolled right, smack on top of me.

I shoved at his shoulders, shouting, "Get off me!"

"Calm yourself," he commanded.

"Get...*off*...me!"

"*Calm yourself!*" he barked.

"And what if I don't!" I yelled back. "You gonna shake me so hard I see stars? Or toss me around?"

"I had another idea to get you to obey."

"Spanking? Whipping? Wait, that might draw blood—"

"Cora—"

"Water torture?"

"No, Cora, *fucking* you so hard you can't bloody breathe and you're so damned exhausted after, you can't move and you're forced to shut your mouth and bloody *listen*."

I snapped my mouth shut.

Shit, I should have never taught him that word.

"That did it," he muttered.

"You want to talk, talk," I invited, my tone surly.

He scowled down at me.

Then he sucked in a breath and started, "I hurt you—"

"Yep," I confirmed. "I checked and I've got the bruises to prove it."

This time the flinch was not nearly imperceptible. This time he flinched flat out.

"Gods," he whispered.

"You can say that again."

His eyes warmed again and his hand came up to cup my jaw. "Love, I'm—"

I jerked my head away, doing my best to angle my body to keep it away.

My eyes tilted to him and I reminded him, "I told you, don't touch me."

"I scared you," he muttered, studying me, his hand dropping to the pillow by my head and I relaxed.

"Yep, you did that too. Shitless."

His brows knit. "Shitless?"

"Yes, shitless, as in, you scared me so badly I was incapacitated. I couldn't think. You made me *cower* in front of you like a weak thing. You scared me so much you forced me to humiliate myself in front of you. So, you've shaken me before, you've spanked me, *twice*, and done other stuff that's not very cool but that, that, Noctorno, I cannot forgive you for. I could fight the vickrants with you, and I'll admit I was terrified out of my brain while I did, but you…it was *you* who scared me so much, I couldn't…fucking…*breathe*."

He closed his eyes slowly and with them closed he whispered, "Cora, sweets—"

"Get off me."

His eyes opened. "My love—"

"Don't call me that!" I snapped and his hand suddenly was back at my face, cupping my cheek, his thumb pressing against my lips and his face dipped lower so it was all I could see.

"Please, let me speak."

I lifted a hand to pull his thumb from my mouth and hurled, "Fuck that and fuck *you*!"

"I'm uncertain I understand all the meanings of this word," he replied quietly.

"I think you get the gist," I guessed.

Suddenly he stated, "We were losing."

I blinked in my surprise, letting my guard down which was foolish. It was foolish because my fingers were still wrapped around his thumb. He twisted his wrist, laced his fingers through mine and then rested our entwined hands on the bed by my shoulder.

"I was in a foul mood because I was concerned because we were losing," he semi-repeated.

"Losing what?"

"Against the vickrants."

This was confusing.

"We were?"

"Yes, love."

"But I thought we were kicking ass," I told him and his mouth twitched again.

Then he informed me, "We were but if that village was a mile further away, they would have overwhelmed us. What we fought was only the first wave. The second wave was coming. I heard it. Salem heard it. They were close. If they made it to us, they were triple in number. They would have overwhelmed us and you would be gone."

I felt my eyes grow wide as my mouth formed the whispered words, "Holy crap."

"I'm not certain what that means but the way you say it makes me think it says it all."

"It does," I whispered.

He held my eyes.

"The second wave was *triple* what we were fighting?" I asked.

"Minerva's hungry," he answered.

Oh dear.

"She needs both the sisters to complete the curse over the land," he continued.

Oh. Fucking. Dear!

"She's waited millennia to do it," he explained.

Now it was oh shit.

"It's been centuries upon centuries that the vow has gone unbroken," he carried on.

Ohshitohshit.

"That would be, I'm guessing, the vow that the soulmates wouldn't see each other prior to the wedding festivities," I guessed.

"That would be the vow," he confirmed.

"Oh *shit*!"

That time, I said it out loud.

His fingers squeezed mine. "She creates the soulmates, love."

I blinked again. "What?"

"Playing. Torture. She does it only so she can tear them apart. She's evil. Pure through to her core. She creates them then plays with them, trying to trick them, showing them the promise of joy beyond measure in the hopes to rip it away."

"My God, that's…that's…" I shook my head, "I don't even know what that is."

"That's Minerva."

"What is she?"

"She was a witch. Through the years, her power grew. Now it so closely rivals the gods', she *is* a god."

"Uh-oh, that doesn't sound good."

"It bloody isn't."

"But you said the gods pick the soulmates."

"No, I said the *she-god* picks the soulmates. Unfortunately, the benevolent ones have been forced to let her into their ranks. We pray to our gods. We fear Minerva."

Crap.

Then it dawned on me.

"And so Dash had planned it all. Rosa was to stay at her, I mean, *our* parents' house and he was—"

Noctorno nodded his head. "You live miles away in the opposite direction to your parents, the church and my father's castle. We stayed the night miles beyond that. Rosa wasn't supposed to be anywhere near there. We were dropping in mostly as a joke. Dash wanted to tease you, guessing you'd sleep in. I knew, however, that you *would* sleep in so, since you were on our way, we stopped by to drag you out of bed."

My eyes drifted over his shoulder and I asked mostly myself, "I wonder how she got there."

Since I asked mostly myself, I was guessing this was why he didn't answer.

My gaze went back to his. "If this was happening for millennia, why didn't Rosa know about it?"

His head tilted to the side and he examined me. He did this closely, intensely. He was a pretty intense guy but this was even *more* intense. It was like he was doing it for the first time, or perhaps seeing something he hadn't seen before that fascinated him.

After he did this awhile, he said softly, "There are delicate souls, some so delicate, you know, even a child just born, how delicate they are. Rosa is one of those souls. Her parents, and even you, throughout her life protected her from unpleasantness that she couldn't handle. She doesn't only not know the curse exists, she doesn't even know Minerva exists."

I thought of tra la laing Rosa and I could see this girl had a delicate soul.

"I met her briefly," I informed him. "I can see this."

"It's hard to miss," he muttered.

Something struck me. Something bad. Really bad. And my heart lurched as my body went solid when it filtered through me.

"Oh my God, Tor," I whispered, my free hand lifting to curl around his neck. "Oh my God."

"What?"

"Oh my God," I breathed.

"Sweets, *what?*"

"Rosa's delicate and Minerva has her."

His jaw got hard. "Yes."

"Oh my God!" I yelled and bucked, trying to push him off.

"Cora—"

I stilled and looked up at him. "We have to go get her!"

His brows drew together. "Pardon?"

"What are we doing?" I cried desperately then blathered on, "Why were we holed up in a cave? *Here?* We have to find her! We have to rescue her!"

"Cora—"

"We have to go!"

"Cora—"

"*Now!*" I shrieked and his mouth came down on mine hard.

This time, his tongue didn't sweep into my mouth. This time, my bones didn't turn to water. This kiss was meant to silence me. It worked because it was hard but at the same time also freakishly tender in a way I liked.

Therefore, my body melted under his and when he felt it, he lifted his head an inch.

"Are you calm?" he asked softly after his blue eyes caught mine.

"Calm…*ish*," I answered breathlessly.

"Orlando is leading the rescue mission to find your sister," he explained. "He has at his command my father's entire army and my warriors, all of them but my personal guard who are at my castle, on alert should you and I need them."

I stared up at him. "You have warriors?"

"Yes."

"Why?"

"I'll explain that later."

Okay, I decided to let that go.

"Is, um…Orlando good at that kind of thing? You know, leading a rescue mission?"

"Yes. If he wasn't, I'd be with him, but he also has my men with him and if he wasn't good, they are."

"So, they'll find her."

He nodded and stated firmly, "They'll find her."

This made me feel better.

So I asked, "Dash isn't with them?" He shook his head and I continued, "Why not?"

"Because Dash is in danger, like you and like me. The full curse starts when both the females are collected but Minerva switches tactics frequently. Generation upon generation, she conjures something new, growing frustrated at her torment being thwarted. She could attempt to take Dash or me. He needs to stay safe and we all need to be cautious. There's no telling what she'll do."

"Oh," I whispered, thinking an unpredictable enemy who had the power of a god was not a good thing.

"And furthermore, he's Dash," Noctorno carried on.

I felt my brows knit. "He's Dash?"

"My brother is a lot of things, nearly all of them good. What he is not is a soldier, and something else he definitely is not is a warrior."

"Like you," I guessed quietly. "Being a warrior, I mean."

"Indeed, love, like me."

And I knew this to be true the way he sat astride a horse and beat back an army of vickrants wielding a sword.

Not to mention, all his scars.

"And," he started and I focused on him to see his eyes lit with something I'd never seen before, "apparently like my wife."

"What?" I whispered.

His gaze moved over my face then his head dipped. I tensed when his lips brushed mine sweetly, slid along the skin of my cheek just as sweetly and ended up at my ear.

"You are valiant," he whispered there and I shivered.

"Valiant?"

"Never in a million years would I think you had that in you."

"Had what?"

His head lifted and his eyes locked on mine. "You fought alongside me and Salem. No hesitation. Quick reflexes, brilliant instincts. You did not recoil. You did not become hysterical. You were no burden. You were a boon. Had it only been me and Salem, they may have taken me or they may have harmed him."

I felt something squishy in my belly at his words but also felt the need to point out, "You're pretty good with a sword yourself, big guy."

He grinned at me. "I've had plenty of practice. You, my love, as far as I know, have never wielded a dagger." His fingers tensed in mine. "Your strokes were awkward, uneconomical, you expended more energy than you needed. You lashed out, were reactionary rather than tactical."

Well!

"Nevertheless," he went on, "you instinctively protected my weak flank and our mount." He gave me another finger squeeze. "You did well, sweets."

My belly was even squishier when I whispered, "Uh...thanks."

He grinned at me and dipped his head yet again to brush his lips against mine.

Damn, but I liked it when he did that.

He lifted his head and I saw his eyes were smiling. "Now, as brilliant as it is to have your soft body under mine in an actual bed, my love, I need to drag you out of it, feed you and we need to be on our way."

What?

"We do?"

"I've given Salem his oats. He's rested. We have to press on."

"Press on to where?"

"My castle."

Oh.

Wow.

"Seriously?" I asked, wanting, despite myself, to see his castle.

"Yes, Cora."

My eyeballs moved around the room then back to him. "But, if this is safe—?"

"It *is* safe but it's rustic, one room and there's no tree cover. The cottage is sacred ground, the land around it isn't. You or I leave the house, we could be spotted. My castle, and the land around it, is bigger, more comfortable and all of it is off-limits thus it's safer."

"Oh."

This made sense.

"Now kiss me quickly, make it good, earn your breakfast and we'll be away."

Uh.

What?

"Are you joking?" I asked.

He grinned and answered, "Not even a little bit."

The squishiness in my belly and the excitement at seeing his castle disappeared and I glared at him.

"So we're back to that?"

"We never left it."

"You let me have a bath, clothes and dinner without earning it," I reminded him.

"You cleaned my cave," he informed me.

Ugh!

"Why is it when I think I can start liking you, you remind me why I don't?" I asked and that earned me another insolent grin but no response.

Drat the man!

"I think I should get a pass considering I helped you hold back the vickrants and put up with your foul temper in the church," I informed him.

The grin faded and the amusement in his eyes died but still he said, "And I think you should stop talking and earn your breakfast so we can be on our way."

I tried to unlace my fingers from his (and failed, by the way) so I scowled up at him. "You forget, I've decided to go it alone."

"And you forget that you foolishly left me, taking my horse while doing it. It's my duty to protect you, you put yourself in danger and doing this, you negated anything you might have earned in our fight and enduring my foul temper in the church."

"That doesn't add up!" I snapped.

"It certainly does," he returned.

"It doesn't!" I shot back and his fingers tensed and stayed tensed in mine.

"The curse has just begun. The Shrew cannot complete it unless she has a half of *both* the souls. She gets you, and it's highly likely, you go on alone, wherever the bloody hell you think you're going, she'll get you. That means my land, my people, will live under that curse in all its fullness until the next divided souls blissfully wed. My people, as yet, are unaware of what has befallen them. They are experiencing unpredictable weather patterns, but as far as I can tell, nothing more. As the curse has not descended for millennia, there is no known record of what to expect *except* whatever it will be will likely mean floods, droughts, crops failing, plague, famine and the only hope would be to endure, for a shred of humanity to hold on as the decades pass until the new souls are united in matrimony. You endangered that, *again*, my love, and for that we return to our terms and you *earn* your keep."

Oh dear.

I didn't know any of that. I'd fucked up again. Royally (in my case, seeing as I was a princess, that was weirdly literal).

Shit.

"Then I'm not hungry," I decided. "We can just go."

"You'll eat and you'll earn it."

"Nope, I'm fine. Thanks for your concern but I'm good."

"Did you eat yesterday?"

No, I did not and, incidentally, I was starved.

I didn't tell him that.

"Cora, you can earn it or I can take it from you."

I blinked up at him. "What?"

"You kiss me or I kiss you. Those are your choices. You have two seconds to decide."

"Don't you dare kiss—"

"One."

"Noctorno, you kiss me, I'll—"

"Two," he muttered, his eyes dropping to my mouth then his lips dropped there.

Hells bells.

I fought it, I did.

Seriously.

And I worked hard at it. And it seemed I was winning.

I kept my mouth resolutely closed no matter how he coaxed (and he *coaxed*) with lips and tongue to get it open.

I was feeling pretty pleased with myself when his free hand suddenly cupped my breast and his thumb, with pinpoint accuracy, swept over my nipple.

Holy crap.

My mouth opened at the shock of pleasure that shot through my system and his tongue swept inside.

Oh shit. I forgot just how stinking much I loved how he tasted and how much more I loved how he kissed.

My body gave in before my mind, my arm curving around his broad shoulders then my back arched to fit my breast more firmly in his hand.

He groaned in my mouth and I loved that too. So much, that was when my mind gave in and he had all of me.

He deepened the kiss and my fingers glided into his hair to hold him to me as his thumb stopped sweeping my nipple. His hand went up, tugged the fabric down then he went back to my nipple, thumb and finger this time, rolling and squeezing.

Oh my.

Nice.

My hips surged up, my fingers still laced in his hand held on tighter and I moaned my pleasure in his mouth.

His lips left mine and I moaned again because I didn't want them to go.

But they didn't go. They just moved to relocate. His hand cupped my breast, lifting it, his body angled down then my nipple was in his mouth and he instantly started sucking even as his tongue swirled.

Oh my God.

That felt freaking *great*.

My fingers still in his hair fisted and I breathed, "*Tor*."

His lips left my breast, his hand cupping it warmly again, just cupping it this time as his mouth came back to mine.

My eyes opened and they stared into the heated depths of his.

"Don't stop," I begged, arching into him again.

"Why do you burn so hot now, sweets, when we must go?" he muttered, his mutter husky with want at the same time I sensed frustration.

"We can delay," I whispered, my hand leaving his hair to cover his at my breast and my other hand squeezing his insistently.

"We can't," he denied.

"Ten minutes," I pushed and watched the desire in his eyes war with amusement.

"My love, what I intend to get from you will take far, *far* longer than ten minutes to get."

Oh boy.

I liked the sound of that.

His hand moved from my breast and he pulled up the material.

Drat!

I couldn't help it. I felt my mouth twist into a pout.

His eyes dropped to it, he stared at my mouth for a scant second and then burst out laughing, throwing his head back and everything to do it.

It totally sucked that he looked gorgeous all the time and laughing was no exception.

"Get off me," I snapped. "I'm hungry."

His laughter turned to chuckles and he dropped his chin to catch my eyes. "I'll give you what you're hungry for, in my soft bed, in my big castle, I promise you that, Cora." His voice dipped sexy, husky deep when he finished, "And I'll take my time doing it."

"I was talking about *breakfast*," I informed him briskly.

"Right," he murmured, smiling down at me.

"Hello? Noctorno? Aren't we in a big hurry?" I called.

This earned me another blasted chuckle but he knifed away from me never letting go of my hand. Therefore he used it to pull me out of bed with him. And he rested me on my feet half an inch from his body, let go of my hand but crushed me to his body with both arms.

I tipped my head back to look up at him.

"What are you doing now?" I snapped.

His eyes searched my face and they did this for a long time. So long, the scrutiny so intense, I started to feel funny but I didn't know if it was a good funny or a bad one.

"Noctorno?" I finally said.

"I prefer you calling me Tor."

I didn't answer.

One of his hands slid up my spine and started to play with the ends of my hair.

Oh dear.

I liked that too.

"My wife is exquisite," he said softly and I felt my body still as I felt my lips part. "That, I always knew. But she's also brave, defiant, clever and amusing. That, my sweet, I did *not* know."

Holy crap!

"Tor," I whispered but didn't say anymore because I didn't know what to say and because his head dropped down so he could again brush his lips tenderly against mine.

"Now I need to feed you," he murmured against my lips.

I sighed against his.

His eyes, which were all I could see, lit with a light that I liked way too much then he let me go, took my hand and led me to the table.

11

Sharing

~

Salem was clip-clopping under us at a sedate canter as the magnificent countryside passed us by.

The clouds had shifted so now the sun shone and the view as far as the eye could see (and the stretch of what we'd already passed) was extraordinary.

Every inch of it.

I had, that day, learned two things.

One, a horse could look contrite. I discovered this when I walked outside and glared my displeasure at Salem. He gave me a look and if he could bite his lip, I knew he would. Instead, he ducked his head.

I let him suffer for about two seconds before I gave in, stroked his long, glossy nose and muttered, "I forgive you, and anyway, you did the right thing, taking care of me and obeying your master at the same time. You're a good horse."

He blew in my neck.

Two, my husband could cook—on an old, iron wood-burning stove, no less. He made me eggs, bacon and thick slices of toast slathered in creamy, melty fresh butter. The food was awesome and not just because I hadn't had anything to eat since the stew at Liza and Rory's pub but because Tor could *seriously* cook. It was just eggs, bacon and toast but somehow he made it delicious.

After breakfast, we both mounted Salem even though there was another horse there (the one Tor used to track us). He left it saying he'd have his "people" deal with it just as they would deal with the dirty dishes we left.

It, obviously, was good being the future king.

I didn't understand why we wouldn't take the horse. I figured we could go much further much faster if we both had our own mounts but he disagreed. He told me if we were attacked, he could guard me much easier if I was close. Considering my inexperience as a horsewoman and warrior princess, I agreed.

As much as I hated it, I had to admit that I liked sitting in the sunshine atop Salem, feeling Tor's big, strong body surrounding me, making me feel safe. Yesterday had been overcast and chilly, I felt the need to be constantly vigilant and I wasn't a brilliant rider, only having been on a horse a handful of times in my life. Salem luckily knew what he was doing but riding was difficult, jarring, exhausting, and it was nice to sit back and enjoy the ride.

Which, watching the splendiferous countryside pass us by as the sun warmed our bodies and Tor held me close, I was doing.

I relaxed further into him and asked, "How long before we get to your castle?"

"If we were able to take the main road, which we cannot for Minerva's beings will be watching it, a day. The route we have to take, likely three," Tor answered and I straightened, twisted and looked up at him.

"Three?"

"Yes, love, three."

Holy crap. That was a serious detour.

I turned back and fell silent. In the distance I saw a bunch of deer lift their heads in our direction, sensing us. Then, as a group, they took off, gracefully running up a hill into a forest.

I'd never seen that many deer in my life. A few here and there, but there had to be thirty, maybe even forty of them.

Outstanding.

My eyes slid across the landscape, experiencing greens greener than I'd ever seen before, wildflowers running riot in the fields around Salem's legs and beyond, a faraway body of water that was the blue of Tor's eyes. In fact, it seemed strangely the very air sparkled like it had tiny pieces of near invisible glitter floating in it.

It was magical.

I sighed.

Then I decided to take a chance and rested my hand on Tor's arm at my belly.

"Can I tell you something?" I asked.

"Anything, sweets," he mumbled and I felt his chin come to rest where my neck met my shoulder.

Oh boy.

That felt nice.

"Can you promise me something before I tell you?" I went on.

"Ask me and we'll see," he replied gently.

Well, that wasn't a yes but it wasn't a no, and it was a maybe said in a tone I liked so I sallied forth.

"Okay, I want to talk about something you don't believe and won't like. But can you just *pretend* you believe or, I don't know, just keep silent?"

I received no response for some time then his arm around me gave me a squeeze and he answered, "I can do that, Cora."

"Really?" I whispered to the landscape.

"Really, love. What do you want to talk about?"

I pulled in a deep breath and then shared what had been niggling me deep in the back of my head for a while.

"I'm not going home," I said softly, his arm squeezed me again and I went on quickly. "No, don't say anything. I know you think I *am* home but I'm not. And every time I go to sleep, I expect to wake up back in my apartment, in my life. But I'm not doing that. And as the days pass by, I'm wondering if I ever will. And there are a couple things about this that are nagging me."

He didn't lift his chin from my shoulder when he prompted, "And those are?"

"Well," I started. "If I'm here, that means the other Cora is there. And if she's like you say she is…um, I don't think that's good. See, my job is in danger. I've been there years and I make okay money but they're looking for reasons to get rid of people. If she doesn't figure out she has to work for a living or decides not to, or figures it out, goes in and doesn't know what she's doing, which by the way in my world she can't possibly know, or by some miracle, pulls that off but pisses someone—"

"I get it, love," he cut me off quietly.

I sucked in breath before I said, "I can't lose my job, Tor. And Lord only knows what else she might get up to. And the longer I'm here, the more time she has to get up to it."

"This is true. The gods only know what the other Cora would get up to," he agreed and I didn't know if it was actual agreement or him humoring me but I didn't ask because I didn't want to know if was the latter (though I figured it was).

"This is important," I told him. "And it's kind of freaking me out."

"Freaking you out?"

"Worrying me," I explained.

He lifted his chin and ordered, "Look at me, Cora." I did, twisting to look up at him to see his eyes tipped down to me. "You have no control over that. Let it go."

"But—"

"Let it go."

"I can't!" I exclaimed.

"I can understand this but do you know how to get back there?" he asked.

I shook my head. "No."

"Do you know how you got here?" he went on.

"No," I repeated.

"Then you have no control over it. *If* you go back," he stated and my heart somersaulted at the same time it clenched, "you'll be forced to deal with it then. Since you have no way of knowing what you'll face, you have no way of strategizing your response. So you simply have to wait and deal with it if it occurs."

He was right. This was logical and wise.

"That's logical and wise," I told him.

He grinned at me.

"I'm still going to worry," I admitted and he chuckled.

I smiled at him because it felt good to unload that, even if I didn't have any firm answers, and I turned to face forward.

We fell silent for a while before I broke it.

"There's something else."

"Yes?"

I stared at the scenery.

Then I swallowed and shared on a whisper, "I don't know if I want to go back."

Tor's body went completely solid behind me and even Salem missed a step before righting himself.

"Pardon?" Tor asked.

I pulled in my lips and bit them. And for some wild, crazy, insane reason, I kept right on talking.

"It's beautiful here. Horses communicate with you. Birds talk to you. It's unpolluted. Life is simple. I would never, not in my life, have guessed that I wouldn't miss cars, cell phones, microwaves, martinis and high-heeled shoes. If you told me I would come to a place such as this, and if I did I'd have to stay, I'd say no way. But now that I'm here, I want to explore. Every sight I see, I like. Every village. Every flower. Every beast. Every blade of grass. Sure, a curse is pending, but you've got that under control, right?"

"Right," he replied, humor in his tone.

"So," I whispered, "if I'm stuck here, when your brother saves Rosa, I think I'm going to go. Travel. Experience this world to its fullest, something I never did in my own."

"Two points to make, Cora," he said in a voice that now held no humor and I twisted to look up at him again. His eyes dropped down to me. "One, I would ask, is there nothing you would regret leaving behind?"

I bit my lip and turned forward again.

"Yes, my parents and my friends," I admitted and whispered, "I'll miss them, a lot. Losing them would suck. Especially since, by all reports, Cora of your world won't be such a great daughter or BFF and they'd wonder what the hell was going on."

I pursed my lips on this thought then kept sharing.

"But I don't like my apartment, my job. My life is colorless. Brian and I broke up and I haven't been asked out on one, single date. I'm not lonely. I don't get lonely. I like my own company. But a lot of the time, I'm alone, and well, I'm getting sick of that. And, if I'm honest, I was getting sick of all of it...until this happened. And being here, seeing this...this *place*," I threw out a hand in front of me, "it's made me realize all of that."

Tor made no response and spoke no further.

Until I prompted, "You said you had two points to make?"

"Yes," he replied. "The second point would be that when Rosa is saved, I'm afraid, love, you aren't going to go, travel, experience this world to its fullest."

This surprised me and I twisted to look at him again. "Why not?"

His eyes captured mine. "Because I'll not let you."

My head tilted to the side and I stared at him before repeating, "Why not?"

"Because, Cora, I'm beginning to like having you around. So I've decided to keep you."

What?

"*What?*" I shrieked and Salem twitched under us.

Tor smiled. "It won't be that bad, my sweet. When I travel, I'll take you with me so you will experience this world. But when I'm home, you'll be with me there too."

"But we don't live together," I reminded him.

"That will change."

"What?" I snapped. "Why?"

"As I said, I like you around."

"We fight all the time," I informed him of something he already knew.

"Indeed, and I like that too."

I blinked at him. "You do?"

He nodded. "I do."

"That's insane."

"Don't you?"

"Hell no," I clipped.

His arm gave me a squeeze, his eyes shifted over my head and he declared, "You will."

"I won't."

"You will."

"No, Tor, I won't."

He looked back down at me. "You will, Cora, because soon, when we argue, and you take it too far, which you do so you will continue, I'll be forced to stop you." He grinned. "And I like the ideas I have on how I'm going to stop you." His eyes warmed. "*All* of them."

"Ugh!" I grunted and faced forward again, noting, "You're pretty sure of yourself."

"Sweets, all I had to do was draw your nipple in my mouth and you were begging for it. Of course I'm sure of myself."

Damn.

I hated that that was true.

"Whatever," I muttered, inching as best I could up the saddle to get away from him, an effort that was for naught when his arm tightened and he pulled me right back. "Release your arm a little," I demanded. "I want to shift. I'm uncomfortable," I lied.

His arm slid up so it was under my breasts and I felt his lips at my neck. "No you're not."

"I *so* am." I kept lying.

His thumb started stroking the underside of my breast at the same time his tongue touched my earlobe and he changed the subject.

"If you want," he murmured huskily in my ear. "I could pleasure you right here."

Oh God.

That sent a surge of heat between my legs.

"Thanks," I tried to sound snappish and feared I failed. "I'm good."

"I'll give you the ten minutes you begged for in bed," he coaxed and I steeled myself against his pull.

I was thinking those ten minutes would be the best ten minutes of my whole, entire life.

I beat the urge back and replied, "Thanks again but...no."

His thumb moved up half an inch so it was stroking my breast right under the nipple.

Oh boy.

I couldn't stop my lids from slowly lowering over my eyes but I fought back the urge to lift a hand to his and take him to target.

"Turn your head and give me your mouth, sweets," he commanded softly.

"No."

"Right, then lift your skirts so I can have the heat of you."

Oh *God*.

I swallowed a moan and ordered, "Tor, pay attention to where we're going."

His tongue slid along the skin under my ear and he whispered in it, "Salem knows the way."

There it was.

A decent excuse.

"Salem, right, he's a good horse. I couldn't possibly engage in any, um... naughty activities with him around."

Salem snorted and I had no idea if it was a "go ahead, don't mind me" snort or a "thanks for thinking of me, Cora" snort.

"It isn't his first time," Tor told me.

Way, way, *way* wrong thing to say.

Way.

My back shot straight, my eyes shot open and Tor took his mouth from my ear.

"Cora?"

I lifted a hand and curled my fingers around his at my breast, pulling them down.

He sighed.

Then he said, "My love, you know you're not—"

"If I were you, Prince Noctorno Hawthorne, I'd keep my trap *shut*."

He, of course, did not.

"I'm a man, Cora, and you've been withholding from me."

"No I have *not*, considering I lived in an alternate universe until a few days ago," I reminded him. "The *other* Cora has. If you were *my* husband, you'd be getting it regular," I announced.

Tor's body went solid behind me again then he asked, "Does that mean what I think it means?"

I twisted and glared at him.

"Yes!" I spat. "You're a prince. You're hot. You're a great kisser. You have a cool horse. You've got great eyes and an even better chest. You have just enough, not too much, chest hair. And when you aren't being a jerk, you can be sweet. So obviously, if we were wed in holy matrimony, I'd be giving it up...*regular*."

His brows drew together. "You'd be giving what up?"

"Me!" I shouted then twisted forward, muttering, "Yeesh."

His mouth came back to my ear, not to play, just to speak. "Well, since you *are* here and you've taken the place of the other Cora and you're apparently stuck here, then I expect to get *you*," he paused and finished firmly, "*regular*. Starting now."

"No, absolutely not," I denied.

"Then you lied?" he asked.

"No," I answered. "But I can't give it when I'm peeved." I twisted to look at him again. "And make no mistake, Prince Noctorno, I...am...*peeved*."

"You're peeved a lot," he observed.

"Learn from that, big guy," I educated and twisted right back.

He chuckled.

I gritted my teeth.

That was when I heard it.

My head snapped to the left and I peered into the trees at the same time Salem took two side steps and blew through his lips.

"Cora?" Tor called and my hand shot up.

"Shh!" I hissed and listened.

There it was again.

"Pull back on the reins," I ordered.

"Pardon?"

There it was. I heard it again!

"Pull back on the reins!" I shouted then kept shouting, "Salem, *stop*!"

Noctorno pulled back on the reins and Salem stopped.

"What do you sense? Danger?" Tor whispered in my ear, his arm fiercely tight at my ribs.

"No," I whispered back. "Aggie."

I broke from his arm, slid off the side of Salem, landed on my slippers and immediately darted around the front of the horse and ran toward the trees.

"By the gods, Cora! Stop!"

I didn't stop.

Instead, I shouted, "Aggie! Aggie, is that you?"

I kept running and heard the hooves of a horse and the boots of a man behind me but I no longer heard the chirps.

"*Aggie!*" I screamed then let out an, "Oof," when my running was halted by an iron arm around my stomach and I was hauled into a hard body. "Let me go!" I yelled, pushing at his arm and pressing forward.

"Cora," he ground out in my ear. "Don't ever—"

"Chirp, chirp, chirp," I heard faintly and I knew it meant, "Cora, help me."

Oh God.

I twisted in Tor's arm to face him as he dragged me toward Salem who'd run off the road with Tor and I.

"Tor!" I cried desperately, tipping my head back to look at him, struggling against his arm and dragging my feet to stop him from dragging me. "I hear Aggie."

"Who?"

"Aggie!" I yelled.

Tor stopped and stared down at me. "Who's Aggie?"

"Aggie, Aggie, Agglethorpe! The bird!"

His brows shot together. "The what?"

"Bird!"

"Chirp," which meant, "Help."

"Tor! I think something's wrong. We have to do something!" I lifted my hands to his jaws, got up on tiptoe, leaned in and begged, "Please!"

He stared into my eyes then he muttered, "Gods," let me go, grabbed my hand and jogged into the wood, pulling me behind, Salem following on a trot.

"Aggie!" I called. "Chirp for us, sweetie, so we know where you are."

I listened. Nothing.

I lifted my hand, cupped my mouth at the side and yelled, "Aggie, honey, *please*. Give us something!"

I heard it, a close, weak chirp right above us. I stopped, tugging on Tor's hand making him stop and Salem stopped with us. I looked up and saw the bright feathers of Aggie about ten feet up in a tree.

"I see you!" I shouted, jumping up and down and shaking Tor's hand as I did. "I see you! Hang on, Tor's going to climb up and get you!"

"Chirp, chirp, chirp," which meant, "Thank the gods."

"I'm going to what?" Tor asked at my side and I turned my head to look up at him.

"You have to climb up and get him," I explained.

He looked up at the tree and then down at me. "Who?"

"Aggie! That bird up there!" I cried, pointing up to the tree. "He sounds weak. I think he's wounded. You have to go get him."

Tor looked up into the tree again, squinted, I noticed when he saw him because he squinted harder then he looked down at me.

"You jest," he stated.

"*Do I look like I jest?*" I shrieked, throwing out an arm. "That's Aggie! You have to save him!"

"Cora, that bird is half dead," he informed me evenly.

"Then that means he's also half alive!" I yelled.

He stared at me for a long moment then he moved into me, pulling me into him with a gentle tug on my hand and he lifted his other hand to curl his fingers around my neck.

"Sweets," he said softly. "Are you attached to this animal?"

"Yes, no, uh…kind of. I've only met him once but he was cute. Does it matter? He needs help."

"You've only met him once?" Tor asked.

"Yes, the morning I woke up in this world. He was in my room. He was there when the curse started. I've never talked to a bird before. He was my first and, um…only, I guess. But it was cool. You can't talk to animals at home, I mean, you can but they can't talk back. He talks back. I mean, he *chirps* back but in a way where I understand him."

"Of course," he replied.

Awesome! He got it!

"So you have to have heard him too! He's in distress!"

His head tipped to the side. "No, Cora, I can't hear small birds. Women can hear small birds, rabbits, deer, cats, mice and the like. Men can hear horses, dogs, wolves, birds of prey, snakes and the like. I can't hear him."

Whoa.

Weird.

I wanted to hear more about that but just not at that particular moment.

"Okay, well, I can and he needs help," I told him.

"Was this bird your pet?"

"Uh, I don't think so. He flew in from outside.

He pulled in breath through his nostrils. Then he got closer and his fingers curled deeper into my neck.

Once there, he said, "Love, you can talk to the wild animals but you can't form attachments to them."

"What on earth? *Why?*" I exclaimed.

His face dipped closer to mine. "Because, my sweet, they're wild and this," he jerked his chin up slightly, "happens and you have to let it happen."

I took a step back and declared, "Oh no I don't!"

"Cora—"

"Please, Tor, I'm asking you to climb up that tree and save Aggie."

"Love—"

"Please!" I cried.

"You shouldn't—"

"I'll kiss you," I bartered.

"It's not about a kiss, it's about nature. This is nature happening and you cannot intervene."

I glared up at him before I pulled free and stomped to the tree, stating, "Fine! *I'll* climb up and get him."

I didn't get within three feet of the tree trunk before my hips were captured in big hands and I was pulled back.

I struggled forward. "Don't try to stop me."

"Woman, you are not climbing up a gods damned tree!"

I looked over my shoulder at him. "You wanna bet?"

He yanked me back and I collided with his hard body. "Yes, I'll bet."

Oh dear.

I wasn't going to win this fight.

So I tried a different tactic and cried pleadingly, "Tor!"

He stared down at me. I tried to stare up at him beseechingly.

Surprisingly, I won.

He let me go and strode to the tree, grumbling, "When we get home, remind me to speak to my physician about the state of my sanity."

"Thank you, honey," I called quietly.

He stopped at the trunk and cut his eyes to me. "You owe me."

Oh shit.

"I'll pay," I promised.

"You bet your beautiful arse you will," he muttered then he climbed the tree like he was a ten-year-old boy yesterday and did it five times daily. He climbed down just as agilely all the while cradling the tiny Aggie in one hand.

I rushed to him and bent my head to an Aggie who didn't look too good.

"Oh, Aggie," I whispered.

"Chirp," meaning, "Cora."

"Baby, we got you," I told the bird.

"Cora," Tor called and I tilted my head to look up at him not noticing I had the fingers of one hand wrapped around the wrist of his hand holding Aggie and the other hand resting on the wall of his chest. "His wing is mangled. Beyond repair."

"Oh God," I breathed.

"You and Salem need to go to the road. I'll take care of Aggie," he continued and I blinked.

"Take care of him?"

"He's in pain. He's been up in that tree for a while, no water, no food. He's not half dead, he's mostly dead. I need to take care of him."

I tilted my head to the side. "Take care of him how?

"Take away his pain."

Oh no.

I was pretty sure I knew what he was saying.

"Are you saying—?"

He must have read the horror on my face for he answered swiftly and gently, "Yes."

"Tor, no."

"It's the right thing to do."

"We'll find a vet."

"Pardon?"

"A vet, a veterinarian. A doctor for animals."

"I know what a vet is, love. What I was trying to ask without saying it is, are you mad?"

I stepped back. "I'm not mad! Maybe something can be done."

"Something *can* be done, and if you would go with Salem to the road, I could do it and put this creature out of its misery."

"Chirp" came from Aggie which unfortunately meant "chirp." Therefore, no clue what Aggie thought of this conversation and his impending euthanasia at the hands of a hot prince warrior.

"Tor—" I whispered.

"Sweets, go."

I shook my head. "We can get him water. Food. Maybe he'll perk up."

"Sweets…*go*."

I stepped into him and put my hand back on his chest.

Leaning in and up, I begged again, "*Please*."

His eyes moved over my face before he said quietly, "I give in, we do this bird no favors."

Oh my God.

Was he going to relent?

"We can nurse him back to health. Get him some seed, water, then to a vet the first chance we get," I suggested.

His jaw clenched.

My hand slid up his chest to curl my fingers around his neck. "Tor, please, he's Aggie. The first being I saw in this world was Rosa, the second, Aggie. I don't have a sister at home and I had Rosa for about ten minutes before she was gone. Aggie was swept away in the wind when the vickrants came. They both can't be gone. I couldn't bear it. It may sound crazy but he's important to me. I can't do anything to help Rosa but maybe I can do something to help Aggie. Help me help him. *Please*."

Okay, truth be told, I was laying it on a bit thick but the reason this bird had been stuck up in a tree for days was because I had inadvertently started a curse that struck up a wind that caught this little creature in it so it was all my fault his wing was mangled (kind of).

Tor held my eyes, lifted his hand and cupped my jaw.

Then he murmured, "Go get the waterskin. Let's get this bird hydrated."

He relented!

Goodie!

I smiled brightly at him, lifted up on my toes, pushed in (careful not to further crush Aggie) at the same time my hand slid to the back of his neck and pulled down. He bent and I touched my mouth to his.

I pulled back an inch and looked in his beautiful eyes.

"Thank you, honey," I whispered, watched his eyes light but I had things to do so I didn't dawdle.

I let him go and raced to Salem to get the waterskin thinking as I did it that maybe Prince Noctorno Hawthorne wasn't all that bad.

12

Bellebryn

~

"Sweets, wake up."

I shifted physically but in my unconscious I executed a lazy breaststroke toward consciousness, decided I liked the warm, safe waters I was in, gave up and floated.

Tor's deep voice again penetrated my slumber. "Cora, we're almost home."

That got my attention and my eyes fluttered open.

I was turned fully to the side in Tor's saddle, snug between his legs and up against his chest, my cheek pressed deep, his arm cradling me, my arm cradling a recuperating Aggie.

I tipped my head back, sliding my cheek against his chest, saw the underside of his strong, stubbled jaw tilt down and his beautiful light-blue eyes hit mine.

"Hey," I whispered.

"Hullo, sleepy," he whispered back.

My stomach melted.

Mm.

I gave him a small smile. He returned a gorgeous one.

My stomach melted more.

Mm.

"We're nearly there?" I asked.

He jerked his chin slightly up and replied, "Turn and see."

I started to turn, thinking that I wished we weren't nearly to his castle.

It had taken not three days to get there, but four.

This was because we stopped at a large village with a veterinarian who looked at Aggie, did his best to set Aggie's wing, gave us some medicinal herbal drops, a kind of rudimentary eye dropper we could use to give Aggie water and some tiny balls made of suet and crushed seeds that we could give Aggie to eat.

Even with this, Aggie had not made a turn for the better until that morning. He took his drops. He took his water. He gamely swallowed down the suet balls. But he hovered at death's door until that very morning when we woke to see him hopping around and chirping, partly, but not fully, back to his old self.

It had also taken us four days because Tor stopped in other villages and a small town.

He did this so we could eat in pubs or, when we were in the town, a surprisingly rather cosmopolitan café that had great pastries.

He also did this in the evenings so we could rent rooms in inns in order to have a soft bed to sleep in at night and, major bonus, hot baths (heavenly).

And in the town, he bought me another outfit. It was much the same as the first except the material was of better quality. The skirt and vest were pale blue with beautiful turquoise, silver and green embroidery around the hem of the skirt and all over the vest, and a flowy cream top that had intricate lace around the bottom of the sleeves. The petticoats were cream and dripped at the bottom with the same lace that adorned the sleeves of the blouse. And the satin slippers were green but had blue bows at the toes the color of the dress.

The whole ensemble was awesome.

The dressmaker, thrilled beyond belief to be outfitting who she thought was the future queen, upon hearing (from me, I was being chatty) that we were roughing it, also gave me a comb made out of bone, a brush that looked basic but its bristles were firm and felt freaking great on my scalp and turquoise satin ribbon to use in my hair, all at no charge.

I thanked her with a hug and kiss on the cheek which bought me a short lecture later on princess behavior from Tor, but I didn't care.

I was thrilled beyond belief to be able to comb my hair, it was nice to have something to hold it away from my face and the ribbon looked great threaded through my dark locks, so if I wanted to hug someone because they did me a kindness, I was a princess and I felt I should be able to.

Sometimes when we were in these towns and villages, Tor would not take us to a pub for lunch or dinner but would buy cheese, bread and fruit and then we'd stop on the way by a lake, a stream or in a wildflower-filled field and we'd have a picnic.

On the third day, it hit me what he was doing.

He was taking his time. Allowing me to chat with townsfolk, window shop, smell the flowers, taste the foods and drink in the landscape.

He was giving me his world.

And in return he didn't ask for a single kiss. He didn't make me pay the debt I owed him for saving Aggie. Nothing.

We slept in the same bed every night, I woke in his arms every morning and I spent nearly every waking minute with him (except when I was bathing or trying on my new outfit). Even as future king, he was not a man who shied away from public affection, often brushing his lips against mine (in public and not), taking my hand, guiding me with his fingers at the small of my back, standing with his arm about my waist.

But other than that, he was the perfect gentleman (albeit an often annoying one; he could be a gentleman but that didn't mean we didn't still bicker, we did, though to all appearances, he seemed to enjoy it).

So that meant he gave his world to me without me asking for it or him making me earn it.

He just gave it, free and clear.

Yes, Prince Noctorno Hawthorne, I decided, wasn't that bad at all.

And I also decided I loved every minute of being out on the road with him, experiencing this world. Yes, even when we were bickering and yes, believe it or not, because I was experiencing it with him.

And therefore, as cool as a castle would likely be, I had to admit I was sad that our adventure was ending.

I noticed the sun was setting as I twisted in the saddle holding Aggie carefully. Dusk was settling. Soon it would be night.

I sat forward, lifted my eyes and stopped breathing.

Oh.

My.

God.

I stared.

It was...it was...*indescribable.*

It wasn't just a castle.

It was a castle and a city.

An actual *city*.

I hadn't seen one of those in this world, and let me tell you, it was a-freaking-*mazing*.

The city started at the bottom of a steep, huge hill. Even at our distance (we were still quite far away), I could see flowers burgeoning everywhere. If my eyes didn't deceive me, even some of the *roofs* had flowerpots.

But there were also colorful awnings on the front of some buildings, some solid, some in stripes, all in different colors. They decorated in lanterns too, also all different colors, dripping from the eaves, and it looked like on the sides of buildings and even on the streets. They also fully utilized black wrought iron, there were iron whimsies shooting in the air, curlicues decorating the sides of buildings.

Magnificent.

A winding, blond, wide, clean cobblestone road led up the steep hill that was covered in what looked like adobe, terracotta tile-roofed buildings with their flowers, awnings, lanterns and iron whimsies. The road, too, was set with flowers liberally and lit with tall, curlicued, black iron street lamps.

And at the top of the hill was the best of it all.

A huge castle shooting straight in the air made of a mellow cream stone with an abundance of arched windows that blinked in the waning sun, high turrets piercing the sky with colorful pennants flying, balconies here, there and everywhere dripping with flowers through their contrasting ivory-stoned balustrades—the entire building made of smooth, rounded edges and circles.

To the left, there was emerald-green sea (yes, *emerald green*) and I could see islands close and far and tall-masted galleon ships (yes, *galleon* ships, also lit with lanterns) bobbing. To the right, fields of forests and rolling hills. Beyond, the landscape was a patchwork quilt of different crops. And to the front, a sea of wildflowers, ablaze with color even in the diminishing light.

Totally something out of an animated movie.

We had *nothing* like that at home.

It was unbelievable.

"My God," I whispered as Salem clattered over a bowed, wooden bridge that spanned a wide, rushing, crystal-clear river.

"Welcome to Bellebryn," Tor muttered behind me.

"What?" I asked distractedly, still dazzled by the view.

"We just crossed the bridge into Bellebryn, my land," he explained.

I blinked, and even though I didn't want to tear my eyes away from the sights they beheld, I twisted to look up at him.

"You *own* all of this?"

Tor looked down at me. "No, I own the castle. But I rule it all."

I blinked again.

"Rule it?"

"It's mine, not part of my father's kingdom. Everything from the river to the sea to the forest is ruled by me."

Holy crap!

"Really?" I asked.

"Yes." He grinned. "Really."

"So, your dad gave it to you at birth or something?"

He shook his head. "No, Cora, I conquered it."

I blinked yet again then whispered, "What?"

"I conquered it."

"You *conquered* it?" I breathed.

"Yes, love."

Holy crap!

I turned to face front and I could see why he would want to. It was amazing.

But I didn't get it. Why would he do that? Was he the marauding kind of warrior?

I didn't know if that was good.

"I don't get it," I told him.

"Get what?"

"Why, when you stand to inherit a kingdom, would you conquer this land?"

"This isn't the only land I conquered and all of it was *my* land, my birthright, wrested from me, or more aptly, my father. I just took it back."

I twisted again to look at him.

"What?"

His arm about me gave me a squeeze and he explained, "Remember what I told you about Dash not being a soldier or warrior?"

"Yes," I replied.

"My father isn't a soldier or warrior either."

Whoa.

Tor went on, "He's a good man. A kind man. A benevolent king, fair and generous. His people love him. But even though he has great skills in some ways as a leader, in others, he does not. Furthermore, he had the misfortune of finding, falling in love with and wedding women who were, by all accounts, lovely, but who had weak constitutions. My mother died while having me."

Oh dear.

"Dash's mother died from flu six months after he was born."

Oh shit.

"And Orlando's mother never fully recovered from his birth and died two years after in her sleep."

God, that sucked.

"My Father loved them all and became more and more heartsick with each loss. He was raising three sons alone, and although he is king, he fully participated in our upbringing and therefore his mind was on other things. The ruler of the neighboring kingdom to our north coveted areas of ours, and with my father's heart not in it, this king was able to conquer vast tracks of my father's...and thus my...realm. My father did what he could in his state to fight but did not succeed in keeping his kingdom safe."

All righty then.

Maybe *everything* about this world wasn't hunky dory.

Tor kept talking.

"King Baldur of the north is *not* a benevolent king. He is not fair or generous. He is greedy and ruthless. His taxes are high. His tactics are cruel. Therefore, our people, as ruled by him, were suffering. So, when I came of age and finished my training, I felt that not only was it my responsibility to re-secure the land that was my birthright, it was my responsibility to safeguard those living on that land who were still my people. Therefore, I petitioned my father to allow me to build a personal army of warriors to do these things. He agreed. I chose my men, trained them and then we advanced."

His eyes went over my head as I struggled to wrap my mind around what he was saying and as he gazed at his personal princedom, he continued.

"It took five years and too many lives, but we did it."

Five years!

Tor looked down at me and continued.

"And now my people are thriving and safe. As this was the most beautiful of all the territory we secured, I petitioned my father, as a gesture of gratitude to my men, to confer Bellebryn onto me. All my men and their families live here. It is not just mine. It is ours, the sun, the sea, the forest, the town bustling with trade, a kind of tranquility after years of war. A gift for their sacrifice."

I stared up into his beautiful, scarred face thinking of the other scars on his chest and back, the way he wielded a sword, how armed his cave was and his recent words.

Oh Lordy. I was thinking that Prince Noctorno Hawthorne was not just not so bad but that he might be pretty freaking amazing.

And I was thinking after all my time with him, all I knew, all I continued to learn, that I was sinking into some pretty deep trouble.

I turned to face forward again, and even though my heart was beating hard in my chest and I was finding it difficult to breathe, I felt something should be said.

So I said something.

"It's beautiful, Tor. Every inch of it. In all the beauty I've seen since I've been here, this is by far the most beautiful. And I'm glad you have it after what you and your men endured. I hope it brings you peace, being home."

He stilled behind me but after a second, his arm slid up to my ribs and tightened and I felt his lips touch my neck in a soft kiss.

Then, in my ear, he murmured, "It does, indeed, bring me peace to be home."

I curved my arm around his, laced our fingers at my side and whispered, "Good."

We fell silent and I watched the city getting ever closer as the sun set and more lanterns and streetlights were lit, illuminating the city and casting a cheerful glow into the darkening night.

And I watched this miraculous vision thinking I had an additional worry to occupy my mind.

It wasn't just what Cora was getting up to in my world. It wasn't that with every passing day it seemed less and less likely I was going home. It wasn't that with every passing day I felt less and less like I *wanted* to go home. It wasn't that I missed my parents and friends and I wished I had the opportunity to say good-bye.

It was that I was thinking I was falling for a black prince who conquered lands, took care of his people, gave in when I wanted to save a tiny bird and took time to show me his world.

And if that wasn't bad enough, the possibility still loomed that I could go to sleep at any time and wake up back home. Which would mean, if I fell for Tor, I would leave behind the man I loved in a fairytale world I could never go to again.

Which would seriously suck.

Therefore I was thinking I had to guard my heart when another thought shoved into my brain and my body went solid when it did.

Shit.

Bellebryn was his home, his city, his princedom.

And I was his princess.

And I, or the other Cora, had been here.

Tor felt me tense.

"Cora?" he called and I twisted to look up at him.

"Do your people know me?" I asked.

He studied my face and answered slowly, "Yes."

"Do they know I'm a bitch?"

He hesitated.

Oh shit!

They knew I was a bitch.

I turned quickly forward again, chanting, "Shit, shit, *shit*."

"Cora—"

"Stop," I demanded.

"Pardon?"

"Stop!" I shouted.

Tor pulled back on the reins. Salem stopped then turned his head to look at us and a groggy Aggie chirped a "What's happening?"

I didn't answer the bird. I was trying to think.

"Love, it'll be fine," Tor assured me.

"I need to, I don't know, brush my hair and, um," I lifted my hand and started pinching my cheeks, "um…" I repeated.

I didn't know!

"Cora, look at me," Tor commanded and I did. "It will be fine."

"They think I'm a bitch," I reminded him.

"No, they don't. The people don't know you. You've been here once. I will admit, you didn't make a good impression…" Fabulous. "But you were simply haughty, a bit cold the short time you were here. They don't think much of anything except that you aren't around." He paused. "Now my men…" he trailed off.

Oh boy.

"What have I done to your men?"

He looked in my eyes. "Nothing, except the fact you refuse to warm my bed. Something they haven't missed nor do they like, considering half my soul is yours. They're loyal to me and wish me contentment."

Great. Freaking great. His warriors hated me because I was a cold bitch who made her man search for it elsewhere.

Brilliant.

I turned forward again and Tor called my name again.

"No," I said, not turning back. "I'm okay. This'll be fine. Just fine."

Total lie.

I was freaking out!

"Love, look at me," he urged.

"No," I denied. "Let's just get this over with."

He paused then he sighed and stated, "Cora, just be this you and they'll change their minds. If you're this woman, they won't be able to stop themselves from falling in love with you."

I stared straight ahead but I could see nothing. I could only feel his words wash over me.

Yes, *feel* them.

And oh, but they felt good.

Oh man.

I didn't respond, couldn't. I was trying to control my rapidly beating pulse and prevent a heart attack.

After a while, Tor asked, "Are you all right?"

"Yes," I lied.

"We can proceed?"

"Sure."

"You aren't…freaking out?"

His using words from my world made my freakout fade and my mouth grin and I turned to him.

"I'll be okay," I said quietly.

His eyes held mine as he murmured, "There's my future queen."

Oh man!

He clicked his tongue against his teeth and Salem proceeded. I turned forward again. Aggie chirped, "Cora, are you sure you're going to be all right?"

"Yes, Aggie, no worries," I whispered to the bird.

Tor's arm gave me a squeeze and his thighs gave Salem a squeeze. The horse moved gracefully from a trot, to a canter, to a gentle gallop.

And Bellebryn got closer and closer.

13

Magical

~

I stood at the balustrade of the vast patio jutting out from Tor's rooms in the castle and stared at the now dark sea filled with its ships, their lights casting long reflections across the water.

I was brushing the moisture from my hair after having just taken a hot, gardenia-scented bath in a huge, oval, ivory marble bathtub.

Tor's rooms were the shit.

In fact, his entire castle was the shit.

In fact, his entire princedom was the shit. If it was amazing from the outside, it was doubly amazing on the inside.

I'd made it through the village (which was relatively abuzz) while sitting atop Salem and held by Tor. Nearly everyone we saw turned and looked, smiled delightedly at Tor and dropped into bows or curtsies.

If their eyes fell on me, though, their faces became curious, which was okay, or they closed or went blank, which was not so good.

I did my best to rectify Cora's reputation and smiled as bright a smile as I could pin on my nervous face. But the entire ride up the winding cobblestone street I clutched Tor's hand.

Upon our arrival at the castle everything went completely out of control. Tor's servants, not knowing he was coming home, descended instantly in a tizzy of excitement.

Watching them, it was clear he was well-liked and completely respected.

It was also clear, when their eyes hit me, Cora was not either of those things.

That didn't matter. Aggie and I were swept away to Tor's rooms (when I would have liked to have had a tour of the castle, though I didn't share this desire). I didn't get a chance to do anything but catch his eyes, see him lift a chin in an "it's going to be just fine" gesture before I was away. And I didn't get the chance to say word one before I was divested of Aggie and led into Tor's suite.

I quickly learned that Tor's servants had gone all out when Cora last visited, and even though she was there for a short time and had not come back, they kept things prepared lest she returned.

Therefore, she had clothes and toiletries at her, and now my, disposal.

I wasn't fond of the scent of gardenia (it was pretty enough, but too strong) but I didn't share this either as a meal was silently served (the first I did not have with Tor in ages, nevertheless, it was scrumptious, with rich sauces and lean cuts of meat, and I was amazed they threw it together on such short notice), a scented bath was drawn and delicate underwear and nightclothes were laid out for me.

They had towels, not made of terry, but of thick, soft, absorbent material that they heated on racks by a fire. They didn't only have bath oil but also soap, shampoo, and, get this, conditioner. (Hurrah! No more frizz!) They even had straight blades so I could shave my legs and armpits (this I did, but very carefully, straight-blade razors were more than a little scary, but I succeeded in nicking myself only once).

The whole place was awesome—if I didn't allow myself to think of the fact that the four women who danced attendance on me didn't meet my eyes, said barely anything and treated me with unfailing courtesy if not an ounce of friendliness no matter how I tried to catch their eyes and give them a smile or engage them in conversation.

They left me to my bath. I allowed myself to luxuriate in it, letting the hot water soothe the kinks of the long ride out of my muscles. I got out, toweled off and turned to my newest outfit.

The city, castle and rooms were awesome. But the underwear, nightgown and robe were more awesome...*by far*.

Not shorts or drawers, laid out for me were actual panties made of pale-yellow silk edged at the bottoms with lace. They fit a bit snug (Cora of this world definitely weighed more than a few pounds less than me) but they still looked fantastic.

And the nightgown and robe were to die for. A soft peach silk, thin straps, fitted simple bodice and a flowing skirt that went to my ankles. Luckily the skirt was flowing but, as with the panties, the bodice and hips of the gown fit snug (clearly, the other Cora was also a cup size smaller than me too). The robe was a matching sheer chiffon with a wide satin sash.

They felt great, and even snug looked great and were relatively comfortable.

So there I stood, brushing my hair with the silver-handled brush Cora had left behind, the scent of gardenia in my nose, the lamps and candles flickering behind me in Tor's bedroom (which was awesome too, decorated in royal blue, silver, black and charcoal gray, it had a mammoth, curtained four-poster sitting smack in the middle of the colossal room, handsome dark-wood furniture, comfortable-looking, plush sofas and chairs scattered around, gleaming ivory marbled floors that were made less cold by thick, intricately woven rugs littering them and warm blue-painted walls) and I stared at the view. There was incense one of the maids set to burning that smelled of sandalwood that mingled nicely with the gardenia.

I was brushing my hair, taking all of this in and I was thinking Princess Cora Goode Hawthorne was a total, freaking idiot.

Sure, her house and the area surrounding it were gorgeous but this, all of it, including the man that came with it...

Total.

Freaking.

Idiot.

I heard a noise, turned to face the room and stopped dead.

Tor was walking through the room completely naked except for a black bath-sheet fastened loose around his hips.

Holy freaking *crap*!

With an unsteady hand, I set the brush on the balustrade and stared.

I'd seen his chest but that was it. I knew he had great thighs and he was hard everywhere, but now I saw he had great calves and the indentations around his hips, the definition of his abs, the veins drifting up his belly and down his forearms and biceps, his jaw cleanly shaven, his long-ish, black hair wet and slicked back.

Yowza!

I tore my eyes from him to see he'd come through one of the many doors that led off his bedroom (I hadn't explored because I thought it was rude and I should ask, but by the time I could, I was alone).

What I knew was, it was not the bathroom door.

Where had he bathed?

In his bathsheet he walked right out onto the patio and, honest to God, he looked straight out of a movie with the candlelit room behind him, the wispy, royal-blue curtains blowing in the light breeze and him being so damned *hawt*.

I struggled to find my voice, found it and asked, "Where did you bathe?"

His head jerked and I belatedly noticed he'd been staring, quite intently, at my body and my words startled him out of a reverie.

His eyes cut to my face and he answered, "My bath."

"You have a bath?" I asked as he got closer.

"Yes."

"Is it somewhere else in the castle?" I inquired, thinking that was weird and also thinking of him walking the vast halls of his home in a towel and leaving swooning maids in his wake.

"No," he replied, stopping in front of me, his big hands going to my waist. "I have a private bath and you have a private bath. They're separate. I used mine..." His eyes slid over my wet hair. "And apparently you used yours."

We both had our own bathrooms?

Whoa.

Cool!

"Cool." I smiled up at him.

His hands slid up to my ribs. "Have you eaten?"

"Yes, have you?"

"Yes."

"The food was really good," I informed him.

"Excellent," he replied. "Now get in my bed."

I blinked. "What?"

"If you don't want me to take you on the balcony, you need, right now, to get that beautiful arse of yours in my bed."

My belly dipped and my knees went weak.

Uh-oh.

"Tor," I whispered and his fingers bit into my ribs as his body edged an inch closer.

"Now, Cora," he ordered low.

"Um..."

"I said now."

I placed my hands lightly on his biceps and suggested, "I think maybe we should take a few moments to discuss where this is going, um…between you and me and all of the ramifications of that, um…considering, you know, that I might be catapulted back to my world at any time."

"And, sweets, I think you should decide how much you like those charming garments you're wearing, for if you don't move toward my bed in three seconds while discarding them, I'll be ripping them off you."

Heat hit my cheeks *and* between my legs.

Uh-oh!

"Tor," I whispered. "This is getting complicated. We need to talk."

"One."

Oh dear.

"Honey, we might be making a huge—"

"Two."

I stared up at him and I knew by the determined look on his handsome face that he was, well…*determined*.

And I had a strong suspicion that when Prince Noctorno was determined to get something, he got it.

And that would include me.

Try as I might, in that instant, after the last four days, I couldn't find it in me not to give it to him.

Therefore I begged, "Please don't rip my clothes. I like them a lot."

"Three," he replied.

I braced but he didn't rip my clothes off. He dipped a shoulder and then I was up and he was stalking to the bed.

Oh God. Now what did I do?

I had to stall in order to set some ground rules.

I didn't struggle but wrapped my fingers around his waist.

God, his skin was soft but his muscles were hard and he was warm all over.

Shit!

"I'm not sure I'm ready for this," I told his back.

"Don't worry, love, I'll get you ready."

Oh boy.

"I think we should…oh!"

I cried out because he tossed me over his shoulder and I landed on my back on the downy covers of his soft bed.

He towered over me, still as a statue except his eyes that traveled the length of me, their path burning my skin like it was a physical thing.

Oh God, I was in trouble.

"Tor—"

"Take off your dressing gown," he ordered.

My brows drew together.

"My—?" I started to ask.

"Take it off, Cora, or I will and I won't be gentle."

Holy crap.

I got up on my elbows. "Tor!"

He pulled off his bathsheet.

I started hyperventilating.

I was not wrong. He had great thighs. And there was something else about him that was great too. So great, just looking at him in all his glory, I forgot to be nervous, scared or wonder what future lay ahead of me.

I just wanted all of that for me.

And I was going to get it. I knew this when he fell forward, his arm coming out to control his fall, his hand landing in the bed beside me, him landing mostly on me.

But he held his body away and he did this in order to untie the satin sash of my robe, doing it with a none-too-gentle yank that jerked my whole body with it.

The heat between my legs intensified and got wet.

Or *wetter*.

Oh my.

"Uh—" I started.

"Quiet," he ordered, shoving the chiffon aside.

"I think—" I tried again.

"Quiet," he repeated then yanked the nightgown up.

Oh...my.

"Um—"

He settled on top of me.

"I don't like this scent," he grunted, a hand gliding up my side. "It reminds me of the you that you used to be. Change it."

"Uh, okeydokey," I whispered and shivered.

"Put your hands on me," he commanded, his knee pressing between my legs.

Oh my!

"Um, okeydokey," I whispered again and slid my hands up his arms and around his shoulders.

God, he felt good. He smelled good too.

Sandalwood.

"You smell good." I was whispering but he didn't respond.

He watched as his hand moved in. Over my ribs, it started up. I held my breath then it changed directions and trailed down my belly.

My breath came out in a rush and then it came fast, uneven and heavy.

I wanted him. Now. God, I suddenly ached with it.

He didn't even have to kiss me.

"Tor," I breathed, his eyes came to mine and they were burning.

I started panting.

"If you're not wet, right now, I'll know," he growled, his voice deeper, rough, husky.

"You'll know wh-what?" I stammered.

His fingers slid inside my panties, gliding right through the heat of me.

My neck arched, my back arched and my arms clutched his shoulders.

"Gods," he groaned, pressing his hard cock against my thigh. "Sodden."

The fingers of one of my hands slid into his hair and I pressed into his hand between my legs as I tilted my chin down and tried to focus on him.

"I need you," I breathed.

His eyes flamed. "Right now?"

I nodded. "Right now."

He needed no more coaxing. He rolled slightly to the side and gone were my panties. Then he rolled back, I opened my legs as he did and his hips fell through. I lifted my knees, his hands at my hips lifted them, his mouth came to mine, not for a kiss but it felt more intimate having his heavy, warm breaths mingling with mine and then I felt the tip of him.

He drove inside.

Oh my God.

Magical.

I clutched him closer and arched my back again, whispering, "Yes."

He rode me, driving deep, his thrusts fast, rhythmic, fantastic, and through it all his eyes held mine, his lips a whisper away, our breaths mingling.

I swung my calves in, pressing my heels into his back to lift my hips and take more of him, my arm clutching his shoulders, my hand fisting in his hair. I couldn't tear my gaze away from the beauty of his eyes and didn't want to.

"Bloody hell, you're exquisite," he murmured, lifting me higher, thrusting harder, driving deeper.

"Oh my God," I whispered as his words and his pounding started my sex convulsing.

I was going to come.

"Bloody hell," he grunted.

"Tor—"

"Give it to me, Cora."

Oh, he was going to get it all right.

"Tor!" I cried.

"Give it to me, it's my right," he growled, a hand leaving my hip to fist at the back of my hair.

I gave it to him and he was right days earlier.

It was an explosion. An orgasm the power of which I'd never experienced before. There was no way to describe it. It burned through me so completely, I was laid to waste and I didn't give that first shit that I'd be annihilated by a climax.

I cried out loudly and clutched him closer with every muscle in my body, my neck arching and then my face shooting forward. I buried it in his neck and whimpered through the pleasure.

When I was done, he tugged my hair gently. My head fell back to the bed, his eyes caught mine again and he kept moving inside me, his breath rough and labored, his neck muscles straining.

I lifted my head again and kissed him, sliding my tongue in, giving him everything I had to try to return a little of what he'd just given to me.

His deep groan of climax drove down my throat as his cock drove up deep inside me.

Unbe-freaking-leivable.

He took over the kiss, gentled it as he slid in and out slowly then his lips trailed down my cheek to my neck. He kissed my earlobe and buried himself deep but stopped moving inside me.

"Furthering your royal education, sweets, *that* is how a princess lets her husband fuck her," he murmured in my ear.

My warm, languid, happy body stilled under the heated weight of his and I burst out laughing.

I felt his mouth disappear from my ear and I calmed my hilarity when I felt his hand at my face, his thumb stroking my cheek. My eyes opened to see his mouth was curved in a small, sexy, contented smile and his eyes on me were warm.

Man oh man, it was happening.

All of it.

Everything.

I was falling in love with a fairytale prince.

Shit.

To cover my panic, I whispered, "I like your castle."

His small smile curved bigger. "I'm glad."

"And I like your rooms."

"I'm glad about that too."

Then it came to me.

This was the now. It was my now.

And it was a magical now.

And, fuck it, I was going to take it and I'd worry about the later…later.

I sucked in breath then joked, "And, you know, I'm always around should you have any further princess instruction to impart on me."

His smile turned lazy and so sexy, I felt it everywhere.

"Good to know," he murmured.

"I'm a fast learner," I promised.

"I noticed that."

"And it's important, seeing as I'm a princess, that I learn all about being a princess."

Tor didn't respond just brushed his thumb across my bottom lip.

Nice.

"And," I went on, "it's important that I learn to do those things well."

"I'm a patient teacher," he informed me.

"You didn't seem all that patient ten minutes ago."

His lids lowered sending his sexy look off the charts then his head lowered and he brushed his mouth against mine but didn't take his lips away when he spoke.

"I'll be more patient next time."

"Next time?"

"Yes, next time," he replied, rolled so he was on his back and I was on top of him. His hand lifted the fall of my hair at the side of my head, gliding back so his fingers cupped the back of my head and put pressure on, bringing my face closer to his, "Which starts right…about…" my lips touched his, "now."

Then he kissed me.

Then he took his time showing me another way to be the best princess I could be.

And it was freaking *magical*.

14

I Wasn't Myself

~

I heard the sound of heavy draperies being pulled back, bright sunlight touched my closed eyelids and I felt my mouth curve in a satisfied smile.

Hell, if it was physically possible for me to purr, I would do it.

I was on my belly, naked as the day I was born. I felt the covers were up over my bottom, exposing my back and I stretched out my arms, arched my back into the bed and opened my eyes.

I was thinking of all my princess instruction, and there was a lot of it, three and a half lessons (the half was Tor going down on me, and it must be said the man could use his mouth), and just how much I liked every nanosecond of my lessons (and boy did I like it) when I looked around the massive room expecting I'd see a handsome (hopefully naked) man letting in the light.

But I didn't.

I saw a buxom woman wearing a kerchief on her head, a long, white apron pinned to the front of her long dress and a dour expression on her face.

Eek!

I yelped, yanked up the covers and whirled to my back, lifting up to sitting.

She crossed her arms on her chest and glared virtual daggers across the room at me.

"Uh..." Shit! "Heya," I called.

"Your breakfast, your grace, will be served in your sitting room," she announced in a cold voice.

"Um...my sitting room?" I asked.

She stomped to a door and slapped a hand on it then turned back to me.

"Sitting room," she said on a near snap. "Of course, I understand, it being *so long* since you've slept in your husband's bed, you'd forget."

Oh dear.

"Uh..." I mumbled.

"I'll leave you to dress but I'll *speak to you* during *breakfast* regarding any of your *instructions* for *my* staff."

She said "my" in a highly proprietary way leaving me to understand precisely what she meant.

They were not Cora's staff. They probably were Tor's but they were definitely not Cora's, and in his absence, whoever she was, they were also definitely hers.

"Um, okay," I said softly.

"If you see one of *my* staff in the meantime, I'll ask you to *delay* in any *instructions* you might have *for them* until you can share them *with me*."

I was thinking Tor didn't pay enough attention the last time Cora was there. I was thinking Tor was wrong about just his men hating her because she didn't warm his bed. I was thinking Cora was an even bigger bitch than ever and that was saying something.

"I can do that," I replied carefully.

She nodded her head once.

"I've laid out your clothes. Those and anything else you may need for your toilette," she stomped to another door and slapped a hand on it, "will be in your dressing room. If you would be *so kind*," she spat the last two words, "ten minutes before you require it, pull the cord so we'll know when to serve your breakfast."

"Sure thing," I said quietly.

She squinted at me, sniffed then stomped out of the room wafting so much frost in her wake, I shivered.

I looked around the room wondering where the fuck Tor was.

Then I slithered around on the bed searching the sides for my nightgown, found it, snatched it up, pulled it on and darted to the privy off the bathroom thinking, *Thanks, Cora. Just what I need, another mess you've gotten me into.*

As requested, ten minutes prior to needing it, I pulled the pale-blue velvet tasseled cord in the dressing room (a very pretty room, a lot smaller than the bedroom, painted a soft yellow accented in pale blues, creams and lavenders with a beautifully painted screen, a chaise lounge covered in lavender velvet and a dressing table topped with a bunch of fancy bottles and other fairytale land beautification detritus).

I found my time in the dressing room a little nerve-wracking considering I didn't entirely understand the clothing that was laid out for me.

I mean, there was a lot of it. I couldn't possibly have to don it all.

Then I realized that it wasn't one outfit, but a selection.

I made my selection and noticed two things. One, these clothes were of far superior quality to what I had been wearing and two, they were very different than what I had been wearing.

And they were exquisite.

So I made my selection. Then I perused the bottles on the dressing table (mostly scent—not all gardenia, a vast selection—so I picked something musky yet floral) but there was some powder, blusher and even kohl pencils.

I dabbed on scent, decided against attempting makeup and started dressing.

After pulling on another pair of lovely panties (these pristine white), I put on a cream, silky, lacy chemise and over that I pulled on a soft purple dress made of a light, flowing silk. The scooped neckline was way low, (indeed, without the lace of the chemise peeking over it, it would almost show my nipples), the waistline was empire (thus accentuating my breasts and drawing attention to the delicate lace) and the skirt was mostly straight with a beautiful drape and a slit up the front that also exposed the cream silk chemise. And last, the waistline was heavily, and magnificently, embroidered in a darker purple with hints of silver.

I slid my feet into deep-purple satin slippers.

After I managed that, I went to the carved box on the dressing table where I'd seen some ribbons and hair clips and selected a pair of clips that were filigree silver with purple stones adorning them that looked like real amethysts. I pulled my hair back on either side but let the back fall long and I looked in the mirror.

I didn't look half bad but I also didn't look like a fairytale princess.

I guessed it would have to do.

I pinched my cheeks on the way to the sitting room, and when I arrived I found another pretty room decorated in blues and peaches. There were comfortable chairs set in front of a wide, arched, multi-diamond-paned window, another chair with a round, button-topped, tassel-bottomed ottoman in a corner and a small, round, spindly-legged table in the middle accompanied by two chairs, their poofy, button-topped seats a plush peach.

This table was laid with ornate silver, china, a crystal vase holding a single, perfect peach rose, and it also held my breakfast, which appeared to be French toast dusted with powdered sugar and covered in sliced strawberries, something rich, creamy and yummy-looking oozing out of the middle, coffee, orange juice and a jug of water with actual *ice*.

My stomach growled and my eyes shot to the other thing in the room. The still dour-faced, buxom, kerchief-wearing, apron-dressed woman who clearly hated me.

I pinned a bright smile on my face.

"Good morning," I greeted and looked down at the food. "This looks—"

"If it pleases your grace," she interrupted me, "I'll say what I have to say while you eat, you can give me your instructions and I'll take my leave."

At her words, my step faltered and I stopped.

I pulled myself together, moved slowly to the table, drew out a chair and seated myself while saying softly, "Yes, please, that sounds perfect."

She approached the table but didn't get too close, either because she couldn't stand being in the same space as me or she thought I had the power to strike out and sink fangs into her.

I poured coffee from a sliver service into a china cup and she began.

"The last time you were here, your grace, you made it very clear that our service was…*wanting*," she started.

Oh shit.

"*This time*," she went on, "we will endeavor to meet your *every whim* to your *exacting standards*. I just require that you relate *those standards* to me *prior* to your *expecting* them so that I can educate *my* staff in what you will be *requiring*. That way, I won't find *my girls* in *fits of tears* or need to talk others out of leaving their employment *on the spot*."

I stared up at her.

Holy crap!

What on earth did the other Cora do?

Jeez!

"Um..." What could I say? "I was..." Shit! "Uh, out of sorts last time I was here. In fact, I wasn't..." Drat! "Entirely myself. It seems that I caused some upset."

"Indeed!" she replied tartly.

"Well..." I started, pulled in a deep breath and leaned slightly toward her.

Instantly, her upper body reared back.

Yep, she thought I could strike out with my fangs.

Yikes.

I decided to sally forth and finished, "I'm very sorry about that. *Very* sorry. I was...it was...unforgiveable, but I want you to know, and please tell your girls, that I am truly, very sorry."

She blinked.

Then she rallied and snapped, "Fine. Now, do you have any *specific* instruction?"

"Um...can I, uh...can you ask me that again in a few days? I'd like to get my bearings."

"With all due respect, your grace, no," she answered shortly. "As I explained, I would like to know exactly what you require *before* you require it."

My mind whirled. Finally I thought of something.

"Okay, well, um, I don't like celery," I told her.

"Noted," she clipped and glared at me as she waited for more.

"And, um, my husband doesn't like that gardenia scent."

Her brows shot to her hairline. "That is, as you know, your grace, your specifically requested scent. You did, as you know, your grace, make rather a fuss about it last time."

Uh-oh.

"It's lovely. I mean, *I* think it's beautiful. Utterly perfect," I lied. "But Tor doesn't like it so, perhaps—"

"Noted," she bit off curtly.

Oh boy.

She wasn't melting at all.

"Okay, well," I kept trying. "I was wondering, if Tor can't do it, could someone take me for a tour of—"

"The kitchens," she finished for me. "Of course, it'll be arranged immediately."

"No, I meant the castle," I explained and her head cocked sharply to the side.

"You had no interest the last time."

Of course I didn't.

"Well, I wasn't, uh...myself the last time."

She nodded once. "Noted."

I bit my lip.

Then I asked, "Where *is* Tor?"

"He has, as you know, your grace," she stated tersely, "been away for some time. He has things *to do* and those things, I hope you don't mind if I be so bold as to inform you, don't all involve *dancing attendance on you*."

Lordy, but she hated Cora.

"Right," I whispered.

"So he's doing them," she concluded.

"Of course," I replied.

"Is there more?" she snapped.

"I don't think so," I answered.

"Last time, there was more."

I bet there was.

"Well, if so, I'll be certain to speak to only you about it," I promised.

"Fine," she clipped. "And how long will you be *gracing us* with your *presence* this time? Will you be leaving this eve?" she asked hopefully.

"Uh...no."

Her expression finally changed but only to obvious disappointment.

Yeesh.

The door behind me opened. She looked over my head, her eyes got big and I twisted in my chair just in time for Tor to get there and pull me right out of it and into his arms.

Then, kid you *not*, right in front of the woman, his head descended and his mouth captured mine in a long, wet, hot, *racy* kiss that left me with my arms wrapped tight around his neck, my body arched against the length of his and my lungs breathless.

His mouth went away nary an inch when he lifted his head and his eyes found mine.

"Good morning, wife," he whispered.

My belly melted.

God, how I wished the last word in his sentence was actually true.

"Good morning, husband," I whispered back.

He grinned and his arms tightened, pulling me even closer.

"How are you this morning?" he asked an outwardly innocent but totally intimate question in a low, slightly husky, intimate voice that meant no one could miss the intimacy.

One of my arms slid from around his neck so I could cup his jaw with my hand.

"Very good," I whispered and the fingers of his hand that was splayed at my hip dug in.

"How good?" he murmured.

"*Very* good," I murmured back.

His grin turned wicked.

The area between my legs pulsed.

"How are you?" I asked.

His fingers dug deeper.

"*Very* good," he growled and I liked that he was, so I pressed into him.

His eyes went to the table then back to me.

"You haven't had breakfast?" he inquired.

My hand slid down to his neck. "I think I slept in."

That got me the wicked grin again before he said, "I have things to do, love. Can you find ways to stay occupied?"

"I think so," I replied, though I wasn't certain since the only person in his castle that I had really talked to clearly detested me and the rest the other Cora had set to fits of tears or threats of quitting, I was wondering if I should leave his rooms.

"Only stupid people get bored," he muttered, my body stilled but I felt my face go soft.

"That's what my mama told me," I whispered.

He grinned at me again. This one wasn't wicked, it was warm. It was a close call but I reckoned I liked the warm one even more.

He turned his head to the side, lifted his chin and asked, "You'll take care of my bride, Perdita?"

Hesitantly, I turned my head to the side and took in the clearly astonished, pale-faced woman called Perdita who was staring at us with rapt attention and complete shock.

"Perdita?" Tor called and she lurched.

"Yes, your grace?" she answered.

"You'll look after Cora?" he queried.

"Of…of course," she replied.

"Excellent," he muttered, gave me another squeeze to get my attention, I looked at him and he commanded, "Now give me a kiss before I go."

I tilted my head to the side and teased, "Earning my French toast?"

His brows drew together. "Your what?"

"French toast," I replied, tipped my head to the table and his gaze followed. "Breakfast."

His eyes came back to me.

They moved over my face, something I didn't understand working behind them then he corrected, "Custard toast, Cora."

"Custard toast?"

"That's what we call it."

"Oh," I whispered.

Yum.

That sounded *way* better.

"Sweets," he called and I focused on him. "My kiss."

Feeling Perdita's eyes on us, I got up on my toes, touched my mouth to his and intended to give him a chaste kiss. But his head slanted, he leaned into me, his mouth opened over mine and chaste was a fleeting memory.

I was breathing heavily when his head lifted.

"Don't get into any trouble," he warned.

"I won't," I panted.

He grinned.

Then he stated, "I'm not jesting, be good."

My head tilted in confusion. "I'll be good."

"Like a princess would be good," he clarified.

I felt my eyes narrow as I snapped, "Tor!"

"Cora," he returned.

"All I can be is me," I informed him.

He stared at me and sighed.

He turned his head to Perdita and announced, "My wife can be stubborn and she gets things in her head. If she tries to save a wounded bird, invite every innkeeper in the city to dinner or the like, stop her. You have my permission."

"Tor!" I cried, trying to pull away but he pulled me back.

"You're a princess. You've got to stop being so damned friendly."

"You didn't complain about how friendly I was last night, *three times*," I returned only to hear Perdita gasp.

Crap!

My head whipped around to Perdita and I babbled, "I'm sorry. So sorry. So, so, so, *so* sorry. That was rude. I shouldn't—"

"It's fine," she cut me off, her dour expression gone, she was—dear God, was I seeing things right—she was *smiling* and it was *glowing*. "Perfectly fine." She bustled to the door repeating, "Perfectly fine." She stopped at the door and looked at me. Then she floored me by finishing, "I'm glad to see, your grace, that this time you're more *yourself*." Her eyes flitted to Tor then to me. She lifted a hand and called merrily, "Cheerio!" and she disappeared.

I blinked at the door.

"What's this about being more yourself?" Tor asked and I looked up at him.

Jeez, did making out with Tor and starting to bicker with him win over the frosty housekeeper?

God, I hoped it was that easy.

"Nothing," I muttered and pushed on his shoulders. "Go, be a prince. Rule your princedom. I have a castle to peruse and innkeepers to ask to dinner."

His arms got tight and he growled a warning, "Cora."

I rolled my eyes then rolled them back to his face. "Oh, all right. I won't ask any innkeepers to dinner."

He studied me then shook his head and his mouth twitched. He gave me another squeeze, a brush of his lips against mine, he let me go and walked to the door.

When he had it open and was halfway through, I called, "Is it okay if I ask their wives?"

He turned and speared me with a glower.

I grinned at him and his glower disappeared when he winked at me. My breath caught at how damned hot he could wink and he vanished behind the door.

"I need to go home. I need to go home. I *need* to go *home*," I whispered my prayer into the falling night as I sat curled up in a padded, iron chair in a secluded corner of one of the many balconies in Tor's huge castle. "I'll miss Tor and I'll hate leaving him but please, please, *please* God, send me home."

The people were lighting their lanterns, windows were beginning to glow and the street lamps were being lit.

And I was crying.

Nope, I wasn't crying. I was *sobbing*.

Nope, I wasn't sobbing either. I was *bawling*.

Because, outside of the day the curse started, that day was the worst day in my entire life—the short one I'd led here and the long one I'd led at home. Both of them.

The worst day *ever*.

And I needed to go back home because the people here *hated* me.

Nope, they didn't hate me. They *detested* me.

Nope, that wasn't right either. They didn't detest me. They *loathed* me.

And they were not to be won over by bright smiles and politeness and I hadn't seen Tor all day for them to be won over by us making out or bickering.

No, that day for the first time since I arrived in this world, I had to go it alone.

And alone I went it, touring the castle and the city before I could take no more, slunk back and decided that I might be falling in love with a warrior prince, and he was pretty magnificent (in bed and out of it) and his world was beautiful, but I couldn't take this.

I couldn't take it.

I had found out that the other Cora had been there three days—*three days*—and in all her bitchiness she had left devastation in her wake. She was cold, imperious, demanding, haughty, impolite, patronizing and even cruel.

In all likelihood she hadn't offended everyone in the entire city. She didn't have superpower nastiness like Minerva had. But she did enough damage to those she came into contact with that it was clear rumor had run rampant.

The further fact (I'd heard whispers) that she had nothing to do with Tor, who was beloved (I'd heard straight-out comments muttered loudly behind my back or around my person) not to mention the future king and therefore responsible for siring an heir to secure the kingdom (which she was stopping him from doing, again, I learned this from straight-out comments) didn't make her popular *at all*.

In fact, people thought there was something wrong with her (as they would, Tor was hot and his princedom was awesome) and whatever was wrong was *no good*.

As with Perdita, they didn't even try to hide their contempt for Tor's wife. I was treated to glares, scowls, catty, loud comments, and one man even spit in the path behind me as I wandered the cobbled streets wishing to explore, be friendly and experience Tor's city.

But the spitting, which was horrid, wasn't the worst.

It was the maids I heard talking as I passed them in the castle after giving them a cheerful smile.

"He doesn't like her gardenia so now she's wearing one of his other women's scents that we left in her room," one whispered loudly and then joined in with her mate's giggles.

One of his other women's scents. That vast collection of bottles were left behind by Tor's other women.

And the collection was *vast*.

And I was wearing one.

That tiny tear in my heart that started our night at the pub, which I thought was long since mended, split painfully further.

I was a friendly person. I was a social person and I considered myself pretty strong. I'd weathered being switched to a whole different world and warrior princessed my way through a fight with the vickrants, for God's sake.

But I was not friendly enough, social enough or strong enough to endure the quantity and intensity of hate coming at me that day.

In fact, in the end, I felt almost unsafe without Tor to watch over me.

And without Salem or Aggie (I was scared to ask anyone where I could find Perdita so I could ask for Aggie, so I didn't), I spent hours with not a single kind soul around me.

And that was enough.

I could bear no more.

So I needed to get home before something bad happened. Like I fell in love with Tor or got stoned to death by his people.

"Please God, send me home," I whispered through my tears as the beautiful vista lay before me. A vista no one in their right mind would ever wish to leave but one from which I *had* to escape.

"Cora!"

I heard Tor's voice shouting my name. It wasn't close but it wasn't far.

Shit!

I hunched deeper into my chair and hastily wiped my face with the drenched, lace-edged handkerchief I'd found in the huge, walk-in wardrobe in Tor's room.

"Cora!"

There it was again. And it was closer.

Crap!

The handkerchief wasn't working so I dashed my fingers across my face, thankful that I hadn't attempted any makeup heroics with the kohl pencil.

I heard boots on marble.

Fuck!

"There you are," he said and I sucked in a steadying breath. "Bloody hell woman, didn't you hear—?"

I pinned a huge smile on my face and turned it to him.

"Heya," I greeted and he stopped dead.

"By the gods," he breathed.

Okay, proof the handkerchief didn't work.

I needed to cover.

"So, uh…how was your day?" I asked fake brightly.

One second he was five feet away, the next second he was right there, I was out of the chair and in his arms.

Um.

Not good. Way too close.

"Cora—"

I looked down and to the side.

"Is all well in your princedom?" I tried to inject lightness in my tone and knew I failed when he spoke next.

His voice was so firm it was steely when he commanded, "Look at me."

I did as he asked, lifting my head and moving it in a swift arc, my eyes catching his for a brief second before I tried to look down to the other side. But one of his hands caught me, fingers at my chin, and forced me to face him.

Foiled!

"Bloody hell," he muttered. "By the gods, what happened to you?"

"Nothing," I replied instantly.

"Nothing?" he asked, his voice dripping with impatience and disbelief.

"Nope, nothing," I repeated. "Everything's cool. How are you? Did you have a good day?"

He stared at me.

Then he stated, "Don't lie to me, Cora."

"I'm not—"

I stopped speaking when he shook me gently but firmly and semi-repeated, "I said, don't lie to me."

I looked into his gorgeous face, into his beautiful eyes, eyes that held mine the entire first time he moved inside me, eyes I could fall in love with, and I lost it.

Completely.

I dissolved into tears in his arms, dipping my chin and shoving my face into his chest, my fingers fisting in his shirt by my cheeks as I wailed.

"Sweets, what on earth?" he murmured into the top of my hair and I jerked my head back so fast he had to jerk his up too.

"They hate me!" I cried.

"Who?" he asked.

"*Everyone!*" I shouted then shoved my face back into his chest, and as quickly as I did, I pulled it out, looked through my watery eyes at his face and yelled desperately, "You have to find a witch! A wizard! There has *got* to be someone here who knows how to send me *home*. There's always some magical type…*person* who inhabits enchanted animated movies that knows how to help!"

I pulled his shirt out then slammed it back in and kept going.

"You have to find someone to help. I *have* to go home. *I have to*."

His body grew rock solid against mine but I was too far gone to notice and kept right on babbling.

"They hate me, God! You cannot imagine how much. The other Cora was *a bitch*!" I screeched the last two words at the top of my lungs. "And I *like* you.

Your world is so *beautiful*. You saved Aggie for me. And last night was so…so…" I hiccoughed through my sobs. "*Good*. The best I've ever had by, like…" I couldn't find words to describe how much so I shouted, "*A lot!* I don't want to have it *once* then *have to let it go*." I slammed his shirt into his chest and kept wailing, "I *told you* we shouldn't *do it*! Now, forever and ever I'll remember what we had and want it again and I'll never have it!" My sobs turned to anger and I yelled, "See! I knew! I tried to tell you but would you listen? *No!* You jerk!"

"Sweets," he whispered.

"You owe me!" I cried. "That's our deal. I gave it up…*three times*…and now *you* have to pay. You have to find me a wizard or a gypsy or someone, *anyone* who knows how to send me *home*!"

Then I dissolved again, my knees buckling and he caught me in his arms, lifted me up and swung around. I shoved my face into his neck and held on to his shoulders with both arms, my body wracked with tears, and I dimly heard the firm, angry beat of his boots hitting the floor as he stalked wherever he was stalking.

"Gods, what on…is she well?" I heard a woman ask.

"Find me Perdita," Tor growled. "I'll want an explanation for the state of *my wife*."

"No!" I cried, lifting my head and looking at his hard, angry profile. "Don't blame Perdita. I think she may be the only one who likes me."

"I gave her charge of you and you're a gods' damned mess." Tor's voice rumbled with fury. "So, my love, I'll bloody well be talking to Perdita."

My hand went to his cheek and I pleaded, "Please, please, don't, Tor. You do, you'll do me no favors."

"Quiet, Cora," he commanded low.

"Please, honey!" I cried, swiped at my tears and tried to brighten my tone. "I'll be okay. It's just stress. It's a wonder I haven't already had a meltdown. I'll be fine. It's out of my system."

"I said quiet," he clipped.

"Totally out of my system, baby, I promise," I assured him on a complete lie.

"*Quiet!*" he thundered and I shut my trap.

Oh boy.

Tor was pissed.

Great.

Now what had I done?

He strode angrily through the castle, up the gazillion winding, gleaming, marble steps that led to his rooms and into his rooms where he laid me gently down on his bed and straightened.

Looking down at me, he stated, "Rest. I'll have someone bring you some wine."

At that, I panicked, sat up and cried, "No! Don't! Don't ask anyone to do anything for me!"

Big, *big* mistake. I knew this when his eyes narrowed ominously.

"Or," I went on, trying to repair the damage, "actually, wine sounds good."

Better to see one of his people, who hated me, than endure Tor's fury, which scared the beejeezus out of me.

"Rest," he commanded.

"Right," I whispered.

He turned on his boot and stalked off.

"Fucking great," I muttered and collapsed back on the bed.

I sat curled into the heavy, comfy chair I dragged out onto the balcony patio and sipped at my second glass of wine poured from a delicately carved crystal decanter with a curlicued handle and a whirly stopper that a scurrying, pale-faced, frightened-looking, silent woman delivered to me and I stared at the view.

Tor had been gone a long time.

I heard the door open and the angry pounding of boots on marble.

Oh jeez.

I turned to look around the chair and watched him prowl to me.

He didn't look any less angry.

I bit my lip and took in a deep breath.

He made it to me. I opened my mouth to speak but shut it when he pulled the glass out of my hand, set it on the balustrade, plucked me out of the chair, sat in it, arranged me in his lap, leaned forward and nabbed the wine, handed it to me and then sat back, glowering at the view.

"Uh, is everything all right?" I ventured.

"It bloody well will be," he growled to the view.

Hmm.

I decided to say no more.

Tor pulled the glass out of my hand and took a huge gulp.

Hmm, again.

He spoke again to the view. "You'll not have any problems in future, Cora. You do, you tell me *instantly*."

Oh dear.

I felt it prudent to agree, quickly and softly, so I did. "Okay, honey."

"Are you hungry?" he asked.

I kind of was. I hadn't had anything since breakfast.

"Um…yes?" I asked back cautiously and his eyes cut to me.

"You either are or you aren't, love," he clipped.

"I am," I whispered.

"Do you want to eat up here or in the dining room?"

I wanted to ask which dining room since, in my lonely tour of the castle, I saw three.

"Where do you want to eat?" I asked instead.

"Up here," he grunted. "That way, when we're done, I don't have to waste time walking all the way up here to get you in my bed."

Hmm.

"Okay," I said quietly.

"Go pull the bell," he muttered.

"Okay," I repeated and scrambled off his lap.

Halfway across the patio, I chanced a glance back and saw him drain my wineglass.

I bit my lip and turned back.

Oh boy.

Tor was up on a hand, arm straight, body at an angle, his weight distributed on his other forearm, which was in the bed, his fingers laced in mine.

And his hips were between my legs, he was inside me, driving deep as his fiery eyes held mine captive.

I was close, so freaking close, God. He was big, he could move and he felt so damned *good*.

"Tor," I breathed, communicating it was coming.

He buried himself deep, my neck arched and he stopped.

"Look at me," he commanded, his voice thick.

I forced my chin down and tried to focus on him.

"Cora, *look at me*," he repeated and I blinked the haze away.

"I see you," I whispered, my hand at his chest running through the hair down to his flat stomach. "Don't stop, baby."

He ground his hips into me and I whimpered.

"Who's inside you?" he demanded to know.

"You," I answered.

"Who's inside you?" he repeated and I blinked.

"Honey—"

His elbow bent and my body took on more of his weight as his face became the only thing I could see.

"Who's *fucking* you?" he changed his question.

I was confused.

"You," I said again.

"Who am I?"

Oh God, I needed him to move!

"Tor," I replied breathlessly.

That earned me a violent stroke and heat surged through me.

He stopped again and kept at it. "Who am I?"

"My husband," I gasped.

Another violent stroke and again, "Who am I?"

"My prince," I whispered.

"Bloody right," he growled and his hips started moving faster, harder.

He moved his weight fully to his forearm and his hand slid from my chest, between my breasts and down to my belly.

"Who does this belong to?" he asked.

"My prince," I repeated.

His hand went up and cupped my breast firmly.

"And this?" he demanded while his cock drove deep and I lifted my knees higher and pressed my thighs tight to him.

Oh *God*.

"My prince," I moaned.

His thumb slid roughly across my nipple and a shaft of pleasure shot through me.

Oh *God*!

"And this?" he continued harshly.

"It belongs to you, my prince," I breathed.

His fingers left my breast, he pulled my hand away from his belly and pushed both of our hands between our legs, his hand over mine cupping my sex so I could feel his thrusts between our fingers.

His mouth came to mine and he stopped thrusting and started grinding. "Who does this belong to?"

Oh God, God, *God*.

I closed my eyes and arched my neck again. "You, my prince."

"Bloody look at me," he ordered. I did and he started thrusting savagely. I felt him pounding, inside and out. "You'll not leave," he ground out, his voice hoarse.

My legs circled his hips but I didn't answer.

"Cora, say it, you'll not leave."

Oh God!

"I'll not leave," I whispered.

His eyes kept mine imprisoned as he kept driving deep and I lost it. My back arched, my neck arched and my heels dug into his back as I exploded.

His mouth went to my ear as I climaxed and I felt the sharp nip of his teeth on my earlobe before he gritted, "You're never going '*home*.'"

Then he shoved his face in my neck and groaned.

When we both came down, Tor guided our hands from between us and let mine go. He pulled out of me then kissed my neck and exited the bed.

I rolled to my side and watched as he strode around the room and extinguished candles and lamps until the only illumination came from the city lights glowing through the huge opened doors.

He joined me in bed and pulled me into his arms, settling me with my cheek on his chest, my thigh over both of his and then his fingers came up and played with the ends of my hair.

I closed my eyes tight.

Okay, shit, what was *that* all about?

I wasn't sure but one thing I knew, I was screwed.

The people of his castle and the city hated me, but I could not leave. I could not complain about them or Tor would do something to make them hate me more, if he already hadn't.

I was stuck on that score.

I wanted to take off, but if I did I might get captured by Minerva and then his world would descend into plague and famine and who wanted to be responsible for something like that?

Not me.

From what just happened, it was pretty freaking clear that Tor wasn't going to go out and find me a wizard or sorcerer to help me get home. Further, *I* couldn't ask anyone because they hated me and they wouldn't help me.

So I was stuck on that score too.

And, blast my luck, his protective behavior when he found me crying settled my black prince even deeper in my heart. I wasn't falling sedately in love with him. I was falling fast and I was going to land soon, and when I did, I'd land hard.

Yes, I was totally screwed.

I had no choice.

I had to tough it up where his people were concerned. I needed to build a shield. I would be my friendly, social self and do my best to keep my chin up. I didn't suspect, considering how deep their hatred went, I'd win them over but I had to find a way to live with it.

And as for Tor, I didn't know what to do.

What I did know was that there was a possibility I was going to go home one day, no warning, no chance to say good-bye.

So, I not only had to take what I could get from my fairytale prince but I also had to give him back everything I could muster. Because when I went home, the other Cora would come back and he, like me, would have nothing.

And I wanted him to have all he could have for as long as I could give it to him.

I opened my eyes and pulled in breath.

So that, I decided, was precisely what I was going to do.

"Sweets?" Tor called, his free hand coming to mine on his chest.

"Mm?" I replied but he didn't answer, or at least not verbally.

He moved both our hands to between his legs and wrapped my fingers around his rock-hard shaft.

Jeez, apparently men of this world had superhuman recuperative powers.

"I'm ready for you again," he murmured.

I felt a spasm between my legs and then he shifted me over him.

I lifted my head and looked into his face lit dimly by the city lights.

God, he was beautiful.

He moved the tip of his cock inside me then both his hands went to my hips and pushed me up to straddling him, and as they did, he filled me.

Oh yes.

I bit my lip as I stared down at him and his hands took control of both of mine, leading one to my breast and the other between my legs.

"Give me what I want," he muttered his throaty order, his hands leaving mine where he wanted them as his moved to my hips, his fingers curling in.

I swiped with a thumb and rolled with a finger at the same time moving up and down in a deep stroke.

It felt so good, my head fell back.

Oh yes.

I was going to give him all I could give him for as long as I could give it to him.

"Eyes on me, my love," he commanded and I tipped my chin down and caught his eyes.

And I smiled.

At my smile, his face darkened and his hips bucked.

Then I rode my prince, giving him all as I could give him for as long as I could hold out.

15

Life Is Good

~

Six weeks later...

"Ready to go, Aggie?" I called to the fully recuperated, but unfortunately now flightless bird who was hopping around on my dressing table.

"Chirpy, chirp," Aggie replied excitedly, which meant, "Ready, Cora!"

Aggie liked our excursions. Being flightless he didn't get out unless I took him, and he'd told me he missed the fresh air, uninterrupted vistas and daily adventures. I couldn't give him any adventures but I did what I could every day to give him a change of scenery so he wouldn't get bored.

I extended a finger to the tiny bird. He hopped on then I lifted my arm as he hopped up it and took his usual place on my shoulder.

With Aggie in position, I left Tor and my rooms and wandered down the wide hall toward the stairs.

I was down half the flight when, around a curve, I saw Lucinda, one of the maids, on her hands and knees scrubbing the stairs with a scrub brush, the marble steps behind her glistening wet and so clean, they could be in a commercial.

"Oh!" I cried and her head shot up.

She spied me and her mouth formed a tentative (what I was sure was forced) smile.

"Your grace," she said through her smile.

"I'm sorry, you're cleaning. We'll use the back stairs," I told her, lifted my skirts and started backing up.

"No!" she cried, straightening and lifting up a hand to forestall me. "It's just fine. I'll scrub up after you. No problem at all. Use these."

See.

There it was.

The smile was totally fake. Like always. She was scared she'd do something to upset me, which would make me complain to Tor, which would mean he'd unleash black prince fury. And she was willing to do anything to stop that. Including letting me tread on her hard work. Cleaning stairs on your hands and knees with a scrub brush had to suck. She didn't even have a pad for her knees!

"No, that's all right," I assured her, continuing to move back as well as starting to turn. "It's perfectly fine. Enjoy the celebrations this afternoon," I finished then I fully turned and jogged up the stairs, hurried down the hall and took the back stairs.

I made it without encountering anyone, moving quickly through the halls to the mammoth entry in order not to run into anyone else, and then I went out the enormous double front doors that had to be at least two stories tall and were open to the sunshiny day.

"It's a beautiful day," I told Aggie, my only friend in this world, as I strolled through.

"Chirp, chirp, chirp," Aggie replied, which meant, "That it is, Cora."

I made it down the wide steps leading up to the castle, my eyes on the sun glinting diamonds off the big, beautiful, circular, gushing fountain in the middle of the courtyard in front of the castle.

As I hit the bottom, a vivid flock of small birds swooped low, flying around me so close, they blew the flimsy pale-pink skirts of my gown forward, my hair flew too as the wind from their wings caused a light breeze to surround me.

I giggled as they flew (this wasn't the first time this happened—the first time I freaked way the hell out, now I was a dab hand) and they chirped, most of their chirps being, "Morning, Cora!"

"Morning, birds!" I called after them as their brightness faded into the sun.

I looked across the courtyard, not noticing (because I'd learned to keep myself to myself) that all the men and women in the courtyard were gazing at me with indulgent smiles, and I spied Salem across the expanse.

"Salem!" I cried with delight, snatched Aggie off my shoulder so he wouldn't go flying (figuratively) and skipped excitedly across the space while holding Aggie carefully in my hand.

Salem watched me and when I got close, I threw my arms around his glossy neck, deftly letting Aggie out of my hand so he could hop up on Salem's back.

Salem whinnied, and when I stepped back and grinned at him, he stuffed his nose in my neck and blew.

I laughed out loud because it tickled.

"Look at you, you beautiful beast. I've missed you. I haven't seen you for a whole week!" I cried.

Salem snorted.

"How do you like that, Algernon?" A deep, handsome voice came from Salem's other side and I ducked under the beast's neck to see Tor standing there, arms crossed on his chest, powerful legs planted wide, eyes on me, his sergeant-at-arms, Algernon, at his side. "My wife flies across the courtyard to hug *my horse* and she doesn't even look *at me*."

Salem whinnied in a way that I could swear was laughter.

I grinned at Tor, moved under Salem's neck, stroking him as I went, and when I cleared him, I flew the four feet to Tor and threw myself in his arms.

I had my face in his neck so I didn't see the indulgent smiles all around widen or the knowing, happy looks that were exchanged as Tor whirled me in a circle, setting my legs and skirts to flying.

He set me down on my feet in front of him.

I leaned close, resting into my arms with my hands flat on his chest and my head tipped way back to look in his light-blue eyes.

"How are you this morning, my husband?" I asked on a smile.

His arms around me gave me a tight squeeze. "Very well, my wife. How are you?"

I leaned closer and whispered, "*Very* well."

His eyes warmed before they scanned my face.

Then one of his hands slid from my back, around my waist, to come to rest, weirdly, palm flat, on my belly.

His neck bent deep and his face was all I could see when he murmured, "How well, my love?"

"Very, *very* well," I replied on a grin, leaned up the inch he left and touched my mouth to his.

I forced myself to pull away and look at the strapping, blond Algernon who would, in return, pretend to like me.

Tor had not been wrong about his men. So the folks of the city and castle loathed me but his men despised me. This I found out in an unpleasant way when some words were uttered in my direction (if not to my face), words, or in particular *a* word (starting with a "c") that I didn't know they even *had* in fairytale lands.

This incident I had been smart enough *not* to share with Tor.

"Heya, Algernon."

He grinned at me and it was a good one. It looked nearly genuine. But it did not meet his eyes.

Then he bowed at the same time he touched his fingers to his forehead and said, "Good morning, Princess Cora."

I smiled at him and looked back at Tor and asked the question I'd asked every day as each of them slid by with two things not happening: me going home (and it seemed pretty clear I was stuck here, it felt like I'd been there forever) and Rosa being rescued.

"Any news of—?"

Tor's eyes went guarded and he gave me another squeeze.

"No, love."

I pulled in both my lips and bit them.

Tor, as he always did, swiftly changed the subject, likely, I guessed, because he knew it upset me.

"What are you up to today?" he asked and I shook my head.

"You can't ask me that question," I informed him.

"I can't?"

"Nope."

His brows drew together. "And why not, wife? I ask it of you every day."

"Yes, well," I smiled up at him and pushed closer, "every day is not my husband's *birthday*."

His eyes scanned my face again as his body went still but his arms got tight.

And today *was* his birthday. I learned he was thirty-eight that day. And it was going to be a day of fun and festivities. There were going to be games and dancing and parties and street vendors, and that night fireworks set off on the ships in the sea.

I was dreading it. I would have to spend all day with his people all around, pretending they liked me. It was going to be torture.

What I was not dreading were my plans for him.

I was going to bake him a birthday cake.

I had no money (anything I bought in the village was tallied up and sent as a bill to Perdita to pay) and I had no way of earning money, and I didn't want him to have to pay for his own birthday present.

So I was going to give him something from my world.

I was going to make him a red velvet cake (without the red, of course, because I was pretty sure they didn't have red food dye). I was going to do this because it was the only cake I knew how to make by memory and also it was a freaking great cake.

I just hoped I could find all the ingredients.

"And what do you have planned for my birthday, my sweet?" Tor asked quietly, regaining my attention.

"Again, honey, you're not allowed to ask." My hand slid from his chest to his jaw and I whispered, "You'll see."

His eyes moved over my face again before he replied, "What I see is, whatever it is, I should look forward to it."

"Oh yes," I returned.

His fingers dug into my hip, he dipped his head to brush my lips with his and when he pulled away he murmured, "Then I'll leave you to it."

I didn't want him to leave me to it.

In this world, I had Aggie and I had Tor.

But Tor was a prince. He ruled a princedom and his sister-in-law was in the clutches of an evil witch-god. He had a number of things to occupy his mind. Which meant, as each day threaded into the next, I had to find ways to amuse myself without him.

Which sucked.

But, when he came to me in the evenings, he found ways to make it all worth it.

I pulled away giving him a bright smile and calling, "See you later."

I smiled at Algernon, gave Salem another stroke, collected Aggie, setting him on my shoulder and didn't quite meet the eyes of my many onlookers as I sauntered away.

"You need to be back, Cora, by noon!" Tor called from behind me.

"I will, honey!" I called back. "*Way* before that!"

I made it three more steps before a fat ginger cat wove through my ankles.

"Brrr morrrrning, Prrrrrincess Corrrra," she purred.

"Calliope, like I tell you every day, you can't eat Aggie," I admonished.

She leaped away but stopped, sat on her fat tush and blinked at me in irritation.

Distracted by Calliope, I caught a vendor's eyes accidentally.

He gave me a seemingly bright smile, tipped his cap respectfully and muttered, "Princess Cora."

"How are you, Boris?"

He straightened from the wares he was organizing and winked. "Doin' well, with the party comin' on. Bellebryn throws a good party, especially for its prince. Wait 'til you see, yer grace."

"Can't wait!" I cried, clapping my hands in front of me and lying through my teeth.

"See you there, yer grace," he called as I moved away.

"Save a dance for me, Boris," I called back and I gave him a bright wave and brighter smile before I moved through the vast, black, wrought iron, silver-crest-encrusted gates and into the village.

As I strode the cobbled streets, I smiled and nodded my head as people smiled back. I returned greetings when they were offered to me. I extended them when I saw someone I knew or was given an opening. I touched little children's heads when I passed them, grinning into (fake) beaming mothers' faces.

Mostly I chatted with Aggie, who chatted back, and I worried I wasn't going to be able to find mascarpone cheese.

And I went to the house with the blue door and knocked.

It was thrown open by a harassed-looking, wide-hipped woman who had a two-year-old, bawling toddler at her hip and a four-year-old, snot-faced child clutching her skirts.

She bobbed a curtsy and looked in my eyes. "Oh, Princess Cora, I'm glad you're here! Thank the gods you could make it on this, of all days."

I tipped my head to the side and stated, "I never miss a day, Blanche, you know that."

And I didn't.

When I'd heard Perdita talking with one of the maids about her cousin Blanche who had two children, a husband away at sea and a frail mother to look after, I'd cautiously offered my services to help out any way I could. Perdita had asked Blanche and then informed me those services were taken up.

So, every day, never missing one, I went to the house with the blue door so Blanche could do whatever she needed to do and I could look after her mother for a spell.

Her face broke into a smile and she muttered, "No, thank the gods yet again, you never do. Bless you. She's upstairs, waiting for you."

"Right, scurry on, you all!" I ordered, rumpling the four-year-old's hair as he passed by. Then Aggie and I went into the house and I jogged up the wooden steps, circled the railing and entered the room where the old woman sat in her rocker, staring out at the sea but seeing, I knew, nothing. "Heya, Clarabelle," I called softly and her sightless eyes came to me, her face wreathed in a genuine smile.

I was wrong. I didn't just have Aggie and Tor. Clarabelle, I was pretty certain, also liked me.

"Chirp!" Aggie chirped his greeting.

"Hullo, my princess. Hullo, Aggie," she called back.

I moved into the room, grabbing the book as I passed it. I dragged a chair toward her, bent to kiss the paper-thin skin of her cheek then lifted my fingers for Aggie to hop onto.

He did. I transferred him to Clarabelle's offered hand, she brought him toward her and stroked him as I sat.

"Do you want me to get right into it? We left it at a good part last time," I reminded her.

"If you want, Cora, my dear. Or, we can chat. Are you well?" she replied.

"Very," I somewhat lied.

There were things that were good (dinner at night with Tor, bedtime, again with Tor, waking up when Tor was there and sometimes I could lose myself in the fantasyland around me) and other things that were bad.

"And our prince?" she asked.

"Um…worried about his brother, I think," I answered, having told her (although no one else knew and I swore her to secrecy) about Rosa, Dash and the evil Minerva.

"I daresay, he would be," she murmured, her voice somehow strange. Her hand came out, searching. I extended mine, she caught it and squeezed it gently. "You sure you're well?" she asked softly.

"I'm perfectly fine," I outright lied. "Happy," I kind of lied. "Life is good."

She squeezed again and let me go with an, "If you say so, my dear."

Hmm.

It would seem I needed to be better with my act, even, maybe especially with an old, blind lady.

"So, shall I start reading? Blanche will be back with the kids before we know it, mayhem will ensue and you won't know if the pirate was able to cow the fair maiden to his will."

She smiled a gentle smile. "Well, I can't miss that."

I opened the book to its marked page and mumbled, "Certainly not."

I heard her quiet chuckle and I reached out a hand and squeezed her knee.

Aggie chirped a, "Read, Cora!" (he liked this story too).

So I let my friend go and started to read out loud.

16

The Only Thing I Needed

~

Tor's hand tightened in mine.

We'd just walked in his front doors and I was pulling away.

"Where are you going?" he inquired.

"I have to do something," I said quickly and he stared down at me.

"What?"

"*Something!*" I cried, getting desperate.

Time was wasting.

He gave me an assessing look then he told me something I already knew.

"Hurry, love, you don't have much time."

I nodded, got up on tiptoe, curled my fingers around the back of his neck, pulled him down to me and touched my lips to his.

"I'll be back," I whispered, let him go and started to rush to the kitchens.

The fireworks were going to start at any minute and Tor and I were going to watch them on our balcony. A balcony that jutted out further than any of the others and a balcony, incidentally, that anyone from anywhere in the village and on the sea could see.

This filled me with dread, being somewhere where everyone could see me with Tor (and they'd be watching).

But I had to admit that the day had been pretty fantastic.

Boris was right.

Bellebryn knew how to give a party.

The streets were filled with music. The businesses and houses were decorated with colorful garlands and bunting. There were puppet booths set up giving free shows. Children dashed around with faces made up with face paint and circling vibrant streamers behind them. There were belly dancers, snake charmers and men eating fire performing for coins all of whom seemed, by the looks of them, to have come from faraway lands. The air was thick with clashing aromas because there were stands selling everything from roasted honey-coated nuts to sausages on sticks to big steaming pans filled with paella to flamboyantly swirling lollipops.

Around every wind of the cobbled street (and, as was his duty during this huge street party thrown in his honor, Tor strolled down and up (and down and up again) the entire street, his hand in mine or his arm around my shoulders or waist), people were dancing, swinging around and even I'd been swept into the frolicking. Though I didn't know the steps, I did the best I could do, laughed at myself, because I had to admit it was kind of fun, and I pretended the joyous looks thrown my way were real.

It was fabulous.

It would have been magnificent if I could have really joined in and believed that Tor's people loved me as much as they pretended to or even a hint of how much they very obviously loved him.

And now it was almost over, I was exhausted and I hadn't had time to present him with his cake. The fireworks were the showstopper, ending the festivities at midnight. I had fifteen minutes to give him his cake or he wouldn't get it on his birthday.

And he had to get it on his birthday.

I pulled up my skirts and I ran to the kitchens, coming to a skidding halt by my cake (I had found all the ingredients in the village, *including* the red food dye, thank God).

It looked magnificent and someone had put small, blue candles in it. I'd talked to Perdita days ago about birthday candles and she'd informed me, looking confused but humoring me, that they didn't do birthday cakes here, but birthday *tarts*, and they didn't do candles, but *sparklers*.

I gave in on the sparklers, and even though some people used them in my world, I was disappointed.

I had wanted to give Tor a piece of my world, which included, traditionally, candles.

And there they were. And next to the cake was an oddly shaped, purple-wrapped package.

"Your grace." I heard from my side and I jumped when I saw Perdita as well as half a dozen of the cooks and cooks-helpers standing behind her.

"Uh…heya, Perdita," I replied, smiled and tipped my head to the women around her. "Eunice, Daphne, Sabina, Winnie, Pauline."

I got a bunch of smiles and mumbled, "Your graces," in return.

I looked back to Perdita. "You found candles."

"Talked to Rocco, the candlemaker, had them made special," she told me and I blinked.

"You had them made?" I whispered.

"Seemed important to you, your grace," she whispered back and I blinked again, this time to blink away the tears that sprung to my eyes.

I knew she was doing it thinking she was avoiding my, then Tor's, displeasure but that didn't make me any less happy that I could give Tor a real from-my-world birthday cake, which was exactly what I wanted most to give him.

I was so happy that I dashed to her and gave her a big hug with a loud, smacking kiss on her cheek.

Still holding her arms, I leaned back and whispered, "Thank you."

Her hands pried mine from her arms but held them between us where she gave them a tight squeeze.

"My pleasure, your grace," she whispered back.

I smiled at her and then cast my smile around to the others before I raced back to the cake, saying, "And thanks for letting me use the kitchens."

"We were honored to have you with us," Eunice stated.

"Yes, it was fun!" Sabina put in and I looked at her.

It *was* fun. I had pretended then, too, when I was baking and they were cracking jokes and making an effort to include me in their frivolity, that it was authentic. I hadn't cooked anything since I came to this world, except basting the rabbit that first night with Tor. I forgot how much I loved to do it. It was even better doing it for Tor. And even better, pretending to enjoy it around people who were pretending to like me. And, in a weird way, the whole thing worked.

"We'll have to do it again," I told Sabina, reaching for the cake.

"Wait!" Daphne cried and the women rushed forward as I stilled.

"This is for you," Pauline said, picking up the package and handing it to me.

"For me?" I asked, taking it and studying her.

"Yes, for you," Winnie stated.

"But, it's not *my* birthday," I told them, moving my eyes to the package in my hand.

"No, but we thought..." Sabina started then faltered.

Eunice picked it up from there. "We weren't very nice to you when you, erm...first got—"

"Just open it!" Daphne exclaimed and I looked at her to see she was bouncing on her toes in excitement.

"Okay," I whispered, worried and wondering what the package would hold, hoping it wasn't poison.

I opened it, and as the wrapping fell away I saw I held an exquisitely carved, purple glass bottle in my hand.

"Your scent," Perdita stated and my body jolted as my head snapped up.

"We asked Josephina, the perfume maker in town, to create something just for you," Pauline put in.

"No gardenia." Winnie smiled.

I blinked at them. Then I opened the stopper to the bottle, brought to my nose and sniffed.

The bottle wasn't exquisite. The scent was. Subtle and fresh, almost beachy but with a flowery essence.

It was sublime.

So sublime, no poison could smell like that.

I looked around the faces.

Did they...could it be?

Did they *like* me?

As in, *genuinely*?

"Do you all...*like* me?" I asked quietly and got confused looks.

"But...of course!" Sabina cried.

"You're sweet," Daphne said.

"And funny," Eunice added.

"And you saved a wild bird," Pauline put in.

"You make our prince happy," Perdita stated and my gaze locked on hers. "Blissfully so," she finished.

My heart leaped.

"Do you think?" I whispered.

"Your grace, I'm sorry, but I took a swipe of that icing and let me tell you, if he wasn't blissful before, which he was," Winnie put in then grinned cheekily. "When he tastes that, he will be!"

Holy crap! They liked me!

"God, I hope so," I breathed and they all laughed.

Yes! They liked me!

All of a sudden Perdita jumped and ordered, "You must go. You don't have long before the fireworks start."

"Oh God!" I cried, set the bottle down and mumbled, "I'll come back for that."

"We'll take it to your rooms," Eunice offered, picking up the cake and handing it to me. "And we'll take the others away," she said. I caught her meaning and my smile trembled as my face got soft and she cried, "Just go!"

Perdita slid a thin stick between my fingers under the cake and said, "The candles are lit in your rooms. You can use that stick to light your cake candles so you won't get any wax on your beautiful icing."

I stared gratefully into her eyes and gave myself a long moment to do it.

Then I whispered, "Thank you," and she smiled and that smile lit her whole face.

All of it.

Even her eyes.

Not fake.

She liked me!

They all did.

Hurrah!

I smiled at all of them and rushed out of the room, balancing the cake as I went, thinking joyous thoughts that maybe, just maybe, I was finally going to be *really* happy in this fairytale world.

About ten seconds later, however, I was cursing how far away our rooms were (because, seriously, it was a trek) when I made it there only to find the candles lit all around the room but there was no Tor to be found.

I checked all the rooms (his bathroom, my bathroom, his dressing room, my dressing room, his sitting room, you get the picture). He wasn't anywhere.

Shit!

Was I supposed to go somewhere else?

I stood by the bed and tried to think of where I might have to go and it hit me that the balcony off his study faced the city proper, not the sea like the one off our rooms did. Maybe I was supposed to go there.

Holding the cake carefully, I lifted my skirts in one hand and ran to his study as fast as I could without dropping the cake.

When I got there, the double doors were mostly closed, one open an inch. I turned and put my booty in it to open it (I'd have to light the candles later, so much for my big reveal, I didn't have the time) and stopped dead when I heard Algernon's voice.

"I apologize for calling you out at this hour but with her performance today..." he paused, "Well, as you know, the men are talking. She's not herself. So not herself, it's strange."

And Tor's answer made my entire body lock.

"She says she's from a different world."

Uh...

What?

I *said* I was from a different world?

He didn't believe me?

I thought he'd come to believe me.

I heard Algernon's sharp bark of surprised laughter before he asked, "A different world?"

"Yes. A different world," Tor replied. "Gods, it's unbelievable. She lives it and breathes it. She's even created words to go with it. She tells me extraordinary stories of the make-believe architecture and fantastical gadgets they have in *her world*."

He paused and my dazed brain imagined him shaking his handsome head in disgust at the same time it hazily recalled the many nights over dinner or when we were in bed when I'd tell him stories of my world and all the things in it when he went on.

"I must admit, it's stunning how clever she is, how sharp her mind. She's astonishingly imaginative and she never forgets a word of it. She has to be making it up as she goes along but every lie she tells, she remembers and uses it again."

Every lie I tell?

"How bizarre," Algernon muttered.

"It's remarkable," Tor said with what, if I wasn't about to melt into a puddle of steaming heartbreak, I would have noted was clear respect.

"So she's playing you?

"Indeed," Tor answered. "I gave her permission to do so and clearly she took me up on the offer."

I stepped away from the door in order to lean against the wall beside it so my shaking knees wouldn't fail me.

He thought I was playing him.

He thought I was playing him!

Weeks of it! Nearly two months of it!

He thought I was playing him!

"You gave her permission?" Algernon sounded shocked.

"Certainly. It's living a lie but living Cora's lie is better by far than living with the old Cora."

"It doesn't make you angry?" Algernon asked.

"Gods no," Tor replied. "It comes with her sweet body, that charming mouth of hers, her skillful tongue and the possibility that she's already carrying my heir."

Holy crap!

"So you're getting something out of it," Algernon stated.

"Every bloody night," Tor replied and I felt pain sharp in my gut, like I'd been punched. "And if my wife lives and breathes her deceits with exuberant imagination out of bed, you can well imagine what she treats me to *in* it."

Algernon chuckled a low, manly chuckle.

But I closed my eyes. Slowly.

He thought I was the Cora of this world.

He didn't believe I was me.

I was falling in love with him...

Fucking shit, I'd *already* fallen in love with him.

And he was using me.

Using me!

Using me to get his heir.

He was trying to get me pregnant and enjoying himself doing it.

I was letting him.

And enjoying myself doing it, too.

But I *loved* him.

And he did not love me.

He didn't even *like* me.

He was *playing* me!

Why, why, why did guys have to be dicks in my world *and* in fairytale world?

Why?

"Well done, sir," Algernon stated as I made up my mind, straightened from the wall and walked right into the room.

Both men started when I did, their heads swinging in my direction.

But I only had eyes for Tor as he stared at me walking across the room carrying the swirly, creamy frosted cake with its blue birthday candles that I'd wanted so badly and worked so hard to make for him (seriously, the kitchens in his castle were warm and jolly but the utensils and appliances were so far away from KitchenAid it wasn't funny).

"Happy birthday," I whispered and even I heard the ache in my voice.

When Tor heard it, I watched him flinch and the flinch was so reactionary he had no hope of hiding it.

He knew I heard.

Good.

"Cora—" he started.

"In *my* world," I cut him off and moved my what I was sure were heartsick eyes to Algernon, "we don't serve birthday tarts with birthday sparklers, as Perdita told me you do here. In *my* world," I looked back at Tor who was frozen to the spot and watching me stop at his desk and set the cake on it, "we serve birthday cake with birthday candles."

I touched the stick to a candle on his desk, lit it and started lighting the birthday candles as I kept explaining.

"So, for your birthday, since I have no money but I wanted to do something special, I decided to give you something that was special to me, a piece of my world, kind of literally. I scoured the city to find all the right ingredients and Perdita had the candlemaker make special candles. So here you are." I gestured to the cake with a flick of the stick. "A my-world birthday cake." My eyes went to his. "My birthday present to you. And now what you have to do is make a wish, blow out the candles and your wish is supposed to come true."

Luckily, there were only ten candles (I guess I didn't explain very fully to Perdita). I'd finished with them so I blew out the stick and set it on the desk.

"Cora—"Tor started again, beginning to move toward me.

"No!" I cried, lifting up a hand, and he stopped.

"I'll just—"Algernon began, my head snapped to him and I dropped my hand.

"Please, don't go, you must have some cake," I whispered, his eyes shot to Tor but he didn't move.

I looked back at Tor.

"You need to make your wish," I told him. "Then blow out your candles."

"Sweets—" he started, my eyes closed and that tear in my heart didn't split. It didn't gently rip deeper.

It slashed through my heart, rending it in two.

I opened my eyes, locked them on Tor's beautiful, blue, playing, deceitful ones and I felt mine fill with tears.

"Make your wish," I whispered.

"Cora—"

A tear spilled over and slid down my cheek.

"Make your wish, honey."

I watched his eyes follow the trail of my single tear then they came to mine and he came at me.

I whirled, picked up my skirts and ran.

"Cora!" he yelled as I dashed out the door and down the hall. "Cora! Gods damn it, stop!"

He was right behind me.

Shit!

It sucked that he was so tall and his legs were so *freaking* long.

The staircase was in sight, the winding one that skirted the circular wall of the mammoth circular hall that led to the front doors. A hall floored in gleaming black marble veined with silver and blue. A hall that could house at least a hundred bodies whirling around in a waltz.

A fairytale hall in a black, hideous fairytale.

I didn't make it to the staircase though. I was caught by the arm and pulled around.

"*Take your hand off me!*" I shrieked.

"Cora, calm down,"Tor ordered gently.

I stilled and tipped my face to look at him, "Fuck you! Fuck calm! I'm going to find a wizard right now! And don't you *fucking* stop me!"

"Cora, gods, calm the fuck down!" he yelled back and it pissed me off that he'd picked up some of *my* language from *my* world that he didn't even believe fucking *existed* that I wanted to go back to and I didn't want *him* to have any part of.

"Take your hand off me!" I screamed again, trying to pull away, but failed when he let me go and his arms locked around me.

"Listen to me," he commanded.

"No! No way! You're not a jerk. You're a *dick*! You're a *player*! I fucking *hate you*! Which really sucks because about ten minutes ago, I fucking *loved you* more than *anything* in this, *and my*, whole, *fucking worlds*!"

His body went solid and I took advantage.

Wresting out of his arms, I turned instantly and started running.

"Cora!" he shouted as I made it to the top of the staircase and I looked back over my shoulder.

"Don't come near me!" I yelled, starting to race down the steps.

"Cora! Gods! Mind the—!"

That's when it happened.

I tripped.

Stupid, stupid, *stupid* me, running in an emotional state down a flight of stairs.

And down I went, crashing, bumping and whirling down a silver and blue-veined set of winding, black marble, fairytale castle stairs.

I landed at the bottom feeling pain in every inch of my body but most especially my head, which slammed, rather violently, against a number of steps on the way down.

Fucking great.

I felt Tor crouch at my side and carefully and tenderly (the asshole), he lifted my torso in his arms, cradling my head in the crook.

"Sweets," he whispered.

I opened my eyes and I looked into his fucking unbelievably beautiful eyes and that was when my vision started to fade.

"I loved you," I whispered.

"Cora," he whispered back.

"I know you don't believe me, you'll never believe me but it's true. I loved you."

"Stop speaking," he murmured.

The black started to permeate, take over. It was coming fast. I was losing it.

"In this world," I kept whispering, "you were the only thing I had but you were the only thing I needed."

"Gods," he muttered, the word sounding dragged out of some deep part of him.

And that was all I heard before everything faded to black.

17

Until You

~

I felt weak light hit my eyes.

I opened them and I saw my light green pillowcase.

I blinked but when my eyes came back open, there it was.

My light green pillowcase.

My pillowcase. From *my* bed. In *my* world.

I shot up to sitting and nearly blacked out, my head was so woozy. I lifted a hand to it and closed my eyes tight until the feeling went away.

I kept them closed thinking, *Well, guess all I had to do to get myself back to my world was give myself a head injury...good to know.*

I slowly opened them and looked around.

Then my mouth dropped open.

My room looked like a hurricane had rushed through it. There were clothes and shoes and accessories *everywhere*. I spied some glossy bags, squinted, leaned forward and my heart slid into my throat.

Okay, well, there it was. The Cora of Tor's world had come here. She hadn't cleaned in two months and apparently she somehow managed to shop at exclusive department stores.

I flopped back to the pillows, whispering, "Shit."

I felt the mattress under me. I'd always liked my mattress. It was firm and comfortable.

What it was not was firm but soft and downy like Tor's.

Tor.

My nose started stinging and I sucked air in through it.

No more Tor (which I told myself was good). No more Aggie (which was not good). No more Salem (also not good) or Clarabelle (ditto) and, of course, all the girls in the kitchen who I had just figured out liked me.

No more fairytale.

A lone tear slid out of the side of my eye, down my temple and mingled in my hair.

"Good," I whispered but it wasn't a convincing whisper.

It was total bullshit.

Now I was home, heartbroken, having been played by the master, the black Prince Noctorno of a whole other world, and it was clear just looking at my bedroom that I had a big mess to clean up, left by the other Cora.

First, I needed to get a cold compress for my head.

Then I would tackle the mess Cora made of my house and probably my life.

I gingerly got out of bed and just as gingerly walked across the room. I flinched at the bright lights of the bathroom when I turned them on. Then I winced when I saw the state of the bathroom (dirty towels, makeup and hair stuff everywhere). I stared at my mustard-yellow bathroom suite, which had obviously not been cleaned in two months, but even if it was sparkling clean, it would still look like crap.

"Goodie, I'm home," I muttered, did my thing, dug through the stuff on the long bathroom counter (Cora, I saw, had also splurged on some pretty pricey face stuff and makeup). Found face soap, washed my face, opened a new toothbrush and brushed my teeth. I took three aspirin and washed them down cupping the water in my hand under the tap to do so. Then I wetted the sole clean washcloth I could find in my bathroom closet with cold water, wrung it out, folded it and wandered back to my bedroom to lie down thinking a quick rest, parents first (if I wasn't disowned), friends second (if they were talking to me), work last (if I still *had* work).

I moved over the threshold. Something caught my eye, I looked up and stopped dead.

Tor was standing there.

Tor wearing a pair of faded jeans (that looked really freaking good on him) and a navy blue, long-sleeved tee (that also looked really freaking good on him).

His feet were bare, his hair was messy and his eyes were on me.

"What the—?" I started to breathe.

"What are you doing out of bed?" he demanded to know in his Tor-like, imperious, deep voice, and I blinked.

This was a mistake for in the nanosecond my eyes were closed, he made it to me (truth be told, my bedroom wasn't that big), had me cradled in his arms, then he walked me to my bed and gently set me in it. He yanked the covers over me and pulled the washcloth out of my hand, studied it a second, sat on the bed beside me and pressed it on my forehead.

I stared up at him and whispered, "Who are you?"

He stared down at me. "I'm your husband."

Oh my God!

Did Cora of the other world find Tor of this world and marry him in two months?

Holy crap!

"You're my husband?"

His eyes moved over my face before he said, "Yes, love, I'm your husband."

Oh no. Oh God. Oh no.

I couldn't live in *my* world with the Tor of *my* world while remembering what a stupid fool I'd been about the Tor of the fairytale world!

That would suck!

How could this situation, already bad, get so much worse? What did I do to deserve such shitty karma?

"Did we, uh…like, get married in Vegas or something?" I asked and his brows drew together.

"No, Cora, actually, *we* haven't been married, something I will rectify the minute *we* get back home."

Oh boy.

"Back home?" I whispered.

"To our world."

Oh boy!

"Our world?" I asked tentatively.

"My world and what will bloody well be *your* world as soon as I discover how the fuck to get out of this dreary, foul place."

Holy crap!

Tor came back with me!

I shot straight up to my feet and jumped off the bed, running over the clothes and shoes on the floor, my head whirling but I ignored it, praying I wouldn't pass out.

Of course, I didn't make it to the door. I was caught with an arm at my waist and pulled back into a hard body. I struggled, Tor's other arm locked around my shoulders and chest, caging me in and his mouth went to my ear.

"Calm yourself," he said quietly.

"*Let go of me!*" I shrieked.

"Calm yourself, love."

"Let...me...*go*!" I yelled, still struggling.

He let me go but only so he could put his hands to my hips, whirl me around and step into me in a way that I had no choice but to back up until I hit wall and then his body fenced me in.

I tipped my head back to scream in his face but his tender voice got there before me.

"You've sustained a head injury not to mention a variety of bruises and swelling. You need to rest."

"And *you* need to step back."

"Cora, I'll step back when you promise to lie down, not get excited and rest."

"How did you get here?" I snapped.

"I've no idea."

"What happened?" I asked, forcing my hands between our bodies and pushing against his chest, to no avail so I gave up and went on. "The last thing I remember is losing consciousness."

He nodded. "You did. I picked you up, carried you to our rooms. Perdita and the women from the kitchens had come out. They heard us arguing and saw your fall. Algernon was there as well and I sent him to fetch my physician. One of the women got you ice for a bump on your head. I was holding you in my arms and the ice on your head when Algernon and my physician arrived. The next thing I knew, your entire body was surrounded by a blue mist. It surrounded mine with yours and then we were in that," his head gave a small jerk backwards, "bed."

I stared up at him. "A blue mist?"

"A blue mist."

"What blue mist?" I asked.

"I've no idea. I've never seen anything like it."

"Never?"

"Never."

"So we didn't disappear when I passed out?"

"No."

Weird.

I turned my head, looked down at myself and saw I was wearing the stretchy, cotton charcoal gray nightie with the dusty pink band at the top that I'd been wearing the last night I went to sleep in my world.

Then I looked to him. "Where'd you get your clothes? Did you wake up in those?"

"No," he gave another jerk of his head and I saw his clothing from his world, including boots, dumped in a corner. "These were in your wardrobe, which, sweets, is incredibly small."

Clothes that fit him perfectly were in my closet?

Oh man.

I didn't think that was good.

"As is your whole dwelling," he went on. "It's also filthy. You cleaned a cave. How on earth do you live like this?"

"Well, *Tor*, I haven't been living in my *dwelling* for two months, now, have I?" I asked snottily then demanded, "Move away."

"Cora—"

I gave another shove of my hands, doing it with such effort it hurt my head (and my, I belatedly realized, aching muscles) but he rocked back only an inch.

Then he came right back. "Not until you promise you'll settle down and rest."

"I'll promise to settle down and rest if you'll get the *fuck* away from me!" I screeched.

His head tilted and his chin went down just as his eyes closed slowly and, God's honest truth, he looked in pain.

It proved to be true when he opened his eyes and locked them with mine.

Yep, he was in pain.

Lots of it.

Ouch.

Man, it totally sucked that I could hate him, see his pain and hurt for him.

His hand came to my neck and I had nowhere to go so I couldn't pull away.

"Please, listen to me," he said softly.

"Fine," I snapped. "Get it over with so I can go to bed and let the aspirin work."

"The what?"

"It doesn't matter. Just say whatever you have to say."

His jaw clenched then his thumb started stroking the side of my neck. That was when my jaw clenched and I glared at him.

"Is it normal, in this world, this...travel between worlds?" he asked.

"No," I bit out.

"Do you know anyone it's happened to?"

"No," I repeated shortly.

"No one?"

"No," I replied. "Get to the point."

"Me either," he said quietly. "Until you."

Oh shit.

I saw his point and that sucked.

When he said no more, I prompted, "Is that all?"

"My love," his thumb moved up to stroke my jaw as his face got even closer, "it was fantastical what you were saying. You have to agree."

"No I don't," I denied.

"Put yourself in my place," he urged.

"Yes, well, sure, for an hour, maybe a day. I'll give you a week," I stated sarcastically. "I can put myself in your place and maybe the Cora of your world could pull something like that off for that period of time. I'll give you that."

"My sweet—"

"But we had *two months* together. I saw the damage she wrought on your staff and the entirety of Bellebryn. I know she was idiot enough to spurn your love. I can look around my house and see what she's capable of. But you can't tell me that she's capable of carrying off *that* kind of deception for *that* long. When I arrived, everything about her had changed, I hope. *Everything*. Even the way she *slept*. And you cannot tell me that you covered my body with yours, moved inside me, looked in my eyes while you fucked me and didn't know the *bloody* difference."

Shit.

Now I was using *his* curse words.

But it worked. I scored a hit. I saw the pain slash through his eyes.

"I wanted to believe—" he started.

"Well, you didn't. I baked you a *fucking* cake because it was the only thing I had to give you on your birthday, I wanted to give you a part *of me*, and I got to your study and heard—"

"Don't," he clipped tersely.

"Yes, you know what I heard," I whispered.

His hand slid up to cup my jaw, his other hand joining it on the other side.

"Take your hands off me." I was still whispering.

He didn't.

He dropped his forehead to mine and started talking.

"Think about it, love, please," he urged softly.

"Think about what? How, while I was falling in love with *you*, you were playing *me?*"

"You love me," he told me.

"Not anymore, I don't," I returned and I watched his eyes smile.

"You can't fall out of love just like that."

"Trust me, Tor, *you can*."

He lifted his forehead from mine and swept his thumb across my lips. I tried to tear my face away but his fingers simply gripped tighter.

"You can't. I know. I fell in love with her and it isn't that easy. I know this because I tried."

"Well, I'm not you," I spat.

"No, thank the gods, you aren't." And his eyes were smiling as his lips twitched.

I looked at the ceiling then back at him.

"Will you let me *go?*" I demanded impatiently.

"Yes, I will, in a moment."

"Now!"

"A moment, Cora," he stated firmly. I glared and he continued, "I will leave you to rest. You need some time away from me. I'll give it to you."

Really?

How was he going to do that? Where was he going to go?

Oh Lordy, he'd probably walk in front of a car or…

"But, I'll leave you with this," he interrupted my thoughts. "If you have a twin in my world then it is safe to assume that there is a man in this world who looks like me. And if he was in your life, if you fell in love with him the instant you saw him, if you were convinced by a prophesy written in the sky that he carried half your soul, just like every prophesy that came true generation after generation for as long as anyone could remember…and then he crushed your heart. Then I was brought into this world and I was charming, amusing, seducing you with every turn of my head, every look, every smile, every move I made, telling you fantastical stories about how I came from another world, what would you think? What would you do?"

"I didn't seduce you!" I cried.

"Cora, love," he whispered, "you're seducing me right now."

That shut me up *and* it made my heart clench.

"Think about that," he said quietly then he let me go and stepped toward the door.

I watched him go and I knew I couldn't watch him go.

Damn it all to hell!

I turned and called out to him (really, I had no choice), "Where are you going?"

He stopped in the doorway and looked at me. "Out."

"Out where?"

"Wherever my feet take me."

Shit!

I turned fully to him and crossed my arms on my chest. "Tor, you can't go out in my world without me. Things are different here. *Vastly* different. You might get…hurt, or something."

His mouth curved up. "Worried?"

"No!" I snapped. "I just figure you're destined to go home soon and I don't want to deprive Bellebryn of their ruler."

"Right," he murmured and started to turn. "I'll be back."

"Tor!" I cried, taking a step to him.

He stopped and looked at me.

"Take one more step *away* from the bed, Cora, and I'll have to be inventive in finding ways to keep you in it and make you rest."

I took a step back and glared at him.

"Don't worry about me, love. I'll be fine. Rest. I'll be back soon."

Then he went to the dresser, opened a drawer, grabbed a pair of socks then nabbed a pair of boots from the floor before he disappeared.

I stared after him. Then I walked back to my bed and collapsed on it.

There, I stared at the ceiling and muttered, "Shit."

18

Thank God You're Home

~

I was pacing my living room and freaking out.

Tor had to get home and he had to get home *soon.*

There were two reasons for that.

One, night had fallen which meant he'd been gone all day. It had been raining or drizzling all day, and I had to admit (damn and blast!) that I was worried about him.

Two, I had a strong feeling the Cora of his world was in some deep shit.

Earlier, after he'd left, I'd lain down, and when the aspirin didn't work, I picked my way through my (filthy, Tor was right, there were used takeout cartons, dirty dishes and other debris everywhere) apartment to the kitchen hoping to make coffee. However, I found no coffee and not much else except sour milk in a carton I was pretty sure *I'd* left behind.

I shook the milk out in the sink and threw the carton away, got some ice water, took some ibuprofen and tried the resting thing again.

But I couldn't rest because my house was so filthy.

So I started cleaning.

Throwing in some laundry, removing the sheets, picking up sodden towels, putting away my clothes and makeup and the other Cora's expensive clothes and makeup, not to mention, tidying the glossy department store bags that still held receipts and seeing just how much money Cora had spent, which nearly gave me a heart attack.

Where had she got so much money?

I found my purse and there was twenty dollars in it which, if I remembered correctly, was how much I'd left in it. I went to my computer and logged into my bank account. All my money was still there. I checked my online credit card statements, all the balances were nil, like I kept them, paying them off monthly.

What on earth?

I went back to cleaning, and when I bent to put away the scattered DVD cases in the cabinet under my TV, wondering why on earth she pulled out what appeared to be every DVD I owned—she must have *really* liked movies—I thought I found it.

Money.

Stacks and stacks of it.

And we weren't talking five or ten dollar notes, here. We weren't even talking twenties.

They were *all* fifties and hundreds.

Holy crap!

I stared at it then sat back on my tush, slammed the doors shut and stared at the cabinet some more.

I went back to cleaning, but now I was cleaning because I was nervous, agitated and trying not to panic. I was hoping I could concentrate on cleaning and not obsessing about all the ways Cora could get that kind of cash, every way I came up with spelling trouble for her and now…me.

But I couldn't stop thinking about it.

How did she get so much money?

And whose clothes were those men's clothes in my closet and, I might add, drawers? There were jeans, t-shirts, suits, dress shirts, shoes, boots, underwear, the whole enchilada. Not many but enough to spell trouble.

Something was wrong and I didn't want to be home alone without Tor whenever that something walked into my apartment.

I only hoped that whoever *he* was, he went with her when she went back like Tor came with me.

I finished tidying, scouring, wiping and vacuuming, and when I finished, I took a shower, lotioned with *my* lotion, blow-dried my hair and put on a pair of jeans and a University of Puget Sound sweatshirt.

The clothes of Tor's world rocked but I had to admit, it felt nice to be in a pair of jeans.

Then I sat down by the phone (why I still had a landline when all my friends had gone totally cell, I didn't know—I just did because my parents did because my dad was sure the cell phone companies were in cahoots with the government, conspiring to take away our civil liberties, and if they could help it, they never called me on my cell).

Right.

Priorities.

My parents.

"Sweetie!" my mom cried when she heard my voice and I was relieved I wasn't disowned. I was also close to tears just hearing her voice. I loved my mom. "My God, where have you been? The last three times I talked to you, you said you were in a rush and you had to go, you'd call me back. Why haven't you been calling me back?"

"Uh..."

"And *who* was that sexy-voiced man who answered the phone, at eleven thirty at night, I might add?"

Oh dear.

"Well—" I started.

"Damn, now *I'm* in a rush," Mom cut me off. "Your father is having car problems and he's stuck out by the bridge. You know, he won't get rid of that dratted Volvo. I keep telling him, it's done. He has to let it go. He's had it for sixteen years! I keep telling him he can buy a hybrid, they're good for the environment, or at least not as bad as other cars. I mean, does he want to be buried in that Volvo, for God's sake?"

Dad and his Volvo. Why did discussing this, *again* (we'd discussed it, like, seven hundred thousand times—Mom freaking hated that Volvo) also make me want to cry?

"So now, I have to beg off but you're coming to dinner," she carried on. "You're doing it tomorrow night. I don't care what you have going on. *And* you're bringing Mr. Sexy Voice with you. I know my girl and *he* is why we aren't hearing from you. I'm so *pleased* you've moved on from Brian. You know, your father and I always thought he was a bit of an idiot. Then again, any man who wouldn't hold on to my beautiful, sweet, funny girl is an idiot."

Oh man, totally going to cry.

"Plus," she went on, "there is the small fact Brian voted for Bush."

"Mom—"

"Gotta go! Our house. Tomorrow. Six. With your man. See you then! Love you, sweetie."

Then she was gone.

I stared at the receiver then I hit the off button. The instant I did, it rang in my hand and I jumped.

Bracing (because it could be anything), I hit the on button and greeted hesitantly, "Hello?"

"Forgot to ask, sweetie, does your man not eat anything? I mean, is he a vegetarian or something?" Mom inquired.

Tor killed two Thumpers for our first dinner together. The man was so *not* a vegetarian it wasn't funny and yet I burst out laughing. Probably hysterically.

Through my laughter, I said, "Uh, no Mom. He's definitely not a vegetarian."

"Oh, okay, well, anything else he doesn't eat?"

I controlled my hilarity and started, "Mom, I need to explain—"

"Explain tomorrow, over wine. Now I have to know this *and* get your father. Is there something he doesn't eat?"

Shit.

"I think he eats everything, Mom."

"Great! I'll get inspired. Promise. Later!"

And again she was gone.

I beeped the off button again.

Oh crap, did I just allow my mother to order me and my other world man (who I hated) to dinner?

Shit!

After that, I set about calling my friends. None of them picked up. I didn't think this was a good sign.

I left hesitant, "I really need to talk to you, something's happened," voicemail messages and hoped.

And after *that*, I took the trash out to the dumpster, ran by the corner store to get staples and came back only to see Tor standing in my living room wearing a very well-tailored suit and looking around at the newly cleaned apartment.

What?

Was he trying on clothes?

He turned and gave me a huge smile.

"Baby," he growled, walked straight up to me, hauled me into his arms and laid a wet one on me.

And I knew instantly it was not Tor because whoever the hell *this* guy was, he kissed weird.

Which meant my body turned to stone.

He lifted his head and looked down at me.

Yep, not Tor.

I hadn't noticed it but he didn't have a scar.

"Hey, princess, what's goin' on?" His eyes traveled down to my chest then shot up to my face. "And what's with that ratty-assed sweatshirt?"

Holy crap. Holy crap. Holy *crap*!

Cora had found this world's Tor! Why? How? *Why?*

"Uh...Tor?" I asked.

"What?" he asked back.

"Tor?" I tried again.

"What the fuck you talkin' about, babe?"

Oh shit.

"Noctorno?" I tried yet again.

"That's me, Cory, Noc, your man. What the fuck? You okay?"

He called himself Noc?

Oh boy.

"Uh..."

"Checkin' in." He gave me a gentle shake, his eyes scanning my face. They were alert as if he was looking for something. "Wonderin' if we're goin' out tonight?"

"Out?"

"To the tables, babe. *Out*."

The tables?

"What tables?" I asked.

He stared down at me.

Then he dipped his face close, "Shit, babe, you don't look too good. What happened? You got a headache or something?"

I latched on to that. "Yes, actually, yes. A bad one."

He looked at the door then down to my hands carrying plastic bags and back at me. "Then what were doin' outside?" he asked, letting me go, taking the bags and dumping them on the dining room table saying, "You don't feel good, you don't go outside. You call your man. I come and take care of you." He came back to me and his arms circled me again when he finished, "That's the gig."

I stared up at him.

Wow.

Cold, bitchy Cora had this guy wrapped around her finger.

In *two months*.

And Tor fell in love with her on sight.

How did she do that?

"Cora, baby, hello? You with me?" he called.

"I'm, um...with you. Listen, what tables were you talking about?"

His brows grew together before he answered with a scary, "Poker."

Poker?

The money in my TV cabinet.

Oh shit!

Cora, or this guy, was earning money, *lots of it*, playing *poker*.

"Right, yes, right, poker tables." I shook my head. "Sorry, um...I'm kind of fuzzy. My head really hurt this morning when I got up and now I'm feeling weird."

"Shit, babe," he muttered then his face was in my neck. "That's what happens when you sleep alone." I felt his lips on my neck and I shivered (not like Tor made me shiver, another kind of shiver) at the same time I prayed Tor wouldn't walk in the door.

"No, actually, that's what happens when..." Damn! What did I say? Then I hit on it, the perfect excuse. "I get my period."

His head shot up. "What?"

"I've got my period."

But I didn't.

In fact, I hadn't had one in...

My body turned to stone again.

Oh.

Shit!

"Babe, you had your period last week," he said suspiciously.

Fuck!

Clearly Cora of the other world and I didn't share the same cycles.

Or, damn and blast, maybe we did.

"Um..." I muttered, my mind awhirl, trying to recall when I had my last period but knowing whenever it was, it was in this world, not Tor's.

Oh dear.

"What's goin' on?" he asked.

"Nothing," I said quickly. "It just...gets like this. I'm, uh...irregular. It, um...sucks."

"Sucks?"

"Yes, sucks."

He studied me as he noted, "Cory, baby, never heard you use that word before." Uh-oh. "You speak proper," he went on and I stared up at him. He grinned and his voice dropped low. "Why I like you. Thought you were an uppity bitch and you are, cold as ice, but with me..." He dipped his head and whispered in my ear, "Wildcat."

Cora was a wildcat for this guy?

Whoa.

I had to get it together and I had to play this right. Until I could figure out what was going on in my life and play him *out* of it that was.

And I also needed to go get a freaking pregnancy test. Stat.

I wrapped my hand around his neck and whispered in his ear, "I'm sorry, um...my love. I just, well...I'm not myself."

He lifted his head and looked at me. Then he lifted his hand and cupped my cheek.

"Can I get you something?" he asked.

Damn, this guy was kind of sweet. How did Cora latch on to him, seeing as she was such a bitch?

"No, love, just...I need to rest."

"Fine, I'll come by later and—"

"No!" I cried, his brows shot together and I hurried on. "No, uh, my sweet, just...I need some alone time. I'm not me. I just feel...not myself. Can you call me later?"

His eyes narrowed and he informed me, "This is two nights you've wanted to be alone. Babe, my clothes are in your closet. You get what that means?"

Did he live at my place?

He, luckily, went on, "I'm happy to give you space, you need it. I got my own. But, you got issues, we need to sort them out. You with me?"

Shoo.

He had his own space. All was not lost.

"I'm with you. And I don't have any issues." Yeah, right. "It's...um, I just don't feel good, Noc. Can you give me some time? When I feel better, everything will be okay."

Fat chance of that.

His eyes moved over my face.

"Yeah, baby, I can give you some time," he said softly.

Damn, he *was* sweet.

"Thanks," I whispered.

"You'll call me, you need anything?"

I nodded and he smiled. It was nearly as good as Tor's.

"Give your man a kiss, yeah?"

Oh boy.

I nodded, bit my lip, went up on my toes and gave him a kiss. His mouth opened over mine and he gave me a deeper, wetter one. I managed to return it which meant it unfortunately got deeper, wetter and hotter leaving me thinking it wasn't weird, it was just different. In my opinion not as good as Tor's but also not bad by a long shot.

His lips left mine and when I opened my eyes, I saw him quickly shutter the surprise in his.

Weird.

What was that?

After searching my face for a second, he kissed my forehead.

Wow. That was sweet too.

He looked me in the eyes. "I'll call you later, babe."

"Okay," I whispered. "Later, um...love."

He grinned at me, gave me a squeeze, let me go and walked out the door.

I collapsed on my sofa.

After I recuperated from Noc's visit (while staring at the TV cabinet like it would explode at any minute and take me with it in its ball of flame), I made myself a fried bologna sandwich with three pieces of bologna and a melted square of American cheese on top. I toasted the bread and smothered it with mustard. Then I made myself another one. After that, I ate a quarter bag of Cheetos. Last, I popped a Diet Coke.

After sucking some back and stopping myself from hyperventilating, I called work.

"The Arthur Broderick Agency, this is Esther. Can I help you?"

Oh crap.

Some chick named Esther answered my extension.

"Um, Esther, is Mr. Arthur there?" I asked.

"Can I tell him who's calling?"

"Cora Goode," I answered.

"One moment," she replied

I waited, listened to bad music and then, faster than I expected, Dave Arthur, my boss, was on the phone.

"Cora?"

"Dave, hello, I—"

"Cora, thank God. Everyone's been worried sick about you!"

Thank God? Worried sick?

"Um…"

"You were no call, no show. You're never no call, no show. Hell, you're never no show! Phoebe went to your apartment, said it looked like a disaster hit it and your car was gone."

Phoebe, my best friend in and out of the office (therefore she had a key to my apartment) came to my place?

And my car was gone?

"For weeks, we've been phoning the police and hospitals," he continued.

Oh dear.

"Why didn't you phone my folks?" I asked stupidly because I should be thankful he didn't. "They're my emergency contacts."

"I couldn't phone Dara and Forrest and worry them if something wasn't right with you," he said, sounding aghast, and I was grateful that my mom and dad knew my boss and they had formed a bond over multiple games of Apples to Apples. "Especially when Phoebe went back, saw some big guy walking out of your apartment. She says he looked like he was living there and when she tried her key, it didn't work. She thought you'd moved out or something really bad had happened, like you got hooked up with this dude and he was bad news. God, I'm so fucking glad you phoned and sound all right."

What?

"Dave, don't you think you'd get a call if something bad went down with me?" I asked stupid, stupid, stupidly.

He paused.

Then he asked, "Yeah, I would. So where have you been?"

Stupid!

"Well, I'm calling to say…" *Shit!* "Something bad went down with me."

"Oh my God! What? Are you okay?"

Seriously, this was why The Arthur Broderick Agency weren't doing all that great. Dave was awesome, he was a creative mastermind when it came to advertising and he could charm a snake, but he was mostly a flake. Boyd Broderick wasn't much better. They were college roommates and they still wore beer bong hats and got toasted in their offices frequently.

"I…" I started, my mind searching then I came up with it. "Got in an accident."

"Holy shit! Were you hurt?"

"No, I mean, yes. I had a head injury."

"Oh, Cora, I can't believe it! That sucks! I can't believe Dara and Forrest didn't phone. They went it alone. That's awful. We could have, I don't know, sent a fruit basket or something. Are you okay?"

"Um, well, I had amnesia for a while so obviously, uh…forgot where I worked…" Pure soap opera, was he going to buy this shit? "And so, no…I'm still recovering and…" Was I going to do this? Damn, I was. "I need a bit more time."

"Whatever you need. We'll activate the extended sick leave policy for you. We had to, you know, stop your pay. HR made us do it, swear. But we'll reinstate it and get you reimbursed for…"

"No," I cut in, feeling like a cheat. "You don't have to do that."

"Of course we do. You've been with us frickin' forever."

God, that was nice.

"No, really, I have special insurance for, you know, that kind of thing," I lied and kept lying. "I'm good. Totally okay. I just need another week. Maybe two. And then, um…can I come back?"

"Yeah, sure, totally," Dave told me. "We have an ad in the paper but we've been getting temps and they, like, totally suck so, abso-freaking-lutely. Can't wait to have you back but you get healthy first, hear?"

My boss rocked.

"Thanks, Dave."

"Good to hear your voice, Cora. Sucks you had an accident but glad you're gonna be okay."

"Thanks."

"Later, Cora."

"'Bye, Dave."

I hit the off button.

Then I stared at the phone.

I started giggling, this, I knew, was definitely hysteria.

I quit giggling and did more laundry, folded clothes, tidied them away and put clean sheets on the bed.

After that, I did another round of phone calls to my friends, none of whom, again, picked up.

After that, I started freaking out.

And after that, I started pacing, waiting for Tor to return and trying not to panic.

And now, it was after eight. He left just after nine thirty, it was raining and he wasn't home.

He was probably in an emergency room, every bone in his beautiful body broken, having been hit by a bus.

Sure he was a dick and an asshole who ripped my heart out and stomped on it, but when I was new to his world, he took care of me. Yes, there was a curse that started and the small fact he thought I was his wife that made him take care of me, but he did.

He killed rabbits for me.

And I let him go out and be hit by a bus.

Shit!

The door opened and he walked through, hair wet, clothes drenched and plastered to him, looking hot.

Not thinking, I ran to him, grabbed his shirt in my fists, pressed to his wet body and tipped my head back to look at him as his arms slid around me.

"Thank *God* you're home," I breathed.

Tor stared into my face.

Then he smiled.

19

Only You

~

After Tor smiled at me, his eyes moved over my face then over my head then they scanned my living room.

His smile faded, his expression went decidedly ominous, his gaze dropped back to me and he growled, "What are you doing out of bed?"

I didn't have time for Tor's ominous look. There was a shitload of money in my TV cabinet. None of my friends were talking to me. Cora had hooked up with my world's Noctorno. And we had a date to have dinner with my freaking parents tomorrow night.

I had to stay on target.

"Where have you been?" I asked, my voice pitched high, my fingers still curled into his wet shirt.

"Out in your world," he answered and before I could say more, he did. "You were right, love, it's colorless."

"I know, but—"

"Gray. So bloody wet. And it's loud."

"I know, listen—"

"And grimy," he cut me off again. "So much filth, even the air doesn't taste good."

"Tor, *I know*, but—"

"And so many bloody people, all in a hurry, all impatient, gods, hideous."

"Tor!" I shouted.

"What?" he asked.

"We need to talk, we have problems," I informed him and his brows drew slightly together as his arms curled me protectively closer.

"What problems?"

I opened my mouth to speak and didn't know where to start.

So I asked, "Have you eaten?"

"No," he replied.

I pulled away, ordering, "Change out of those wet clothes, I'll make you a bologna sandwich and we'll talk."

"A what?"

That's when I lost it.

"Just change out of your clothes!" I cried.

The instant I finished my last word, his hand cupped my jaw and he bent to put his face in mine.

"I'll change, Cora, calm down. Whatever it is, we'll sort it out. Right?" he said softly.

I looked in his eyes, sucked in breath and nodded, hating that his quiet, powerful strength could calm me but having to admit that it could.

His hand dropped away and he sauntered into my bedroom.

I dashed into the kitchen.

I was toasting bread and frying bologna when he walked in wearing another, more faded pair of jeans (that were, incidentally, even hotter on him than the others) and a white, long-sleeved tee that was tighter than the other one. And seeing as I'd never seen him in anything but black or, this morning, navy blue, its brightness against his tanned, olive-toned skin looked so good, it struck me momentarily speechless.

I pulled it together when his eyes dropped to the frying pan and he asked, "What, by the gods, is *that*?"

"Bologna," I answered. He looked at me, I knew my answer meant nothing to him so I explained, "It's a kind of meat."

"It's round," he observed with barely concealed distaste.

"Uh…yes."

"Meat is not round," he declared.

Well, he was mostly right.

"Can we not talk about bologna?" I asked.

He held my eyes for a second then he crossed his arms on his wide chest and leaned a hip against the counter which I took as an affirmative.

I flipped the bologna, snatched the toast out when it popped up and started talking.

"I think Cora is in trouble. I found a big stash of money in my TV cabinet. A *lot* of it, Tor. Too much to earn in two months in any legal way. I found out she's playing poker and I think that's how she's getting it."

I squirted mustard on the bread and turned my head to look at him.

"Poker?" he asked.

"It's a card game. Gambling."

His brows drew together and he clarified, "A game of chance for money?"

I nodded.

His lips thinned.

Oh boy.

"What?" I asked.

"Cora has a gift. Most would use it for good. I could see she would not."

That didn't sound good.

"What gift?" I asked.

"She excels with numbers."

Oh dear.

That could mean Cora was counting cards. Cora was playing poker and counting cards.

Shit!

"This isn't good," I muttered, grabbing a slice of American cheese and unwrapping it from its plastic.

"What's that?" Tor asked and I looked at him to see his eyes on the cheese.

"American cheese."

"And that clear sheet you're removing?"

"Plastic wrap."

His hand came out and he took the plastic from me. I slapped the cheese on one of the pieces of bologna and went for another slice as he rubbed the plastic between his fingers.

"Extraordinary," he murmured.

"It doesn't biodegrade," I informed him. His eyes came to me, brows up and I slapped the second slice of cheese on another piece of bologna and continued. "Biodegrade, meaning break down. Return to nature. It never goes away. It's man-made. It's part of the reason this world is so...colorless."

He looked at the plastic and then set it aside.

Acutely aware in a way I'd never been before of the waste I was creating, I opened another slice and slapped it on the last piece of bologna. Gathering the pieces of plastic, I took them to the garbage thinking I was never going to buy American cheese again and then I decided to take us back to target.

"If Cora's gambling and counting cards, that wouldn't be good if someone suspects. But we have another problem," I told him.

"And that would be?" he asked as I went back to the frying pan, turned off the burner and used a spatula to slide the pieces of bologna on the bread.

"I had a visitor today," I told him. "The Cora of your world somehow managed to hook up with the Noctorno of this world. They're together. The clothes you're wearing are his. He's the one who told me about the poker. It seems while you've been carrying on with me, she's been carrying on with him."

The air in the room suddenly changed and it was not a good change. It was also not a bad change.

It was a *very* bad change.

I turned my head to look at his face and I instantly realized my mistake.

He'd been in love with her. Maybe, by the look on his face, he still was. The news that his wife was cheating on him, regardless that he'd flagrantly cheated on her, was not going down very well.

Still, I felt for him and whispered, "Tor—"

"He visited today?" he asked in a soft, dangerous voice.

"Uh…yes."

"He was here?"

"Um…yes," I breathed for his expression nor tone had changed.

"With you?"

Uh-oh.

"Uh…"

"With you, Cora?" he pushed.

"Yes, of course, we…talked."

"And you know they, as you put it…hooked up?"

"Uh…"

"How do you know this?"

Oh boy.

"Tor—"

"How do you know this?"

I wasn't going to get out of it.

So I answered, "He kind of...hugged me and, uh...kissed me." I watched Tor's face turn to stone and finished lamely, "Twice."

The air in the room changed again. It got heavier. So heavy, it was hard to breathe.

"He touched you?" he whispered.

"He surprised me," I said quickly. "I had to, uh—"

"Put his mouth on you?"

"Tor—"

His eyes narrowed. "*Twice?*"

"Um—"

Suddenly I was across the kitchen, my back to the wall and Tor was in my space, his hands on my neck, his thumbs in my jaw forcing it up so his eyes could lock on mine.

"He does not touch you again," Tor growled.

"Tor, he doesn't know what's going on. I had to—"

His fingers tensed and his face came to within an inch of mine. "He does not touch you again."

"Okay," I whispered.

"Repeat it," he commanded harshly.

"He does not touch me again." I kept whispering.

"I will deal with him."

What?

"What?" I asked. "How?"

"I don't know but I will. *You* do not deal with this man. This man does not touch you. He does not see you—"

I wrapped my fingers around his wrists and interrupted, "Tor, he can't see *you* either. You both look exactly alike!"

"Precisely," he clipped. "You're in love with *me* and I'll not give this...*other* bloody *me* an opportunity to muddle your head."

There it was.

He wasn't jealous and hurt about Cora cheating on him. He didn't care about that at all.

He was thinking about me.

God, I hated it that he could still be sweet, protective and possessive, all of which I liked when I was trying to convince myself I hated him.

"Tor!" I cried. "He's not going to—"

"Cora, we're not discussing this."

"This is insane! If he sees you, he'll freak! You can't—"

"Leave him to me," he ordered.

"Tor, seriously—"

His fingers tensed again and he growled low, "Cora, I said, leave him to me."

I glared at him, my mind conjuring the vision of a Noctorno to Noctorno faceoff and just how freaking weird that would be.

Then I snapped, "Oh, all right!"

He relaxed but his hands brought my face up the inch it needed so he could brush his lips against mine.

My lips tingled.

God, I liked it when he did that.

"Stop kissing me," I whispered, staring into his eyes.

"No chance of that, love," he whispered back then let go and walked to his plate. "Is this finished?" he asked, pointing to his sandwich.

I stood where he left me, glaring at him. Then I stomped to the bag of Cheetos.

"Not yet," I stated, shook out some Cheetos on the plate next to the sandwich, dropped the bag on the counter, rounded him and got him a can of Coke from the fridge. I picked up the plate and offered it and the Coke to him. "Now it's done."

He was staring at the plate, and before he had to ask, I answered.

"Cheetos. They're kind of cheese-flavored snacks."

He took the plate and can and his eyes came to me. "The only thing I recognize is the bread. The rest is clearly not natural."

He was right about that.

"We'll go to a grocery store tomorrow. Now you're eating processed food because the selection isn't all that hot at the corner store."

"You went to the market?"

"Yes."

His face turned slightly ominous again. "Cora, I told you to rest."

"I know you did, Tor!" I snapped impatiently. "But I couldn't. My house was a mess. My bathroom a pit. My sheets dirty. And I had to figure out what Cora had done with two months of my life. I couldn't lie in bed and rest. I tried. My mind wouldn't let me. I had to get things sorted so I sorted them. I survived. I'm breathing. So now, will you do me a favor and just *bloody* eat?"

He stared at me. Then he grinned.

"My wife likes order," he noted.

"I'm not your wife," I shot back.

His grin turned to a smile as he turned to the door and muttered, "You will be."

I looked at the ceiling.

Bloody hell.

I followed him to see he was moving to the round, four-seater dining room table I had in the corner.

"What are you doing?" I asked.

He stopped and turned to me.

"Preparing to eat," he answered.

"I don't eat at the table," I informed him. "No one in America eats at the table unless it's Thanksgiving, Christmas, a birthday or they're weird."

He looked at the table in a way that nonverbally said he felt it was strange I owned a set of furniture that I would use only three days of the year (this, a look from a man who had *three* entire dining *rooms*) then he looked at me. "Where do you eat?"

"On the sofa in front of the TV," I replied, walked to the sofa and, no other way to put it, collapsed mainly because I needed to. I was exhausted and my body was beginning to ache again.

He followed, sat next to me, looked about him and then lifted his bare feet up to the coffee table and put his plate on his lap. I took the can from him. He watched as I popped the tab, his brows going up at the hiss then his lips twitched. He took it back, sipped at it, swallowed, shook his head, set it on my side table and commenced eating.

I watched, waiting for a response.

After three Cheetos and his second bite of sandwich, when I got no response, I prompted, "Well?"

He swallowed his bite of bologna and cheese sandwich and stated, "It's not bad."

I felt my mouth form a small smile.

"It's also not good," he went on and for some reason, I burst into laughter.

When I was done laughing I noticed Tor was not eating. He was watching me with a look so tender it was a shock when I felt it slice clean through me. The pain was so perfect, it felt exquisite, better by far than any orgasm he'd given me (and he'd given me lots and all of them were good) so I bit my lip and looked away.

I was trying to shove that feeling out of my soul when Tor murmured, "Only you."

It took a lot but I forced my eyes to his face to see his were moving around the room.

I shouldn't ask. I really shouldn't ask.

But I asked.

"Only me, what?"

His eyes came to me. "Only you could put color in a colorless world."

My lungs seized and then I followed where his gaze had been and I saw my space through his eyes.

I'd painted the walls a soft peach.

I'd strung string after string of fairy lights covered in sherbet-colored daisies all around the top edges. I'd chosen carefully selected, but all fanciful and vibrant, prints for my walls. I had a comfortable armchair in bright pink with a deep purple chenille throw tossed over it, at its foot, a grass-green, poofy, rectangular ottoman. We were sitting on a peacock-blue sofa with sunshine-yellow and orangey-red toss pillows. On the square coffee table in front of us was a collection of glass orbs, all of different sizes and colors.

The dining room table was glass topped but the chairs were covered in raspberry fabric, a huge glass vase in the middle of the table with whirls of multiple colors swirling through it.

There was a wide rug over the wood floors that reflected nearly all of the colors I'd chosen for the room. Not in a dizzying way, but a subtle one (I thought). And all the lamps in the room had different bases and different colored shades, turquoise, lilac, pink, royal blue.

Oh fuck, there was that exquisite pain again.

I turned my head to him, saw him sitting on my sofa in jeans and a tee, feet up, eating bologna sandwiches and Cheetos, chasing it with a Coke, looking relaxed and totally at home after a day out, by himself, in a world that couldn't be any more different from his home and it hit me.

"And only you," I blurted.

His eyes held mine when he asked quietly, "Only me, what?"

Oh well, might as well say it.

"Only you could be catapulted into a different world, a world totally unlike your own, and take it all in stride."

He wasn't just taking it in stride. Just like in his world, he seemed in command of the situation. Not only at ease, but like he had it all under control, and I suspected, with very little effort, if he didn't have it under his control, he would.

Just like always.

I loved that about him and I hated that I loved it.

Hoping to hide my feelings, I babbled on, "When I got to your world, I was totally freaked out. The first ten, fifteen minutes, I thought it was a dream. The rest I knew wasn't and I was scared shitless."

"You forget, my love, I was prepared for your world," he told me and I felt my brows draw together.

"You were?" He nodded. "How?"

"You told me about it. About the cars and the buses and the planes and the asphalt and the sidewalks. You told me about the buildings made of glass rising into the sky. People talking to other people on their phones in the streets. Others sitting in front of those..." he hesitated, "boxes, tapping at them with their fingers."

"Computers," I reminded him, stunned.

He remembered everything I told him.

Everything.

He smiled. "Computers."

"You thought I was making it up," I whispered and his eyes went dark.

"But now I know you were not."

"You thought I was," I semi-repeated.

"But now, Cora, I know you were not," he also semi-repeated, this time softly but also firmly, that tender look back in his eyes.

I swallowed.

It was Tor's way of apologizing.

And it was a good way.

I decided I'd had enough. I couldn't take more. He was going to get to me and he couldn't. What he did hurt too much. And anyway, he didn't belong in my world and I didn't belong in his. It was unnatural and anything could happen. Nature had a way of righting itself, sometimes violently.

I'd given in once, giving him all I had and taking what I could get in return.

And I loved it.

But it could be taken from me. *He* could be taken from me. At any moment a blue mist could form and whisk him away.

I had to stay on target. I had to sort out my life. And I had to guard my heart.

Which was going to be hard with a seasoned warrior obviously intent on laying siege to it.

But I had to try.

"Do you want to watch TV?" I asked into the void, his eyes flashed his displeasure at my change of subject then they settled.

"Will you rest if we watch this…TV?" he asked back and I nodded. "Then yes, I'd like to watch TV."

I sucked in breath then turned, leaned down the couch, opened the drawer to my side table and grabbed the remote. I hit the button and resolutely ignored him as I switched channels until I found an innocuous sit-com.

I settled in, partly turned away from him, and focused on TV (mostly for my sanity).

Not long after, I heard his plate hit the coffee table then the remote was slid from between my fingers.

My head twisted to him and I cried, "Hey!" but like a man, of his world or mine, he took over the technology, hitting buttons on the remote so the channel changed, the contrast changed, the volume changed and then he found a decent volume along with a cop show.

Figures.

He tagged me around my chest and pulled me down to lying beside him, wedged against the back of the couch, as he stretched out on his back, head to a pillow against the armrest.

I pushed up and snapped, "I was comfortable."

"You're more comfortable now," he returned, telling the God's honest truth.

"Am not," I lied, pushing up on his chest.

"Cora, you are."

"Am not!"

The hand attached to his arm that was wound around me slid up to the back of my neck and he pulled me inexorably forward until I was close to his face.

"You promised, we watch this TV, you'd rest," he reminded me.

"Yes!" I clipped.

"Then…*rest*," he commanded.

I glared at him, and as I did I saw the determined look on his face.

I knew what *that* meant.

So I informed him, "You're annoying."

He chuckled and forced my cheek to his chest.

I kept my body perfectly solid to communicate nonverbally that he was a jerk.

That was, I did this until I fell dead asleep.

20

Crash into Me

~

We were on our way to my parents' house, Tor driving.

Yes, Tor *driving*.

Earlier that day, when we went out to my car (which had not disappeared but had enough pop cans, chip and candy wrappers in it to water and feed an army—taking them all in, and thinking of all the takeout cartons I tossed out the day before, I was thinking the other Cora was no longer skinnier than me), Tor flatly refused to sit in the passenger seat.

He demanded a lesson and refused to believe that he'd need more than one lesson and practice (much less an actual license) to drive around in a city.

With no choice (he didn't give me one), I showed him around the console, explained the basics, he started up the car and away we went.

No joke.

He was a natural. He even figured out the road signs and traffic signals and only asked what a few of them meant.

I was not freaked out that I was sitting in a car with a beginner from another world behind the wheel.

No, I was freaked out about the fact that I decided to tell my parents the truth hoping—since they were hippies and had open minds—that they wouldn't think I'd gone around the bend.

And I was also trying not to think about my day with Tor.

Which had been, even in my gray, dreary, colorless world, what only Tor could give me.

Magic.

I woke that morning in my bed to a mild headache, a few aches and pains and to hear my shower going.

The shower meant Tor hadn't been flung back to his world sometime in the night.

I rolled to my side, glanced at his pillow and saw the dent.

I knew Tor, after watching television late into the night, had carried me to my room. When he put me on my feet by the bed, still exhausted and half asleep, I disrobed, found a clean nightie, yanked it over my head, then collapsed into bed, falling back to sleep the instant my head hit the pillow.

And seeing the dent, it was apparent Tor slept with me.

Oh well, whatever.

I decided, since the ibuprofen had eventually worked the day before and I now had coffee, that I would head to my pill stash in the kitchen which was a room that fortunately also housed the coffeemaker. So this was what I did.

Tor came in after I set the coffee to brewing and he was wearing nothing but one of my forest-green towels (they weren't girlie, which sucked, I liked girlie, but they were the only thing (as well as the rust accent colors I used) that didn't look putrid against my bathroom suite).

As I stared at his chest coming my way, he greeted, "Morning, wife."

My body jolted to alert but not in time. I was swept up in one of his arms and his head was descending. He gave me a hard, warm, close-mouthed kiss then broke his mouth from mine.

As I tried to get my head together, he glanced at the filling coffeepot, opened the cupboard over it and pulled down two mugs, not loosening his arm while saying, "I like these indoor waterfalls you have."

"What?" I asked dazedly and his light-blue eyes came back to mine.

"Your indoor waterfalls. These, and your front room, the color of your sheets and the night garments you wear, so far, are the only things I like in your world."

"Um...you mean shower," I told him.

His brows went up. "Shower?"

"Yes, like a rain shower except it's a bathroom shower."

"Ah," he murmured, his lips twitching. "Clever play on words."

I hadn't thought of it like that but it was true.

"Tor—"

"I need food," he announced, moving to the refrigerator, opening it and he did this taking me with him with his arm still around me.

"I'll make you breakfast. Now, Tor—"

He was digging through the fridge (which held milk, Diet Coke, regular Coke, bologna, American cheese, condiments and nothing else) and he didn't even look at me when he interrupted, "I'll need new clothing. I do not want to wear the other me's garments."

"We'll go to the mall. Now, Tor—"

He looked down at me and he was grinning and looking weirdly happy so I snapped my mouth shut because it was a good look.

"So, you're going to cook for me?"

"Uh...sure."

"Do you have eggs in your world?"

"We do. But I don't have eggs in my apartment. I'll have to run to the corner market."

He let me go and turned to the door, stating, "I'll go."

I stared at his muscled back.

Then I cried, "Tor!" and followed him. When I hit the living room, he was crouched by the open TV cabinet and reaching in. "What are you doing?"

His head tipped back so he could look at me. "I assume in your world, like my world, vendors expect payment?"

"Well, yeah."

"Then I need coin," he said, pulling out a wad of fifties and looking at it. "Paper. Unusual," he muttered and looked at me while straightening out of his crouch. "King Baldur prints paper funds. It's worthless. It's printed at vast amounts beyond the gold and silver in his reserve. He expects tax payment in coin and trading in paper. This way does not work and his people are becoming restless."

That was fascinating but I was more focused on him using Cora's money.

"Um...maybe we should leave that money where it is. I've got a twenty in my wallet. I'll give you that," I told him and started to my purse.

"You will not," he stated firmly.

I stopped and blinked at him.

"So, what are you going to use? You can't get a job at a fast food joint and make enough to buy us breakfast in time for said breakfast."

"Cora's money is our money. We'll use that," he told me.

"No, actually, I think we should figure out what's going on with it and not use it. It isn't ours."

"She owes us," he declared.

"How?" I asked, confused.

"I don't know. I just know she does."

"What?"

He walked to me. "Cora, whatever is happening, to you, to me, is her doing. I know it. This blue mist, this is at her command or her request. I don't know if she has the situation under her control or if it has started controlling her. Unless you study under an apprentice for years and pass exams, it's against the law in my world to practice magic. It's against the law because it's very dangerous. I know that Cora has not done this. What I also know is that, whatever is happening, she's behind it. So, if she has earned this money through nefarious means or not, she owes it to us. And furthermore, you as my wife do not pay for your keep, except..." he paused and grinned, "with a kiss."

"Tor—" I started to remind him I actually wasn't his wife and to ask about this apprenticing magic business (I knew they had wizards or something in his world!) but stopped when he bent in and brushed his mouth to mine.

When he lifted up, he started to my bedroom.

"Tor!" I snapped.

"I'll dress, go to this store and be back in a minute."

"Tor!" I repeated, my voice rising and I stomped to the bedroom doorway.

Tor had his back to me and was whipping off the towel. I saw his sculpted, fine ass and decided, what the fuck? He wanted to use Cora's money? I'd let him.

Then I ran to the kitchen.

When Tor got back from the market, he brought with him eggs and a packet of bacon.

However, considering he carried three bags in each hand, I knew he bought much more.

"Jeez, did you buy everything in the store?" I asked as I followed him to the kitchen.

"This store is curious. Everything is wrapped. You cannot see the wares you're buying except, in some cases, through little windows. How do you know all is as it should be?" he asked, pulling out a box of donuts then a bag of chips then out came a gargantuan candy bar.

"You just do," I told him. "If it isn't, it's against the law, I think. False advertising or something."

He turned his head to look at me.

"Curious," he muttered, pulling out a stick of beef jerky.

Oh boy.

"I'm taking a shower," I announced.

At my words, slowly, his head turned to me, his eyes unfocused and directed at my body, then they lifted to mine and he smiled.

It was wicked.

I ran to the bathroom and when I got there, I locked the door.

After breakfast (eggs, bacon, toast and donuts), I took Tor to the mall.

This was a bizarre experience.

I had figured it would be fascinating to him and he'd be looking around, wide-eyed and amazed.

But like everything else, he took it in stride and acted just like a man. He strolled through the corridors with his arm around my shoulders and followed me through the stores intent on one thing, getting his clothes and getting the fuck out of there.

I guessed Tor wasn't into shopping.

He took wads of the other Cora's cash with him and we bought him jeans, tees, shirts, underwear, socks, pajama bottoms, boots and running shoes. We also bought him a money clip, a comb, a brush and an electric razor (the last being the only thing he showed even the slightest bit of interest in).

We were loaded down with bags, him carrying the heavier ones, and headed back to the car when I noticed something strange.

People were staring at us.

If they were simply staring at Tor, I wouldn't have been surprised. He was a big guy, he had a scar, not to mention he was hot.

But they weren't just looking at him (well, some of the women were).

They were looking *at us*.

I was trying to figure out why when Tor spoke.

"Your clothing yesterday, love, I must say, was not to my taste. But today, what you're wearing…" I tipped my head to look up at him to see he was looking down at me. "Your hair," he went on, "what you've done with your face. I like it."

I quickly looked away.

I'd gone all out telling myself it was because I missed my stuff and anyway, we were going to my folks for dinner that night so I had to look nice.

The truth of it was, I had planted myself firmly in denial to the fact that I'd dressed for Tor.

I was wearing a cute little lilac dress with a tiered, full skirt that hit me at the knees, a low, square neckline and cap sleeves, over it a thin, dusty-blue cardigan and a pair of spike-heeled, very strappy purple sandals. I'd blown out my hair and put on light makeup.

He capped it by muttering, "You're by far the most beautiful woman I've seen in this world." My step stuttered, his arm tightened around my shoulders to steady me and he murmured, "All right?"

"Yes," I lied.

But I was not.

We were at a mall and there were a number of hot babes there, including several who'd waited on him in stores, practically pushing each other out of the way, I might add, even with *me* standing *right there*. Not to mention the fact that he'd been out all day yesterday and clearly seen a number of people.

Knowing that, it was the nicest compliment anyone had ever given me.

Then he said, as if to himself, his eyes taking in the eyes of the other patrons taking us in, "This makes me wonder…" He trailed off and didn't continue.

"What?" I asked.

"Mm?" he asked back.

"What makes you wonder?"

He squeezed my shoulders and said distractedly, "Nothing, my sweet."

I watched his face and saw he looked as distracted as he sounded.

I let it go.

We made it to the car, loaded it up and went to the grocery store.

Tor had far more interest in the grocery store and we perused every aisle, Tor picking up stuff, studying it, reading labels, turning it in his hands and tossing it into the cart if it held any interest to him at all.

I knew Tor liked his food. When we were at the castle, the meals were sumptuous, there was always dessert and his portions were manly.

But when our cart in the grocery store was filled to the point we needed another one, I felt the need to intervene.

"Tor, this is a lot of food."

"Indeed," he said, studying a bag of spiral pasta.

"We have no way of knowing how long you're going to be in this world and it'll take *me* a year to eat all of this," I pointed out and his eyes sliced to me.

"If I go back, you'll be coming with me," he declared.

"We don't know that," I replied.

"If I go back, you'll be coming with me," he repeated, more firmly this time and with his face set hard.

I didn't want to have an incident in the grocery store, which by the set look on his face, I was pretty sure we would have if I told him that firstly, he couldn't know that and secondly, I didn't want to go back with him, not anymore.

So instead, I said, "Okay."

He scowled at me then threw the pasta in the cart.

I rushed to get another one.

We loaded the car full to bursting with our grocery purchases and on the way home, my cell rang. The display said, "Noc."

"Excellent, your gadget is sounding," Tor noted.

"Not excellent, Tor!" I cried, holding it out to show him the display, thankful we were stopped at a red light. "It's Noc!"

His eyes slid to the display then to me. "Noc?"

"The other you!" I exclaimed.

"Is it necessary for you to answer it?" he asked logically.

"Uh...no."

"Then don't answer it."

Good advice.

It quit ringing but binged a few seconds later, telling me I had a voicemail.

I hit the screen in order to listen to the voicemail.

"What are you doing?" Tor asked, executing a perfect left hand turn.

"Listening to voicemail," I told him.

"To what?"

"Shh!" I hissed. "He's left a message."

"Cory," Noc said in my ear. "I'm standing in your apartment and you're not here. What the fuck is goin' on? I got shit to do. I'll be back tonight. You get this, call me."

The last was growled.

Noc was not happy.

Oh dear.

And I'd forgotten about him having a key.

"What was his message?" Tor inquired.

"He's at the apartment. He has a key. He says he's leaving but coming back tonight. Tonight! What do we do?"

"First, we deal with his access. How do we do that?"

"Uh...get my landlord to change the lock. But he's lazy and returns phone calls about a millennium after you leave a message. He'll never do it by tonight."

"Why does he have to do it?"

"Because I don't know how and he owns the building."

"We can't wait a millennium," Tor pointed out.

"I know, Tor!" I cried.

"Calm down, sweets, how difficult is this lock changing?"

"I don't know that either. I don't know how to do it."

"In this world, there are vendors who sell everything. In fact, outside of houses and places to eat, that's practically all there is in this world. Is there a place where we can purchase what we require?"

Jeez, it sucked that Tor was the sensible and logical one, even in my world.

"Yes, the hardware store," I informed him.

"Tell me how to get there. We'll acquire what we need and I'll change your lock. He won't have access, one problem solved."

Yep, it sucked that Tor was the sensible and logical one, even in my world.

"Turn right at the second light," I replied.

He turned right at the second light then into the silence he called, "Cora?"

"Yes," I answered the side window.

I felt his strong fingers give my thigh a firm squeeze and he murmured, "My love, everything will be all right."

He couldn't know that either.

But I didn't tell him that.

I stayed silent and directed him to the hardware store.

Tor refused to allow me to carry the bags up to the apartment (two flights!), informing me, "Men do manual labor. Women do not unless they're servants or common."

I glared at him then let him do it. He wanted to lug a gazillion shopping bags and a million pounds of groceries up two flights of stairs? That was okay by me.

I turned on music and got out the toolbox my father bought me when I moved out of my parents' house. I'd used the hammer and a couple screwdrivers but other than that, the set of tools in it were nearly new.

After Tor brought up the stuff, I handed him the toolbox. He perused it with some interest and I put all his clothes and the groceries away while he inspected the lock and then, like all things Tor, changed it without any ado.

He was testing it when I wandered to my answering machine because I saw it blinking. The numerical display said I had two messages. I stood by the box, hit the button and Noc's (in other words, Tor's) voice filled the room and I watched Tor still as he listened to it.

"Cory? Hope you're feelin' better, babe. On my way over. See you in five."

"Is that me?" Tor asked.

"No," I answered and his eyes went from the answering machine to me.

"No, sweets, I mean the other me," he explained.

"Then, yes," I replied and the next message came on.

It was my friend Selena.

"Got your message and just wanna say, don't call back 'cause I got your *other* message loud and clear. I can't believe you have the balls to call me after you did what you did. Don't call back, Cora, *ever*."

I stood frozen to the spot, staring at my machine.

"Cora?" Tor called.

I didn't move.

I felt his hand on my back. "Cora, who was that?"

"My..." My nose started stinging. Oh shit, I was going to cry again! Damn the other Cora! "My friend, Selena."

"Love—"

"What'd she do?" I whispered, staring at the answering machine.

"Sweets—"

I looked up at him, tears swimming in my eyes and whispered again, "What'd she do?"

A tear fell, then another because I could tell my parents (maybe) that I'd been in another world but I couldn't tell my friends. They'd never believe me. They'd think I was insane or making crazy excuses for whatever the other Cora did.

And whatever Cora did, it sounded bad and I knew from experience Cora's bad was the worst that bad could be.

Tor pulled me to the couch, sat down in it with me and gathered me in his arms. I pressed into his chest and held on to him while the tears fell silently.

"I hope I never meet her," I whispered after a while.

"I hope you don't either, love. It's rarely a pleasant experience."

After he spoke, for some reason, I just sat there, cradled by Tor, and thought about the fact that none of my other friends had bothered to call back, knowing now what that meant.

I tried to think of how to rectify whatever happened.

Then I realized I was right back where I started in Bellebryn when Tor first took me there. But this time, it wasn't a bunch of people I didn't know who hated me. It was a bunch of people I cared about. A lot.

I sighed into Tor's chest.

Tor murmured, "This musician is a poet," and I lifted my head and looked at him.

"What?" I asked.

His eyes came to my face then his hand came to my face and he used his thumb to wipe away the wetness as he answered quietly, "That song that was just coming from your box," he tipped his head to my stereo, "the musician is a poet."

I tilted my head to the side because I'd been so deep in thought I hadn't heard what was playing. Then I twisted and reached for my stereo remote in the side table drawer. I used it to go back to the song before the one playing and the guitar strums of The Dave Matthews Band's "Crash into Me" started.

I looked up at Tor who was studying the remote. He felt my eyes, his came to mine and I smiled.

"I love this song," I told him.

His eyes dropped to my mouth then without a word he slid the remote out of my hands and tucked my face back to his chest.

Held by Prince Noctorno Hawthorne on my sofa, in my world I listened to a beautiful, sexy song.

When it was over, almost immediately the guitar strums sounded again (clearly Tor had mastered the stereo remote) and we listened yet again. The words washing over me, I heard them not for the first time but I heard their meaning for the first time. They were words full of yearning, passion, admiration and a love that sounded like worship.

And again, when it was over, the guitar strums came back, but when they did this time, Tor dropped the remote on the side table, pulled me out of the couch, put his hands to my hips and slid them around so he could fit me into his arms.

I tensed, thinking he was going to try to start something, maybe kiss me.

But he didn't.

He pressed his jaw to the side of my head and his hips started swaying, his hands at the small of my back moving me with him.

Holy crap, he was dancing with me in my living room.

I didn't even wait a second before I closed my eyes and moved, telling myself, just this moment, just this time, just this five minutes with Tor and The Dave Matthews Band and a freaking fantastic song.

Just these five minutes.

So I bent my neck and rested my forehead to his shoulder.

He took my hand, laced our fingers together, held them to his chest, his other hand pushing into the small of my back, fitting my hips snug to his. I slid my other arm around his shoulders and turned my head so my forehead was against his neck. At this, he bent his neck and rested his lips against my neck.

And we swayed. Even when the tempo of the song increased, Tor kept our movements slow, fluid and in my little, colorful living room, the rain beating outside, the day gray, the streets grimy, with the help of The Dave Matthews Band, Tor created magic. I felt it with every strum of the guitars, every longing word, every sway of our hips, the hardness of Tor's body pressed to mine, the warmth of his hand at the small of my back, his strong fingers holding mine tight.

It was the most astonishingly beautiful moment in my life, unbearably sexy, and even though I'd spent nearly two months in a glittering fairytale world, in that moment's enchanting simplicity, it was by far and away the most magical.

And when the song faded away, I didn't want it to end. I wanted to snatch the notes back. I didn't want five minutes. I wanted ten. I wanted an hour.

I wanted a lifetime.

Tor's hips stopped moving and his hand pressed mine flat to his chest before it came to my chin, lifted my face up to his and I could see, clear in his eyes, he'd felt everything I'd felt and that exquisite pain I experienced last night again slashed through me.

Then he declared quietly, "The man who wrote the words in that song has given half his soul to his woman. There is destiny you cannot control but this man, he found the woman who completed him and he gave his soul at his liberty."

And he said this like he knew it from experience.

And he said it looking at me.

He bent his head and touched his lips tenderly to each of my eyes in turn, both of them closing and staying closed even after he let me go. I heard his boots beat on my floors and then I heard the electric razor coming through the bedroom from the bathroom.

I realized my chest was rising and falling deeply, my eyes slowly opened and I stared at my wall as I allowed myself one more thing.

I allowed myself to feel that exquisite pain at the same time the shadow of the touch of Tor's lips on my eyes lingered.

Then I went to my bathroom to share the basin with Tor as I fixed my makeup and decided not to share with him that "Crash into Me" had hints of voyeurism at the same time I decided, forever and always, that song would mean to me exactly what it meant to Tor.

And now we were in my car, heading to my parents' house and I was, again, freaking out.

And I was tired of freaking out.

So damned tired of it.

Tor's hand came to mine and his fingers laced through while he noted softly, "I like this transport." I turned to look at him and watched him lift my hand and brush his lips against my knuckles.

Damn.

There it was.

That exquisite pain was back.

He dropped our hands to his thigh and without taking his eyes from the road, he continued, "But I prefer Salem. In your car, you're too far away." My breath caught. "On Salem, you're right where you're supposed to be."

I closed my eyes, looked away then sighed deeply.

I wished he'd quit saying (and doing) things like that at the same time I wished he'd never stop.

Damn.

My folks' house came into sight and I whispered to Tor, pointing with my hand not held in his, "It's that one, right there. You can park in front."

With ease, Tor guided my car to the curb.

I stared out the window at my parents' house, trying to force myself toward calm.

I felt Tor squeeze my fingers and my head swung to him.

"It'll be all right, my love," he assured me quietly.

"Right," I whispered, not believing him.

His hand brought mine to his chest as his other hand came out, hooked me around the neck and pulled me to him.

"If it isn't, I'll make it so," he declared. "That's a vow."

I held my breath. Tor smiled at me.

And, damn and blast, looking at his smile and the ease behind his eyes, I found calm.

21

Meeting the Parents

~

"You *what?*" my father shouted at me then his eyes sliced to Tor, his fists hit the table, he shot out of his chair and bellowed, "Get away from my daughter!"

I closed my eyes tight.

Let's just say that dinner was *not* going well.

It had started okay.

Sure, Mom and Dad had been a little overawed in an obvious way when they first laid eyes on Tor. For one, he was a lot taller than any of my other boyfriends (a lot). For two, he was also a lot more powerfully built (a lot). And three, he was a lot scarier-looking (a lot).

Tor was hot but that didn't mean he looked like a guy you messed with. All of my boyfriends were relatively good-looking but they were also laidback, easygoing and fun-loving.

Tor looked like what he was. A warrior dressed in jeans, boots and a nice shirt.

His scar, no matter how sexy, obviously helped.

But my parents seemed game and were themselves, friendly and charming.

Things disintegrated when Tor was, well, *Tor*.

He was touchy, very much so. He was also attentive, very much so. And he was possessive, clearly so.

I couldn't really explain how he demonstrated the last, he just did. And Mom and Dad caught it.

And Mom, who for two decades of my life (to my utter embarrassment as a teen) didn't wear a bra, and Dad, who read Mom's newsletters from the National Organization for Women from cover to cover (sometimes taking highlighters to it just so Mom, during her perusal, wouldn't miss things Dad thought important she note), didn't take to it too well.

It didn't help matters that I was freaked out, worried, confused and my life was in a turmoil…and it showed.

They noticed and didn't take to that too well, either.

They started to pry into the last two months of my life, specifically how I hooked up with Tor, and, wanting to pick the best time to deliver the news that Tor and I were at the mercy of unpredictable blue mist magic, my answers were cagey. Tor took my lead and kept completely silent on the subject.

Again, they didn't take to that too well.

Conversation became stilted. Mom and Dad exchanged unhappy glances. Tor was catching my eye, communicating to me that if I didn't do something, he would.

I didn't want him to do anything Tor-like which would likely not go over very well either, so after eating Mom's delicious herbed chicken, cheesy-garlic mashed potatoes and steamed greens, but before she moved us onto dessert, I told them that Tor was from a parallel universe, the same parallel universe I had been hurled into in my sleep and resided in the last two months, and we were at the whim of blue mist magic.

"Forrest!" Mom cried when Dad finished shouting.

"Dad, please sit down and calm down," I urged.

"No!" Dad returned to me. "What hold does this man have over you?" he asked then didn't allow me to answer and looked at Tor. "What are you doing to my daughter? Why haven't we *seen* or *heard* from her in two months? Why does she *believe* this crazy story? Are you drugging her fruit juice?"

I didn't drink fruit juice primarily because I preferred to chew my calories unless they were alcoholic (not that I chewed very much fruit, but you get what I'm saying) and my dad knew that (not about the calories, just that I didn't drink juice). He was being dramatic. He was also being *loud*.

"Pardon?" Tor asked, his tone quiet but also deadly. He didn't like my father's words or the way they were thrown at him. He was the future king after all, and a prince to boot, and well, *Tor* and I could see him struggling for control.

"Drugging her fruit juice?" Dad continued. "Addling her mind? A parallel universe! That's insane! Are you in some kind of cult?"

"Dad!" I exclaimed. "Tor's not in a cult!"

My father ignored me.

"What kind of name *is* Tor, anyway? Were you born with that name?" Dad asked Tor, forgetting, in his histrionics, that he had for a brief period of time called himself (and made others call him) Eaglethorn (Mom had taken the name Jasminevine, luckily they stopped doing this before I was born).

"No," Tor replied calmly then announced in his deep, commanding voice, "I am Prince Noctorno Allegro Hawthorne of the House of Hawthorne, heir to the Kingdom of Hawkvale and ruler of Bellebryn. Those close to me, including Cora, call me Tor."

Uh-oh.

What he said was true but it was not the right thing to say. I could see it because my mom went pale but my dad went beet red.

"Prince...Prince...what the hell!" he boomed. "It's *you* that's insane and you're with my *daughter*!"

"Sir, I am far from insane," Tor gritted between his teeth.

"Dad, he's not insane," I rushed to put in. "I know this sounds..." My mind searched for a word, my eyes found Tor's and then it came to me, "*Fantastical*." I heard and saw Tor draw in an annoyed breath and my eyes shot to my father. "But it's true."

"Um, maybe...uh, Tor," Mom cut in, "I don't wish to be rude but considering things are, uh...*intense* and we haven't seen Cora in a while, perhaps you could go so we could have some time alone with our daughter?"

"I'll not do that," Tor replied immediately.

"And why the hell not?" my father returned just as immediately.

"Because, sir," Tor stated slowly, visibly fighting for control. "As Cora explained to you, we are at the mercy of magic and I do not want to be far from her should it start to take her...or me."

Dad glared at him then he turned his glare to my mother. "The mercy of magic. This is *insane*," he breathed with disgust.

"I would thank you to stop saying that," Tor said softly and Dad's eyes cut back to him then he leaned into him, hand on the table and everything.

"And *I* would thank *you* to get up from my table and get the hell out of my house *but especially*, while you're doing that, out of my daughter's *life*!"

Tor's face turned to stone, he rose out of his seat, tossing his napkin to the table and I knew it was time to intervene.

So I shot out of my chair and rushed around the table to put my hand on my father's arm.

"Dad, listen to me," I begged.

He didn't even look at me, just glowered up at Tor. "I'm busy, sweetheart. I'm about to escort this *man* out."

"Dad," I squeezed his arm, "listen. Please, listen. It's true. All of it. I woke up in a parallel universe. A fairytale land. A fantasyland. Where they ride horses and birds talk to you and the air shimmers like it has glitter in it. But there is a me there like there is a Tor here. All the same people are in both worlds, I reckon, and I was switched with the Cora of their world."

Dad slowly swung his head to face me and the look in his eyes made my heart clench. He genuinely thought I'd gone around the bend and this thought pained him.

So I got closer and pulled him around to face me, lifting my other hand to take his other arm.

"I know it sounds crazy, trust me, *I know*. But it isn't. I woke up and all the furniture in my room was wonky, like out of an animated kid's movie. And it wasn't *my* room. And then my sister came dancing in and she was so beautiful, so graceful, it was unreal. Her name was Rosa and..."

I stopped because the minute I said the name "Rosa" Dad's body got still under my hands, his eyes shot to my mother and the air in the room grew heavy.

"Rosa?" my mother whispered and I turned my head to look at her. "In this parallel universe, you had a sister named Rosa?"

"Uh...yes," I replied, looking at my mom who was even paler, and when I did her eyes moved swiftly to my father and she put a hand out flat on the table.

"Mom?" I called and released my dad in order to go to her because she looked like she was about ready either to burst into tears or pass out.

"Rosa," my mom whispered again when I got to her and crouched down. Her eyes were tipped up to my dad and I covered her hand on the table with mine and squeezed. When I did, her head slowly turned to me. "Rosa was alive in that world?"

Oh.

My.

God.

"By the gods," Tor murmured.

I looked to him to see he was gazing at my mother, his face contemplative but his body had lost its angry energy.

I looked back to my mom and whispered, "Is there something I don't know?"

Tears trembled in my mom's eyes before she replied, "We had a little girl." Oh my God. "She died at birth." Oh my God! "We named her Rosa."

I closed my eyes then opened them.

"Why didn't you tell me?" I asked.

"I-I couldn't. I couldn't talk about it. It was bad, sweetie. The birth was bad. For me, too. After that, I couldn't have any more kids. Your dad and me, we wanted a whole houseful and we lost that and we lost Rosa and I…"

"Stop," I whispered when her tears spilled over. "Stop, Mama. I understand."

"It wasn't like I was trying to keep anything from you. It was just—"

I cut her off again. "Stop, Mom. I understand."

She blinked and more tears fell then she turned to Tor. "Rosa is alive in your world?"

I tensed, for Rosa *was* alive but she was also the hostage of a cruel witch-god but Tor simply said, "Alive and beloved. The only beauty in the land more exquisite than hers is Cora's. The only qualities in the land more dear are those of *my* Cora, the Cora of this world."

I felt my body start at his words and I whispered, "That last part isn't true," and Tor's gaze came to me.

"It is, my sweet."

"It isn't. Most everyone hates me," I reminded him.

"No, Cora, everyone hates the Cora of that world."

I rose, telling him, "But they think she's me."

"Indeed, they do but it has been *you* gracing my castle for the past weeks and it was *you*, and your rabid, not befitting a princess behavior that you displayed in towns and villages for miles that people have been experiencing. Word travels. They used to call you Cora, the Exquisite due to your beauty. Now, you're becoming known as Cora, the Gracious."

Cora, the Gracious?

Wow. I liked that.

"Really?" I asked.

Tor's eyes grew warm. "You read to blind women, love, and rescue wild, wounded birds and make them your pet. You smile at every child you see and touch their cheeks or ruffle their hair, which, by the way, you must stop doing." Even if his words were melting my heart, my eyes still narrowed and he smiled at me. "You are friendly, you are polite, you are kind and you are merciful. You *are* Cora, the Gracious."

Oh my.

I was Cora, the Gracious.

How freaking cool!

"How freaking cool!" I cried, grinning at him.

He shook his head and looked at my mother.

"This language and her stubborn bent at being uncommonly friendly to everyone she encounters is not behavior befitting a princess. I persist in telling her this but she doesn't listen. I assume I have you to thank for that."

"I, uh…uh…um…" Mom stammered, looking up at Tor, and I could see coming to the realization that she had a being from a parallel universe at her table. "My daughter's a princess?"

"Of course. She's my wife," Tor replied.

"I keep telling you, Tor, I'm not your wife," I snapped and his eyes cut to me.

"And I keep telling you, my love, that you're going to be, and as far as I'm concerned, you already are."

"You're married to my parallel world twin!" I cried.

"This will be severed officially upon our return. Luckily, Cora and I were wed in Bellebryn and the person who grants annulments in Bellebryn is *me*. Therefore, it will simply be a signature on a piece of paper and then you and I will be wed."

"You're marrying him?" Dad asked.

"No!" I exclaimed hotly.

"Yes," Tor answered.

"I am not!" I stated, my voice rising.

"My love, you are," Tor said to me.

"No I'm not. You can be a jerk," I informed him.

"And you're not a handful?" he returned.

"No! You just said I was Cora, the Gracious," I retorted and Tor looked to my father.

"She's exceedingly friendly to every creature in my realm. Even the birds flock down to tell her good morning and my horse has told me he'd die for her. But to me, she can, at times, be extremely vexing."

"Salem said that?" I whispered, feeling my heart squeeze and Tor's eyes came to me.

"He cares deeply for you," he whispered back.

Then something else he said came to me and I snapped, "I'm not vexing!"

He crossed his arms on his chest and leveled his gaze on me. "Cora, you cleaned my cave and scraped your feet raw in doing so. You fled after our fight with the vickrants and put the entire kingdom in jeopardy. You made me climb up a tree to save a half-dead bird—"

"All right, all right, I can be vexing," I gave in then fired back, "But you're *more* vexing!"

It wasn't good but it was all I had.

"And how am I vexing? Except," he said swiftly when I instantly opened my mouth to speak, "when I'm not giving you your way."

"Tor, you bought two carts full of food at the grocery store."

"Did you pay for this food?" Tor asked.

"No," I answered tersely.

"Did you carry it up to your rooms?" he went on.

"No!" I snapped.

"Then why is that vexing?" he inquired sensibly and logically.

My neck twisted so I could look at my mother and I announced, "He's the sensible and logical one, even in *my* world. I tell you, Mom, it's annoying. When I hit his world and the curse started to fall, I freaked *way the hell* out. I was a wreck! But Tor here?" I leaned back and shook my head. "No." I drew out the "no" for about twelve syllables. "*He* doesn't freak out. He wants to drive a car, I show him the ignition and the turn signals and," I lifted a hand and snapped my fingers, "he's driving a car. We need to change a lock, we go to the hardware store, get the stuff, go home and," I snapped again, "he's changed the lock. I'm telling you, it drives me mad."

Tor called my attention to him by asking, "Sweets, would you prefer that I was quivering, scared of my shadow and incapable of providing for you?"

"No! But you could give me *something*."

"Why? You didn't give *me* anything. You kept the fire burning. You cooked the rabbits on the spit. You cleaned the cave. You say you were a wreck, my love, but I saw none of that. By the gods, you wielded a blade and fought the vickrants with me."

"A blade?" Mom whispered.

"Your daughter is handy with a dagger," Tor informed Mom proudly and I turned and grinned down at her.

"Totally, Mom. You should have seen me," I bragged then pointed at myself. "Warrior princess, in the flesh."

"Bloody hell, warrior princess," Tor muttered and my eyes shot to him.

"Well, I was! You even said so!" I cried.

"I need whisky," Dad put in at this point.

My body went ramrod straight and I looked at my father who had an expression on his face I'd never seen before. I was guessing he now wished that I was actually simply insane or had hooked up with the leader of a cult who seduced feeble-minded women and convinced them he was from an alternate universe instead of being hooked up with an actual warrior prince from a parallel world.

"Dad—" I started but Dad was looking at Tor.

"Do you drink whisky?" he asked Tor.

"I do," Tor replied.

"Comin' right up," Dad muttered and turned to the liquor cabinet on the wall.

My eyes went to Tor and his came to me. His face went soft, one of the sides of his mouth curled slightly up and he winked at me. I took in a deep breath and smiled back. He tipped his head to my chair and waited until my bottom was in it before he resumed his seat.

Dad came back with two whiskies and he brought the bottle. Mom refilled her and my wineglasses.

Dad threw back his whisky like he was doing a tequila shot then refilled his glass.

His eyes came to me.

I watched him take in a breath.

Then he said quietly, "All right, sweetheart. Let's start at the beginning."

I pressed my lips together and looked at Tor. He sat back and sipped his whisky, his eyes watching me over the rim of his glass the entire time. I took a sip of wine, looked between my mom and dad, and I started at the beginning.

Dad and Tor were in the dining room, drinking whisky.

Mom and I were in the kitchen, doing the dishes.

I didn't want Mom to have to do the dishes by herself but I didn't think it was wise leaving Tor with my dad.

I'd told our story and my parents believed it. They were shocked by it, but they believed it.

This was good.

I had left out the part of Rosa being kidnapped by the evil Minerva but Tor had gone into some detail of what a sweet-tempered, lovely young woman she was, how she was destined to marry his brother and how much she was loved by her family, those around her and especially her husband-to-be. This made both my parents' eyes get wet. It also, with the information I'd already communicated about Tor taking care of and protecting me, made them like him. And from the way they were looking at him, I was guessing they liked him a lot.

This I wasn't sure was good.

"Do you think it's a good idea that we leave Dad and Tor in the dining room..." My mother's eyes came to me and I finished, "*Alone?*"

"Why wouldn't it be a good idea?" Mom asked.

I grabbed a wineglass and started drying it, muttering, "I don't know."

Mom hesitated, rinsed a plate and put it in the dish drainer before asking, "Is there something you aren't telling me?"

I bit my lip, put the glass away and I reached for the plate.

Then I lied, "No."

"Cora," Mom said softly and I hated it when she said my name like that. Soft with disappointment. I hated to disappoint my mom. That was the worst.

I dried the plate, put it away, turned my side to the counter and leaned into it.

I found my mother's eyes and I whispered, "I'm in love with him."

My mother, who never hid her expressions from me or anyone—she was who she was, she thought what she thought—didn't do it then either. And her face looked at war. She looked hopeful and happy at the same time she looked frightened and concerned.

She pulled the towel from my hands, dried her own, dropped the towel on the counter and got close to me.

"You're in love with him?"

I nodded.

"If you're in love with a man who obviously adores you for everything you are, sweetie, why do you look like your dog just got run over?"

"Things are…complicated," I explained.

"You got that right," she muttered and I shook my head.

"No, it's not just the alternate universe thing," I told her and her brows drew together.

"Things are *more* complicated than the alternate universe thing?" she inquired and I nodded. "How?"

"Well…" I started, quickly weighed the pros and cons of confiding the fullness of my history with Tor to my mother, then I decided to do it. I had no one else to talk to about it. My mom was awesome, she was also wise so who else would I choose? "In his world, I was up front with him about who I was, where I came from. He didn't believe me."

Her head tipped to the side. "And?"

"For *two months* he didn't believe me, Mom. The Cora of his world is different than me. *A lot* different. She isn't a very nice person and…he doesn't like her much."

Her head straightened, her eyes went alert and she repeated, "And?"

"But he *used* to love her. But she spurned his love. I get the gist that she wasn't nice about it and they were prophesied to marry so he was kind of stuck with her. I got there. He didn't know I was me. I told him I was me and he thought I was her playing a game with him. So he played one with me. He pretended that he was into me. During this time, I fell in love with him. I found out right before we both came to my world that he thought I was a liar and he was playing me."

"Well, I'm guessing he knows you're not a liar now," she replied.

"Yep, he knows," I affirmed the obvious.

"So this is a problem…?" she trailed off and her brows went up.

"Mom!" I hissed, leaning into her. "He thought, for two months, that I was *lying* to him. He played the devoted, adoring husband and the operative word in that is *played*. He never believed me but he led me to believe that he did!"

At this, her brows drew together. "Yes, sweetie, I get that. But that was then. This is now."

I leaned back and whispered, "What?"

She took my hand and held tight. "Cora, that man in there doesn't think you're a liar and he's not *playing* at the devoted, adoring anything. I don't know what went on between you two in that other world, but whatever it was, he's seen it for what it was, he's seen you for who you are and now he's just plain *devoted* and *adoring*."

I sucked in breath and stared at her.

She squeezed my hand.

"Love is a mighty thing," she carried on. "When we deal with the people we love, everything they do, no matter how slight or how huge, has awesome power over us, our emotions, our behavior, our reactions. You love this man and you feel betrayed that he didn't believe you but pretended he did. I get that. I even get why you'd hold on to it and the power that betrayal would have over you. But, sweetie, you'd told him you were from *a different world*. If Rosa was not in that world, our dinner in there," she jerked her head to the wall between the kitchen and dining room, "would have had a far different ending. There is no way in hell you, or Tor, would have been able to convince your father or me that he was from another world. I still find it unbelievable. And the only way I can make it so it doesn't freak me out is to understand the little girl I lost wasn't lost in that world. She has a beautiful life in that world. The rest of it…" she trailed off and shook her head.

"I'm sorry it freaks you out," I whispered.

"I'm sorry you're going through this. And I'm worried you're going through this," she whispered back.

"Me too," I agreed with considerable feeling.

"But I have to tell you, sweetheart, that if you have to go through it, I'm pleased as punch you're going through it with that man in there."

I blinked. "You are?"

She nodded. "That man in there would run through fire for you."

Oh my.

"Do you think?" I whispered.

Her head tipped to the side again. "Don't you?"

"I—"

"Let that go," Mom interrupted me on a shake of my hand. "Cora, you could close your eyes tonight and be anywhere tomorrow. The only way I'm going to be able to live with this is to hope to all that is holy that wherever you wake up tomorrow, that man is with you."

I felt my nose stinging (yes, again!) and whispered, "Mom."

"I'm being straight with you. I could…I could…hell, I *did* lose you for two months and…" she trailed off and her eyes filled with tears.

"Mom," I whispered again and pulled her into my arms.

Her arms went around me tight and we both held on as we cried.

She suddenly let me go but her hands came up. She grabbed both my cheeks and she got right in my face. Her eyes were bright and intense and at the sight of them, my breath hitched.

"I could lose you tomorrow and never see you again," she told me fiercely and my breath hitched again. "And the only thing I can hold on to to be able to rest my head on the pillow at night is the thought that wherever you are, you're with him and he's riding his horse or driving his car or flying his spaceship, I don't care, but he's doing it with you, he's not letting you go and he won't let any harm come to you. That's the only thing I have. And right now, that is what your man is giving your father. So, I think it is *very* wise to let your father have as much peace of mind as your man can give him before whatever happens next, happens." Her thumbs swept my cheeks and she finished on a whisper, "Do you get me?"

I nodded and my fingers came up and curled around her wrists. "I get you, Mom."

"Promise, whatever happens, you'll be safe," she demanded fervently.

"I promise," I promised on another hitch of breath.

"No more wielding daggers," she ordered and I pressed my lips together because who knew what could happen? I couldn't promise that.

"How about, I promise not to wield daggers unless absolutely necessary?" I replied.

She stared at me a second then she burst out laughing and wrapped her arms tight around me again.

I shoved my face in her neck, and when her hilarity calmed, I said into her skin, "I love you, Mom, and when I was gone I missed you, and the worst thing about being gone was thinking I'd never see you and Dad again and I didn't have the chance to say good-bye."

Her arms gave me a squeeze and she whispered, "Oh, sweetie."

My arms gave her a squeeze and I whispered back, "So, if we go again, I want you to know, and never forget, that I'll miss you and I'll always love you. Always."

She shoved her face even further in my neck and held on even tighter.

Moments passed as we held each other and just when I was about to let go, she said, "One more promise, Cora."

"Anything, Mom," I replied and her head went back but her arms stayed around me.

"Hold on to him tight. Don't let that man go. For me, for your dad and mostly...mostly, my beautiful, funny girl," her hand came up to cup my cheek and her eyes stared deep into mine, "for *you*. Yeah?"

I bit my lips and even between my lips, they trembled.

I let them go and said quietly, "He could be lost to me."

"Then hold on tight."

"It might not—"

Her arm gave me a squeeze. "Hold on tight."

"He—"

"Cora, learn this from your mother. There are not many men like him in this world or his, I'd guess. Men like him don't come around very often. Men like him who look at my girl like she holds the other half to his soul and he couldn't exist without her are even more rare." I held my breath at her words, a part of both Tor and Rosa's story I did not share, but words she used anyway while she concluded, "So hold...on...*tight*."

"Okay," I whispered.

Seriously, what else could I do?

"Promise?" she pushed.

"Promise," I gave in.

Mom smiled.

Boy, I was screwed.

Mom let me go and turned back to the sink, wiping her face and saying, "Okay, let's get this done and get back in there. It's good they're bonding but they're doing it with whisky. Whisky makes your father talkative. Talkative means he might get out photo albums. And you went through that unfortunate punk phase when you were fifteen. We don't want Tor seeing *that*."

Oh crap.

No. Agreed. We absolutely, definitely did not want Tor seeing photos of me with ratted out hair, too much black eyeliner and torn clothes held together with safety pins.

I snatched a plate out of the drainer and dried it, urging, "Hurry, Mom. Dad had three before we even cleared the table."

"Right," Mom muttered and started wiping silverware.

And I finished the dishes with my mom and while I did it I memorized every freaking second.

22

Something to Celebrate

~

I was silent on the ride home mostly because I was thinking of all my mother had said, all that had happened between Tor and me and about the words to "Crash into Me."

It wasn't until Tor unlocked the door to my apartment that it hit me Tor had been silent all the ride home too.

He opened the door for me. I preceded him and he closed it, locked it and stalked, yes, *stalked* to the kitchen.

Hmm.

It seemed I'd missed something.

I saw the light go on there. I switched on a few lamps in the living room then I followed him and stopped in the doorway to see he was opening and closing cupboards.

"Can I get you something?" I asked quietly and his eyes sliced to me.

They were broody and intense.

Oh boy.

"Do you have spirits?" he asked back.

Oh boy!

"Um...you had whisky with my dad," I pointed out.

"Yes, and I knew I would be operating that vehicle, undoubtedly in the rain, which it does all the bloody time here, so I did not have as much as I would have liked for operating that vehicle inebriated would not be wise," he returned.

He was right about that.

"In the cupboard by the wall," I belatedly answered his question.

He went to the cupboard, sorted through my myriad of bottles, pulled out some bourbon, opened it, sniffed it and went to the cupboard that held my glasses.

I watched him pour himself a rather healthy dose as I grew uncomfortable.

Tor was being broody, something he could be but he was usually kind of… *openly* broody. As in, it was rare he didn't tell me what was on his mind.

And he'd just had an emotional dinner with my parents and he wasn't telling me what was on his mind.

"Is something on your mind?" I asked after he swallowed a large swig.

He looked at me and declared weirdly, "Things here, in your world, are more advanced."

"Well…yeah," I replied.

"Is this true with medicine?"

My head tipped to the side. "Medicine?"

"Do you not call it medicine?" he asked, didn't wait for me to answer and he went on to explain using the word, "Healing."

"Yes, we call it medicine and yes, it's more advanced."

He scowled at me a second then drained his glass and poured another healthy measure.

"Tor," I started hesitantly, not sure what to do with him in this mood. "Has something upset you?"

He answered immediately, "While you were with your mother in the kitchen, your father was verbose."

Uh-oh.

Dad could have told him anything. About my punk phase, or worse, my militant vegetarian phase, or worse, the excruciatingly uncomfortable time he found Tad Millstrom getting to second base with me in our basement.

"And?" I whispered.

"And, he told me about Rosa. Your Rosa, the sister you did not have."

"Seriously?" I asked softly, surprised by this. Dad could get chatty while smashed but that was an overshare, even for Dad. I knew this because I'd been around Dad while he was hammered a bunch of times and he'd (obviously) *never* mentioned Rosa.

"Seriously," Tor replied then sucked back another large swallow.

"Tor, I don't—"

His eyes sliced to mine and the look in them made me snap my mouth shut.

Then he announced, "You're carrying my child."

My body went statue-still except my eyes. They blinked.

God, I forgot about the pregnancy test. How could I forget something like that?

"I—" I started, that one syllable trembling.

"You've been in my bed every night for six weeks and I've been in *you* every night for six weeks and we've been together day in, day out for even longer. You have not once had your cycle."

Oh God.

"Tor—"

"Your mother nearly died having your sister who *did* die."

My stomach dropped.

"She did?" I asked and he glared at me. "My mother almost died, I mean."

"Indeed," he clipped and threw back more bourbon.

Although this news upset me, greatly, I felt the need to stay focused on whatever was bothering Tor.

"Tor, I don't—"

He gave me his eyes again and I again snapped my mouth shut.

"Women in my world regularly die during childbirth. It happens so often, the midwives petitioned my father, in his kingdom, and myself, in Bellebryn, to make a law as the situation is fraught and the decision, save mother or child, is emotional. They felt the man was in no state during this time to make such a grave decision. And those around him could give thoughtful advice or this advice could be selfish or misguided. After much weighing of the matter and debate, and you can well imagine, considering my father's history with his wives, that there was *much* weighing of the matter and debate, my father and I agreed that the midwife should always save the mother. So this was made law."

My heart clutched and I knew why he was broody and struggling with his mood.

I also understood why he was being so romantic and wonderful and protective and…and…all of it.

Because he thought I was pregnant with his heir and he was trying to win me and take me back to his world not for *me*, but to keep me sweet so he could have what he wanted most in the world.

An heir.

And now he was thinking that if I were to carry that heir and we were transported to his world, he himself had created a law that, should I have difficulties, they would have to save me not his bloody precious heir.

My hand lifted and my fingers curled around the doorframe as I stared at him wondering why I kept searching for hope with this guy and always getting kicked in the stomach.

"I just don't believe you," I whispered, my voice trembling now for a different reason.

His brows drew together. "Pardon?"

I glared at him.

Then I shouted, "I don't believe you! You're not a jerk or a dick or an asshole. You're a *pig*!"

I turned on my foot and stomped to my bedroom. I was halfway to the bathroom when I was halted with an arm around my waist and turned to face Tor.

"Would you *stop* doing that!" I yelled. "If I want to go somewhere, I should just be able to *go*!"

"Cora, what the bloody hell has you in this state?" Tor growled.

He was angry, clear to see, and mystified too, equally clear to see, the pig.

"You!" I snapped then flung at him. "But you're also lucky, seeing as you're the big man in Bellebryn. *If* we go back, then along with annulling your marriage to the other Cora, you can quickly change the law so it's the child that's saved, not the mother. So, if I have a difficult childbirth, you'll be certain not to lose your precious heir!"

His head jerked like I slapped him then his eyes burned into mine before he said in a low voice, "Please tell me you did not just say that."

"I bloody did!" I shot back. "We both know I am and always have had one purpose for you. To be the vessel that safely delivers your successor."

"Now I need you to tell me you did not just say that," he ground out.

"Don't pretend it isn't true," I hissed and he let me go like touching me was akin to getting burned with acid and he took a step back.

Then he said softly, his eyes locked on mine, "You've convinced yourself about me so you'll not believe this but given the choice, both then and especially now, to save our child or to save you, I wouldn't have to think about it even for a second. I would save you."

I sucked in breath, my head got light and the only reason I didn't go down was that I stayed focused on him.

He went on.

"Then, because I could pretend during the days when you were away from me, but especially during the nights when I had you, that you were the Cora I needed you to be. And, my sweet, you'll not believe this either but the truth of the matter is, I enjoyed every *fucking* second of it. And now, because I know you are."

Oh my God.

"Tor—"

He lifted a hand. "You've said enough."

On that he turned on his boot and stalked out of my room.

I blinked at the doorway, frozen in shock at what he'd said. I heard the outside door open, close and the lock turn. I came unstuck way too late, ran through the bedroom and living room, unlocked the door and rushed into the hall.

Tor was gone.

I ran to the stairwell and down the two flights of steps (too slowly, drat my high-heeled sandals), through the foyer and out the front doors of my building.

I looked down the sidewalks to my left then to my right.

And again, Tor was gone.

I stared at the slick sidewalk as the misty rain made my skin and hair damp. Then I raced back into the building, up the steps, into my apartment and I grabbed my purse.

I ran to the corner store and bought a pregnancy test.

Thirty minutes later, my hands gripping the steering wheel tightly to stop them from shaking, I was in my car going *back* to the grocery store even though half of its goods were stuffed into the cupboards and fridge of my kitchen.

But we hadn't bought the ingredients to red velvet cake.

And as crazy and uncertain as our worlds were, Tor and I had something to celebrate.

That was, if he came home.

I was curled up in my pink chair, the purple throw tucked around me, dozing, when I heard the key scrape the lock.

My eyes opened. I sat up, putting my feet to the floor, my heart sliding up into my throat when I heard and saw the doorknob turn. I held my breath, my mind trying to recall one of the ways I came up with while making the cake as to how to apologize to Tor when the doorknob turned again.

I tipped my head to the side, staring at it and then heard the key in the lock again.

Uh-oh. Tor's new lock wasn't working.

I jumped when I heard a banging at the door.

"Cory, babe, open the door!"

Oh crap. It wasn't Tor. It was Noc.

I froze.

There was more banging and then, "Cora! I see the light coming through the bottom of the door. I know you're awake. Open up!"

My eyes flew to my DVD player and I saw it was nearly two in the morning. What was he doing there at two in the morning?

"Cora! Fuck me, babe, open the fuckin' door!" he shouted then more banging.

I stared at the door, my body unmoving.

He was a big guy, just as powerfully built as Tor. My door was crap because my landlord was crap. He could bust down my door, easy.

Shit!

There was silence then he called through the door, "Right, locks changed. I get it. Ice cold."

Oh shit.

"Do me a favor," he went on. "Pack my shit in a suitcase and put it in the hall. I'll be back tomorrow to get it."

There was one loud thump on the door and nothing.

I held my breath. When I was about to pass out, I sucked in a deep breath and held that. When I heard nothing, I threw off the blanket, tiptoed (focused on the tasks at hand, I still hadn't taken off my sandals) to my purse and pulled out my cell.

Tomorrow, should Tor come back (and, God, I hoped he came back), we were going straight back to the mall and getting him a blasted cell phone.

I looked at my phone and saw I had five missed calls while my phone was in my purse at my parents' house, no voicemails. Checking the history, I saw that four were from Noc, one was from my friend Phoebe.

Phoebe.

Holy crap!

It was too late to return Phoebe's call so I shut the phone down, dropped it back in my purse, tiptoed to the kitchen, grabbed the biggest, sharpest knife I could find and I tiptoed back to my living room. I turned off the lamps then settled back in the chair, tossing my throw over me.

I stared at the door, my fingers curled around the handle of the knife and I waited for Noc to come back.

About a half an hour later, I fell asleep.

23

We'll Have It for Breakfast

~

My eyes opened when Tor lifted me to cradle me in his arms.

"Tor?" I asked sleepily.

"Just so you know, love, a true warrior princess would not allow a man to approach and disarm her while she carried on sleeping."

Hmm.

I didn't know what to make of that except for the fact that it was true.

He walked us to my room, and as he did last night, set me on my feet by the bed. Then he made as if to move away, but I shook off the residual sleep claiming me and stopped him by lifting both hands and wrapping them around his neck.

"Honey?" I whispered and his hands came to my hips, fingers digging in.

Then I felt his forehead drop to mine.

I sucked in breath.

"I missed you calling me that," he murmured.

My heart leaped.

"You're not angry with me anymore?" I asked, my voice tinged with hope.

His forehead left mine.

Uh-oh.

"What you said was cruel," he informed me and I couldn't read his tone.

My fingers at his neck gave him a squeeze and I whispered, "I know."

"And untrue," he went on.

I took a risk and moved slightly closer to him.

"I know," I repeated not because I knew then, just because I knew now.

"I want an heir because it's my responsibility to provide one. But mostly I want an heir because I want children," he told me.

"Okay," I said softly.

"But more than that, I want you," he finished, his fingers digging deeper into my flesh and I pressed my lips together as my heart didn't leap…it flew.

"Really?" I breathed.

"Cora, my love," he started and I saw his shadowed face get close. "I know your life is in turmoil, but you really must start paying attention."

As much as it pained me to admit it, he wasn't wrong about that.

I swallowed then quietly I agreed, "Okay."

His fingers squeezed again and started to release so my fingers pressed in and I got on tiptoe so our faces were even closer.

"Please, don't be angry with me anymore," I whispered. "I shouldn't have said what I said. Not at all but especially with what happened to your mom and your stepmoms. I'm really so, so sorry."

He nodded. "All right, Cora." And again he started to move away.

I held tight and got higher on my toes so my lips were a breath away from his.

"Don't be angry with me anymore," I repeated and he stilled.

"I'm not angry, sweets," he whispered.

I touched my mouth to his and said yet again, "Don't be angry with me anymore."

His fingers flexed into my skin again and he replied softly, "Cora."

I touched my mouth to his again, my fingers sliding from his neck up into his hair, my body moving in two inches so it was against his.

Tor got the message. I knew this when he groaned against my lips, his head slanted, his mouth opened over mine and his tongue slid in.

Yes.

I moaned into his mouth and the kiss went instantly wild. His arms closed around me and crushed me to him then I burrowed closer, pressing my fingers into his hair to hold his mouth to me as he drank from me and I gave to him everything I had.

Suddenly, he broke his mouth from mine, turned me so my back was to him and with a hand between my shoulder blades, he shoved me forward. My arms went out to break my fall, my hands hit the bed at the same time he tossed the skirt of my dress up.

Oh God.

My knees trembled and I felt wetness saturate between my legs.

He yanked my panties over my ass.

My knees nearly buckled.

"Tor," I breathed.

He jerked my panties down my legs.

"Step out of them," he commanded, his voice thick.

I stepped out of my panties then he pushed against me with his hips and I mounted the bed on my knees. I felt his hand working at my behind then *he* mounted *me*, filling me full.

My head jerked back at the feel of him.

"Yes," I whispered.

He shoved in with his body and got on the bed on his knees then leaned forward. Wrapping an arm around my chest, the other around my ribs, he hauled me up, still impaled on his cock.

"Mouth," he growled.

I twisted my head and the instant I did, his mouth found mine and he kissed me.

This kiss was wilder, no control, not from Tor, not from me, and I loved every *fucking* second of it.

His mouth broke from mine and he ordered, "Discard your dress."

With trembling hands, I pulled off my dress and flung it aside.

"Now this," he demanded, tugging at the cup of my bra.

Arching my back (which also succeeded in sliding him deeper inside me which felt freaking *great*), I reached for the hooks at the back of my bra. I undid them clumsily, pulled it down my arms and tossed it aside.

One of his hands went to cup my breast warmly, the other hand slid between my legs, his middle finger hitting the core of me.

At the sensations these caused, my back arched again and I whimpered.

His thumb and finger found my nipple and he pulled. "Who's inside you?"

"My prince," I breathed, twisting my neck, tucking my forehead into his neck and covering his hand at my sex where his finger was working magic.

He pulled my nipple again and fire shot straight through me.

"Bloody right," he growled, his hips dipping, he drove back up inside me.

"Baby," I whispered, my hand tensing on his.

"Who are you?" he asked on another pull on my nipple causing another shaft of fire.

"Your princess," I answered immediately, wanting my reward.

I got it, another heady stroke of his cock.

"Who are you?" he repeated and I closed my eyes as his finger between my legs twitched relentlessly and I ground into him.

"Honey," I breathed.

I was losing it.

Another pull at my nipple, sharper, harder, *better*, then, "Who are you, Cora?"

"Your wife," I whispered, his hips dipped and he surged up again, pulling at my nipple and rolling my clit at the same time and I cried out, "Tor!" as it overwhelmed me.

I barely started coming when he shoved me back down into the bed and then started moving inside me, rolling his hips as he did it, his hands at my hips yanking me back while he drove in.

God, beautiful.

I lifted up on my forearms, arched my back, lifting my ass for him and he reached forward. His fingers curling around my shoulder, he pulled me back into him, this allowing him to thrust deeper into me. I shuddered and finished my climax as he plunged in, his rhythm slow, steady, his hips rolling, his hand at my shoulder driving me back as he drove forward and it started building again.

"Baby," I gasped breathlessly into my comforter.

His hand left my shoulder and both curled around the sides of my ribs.

"We go back to my world, we find someone who can make you more of these shoes," he declared huskily.

"Yes," I breathed.

His hips rolled and he thrust deep.

"Dozens of them," he went on.

"Yes," I repeated.

"My wife has a beautiful arse," he grunted, his hips rolling and thrusting again.

I closed my eyes, arched my back and stretched my arms straight forward, pressing back even as he pulled me to him.

"Fuck me," I whispered and his thrusts quickened. "Yes," I breathed.

"And the wettest, sweetest fucking cunt," he growled, his voice hoarse, his thrusts coming faster.

My head jerked back, my hair flying, my sex spasming.

"Oh my God," I moaned.

"That's it, my love." His fingers at my ribs flexing tight, yanking me back violently. "Give me what's rightfully mine."

"Okay," I breathed then my body bucked and I cried out yet again as a stronger climax washed through me.

Tor pounded into me, hauling me back into him, his thrusts savage as I heard him grunt and he drove in hard, once, twice, three, four, five, six times then he stayed planted and groaned.

My eyes slowly closed and just as slowly a smile curved my lips.

He waited until my breathing slowed then he pulled me up again, arms tight around my chest and ribs, bodies still joined and his face went into my neck.

"Would that we would be transported to a world where you could spend your days with my seed planted deep inside you," Tor whispered into my neck.

I closed my eyes again as renewed heat flooded my system.

"Which would mean," Tor went on quietly. "I would spend my days planting it there."

My body trembled and then I swallowed.

Tor kept speaking.

"Are we understood, you and I?" he murmured.

"Yes, Tor," I whispered, lifting a hand to place it lightly on his neck.

And we were. Or, at least, I hoped we were.

His lips went to my ear. "We have enough challenges ahead of us, my sweet. We do not need to be striking out and wounding each other."

Boy, was he right.

"You're right," I agreed softly.

His arms gave me a squeeze then the one at my ribs loosened, his hand sliding down to rest on my belly briefly at the same time he kissed my neck. He lifted me off him, set me on my knees in the bed and fell to his side grabbing my hand as he did so. I went down and he rolled to his back and pulled me in his arms so I was pressed into his side, one of his hands coming up to play with the ends of my hair.

"Uh...Tor?" I called.

"I'm right here," he answered and I snuggled closer, because he was.

Then I told him something I had to tell him but didn't want to.

Still, I had to.

"Earlier tonight, uh…Noc came around."

"I know."

My head shot up and I looked at him through the shadows. "What?"

"I ascended the stairs when he was shouting through your door. I hid, watched, prepared—should he lose his temper—to intervene. He did not. He left and I followed him."

My hand lying on his chest fisted. "You followed him?"

"I did. And Cora, I will say it's very strange seeing another you," he told me.

I was sure it was but I was also stuck on Tor following Noc.

"You followed him?" I repeated and he sighed.

"Yes."

My fist opened and I slapped his chest. "Why would you do that?"

"The same reason I spent a day wandering your world when I first got here. You do not wage battle unless you know the lay of the land. And you never battle an opponent you do not know and understand even better than he understands himself."

What he said was very wise and everything but I still glared at him through the dark. "But, he could have seen you! He could have freaked out! He could have lost it! He could be a bad guy and led you someplace you shouldn't be." A thought struck me and I asked, "Where did he lead you?"

"He led me to what you call a police station."

I blinked.

Then I breathed, "What?"

"He led me to what you call a police station," Tor repeated.

What on earth?

"Why?"

"From observing through the doors when he went in, it appears he is known there so my guess would be, he goes there often."

My voice got high when I asked, "He's a *cop*?"

"A what?"

"A police officer. An officer of the law. A—"

"Do these men carry gold emblems?" Tor interrupted to inquire.

"You mean a badge?" I asked back.

"Perhaps. He carried such as this on his belt."

"Yes, a badge and yes, cops carry badges."

"Then yes," Tor stated. "It would seem this man is a...*cop*."

Holy crap!

I whirled to sitting and stared into the darkness.

This, I reckoned, was *not* good.

Tor sat up and called, "Cora?"

I focused on his shadow. "I don't think this is good, Tor."

"I would say there's no thinking about it, my love," he replied and I stared at him.

Great.

"Why would you say that?"

"Is this poker illegal?" he asked.

"Um...no, if it's done in a casino, of which there are some around here. But, yes, if the games are illegal."

"Then Cora is attending illegal games," Tor declared and I blinked.

Then I cried, "How could she even *find* illegal games? And how did she even learn how to *play* poker? She was here less than two months! *I* wouldn't even know where to *begin* to find an illegal poker game and I never understood poker. And...and...not only how but...*why*?"

His arms came out and he pulled me to him, saying, "The Cora of my world is what she is, and she does what she does, and very little of it is good. We cannot waste our energy trying to understand *how* or *why* because the answer to the first is superfluous and even if we knew the answer to the second, we would not comprehend it. What we need to expend our energy on is what kind of danger she has placed *you* in."

Okay, it must be said, sometimes Tor being sensible and logical was a good thing.

"Right," I agreed.

"Share your thoughts," he demanded and I relaxed into him.

"Well," I started, processing them in my head. "The best case scenario is that he's a dirty cop and he's in on whatever she's in on, they're playing at it together. This would be good since *I* won't be going to any games, I'm making it clear he's out of the picture and he'll have to find another sugar mama who can count cards."

"Go on," Tor urged when I stopped.

"The worst case scenario, and the one I'm thinking it is, is that he's undercover and he's either investigating her activities or using her as an in to bring down some illegal gambling racket."

"This would be bad," Tor muttered.

He had *that* right.

"But I would like to know why you think it's the worst case scenario," Tor stated.

I moved so I could see his face (kind of) and explained, "Well, you said she was cold. He even said she was cold. And you said that, um…she was not much to write home about in the bed frolicking department."

I felt his body shake with laughter and heard his voice shake with it when he confirmed, "Indeed, she's not much to write home about in the *bed frolicking* department."

I slapped his arm. "Tor, this is serious!"

"Yes," he agreed, his voice still shaking. "Talk on."

I sucked in an annoyed breath and told him, "We have no way of knowing, since she's so different from me, what he's like. I was only around him a few minutes but he seemed, I don't know, *sweet*."

His arms tensed around me and I quickly forged ahead.

"Anyway, she is who she is so my guess would be, she thinks she's playing him. He said she was a wildcat. If she was a wildcat and he was into her, and he's even a little bit like you, then no way that a few missed phone calls and Cora not opening the door would mean he'd give up and tell her to pack his clothes in a suitcase and put them out in the hall. That's saying it's over and he's fine with that. If she's giving it to him like he likes it and he's into her, he's not going to give up that easy. Unless she's *not* giving it to him like he likes it, he's *pretending* he likes it as a means to an end, she's giving him the heave-ho and he's sensing trouble, which as a cop he would do, so he's cutting his losses and taking off."

"This would make sense," Tor replied.

"Yes," I agreed.

"This would also mean trouble," he remarked and my head tilted.

"Trouble?"

"Love, we have no way of knowing how much time he invested in this… situation. What *I* know from experience is that it is highly unlikely Cora of my world could play that kind of game, especially if she took him to her bed, and be convincing. Perhaps to a normal man but not one who is trained to scrutinize human behavior and is on the alert for the sake of his own safety and the success of his endeavors. I don't think after he devoted time and energy to his inquiry at the same time enduring her…limited charms…that he would be willing to cut his losses, as you put it."

This made sense but I didn't get it.

"I don't get it."

"He won't be conceding. He'll be watching you."

Oh shit.

"Which means," Tor carried on, "if we aren't careful, me."

Oh shit!

"Tor," I whispered.

"Therefore, we must be careful," Tor concluded.

"What if he's already watching and he's seen you?" I asked.

"Considering the uncomfortable feeling seeing another me gave *me*, and I knew he existed, I would surmise that we would know if this was the case already."

I sucked in breath. Then I nodded.

"So what do we do?" I inquired.

"I don't know. I need to think on it."

I stared at his shadowed face a second before I nodded again.

He started righting both of us in the bed. "But to think clearly, I need sleep."

I gently pulled away from his efforts to right me in bed.

He might need sleep but he wasn't going to get it. At least, not for a while.

"Cora?" he called.

I shoved my hand under the pillow and pulled out my nightie, saying softly, "Just a minute."

Luckily, with only a searching look at me, he let it go. I pulled the nightie on while he rolled off the bed to disrobe. Then I sat on the side of the bed, took off my sandals and dashed to the bathroom to grab the white stick with the pink plus sign on it. I dashed out of the bathroom to the kitchen being certain not to look at him on the way and also trying not to hyperventilate because I was nervous.

In the kitchen, I lit the two birthday candles on the top (one pink, one blue—he wanted a son, but Lord knew, at this point, it was a fifty-fifty shot). Then I walked the cake slowly back to my room.

When I got close to the bed, I saw Tor was sitting up in it. His eyes I could see by the minimal candlelight were not on the cake. They were on me.

And they were burning.

"Love," he whispered, his deep voice strange, like there was an ache in it.

I sat on the bed and held the cake between us. His gaze finally went to the cake.

Then it came back to mine and there it was.

Definitely an ache.

"You did not need to do this to apologize," he said softly, his attention went back to the cake and I understood the ache. He was remembering the last time I walked into a room with one. "*Especially* not this," he finished.

"Honey," I replied quietly. "I didn't make it as an apology. I made it for a celebration."

He looked at me. "Pardon?"

I balanced the cake on one hand and lifted the white stick with the other.

"In my world, you can buy pregnancy tests at the drugstore. When you left, I bought one, took it and—"

Just like that, the cake was whisked out of my hand, the candles flickering out as it was swiftly deposited on the nightstand. Then the white stick was yanked out of my other hand and Tor tossed it to the floor.

And last, I was on my back with Tor's body covering mine.

His hands framed my face.

"It is confirmed, you're carrying my child," he declared.

"Uh...yes," I whispered.

"And you feel this is cause for celebration," he noted, his voice husky.

"Um...I'm scared," I whispered my confession. "But...uh...yes," I agreed shakily.

I barely got the "s" out on "yes" when Tor's mouth slammed down on mine and he kissed me, deep, wet, rough and thorough, and while he was doing it, his arms closed around me and he rolled so I was on top.

His hands went into my nightie, yanking it up, and I had to break free of his mouth when he pulled it over my head.

"Tor, the cake—" I started.

One of his hands fisted in my hair, the other one curled into the flesh of one of the cheeks of my bottom.

"We'll have it for breakfast," he replied.

"You can't eat cake—"

His fingers on my ass flexed. "Quiet."

"But—"

He rolled again so he was on top, shifting his hips insistently until I opened my legs and his hips fell between.

"Quiet," he repeated on a growl, "I'm about to fuck my wife and the only words I want her saying when I do it are 'yes,' 'Tor,' 'my prince,' 'baby,' and 'oh my God.' Am I understood?"

God, he was bossy.

"God, you're bossy," I snapped.

He slid inside me and my neck arched.

Damn, but I loved the feel of him inside me.

"Cora, am I understood?"

"You're understood," I breathed.

His mouth came to mine and he whispered, "Good."

Then he kissed me and started to move and for the next half an hour the only words I said were "yes," "Tor," "my prince," "baby," and "oh my God."

Weak sun was touching the sky as my eyes drifted closed and sleep started to claim me.

"Sweets?" Tor called and my only answer was to press closer. He nevertheless heard my answer loud and clear and kept talking. "That cake was superb."

My eyes opened and I saw the wall of his chest.

He'd made love to me then I'd gone to the kitchen, got a knife, cut a slice of cake and fed him with my fingers. I cut another one and he fed me. Then I licked his fingers clean. His eyes watched my mouth through every second of me doing it. They darkened in a way that was too sexy for words and when his fingers were clean, he made love to me again.

Now I'd had four orgasms, a piece of damn good cake (even if I did say so myself) and the man I loved was in my arms. And, according to my mother and finally paying attention, it appeared the man I loved was both devoted to me *and* adored me.

All was not right in my world but all was pretty freaking great in my now.

I slid my hand through the hair on his chest and replied quietly, "I'm glad you liked it."

"'Like,'" he muttered on a squeeze of the arms he held me with. "Is not the word I'd choose."

I didn't think he was talking about just the cake.

I smiled against his chest and my eyes started to drift closed.

"Cora?" he called again.

"Yes, baby," I whispered, not opening my eyes.

"Who are you?" he whispered back.

"Your wife," I answered sleepily and burrowed closer.

"Bloody right," he muttered and I smiled again then drifted off to sleep.

24

The Only Hope We Have

~

The loud banging at the front door jolted both of us awake.

I blinked, rolled out of Tor's strong arms and away from his warm body, feeling like I had an hour's sleep (which, with a glance at the bedside clock, was close to the truth).

Tor had a different reaction.

He threw back the covers and growled, "By the gods, what the bloody hell now?"

With sleepy fascination, I watched him pull up a pair of drawstring pajama bottoms then, still with sleepy fascination, I watched him prowl toward the door.

I suddenly was not sleepy or fascinated anymore because I instantly freaked out, threw the covers back, jumped out of bed and snapped, "Tor! Where are you going?"

He stopped and turned his head to me. I started searching for my nightgown and panties, found them on the floor and tugged the panties on in a flurry of motion, my head tilted back to look at Tor when he spoke.

"I'm getting the bloody door."

I pulled down my nightgown only to see he'd resumed prowling and was out the bedroom door.

I raced after him, hissing, "You can't! What if it's Noc?"

Tor stopped at the door, lifted a big hand and pointed a long finger at my peephole.

"You have a tiny porthole," he replied in a low voice, his blue eyes on me.

Oh.

Right.

I did. I had a tiny porthole.

The banging came back as he bent and looked through it then his head turned to me, his expression unreadable.

I stopped trying to read it when I heard Phoebe shouting, "Cora! I know you're in there! Open up! I don't have all day."

Phoebe!

My heart started racing.

She'd called last night. Now she was here.

I didn't know whether to be terrified, happy or to brace.

My eyes refocused on Tor just as he unlocked the door, pulled it open and when he did, I decided my best option was to brace.

At that point I saw my petite, dark-pixie-cut-haired, adorable-faced, gorgeous-platform-pumps-with-skinny-jeans-and-kickass-sweater-wearing friend standing at the door, one hand raised ready to knock again, one hand holding a department store bag by the handles, body arrested and head tipped way back with mouth falling right open when she caught sight of Tor.

Oh boy.

She blinked then her eyes did a top to toe scan. They stopped on the way back to the top, arrested on his chest, she blinked again, and I had a feeling she also started salivating (I had this feeling because that was what I did when I saw Tor's chest).

Finally, her eyes slid all the way up, they moved over his face and she whispered, "Dude. What happened to you? You didn't have a scar the last time I saw you."

Oh boy!

"Phoebe," I said cautiously, moving into my living room and her head jerked my way, her eyes lost their wonder and her face instantly closed down.

My heart clenched and I stopped moving.

I'd been right to brace. Cora had done something to her.

Really, really, God, *really*, I hoped I *never* met that *awful* woman!

She opened her mouth to speak but Tor got there before her, shifting slightly but the movement was hard to miss since he was a big guy, but also because it was vaguely threatening.

Phoebe didn't miss the movement or the vague threat. Her head jerked back as her eyes cut to him and I watched her body go still.

"You are clearly an acquaintance of my wife and we are not unaware that others of her acquaintance are unhappy with her, or, the *other* her. What *you* must be aware of is that I will not tolerate you being unkind to her, that is to say, the *real* her," Tor declared.

Phoebe blinked yet again and I snapped, "Tor!"

He looked to me and asked, "What?"

I didn't answer and this was because Phoebe whispered a shocked, "Your wife?"

I looked from Phoebe to Tor, pointed to my friend and said, "That's what."

"What's what?" Tor returned.

"Your wife?" Phoebe repeated.

I walked three more strides into my living room, stopped and planted my hands on my hips. "You can't go around telling everyone we're married."

Tor turned to me, crossed his arms on his chest, tilted his head slightly but dangerously to the side and asked back, "And why not?"

"Because it freaks them out!" I semi-shouted.

"The other her?" Phoebe asked.

"Oh for goodness sakes," I hissed and stomped to the door. I reached to Phoebe, grabbed her arm, pulled her in and turned to her. Then I introduced my friend to my parallel world husband, throwing my hand out from one to the other and back again as I spoke, "Phoebe, my kind-of husband, Tor. Tor, my hopefully still best friend, Phoebe."

Phoebe blinked again and asked, "Kind-of husband?"

"It's a long story," I muttered.

"I'm not her kind-of anything," Tor stated at this point. "I am her husband and she is my wife and the mother of my unborn child."

Oh my God!

Phoebe's eyes bugged out of her head.

I whirled and exclaimed, "*Tor!*"

"What?" he growled, losing patience.

"You also can't go around telling everyone I'm pregnant!" I cried.

"The little white stick said you were and I *knew* you were even before that contraption confirmed it so why the bloody hell not?" Tor returned.

"You just can't," I shot back.

"You're pregnant?" Phoebe whispered and I turned back to see her face pale, her eyes still big and they were on me.

"Uh...yeah," I whispered back.

Her big eyes darted to Tor then back to me then back to Tor then to me.

I knew she came to a decision (and not a good one for me) when she straightened her shoulders and pulled in breath as I watched her face close down.

She lifted up the bag and informed me, "Dave said you were back. He also told me some stupid story about how you had amnesia or whatever. Total soap opera but he bought it because he's a big dork. So, whatever. I'm here to return that Coach bag and that blouse you loaned me. Then I'm gone." She shook the bag. "Here it is."

I didn't look at the bag. I kept my eyes glued to my friend.

The other Cora had done something to her, obviously. I just had no clue what.

And I also had no clue what to do to make it better.

What I did know was that I couldn't bear thinking she was mad at me at all much less leaving her in this world after whatever happened to me and Tor knowing she would always hate me for whatever the other Cora did, so I had to do something.

"Take it," she said, shaking the bag again.

"She hurt you," I whispered.

"All right, don't take it," Phoebe stated, moved further into the living room, dropped it by my armchair and hitched her purse up on her shoulder, muttering, "Have a happy life with your hot guy, kind-of husband."

She started toward the door Tor had not yet closed.

"His name is Prince Noctorno Allegro Hawthorne. He's of the House of Hawthorne, heir to the kingdom of Hawkvale, ruler of Bellebryn," I announced.

Phoebe's shoulders went up her neck as I spoke, she stopped and slowly turned to face me.

I kept talking.

What the hell?

I had nothing to lose.

"Obviously, all this is in an alternate universe that, evidence is suggesting, has the same people in it as we have here but even though they look the same, they're different. I was transported there in my sleep two months ago and the Cora from there was sent here. She's a bitch, like, an all 'round bitch. She doesn't discriminate with her bitchiness. She's a bitch to everyone, here and in the other world. Tor's world. Everyone hates her there but she's had a lifetime of building that. It proves the true strength of her bitchiness considering she'd been here for just under two months and succeeded in making everyone hate me."

Phoebe stared up at me and said not a word.

So I kept right on going.

"Anyway, we still don't know what's going on but a quick update. I was transferred there and within minutes, I accidentally started a curse that, if it comes to fruition, will bring plague and famine to everyone in Tor's land. Tor is married to the other Cora but he hates her as in, *a lot*, so, since this world-hopping business is about as usual there as it is here, that is to say, *not at all*, he thought I was her so he didn't like me either. Obviously, since I'm now pregnant, he got over that. Then we were both transported back here and we don't know why that is either. We also don't know how to get back. What we do know is that when we do, he's divorcing her, marrying me, and I'm having his baby. So, I'm kind of his wife—"

"Cora," Tor growled from behind me, interrupting me and successfully expressing his displeasure at my turn of phrase.

Therefore I hurriedly explained, "Though Tor isn't fond of the 'kind of' part and just considers us hitched."

Phoebe blinked. Then she looked up at Tor and blinked. She looked back and me and when she didn't blink, I kept talking.

"So, as if uncertain travel between parallel universes isn't enough for us to deal with, the Cora of that world, when she was in *this* world, was bitchy to all my friends, including, obviously, you. And now they all hate me. She also left my house and car a *total* pit, which was not nice but luckily at least that was easily remedied. She also got herself into some kind of trouble. We think playing poker. The Noctorno of this world is a cop and he's involved with her somehow. There's a shitload of money in my DVD cabinet and he's, that is the other Noctorno, or I mean, the Noctorno of this world is coming back to collect his clothes sometime later. He can't see my Noctorno," I gestured behind me, "mainly because he'd freak. And now we need to get back to make sure the curse doesn't befall Tor's land and do it before getting arrested or whatever."

Phoebe said nothing, just stared at me.

I held her eyes and tried to read something there, anything.

There was nothing. She was just staring at me.

My heart lurched.

But my mouth whispered, "I know it sounds crazy but it's true. I can't prove it except to point out the other Noctorno you've seen doesn't have a scar and my Noctorno does. So, you might believe me if you saw both Tor and Noc together but I can't give you that so…well…" I threw out a hand. "I don't know what else to say. Except I hope one day, when you know I'm gone, you'll know I'm back there, with Tor, in his world, married to him and making a family because I love him and you'll know it wasn't me who hurt you but it *was* me who always loved you and I'll be missing you."

She continued staring at me, unmoving, unblinking.

I had nothing else to give.

Then she asked softly, "You're pregnant?"

"Yes," I said softly back.

"With a hot guy's kid?"

I pressed my lips together and tried not to hope.

I couldn't not hope.

I nodded and felt the tears stinging my eyes as the hope clogged my throat.

"In Tor's world," I whispered, "I'm also a princess. I can talk to birds and they talk back. The air shimmers like there's glitter in it and my clothes kick ass."

Phoebe stared at me a moment before she asked quietly, "You love him?"

I pulled in breath through my nose and felt Tor's heat get close to my back.

Then I nodded.

Suddenly she tipped her head back and screamed at the ceiling, "*My best friend is knocked up with a hot guy's kid and she's a princess in an alternate universe!*"

She tipped her head down and launched herself at me, bursting into tears, holding me tight and rocking me violently from side to side.

I heard Tor close the door about half a second before I also wrapped my arms around her, burst into tears but mine were relieved as well as joyous.

We rocked back and forth crying for a while then she reared back, grabbed my forearms, shook them, her eyes darting to Tor and back to me before she shouted, "Look at him! He's tall, hot, those scars are *way* hot, I've never seen *any* man wear pajama bottoms that well and he has just the right amount of chest hair! Girl, you did *all right*."

See!

There was a reason Phoebe and I were BFFs.

"Girl, I *know*!" I shouted back.

"Sweets," Tor murmured from behind me and I felt his hand warm on the small of my back before I twisted my neck to look up at him. "You may wish to calm down and rejoice far more quietly."

"Sweets," Phoebe whispered reverently. "*Hot*."

I smiled at Phoebe's words but my eyes didn't leave Tor's face and I saw his eyes smile back before I said to him, "Right. That would probably be prudent."

"Right," he replied, leaned in and touched his mouth to mine.

"*Hot*," Phoebe breathed, and incidentally, didn't let go of my arms.

Tor pulled back, his eyes slid to Phoebe and back to me before he muttered, "I shall get dressed."

Phoebe finally stepped away from me and as she did so, she stated, "Please, if you're doing that on my account, I'm totally cool with you *exactly* the way you are."

Tor looked at her then he looked at me and his mouth twitched. He shook his head, made no response and strode to my bedroom.

Phoebe and I watched.

While we did this, I heard Phoebe repeat a breathless, "*Hot*."

I looked at her to see she was looking at me.

And, as often happened, sometimes for no reason whatsoever, we both dissolved into giggles.

Our giggles went uncontrolled when we both heard muttered from my bedroom, "Bloody hell."

In fact, at that, we collapsed into each other's arms and roared with them.

So much for being quiet.

I made my prince and my best friend blueberry pancakes and bacon and we went overkill by following this with red velvet cake.

But, whatever, it was time to celebrate. I was in love with a hot guy prince and future king, pregnant with his child, and I still had my best friend.

If that didn't say celebration, nothing did.

And furthermore, if there was a time I could overeat, now was it.

While Tor showered, I filled Phoebe in on more detail about Tor and she breathed the word "*hot*" or drawled the word "*nice*" about seven thousand times while I was doing it.

While I cooked and we ate (standing up in the kitchen with our plates close to our mouths, something else that made Tor's lips twitch), I filled Phoebe in with more detail on everything else.

After that, we retired to the living room.

Tor was dressed in jeans and a cool, light-blue shirt he didn't tuck in. I was wearing my nightie with my short robe tied over it and we were sipping after breakfast/after cake coffee.

Phoebe was curled in my armchair. And I was tucked tight to Tor's side on the couch, the soles of my feet to the cushion, my legs having fallen into his thigh. His arm was curled around me holding me close when it occurred to me.

And what occurred to me was that my best friend was definitely crazy, a certifiable nut. But, even so, she'd bought our equally definitely crazy story really easily.

And that was weird.

"Uh...Phoebe," I called when she'd taken a break from updating me on her life (doing so at the same time educating Tor to the fact she was definitely crazy and a certifiable nut) and was sipping from her cup.

"Yeah, babe," she replied.

"Not to look a gift horse in the mouth because I'm glad you believe our story but *why* do you believe our story? I mean, when we told him, Dad freaked as in *totally* freaked. He accused Tor of being the leader of a cult and tried to kick him out of the house. You didn't even blink."

Well, she did blink, repeatedly, but she didn't freak.

She grinned at the cult comment then threw out a hand and, as if she was not rocking Tor and my worlds, she blithely said, "Because Brianna's friend Marlene's friend Circe lives in an alternate universe."

This time I blinked and I also felt my mouth drop open.

Tor's body went solid at my side.

"What?" I whispered.

"Pardon?" Tor growled.

She studied us, eyes going back and forth as she repeated, "Because Brianna's friend Marlene's friend Circe lives in an alternate universe."

Tor leaned forward, and since his arm didn't move from around me, he took me with him.

"Explain," he ordered, his voice low and commanding.

Phoebe's eyes didn't move from him as she whispered, "Well, I mean, I don't know Circe and I've only met Marlene once at a party. But everyone in that circle knows Circe went to bed one night and another Circe was there the next day and the here Circe was *gone*. The here Circe also came back home. So for a while there were two Circes then the here Circe went back there. She's there now, as far as I know." She tore her gaze from Tor and looked at me. "She was also knocked up when she got back, by the way."

I stared at my friend.

"More," Tor demanded, his tone not having changed and Phoebe's eyes shot back to him.

"I...well..." She sucked in breath then she looked at me and went on, "I don't know the whole story, and from what you said while you were making breakfast, Cora, it seems her other world is different. Maybe it's another one. I mean, birds don't talk to her, I don't think. The air didn't glitter either. Definitely. From what I heard, it was primitive, savage even. The place she went to was barren with rocks and stuff. They lived in tents and a lot went down when she was there, like, serious stuff and when I say that I mean, like, *NC-17 rated* stuff. She's a queen, though, married to the king of what I think Marlene called a horde."

"Korwahk," Tor whispered.

I looked to him and asked, "What?"

He sat back (again taking me with him) and turned to me. "She describes Korwahk."

"That sounds familiar," Phoebe put in and we looked at her. "She's, like, the Golden Queen?" she asked as if we could confirm then she shook her head and muttered, "I don't know, something like that."

"The Golden Warrior Queen of The Golden Dynasty," Tor stated and I looked back to him to see he was looking at Phoebe. "Is she fair with golden eyes?" he asked.

"I don't know about her eyes, but yes, I think she's blonde," Phoebe answered.

"Honey?" I prompted Tor and his eyes came to me.

"It was reported through diplomatic dispatches while you were with me in our other world that Dax Lahn, the king of Korwahk, they are known as Dax in their language, has finally claimed his queen. She is known as the Golden Warrior Queen and it is said he's also claimed their union begins The Golden Dynasty."

Wow.

That sounded cool.

"That sounds cool," I said quietly but a strange flash in his eyes made me think it was anything but cool so I asked, "What?"

"It is nothing," he muttered, turning his attention to his coffee cup and therefore I knew he was also totally lying.

So I repeated, "What?"

He took a sip and his eyes came to me. "It is nothing, my love."

But his eyes were troubled.

I didn't need troubled eyes. We had enough trouble.

So I repeated, sharper this time, "Tor, *what?*"

He held my gaze a moment then he looked to Phoebe, "She returned to the other world?"

I looked back to Phoebe to see her nod but she replied verbally too, "Yep."

"Did she *wish* to return?" Tor asked.

This was an interesting question and his stress of "wish" made it more so.

Phoebe shook her head. "I don't know. I mean, I'm not sure."

"Do you know *how* she returned?" Tor went on.

Now that was an *excellent* question.

Phoebe shook her head again. "No, but I can ask Brianna to ask Marlene."

"Please do so," Tor murmured. With eyes locked on Phoebe, he finished, "Immediately."

"Righty ho," Phoebe whispered because my friend might be a nut but she was far from stupid. But even an idiot could read Tor's intensity.

So she immediately pushed herself up, put her cup down on the coffee table, turned and twisted to hang over the arm of the chair to grab her bag from the floor and get her phone.

Tor took another sip of coffee and it wasn't hard to read that he was doing this to avoid me even though I was pressed to his side.

"Baby," I called.

"Mm," he murmured.

Totally avoiding me.

"Uh, Tor," I called again and he turned his head to me. "What aren't you telling me?"

Finally, he answered, it was just not the right answer.

"What it is is not for your ears."

"Tor—" I started warningly.

He put his mug down on the side table, twisted his torso so he was facing me and placed his other hand light on my hip. "Cora, it is not for your ears. Trust me."

"Uh, big guy, do you think there is anything that has to do with any of this that I shouldn't know?"

"Yes," he replied immediately. "This."

"I'm a big girl. I can take it."

"My love, I don't *want* you to take it."

"I'm not certain that's your choice," I returned.

He held my eyes and I held his right back.

Then he sighed.

As Phoebe got up, murmuring into the phone and moving toward the kitchen, Tor spoke.

"If this world your friend's friend's friend knows is indeed Korwahk and this Circe was claimed by the king of that nation, I have concerns."

"What concerns?"

"Korwahk is in the Southlands, far away from Bellebryn and Hawkvale. Things are very different there. Uncivilized, some would consider it primitive, but it actually isn't. It is only different. What it is, is *savage*."

I sucked in breath.

That didn't sound good.

"Do you think she's been—?" I started.

"What I know is, any warrior of the Korwahk Horde, most definitely their king, gets his wife one way."

He paused.

I leaned in closer.

He saw he wasn't going to get away with not telling me the whole story so he finished, "He hunts her."

"Oh my God," I whispered, leaning back.

"Yes," he muttered his agreement.

I just stared at him.

On a sigh, he kept talking.

"This Wife Hunt is well-known, my love. It is even attended by spectators who travel far to watch, though I cannot understand what they would get from this. To my culture, this practice is sordid, although it is perfectly acceptable in the Southlands and has been happening for centuries. Women are gathered, paraded through the warriors of the Horde, let loose, the warriors hunt them and claim them by fighting their brothers-in-arms for them and then, if victorious, they take the women on the spot."

"Oh my God," I whispered again. "Take them as in…?" I trailed off, hoping he got me without me having to say it, and I knew he got me when his fingers squeezed my hip and he nodded. "Oh my God," I breathed it this time.

"I would assume this is also not common practice in your world," he stated.

Hunting women and raping them?

"No!" I cried.

"It is not in my land or any of the countries of the Northlands," he muttered then his eyes caught mine. "She, this Circe of this world, if she was switched before the Hunt, would endure that, love. I've no doubt about it."

Oh my God!

I looked away and closed my eyes, now worried about Circe, a woman I didn't even know!

"Cora," he called and I looked back, opening my eyes. "As I explained, this concerns me. But Dax Lahn has declared his union with this Circe is the beginning of The Golden Dynasty. He is said to brag greatly of her beauty and spirit. It is said he cares deeply for her. He is known and what he is known for is being brutal, unforgiving and that he has the strength of ten men. There are many who think he is a god on earth, an unbeatable warrior, a formidable ruler, a cunning leader. He has great strength but he also has great intelligence. Even so, he rules a savage land with savage practices. Yet, the reports state his bride is adored, not only by her king but by his people. It is said she holds noble magic and is goddess to his god. He is said to display tenderness toward her, even publicly, which is not always the practice of the warriors of that Horde but definitely not a characteristic he has ever shown. And it is said she brings him humor." He leaned closer to me. "Perhaps it is somewhat like us. Perhaps, sweets, he or she has found a way to break through. Perhaps she is pleased she carries his child and wished to return."

"I hope so," I whispered.

"As do I," he whispered back.

"Welp!" Phoebe called from the doorway from the kitchen. "The gig is, Circe's alternate universe guy, who, Cora, by the way," she looked at me, "apparently is also *way hot*." She took us both in and continued, "It was him that found a way to get her back. She was at a party and just," she lifted her hands and even with the one holding her cell phone, she wriggled her fingers, "melted away."

"Bloody hell," Tor muttered.

But all I could think was, *melted away*.

I didn't like the idea of the blue mist and I wasn't conscious to see that. I certainly didn't want to *melt away*.

"That's the bad news," Phoebe announced then stated, "The good news is, when she was gone, her dad and the alternate universe Circe found a witch here who knew how to bring her back. They just never got the chance since the here Circe came back on her own somehow."

Both Tor and I straightened but it was me who asked, "Really?"

She nodded, coming to stand behind my armchair and putting her hands on the back of it. "Yep, Brianna is calling Marlene now to get the full scoop and to tell her about you. Brianna's gonna sort it all out and we're gonna meet them for coffee later."

"Excellent," Tor stated and my head shot around to him.

"Excellent?" I queried.

He looked to me. "Of course. This is good."

"How is this good, Tor?" I asked. "We don't have magic in our world! This witch is probably a charlatan or something!"

"Uh, we so totally do have magic, girl," Phoebe put in. "You were at Selena's party with me when that chick put the whammy on that other chick for flirting with her boyfriend and she fell down the stairs."

"Her 'whammy,'" I lifted my hands and did quotation marks even around my coffee cup before dropping them and reminding my friend, "consisted of her *pushing* the flirting chick down the stairs."

"She wasn't anywhere near," Phoebe returned.

"That was what *she* said but the other girl said she was totally there because she felt her hand in her back *and* she saw her at the top of the stairs when she was on her way down," I fired back.

Tor (wisely) cut into this exchange stating, "There is no harm speaking to this Marlene and then to this witch."

I looked to Tor and told him, "Okay, you're right, honey. But what if we find out there *is* magic in this world. This woman is untried. What if she messes it all up? What if she sends us to, I don't know, some other place? What if she sends you someplace and sends me someplace else? What if Circe isn't in Korwahk but some other savage, barren place with primitive hordes? What if one of us gets sent *there?* I don't want to go to a savage, barren place with primitive hordes!"

Sensing my rising panic (though it was hard to miss), his arm around my back shifted up and his fingers curled around the back of my neck as he leaned close and said gently, "There are many what ifs, my love, but this is also the only hope we have. Right now, we are powerless. But if there is any possibility this witch can control the blue mist then we must speak to her, ascertain if she can control it, and if she can, convince her to use it to send us home."

I stared into his eyes thinking he was right at the same time thinking that sucked.

Therefore I sighed, Tor knew that meant I was giving in and he grinned, giving my neck a squeeze and pulling me to him until my cheek was resting on his shoulder.

"You guys are totally cute," Phoebe announced, smiling brightly at us then her gaze slid to Tor. "Dude, you are, like, crazy hot in a scary macho way, but still, you know how to work the cute."

I couldn't help it, I was freaking out but still, what Phoebe said made me giggle.

Then her phone rang, she jerked it up, looked at it and said to us, "Brianna." She stabbed at the screen, put it to her ear and wandered back toward the kitchen ordering bossily, "Talk to me."

She disappeared.

I heard Tor mutter, "Your friend is very strange."

Still freaking out but also still unable to help it, I wrapped my arm around his abs, pressed close and burst out laughing.

25

You Hold the Other Half of My Soul

~

We sat in the coffee house, Tor resting back against his chair, legs straight out, ankles crossed, sipping regular coffee, calm as you please.

As for me, I had my legs crossed, foot bouncing, fingers of one hand tapping on the table while slugging back my third latte (decaf due to confirmed pregnancy—yikes!), not calm by a long shot but wired like I'd actually had a shitload of caffeine.

"Love," Tor called and I turned my head to him, surprised to see his eyes on me. A minute ago, he was taking in the bustling environs of the coffee house and the busy slick sidewalks outside with avid interest.

"Yes?" I replied.

He leaned in as his hand came out and covered my tapping fingers, his fingers wrapping warmly around mine.

"Calm," he said quietly.

Yeah, right. Calm.

We were waiting for Brianna and her friend to show at the same time we were waiting for Phoebe, who was hanging at my place, having volunteered to hand Noc his packed suitcase personally and see if she could pump him for information.

I wasn't all fired up about this controlling blue mist magic business, and I wasn't because anything could go wrong.

What if the world this Circe had been to *wasn't* the Korwahk on Tor's world? What if there were a bunch of worlds and Tor and/or me were sent to one of those—where there were savages and mighty kings with the strength of ten men?

Not to mention, what if Phoebe did something to alert Noc to the fact that all was not right with the Cora he knew and set him to doing something that would not bode well for Tor and me?

And, I should mention, I wasn't hip on Phoebe being involved in any of this, especially not Noc investigating the other Cora. My friend wasn't exactly a super-sleuth. She was an administrative assistant, like me. And she couldn't be swept away to a safe fairytale land, like me. She would be stuck behind, maybe considered an accomplice in whatever Cora was up to…or something.

But Phoebe had no qualms about wading in and actually seemed excited to be in on it all.

Then again, as I had mentioned before, Phoebe was more than a little nuts.

But too much could go wrong. I wasn't all fired up to be at the mercy of blue mist magic or whatever Noc was doing with Cora, but I was equally not fired up about sticking my nose in where it might not belong.

And, it had to be said, I had no interest at all in *melting*.

"Tor—" I started, his eyes slid to the side and his jaw went scary hard.

I looked to where he was looking to see a man holding a paper cup with a cardboard sleeve staring at my crossed legs as he passed by. Tor moved, the man's eyes moved to Tor, his face blanched and he hurried away.

I looked at Tor to see him turning in his seat in order to continue scowling frighteningly at the man's back and I twisted my hand so I could squeeze his fingers.

"Honey," I called softly and his gaze sliced to me.

"Although your garments are becoming, Cora, I do not like the amount of skin they expose," he growled.

"Tor—"

He cut me off with, "You have lovely legs."

Wow.

That was nice.

I smiled at him. "Thanks, baby."

His face went as hard as his jaw.

"*Too* lovely," he went on. "And they are mine and I do not like that other men gaze at them."

Oh boy.

"Tor, this is how we dress in my world," I told him something he had to know for I was wearing another little dress with a light cardigan and high heels but there were other women around us in Capri pants, mini-skirts, skintight tees or tops with huge-ass cleavage. It wasn't like he was blind.

"I am aware of that, Cora, but that does not mean I have to *like* how you dress in this world."

I held my breath, waiting for him to say something Tor-like to piss me off, like I had to go home and change into something he preferred, say, a floor-length granny ball gown that covered me from neck to wrist to ankle. But, surprisingly, he did not say this. He let my hand go and his eyes slid around the room.

The anger faded from his face and it grew pensive.

"Tor?" I called and his focus shifted back to me.

Before I could ask what was on his mind, he told me.

"Why are you not taken in this world?"

"Sorry?" I asked.

"You are very beautiful," he stated as if this was fact and my belly melted and continued to melt as he carried on, "Far more beautiful than any woman I have seen not only in my own world but especially in this one. There is no compare."

"Tor," I whispered, my heart growing light.

"This does not make sense to me. If the Cora of my world had not been destined for me, men would fight battles for her. They *did* write songs and poems to her beauty. She might not be likable but that didn't mean her beauty was not desirous and greatly admired. You hold not only her beauty but a kind heart and a sharp wit. It is..." he paused, "*strange* that no man has claimed you."

Jeez, I loved this guy.

"Um...the dating game is different in this world and—" I started.

"Dating game?"

"Uh...wooing," I explained. "You know, courting."

He shook his head and stated, "Rubbish."

I tipped my head to the side and replied, "No, honey, it's true."

His eyes held mine. Then he leaned in, reached across the table between us and again took my hand. I studied the look on his face and twisted my body to face him, leaning in too, giving him my full attention.

When he had it, he spoke. "Cora, I have been thinking about this, noting your men's response to you, your people's response to *us*, and it occurs to me that there may be other powers at work here."

Great. Other powers at work.

Fantastic.

Just what we needed.

"What do you mean?" I whispered.

"You are not claimed in this world. This is unnatural. With your beauty, your character—"

"Tor, honestly, it's different here. It's *totally* natural. Good women constantly—"

He shook his head and squeezed my hand. "It is unnatural."

"Tor—"

"I'm a man, in your world or mine. Believe me, my love, this is *unnatural*," he stated firmly.

Okay, I couldn't argue with him being a man. He was definitely that.

I leaned in further and asked, "What are you thinking?"

"People observe us," he remarked. I pulled in my lips and bit them because I'd noticed this too. "It is strange. I could understand men gazing at you. You're beautiful, this happens in my world too. But the way their eyes are drawn to us, not only men but women—"

"I've noticed that too," I told him.

"Something is not right about this," he told me he was feeling the same thing I was feeling.

"Why do you think that?" I asked.

"I don't think it, sweets, I *feel* it."

Oh boy.

Yeah, he was feeling the same thing I was feeling.

"And what do you feel?" I asked hesitantly.

"You do not have destinies written in the sky in your world, do you?" Tor inquired and I shook my head. "And therefore, souls are not split in this world."

I shook my head again and Tor studied me. Then he said softly, "Cora, I think you hold the other half of my soul."

I sat back swiftly, my heart clenching then beating madly.

I stared at him and said in a high-pitched voice, "*What?*"

His hand tugged mine and I leaned back in. "Minerva's magic is blue."

I shook my head but kept my eyes on his. "I don't get it."

"The vickrants aren't born, they are made. Same with the toilroys. And the hewcrows. Minerva creates them. That is why, when struck, they bleed blue magic. That is why I was offended when you suggested I bled blue."

"That's a saying in my world, Tor, about royalty—"

He squeezed my hand and I quieted. "I know, love. But this mist that took us, it is also blue."

Oh shit!

I hadn't thought of that.

"Oh my God," I whispered.

"And Minerva, she is impatient. She's been thwarted generation after generation. And I'm thinking that she knows of this world and knew of your existence. And therefore, to feed her need for evil, she split my soul but the other half she did not put in the Cora of my world. She put it in *you*."

I wanted this to be true. I really did.

But I didn't think it was true.

"Tor," I reminded him gently, "you fell in love with her on sight when you met her."

"I didn't know another her existed and I had grown up from the time I could comprehend to the time I laid eyes on her being told she was my one true love, my only, my destiny, the being that held half my soul. It would stand to reason having this ingrained since I could remember that my mind would conjure a love that was not actually there."

"She hurt you," I said softly. "You can't hurt someone if—"

"She is beautiful and I wanted the magic that was supposed to be mine but never, until I met you, did she vex me so thoroughly, unless it was shaded with disappointment as to a lost dream. Never did my blood heat with her every move, word and smile. She never wept in my presence, but every tear I saw *you* shed scored my soul and I cannot believe if I saw her weep I would experience that same feeling."

"Tor," I whispered, my hand tensing in his just as his words scored at *my* soul, but I couldn't say it wasn't a beautiful pain.

"I do not wish to remember this or remind you of it, my love, but when you came into my study carrying your birthday gift, the look on your face..." He shook his head. "I felt your hurt and I felt it so deeply, I must have felt it just as keenly as you did."

My hand tensed harder and I felt tears sting my nose. "Honey."

"And I have been away from her for great periods of time," he continued. "But I have not felt the pain that Dash shares he feels when he's separated from Rosa. And my brother wouldn't even consider another but Rosa. They have not known each other intimately, but since he's met her, he's not shared relations with any other. The very thought, he's shared, is repugnant to him. I have had others, and in doing so, for the other Cora I've felt..." one of his broad shoulders lifted in a slight shrug, "*nothing*."

I had nothing to say to that because there was nothing to say.

Except the fact that, if I was who he thought I was to him, and the idea of another woman was repugnant, that was a little bit of a whole heck of a lot of *all right*.

Because I felt the same.

It was only Tor for me.

And I knew down to my soul that was the way it'd always be.

Tor interrupted my thoughts by repeating what he thought I was to him.

And he did it like the future king he was.

Decisively.

"You are my other half, Cora,' Tor declared.

I felt the tears fill my eyes.

"Oh, baby," I whispered.

"These people, your people," he tipped his head to the side to indicate the patrons of the coffee house, "they see this or sense it. This magic we have. This connection of souls. They do not understand it but they sense it."

I felt my brows rise. "Do you think?"

"Yes, I do."

"But...what would Minerva get out of that?"

"What she has got for the last five years since I met the other you. The opportunity to feed on my frustration, my heartbreak. It isn't an entire kingdom filled with despair but it's something. And if she did this, she would have my lifetime of frustration for I would never have you."

"But if the blue mist—"

"She toys," Tor interrupted me. "What, my sweet, is worse than not having the love you always knew you would have?" He didn't wait for my answer but answered himself, "What is worse is having it for a time and then having it taken away. My father taught me that with nearly every day he existed without one of his wives."

Oh *God*.

He was right.

"So, you don't think Cora is behind this?" I asked.

"I am uncertain. What I think is that Cora is as lazy as she is unkind as she is *greedy*. What I think is that Cora *does* care, too much, for my brother, which would provide added evidence that *she* is not the other half to *my* soul for she would not feel this way about Dash if she was. I have always found this strange for *I*, until I met you, have never held feelings for any other than her, and until we came to your world, I thought you *were* her. This," he squeezed my hand, "would explain her feelings for my brother."

This was true.

Tor continued.

"What I also think is that Cora may have colluded with Minerva for some gain or so she herself would not have a lifetime of watching her sister and her love be wildly happy together. What I think is that she may be sly but she has nowhere near the sharp wit you have. What I think is that Minerva chose that Cora carefully, and in doing so chose *you* carefully, knowing all this would happen. What I think is that Cora would convince herself she could play Minerva but Minerva is manipulating Cora and feeding off her unrequited love or her greed or her malice, or all three."

"But that would mean you think Cora would bring down the curse," I remarked.

He shook his head.

"I couldn't imagine even Cora would do that. She knows how the curse works. She knows me. I did not consent to meet her until after I re-secured my birthright. She knew the warrior I was. She would know I would do everything in my power to stop the curse. It is my conjecture that Cora agreed to leave that world so as not to have to watch my brother with her sister and she would assume

I would stop the curse. Either way, her being here would mean she wouldn't be in Minerva's clutches therefore the curse would never fully culminate."

"Maybe she didn't do any of that, Tor. Wouldn't Minerva just do as she wished to toy with whoever she wanted?"

"The gods are all-powerful, my love. The she-god, whose power is immense but it comes from her own conjured magic, is not. Regardless, all the gods grant us free will and we use it as we see fit, for right or for wrong. Minerva, however, capitalizes on the wrong. She insinuates herself and manipulates. She needs a being to make the wrong choices, or she uses malicious means to guide the weak to make wrong choices so that she can exploit those choices. And the other Cora, as I think you know, sweets, is very good at making the wrong choices."

Something hit me. "Do you think she had something to do with Rosa being at her house the day of the wedding?"

"Yes," Tor answered promptly. "It could be payment for Minerva agreeing to take her to your world."

"But that would start the curse! She'd have to know that," I cried.

"This would be a hideous thing to do, even for Cora, sending her delicate sister into the clutches of Minerva. But I think you have learned that Cora is not above doing something hideous, even to her own sister. That said, she would also know that I would see to it that Rosa was rescued, which I did."

The entirety of my body froze except my eyes. They blinked.

Then I whispered, "What?"

Tor studied me and as he did so I could actually feel the blood rushing to my face as the mounting anger rushed hot through my veins.

"Cora, love, listen to me," he urged, his hand holding mine so firmly I had no hope of pulling mine away which pissed...me...off.

"She's been rescued?" I asked, my voice quiet and trembling with anger.

"Yes," he answered and my eyes narrowed. "Orlando was faltering. I sent him a missive and called him to Bellebryn. I met with him and my warriors, in secret from you, and we devised a strategy. They carried this out and it was successful. Rosa was delivered safely to her parents some weeks past. Since then, she has been engaged in the re-planning of her wedding. She and her parents were asking after you but I sent a missive explaining you were not yourself and when you were better, I would take you to her."

Hmm.

It seemed during his days away from me my warrior prince had been busy.

The big, fat *jerk*!

"She was rescued some weeks past," I stated softly.

His hand gave mine a gentle tug. "Cora—"

"*She was rescued some weeks past!*" I shouted and felt the eyes of the customers swing our way.

"Cora, calm down," Tor commanded tersely.

"Calm down? Are you nuts?" I snapped. "I was worried *sick*! And you *lied* to me, telling me nothing had changed! Leading me, I might add, to believe my *sister* was in the evil clutches of a she-god!"

I felt more attention come our way as Tor leaned closer to me over the table.

"And I did not know that *you* were *you*," he reminded me. "And you did not one thing to stop Rosa from seeing Dash. I know now you didn't do anything because you had just woken in a new world. I thought then that you didn't do anything because you were *her*. I could only assume you did this because you meant Rosa harm. I could also speculate that you were united with Minerva for some despicable purpose. Because of this, I could not give you that information. You must understand that."

"What I understand, *Tor*," I hissed, trying and failing to pull my hand from his which pissed me off even more because I was sick of how bloody, stinking *strong* he was. "Is that we've been *here* and you've known *I* was *me* for two and a half days and you did not share this *information with me*!" I was fairly shouting my last and his hand gave mine a rough jerk.

"And why, my love, do you think that is? Perhaps because you're reacting the way you're reacting right now? Or, could it be that I had hurt you gravely prior to us coming to this world, so gravely, you fled from me and I watched you tumble down a flight of marble, *bloody* stairs, smashing your head and bruising your body in the process? Bruises you still carry on a beautiful body that is bearing my child? A child we were both extremely fortunate didn't abort upon this accident? And, just after that, holding you unconscious in my arms and wondering if you'd ever wake up, suddenly I was in a new world, with you angry and hurt, pushing me away. And, by the gods, I'd just come to understand you were who you are and I was in love with you. So perhaps I had other things on my mind than the fact that your sister is happy, healthy and has decided to change her wedding bouquet from orange blossoms and jasmine to roses and daisies because she thinks the scent of jasmine will clash violently with the blossoms?"

I stared at him.

Then I breathed, "You're in love with me?"

"Gods, Cora, I just told you you're the other half to my soul."

"You're in love with me?" I repeated.

He leaned back in his chair then tipped his head and looked at the ceiling to which he muttered, "Deliver me."

"Tor," I called, tugging his hand lightly and feeling something swelling inside me. Swelling fast. So fast, I was going to burst at any second.

He looked at me and raised his brows.

"Everything is right in your world," I told him quietly.

"Yes, Cora, everything is right in my world."

"The curse is no longer pending. Rosa is saved," I went on.

"Yes, love, I just told you that."

"So if we can get back, get Dash safely married to Rosa, then the land will be safe for our generation."

"And you married to me," he stated firmly.

"And me married to you," I whispered softly.

He glared at me.

"Then all will be well," I whispered.

"Yes, Cora, all will be well," he semi-repeated with obvious strained patience.

"So that means," I kept whispering, "I can tell Mom and Dad and Phoebe that, when I go back with you, it will just be you and our child and me and my sister, alive and happy, in a fairytale land and they'll feel better letting me go."

I watched Tor's body go still. Then I watched his face get soft and his eyes get warm.

Then he whispered, "Yes, my love, that's what it means."

"That will make me feel better," I whispered back.

He stared at me about a nanosecond before, without letting my hand go, he stood, rounded the table, pulled me out of my chair and into his arms where he plastered me to his body and laid a wet, hot, fantastic and very long kiss on me that I returned all the while melting into his arms.

When he lifted his head, I looked in his eyes and whispered, "I love you, my prince."

At my words, Tor smiled his freaking unbelievably beautiful smile.

At that moment we were hit with a wave of sound when a loud, spontaneous cheer went up in the coffee house.

"All right, dawg!" some guy yelled.

I felt heat hit my cheeks and I pulled in my lips. Tor's smile just got bigger.

"Jeez, you guys. Seriously. You keep that up, you need to get a room, like, *pronto*," Phoebe said and I turned my head to see my grinning friend, her friend Brianna who I had met a couple of times and another woman joining our table.

The other woman was gazing with open fascination at Tor and I knew she was the Circe back in the other world's friend. And I knew she knew Tor was from a parallel universe.

And I also knew that my crazy life was about to get better…or decidedly worse.

Oh boy.

26

Torn Away

~

I was sitting on the armchair in my living room, feet up on the coffee table, legs bent, pad of paper on my knees, making lists.

Tor was stretched out on the couch, his fingers wrapped around a bottle of beer that was resting on his abs, his eyes on a baseball game on the TV.

So...totally...*a man.*

This was after our conversation with Phoebe, Brianna and Marlene.

It was after we had gone by the mall to get Tor a cell.

And after we had come home, Tor stopping blocks away and getting out of the car to walk back just in case the apartment was under surveillance (somehow, he was standing outside my door by the time I got in the driver's seat, drove home, found a place to park on the street and walked up to my apartment proving he wasn't just strong, my man was fast, and I hoped stealthy).

I'd made Tor a dinner of spiral pasta, spaghetti sauce with meatballs, garlic bread, salad and beer (for him, diet root beer, for me) and Tor had shared he liked this meal far more than bologna sandwiches and Cheetos.

Obviously, we followed dinner with red velvet cake because that cake could be a week old and it would still kick ass.

At the coffee house, we had learned from Phoebe that Noc had not given her anything.

Not that first thing.

Except he appeared pissed that, first, she was there and not Cora (as anyone who was getting the boot would be) and second, that he was getting the boot without explanation and for what appeared to be no reason.

She'd tried to pry but he was closed up tight, and after his hand gripped the handle of the suitcase, he didn't hang around long.

She did stress, however, that he *appeared* pissed but she got the sense he felt relief and that mostly he just wanted his stuff. She also reported that he seemed distracted, acted like he had better things to do and that he just wanted to get the hell out of there.

This was a disappointment but not unexpected.

What was *not* a disappointment but was a shock (some of that shock good, as in possibly very good, some of it was bad, as in really bad) was all that we learned from Marlene.

First, we learned that the alternate Circe, in an effort to bring back the, uh, *real* Circe, had gone all out to find a witch in this world who would be able to bring the real Circe back to her world (how's *that* for confusing).

Then we learned, thankfully, as Tor confirmed from Marlene's additional information, that this world *was*, indeed, Korwahk. And the witch had provided the information that there weren't an infinite number of worlds. There was Tor's and there was ours.

Then it was confirmed that Circe was sent back not by the witch. Circe's King Lahn had found some means to transport her back to him.

However, the witch had, with great confidence, assured Circe's father who assured Marlene that Circe was safely back where she wanted to be. That said, although the witch did not send Circe back, Marlene was relatively certain (relatively, yikes!) that she had the power to send Tor and I back.

And Marlene had also, prior to meeting with us, called Circe's dad, found out the location and swung by this witch's trailer (yes, *trailer*) only to discover she was no longer there. In fact, the whole trailer was gone.

This was bad.

What was a surprise was that Marlene had said the witch was old, she was blind and her name was *Clarabelle*.

At that, I gasped and Tor's eyes sliced to me. He showed and shared no response even when I quizzed him about it later in the car telling him I thought this was good news.

His reply was simply, "You are not the other Cora, this Noc is not me and this witch is not the other Clarabelle. We have no idea of her character. What we do know is she is a witch and anyone who dabbles in magic is suspect. We must tread cautiously."

I had to admit, I was totally down with that.

I questioned Marlene more about Circe's other world and learned that what Tor and Phoebe had said was true. Things for Circe, like me, had not started out all that great with Circe and her King Lahn and this was to say the least (she was, indeed, hunted, "claimed,"—as in *raped* by this King Lahn—then installed as his queen).

But somehow he rallied and they ended up getting on well, as in *very* well. So well she was desperately in love with him, desperately heartbroken when she'd left him, totally into having his child and apparently blissfully happy when she got back, gave him twins and was living her life like a queen (literally).

She was so happy, she was totally fine with leaving everything behind and living with this guy in his primitive world for the rest of her natural-born days.

The semi-good news about all this was that Circe's dad had been able to get a message to her in her world and she was able to return one, setting her dad (and Marlene's) mind at ease about her situation.

The reason this was *semi*-good news was that, although Circe had been back there for a while, communications between worlds were unpredictable, and although Marlene told me that Circe's dad kept trying and Circe had promised her dad she would too, he had not heard from her again.

This sucked.

However, where there was hope, well...there was hope.

Obviously, Queen Circe (or Queen Circe, the True Golden Warrior Queen of Korwahk, how's that for a kickass title), her brute king and their growing brood didn't take vacations in Seattle, which also sucked.

We learned from Marlene the reason Circe did not go back and forth was because the witch, Clarabelle, informed Circe's father—and the *other* Circe (who was, more news, a sorceress) corroborated this—that it took vast amounts of power to travel between worlds.

There was not only little communication with the other world, what little there was was random, not in anyone's control and therefore the witch did not know who was controlling the travel from the other side, and she could not guarantee she could get messages from there or to there to bring anyone back. And even if she did, it would be a one-way trip as, once she brought them here, she couldn't get them home as getting them here would use up all her magic. It would take decades for her magic to recover enough for her to attempt another trip.

See?

Totally sucked.

So, when Circe made her decision to send the message to her father that she was staying, this meant Circe knew it was King Lahn's world or her own.

Circe chose King Lahn.

I got where she was coming from though I would have preferred to be able to travel back and forth at will, say, having my child in my world where medicine was more advanced and so my parents could meet him or her. And, of course, when the Oscars pre-shows were on because that was my most favorite event of the year (it was all about the dresses and, I might add, the hairstyles and jewelry).

Alas, this was not possible.

But I'd already made my choice, no matter how difficult. And I made it because Tor could not be a prince in my world, his people depended on him and he'd expended great effort (and had the scars to prove it) to rebuild his kingdom. I couldn't ask him to give up enjoying the triumphant result of something he felt so strongly about. He gave it five years of his sweat and blood and his efforts to regain it were marked on his face and body. Nor could I ask him to give up the eventual succession to rule a kingdom that was his birthright.

I was an administrative assistant, only Dave depended on me and the only wounds I ever got were from paper cuts.

I didn't think about my parents or Phoebe or Dave or the Oscar pre-shows or any of that. I couldn't. I had to focus. I was in love. I was pregnant. My man was far away from his family, who he cared about, and his people, who depended on him.

And I had a sister to get to know.

The rest I would deal with when the time came. And if I couldn't then I knew Tor would help me, or at least do everything he could to try.

Before we left the coffee house, Marlene had turned to Tor.

"You hear tales of her?" she asked.

"Indeed," he answered.

"And she's, um...*happy?*" she went on, her voice low, her eyes intense and Tor's answer obviously meant the world to her.

At this, I tried not to look at Phoebe but that didn't mean I didn't search for her hand on the table, find it and hold it tight.

"They are said to be a love match. She is revered as a goddess. So yes, I would assume she's happy," Tor replied quietly.

She nodded then inquired, "Is Korwahk far from your kingdom?"

"Very far," he answered and she looked disappointed but nodded again then she licked her lips and looked away.

So I called her name and when I had her eyes, I asked, "Is there something you want?"

Marlene studied me. Then she nodded.

"I'd like to get a message to her, just...to let her know I miss her and I'm glad she's happy," Marlene said quietly.

Hmm.

Marlene was sweet and seemed quiet, unlike Phoebe who was a different kind of sweet but not all that quiet. But it would seem Marlene was Circe's BFF just like Phoebe was mine. This made me smile at her but it also made my hand grow tighter in Phoebe's.

"We will see to that upon our return," Tor offered. Marlene looked hopefully at him, but Tor went on, sharing honestly, "However, this land is far away, routes of communication are not dependable, this king is nomadic and therefore I cannot assure you it will reach her but I can assure you we will try."

I fought the urge to kick him under the table for it was cool he was being honest but she didn't have to know about the undependable routes of communication, for goodness sake.

She nodded at Tor and looked at me. "He took her when I was with her. I was actually standing right next to her. I saw her disappear. She just...melted away."

Holy crap!

There it was again!

Marlene continued.

"And we'd just been talking about how she didn't want to go back when, suddenly, she was gone."

At this, Phoebe clenched my hand and I clenched hers right back.

"I know everything is okay with her now and she's happy but..." Marlene shrugged. "It would have been cool for her to, you know, meet someone from home, to, like, know she wasn't alone. It sucks your kingdom is so far away."

"Maybe, after I have the baby, Tor and I can take an adventure," I suggested to bring that hope back to her face. It worked, her face brightened but Tor's grew dark. "Just saying, maybe..." I muttered in his direction.

His eyes went back to the ceiling.

When Marlene left she promised to do what she could to find this Clarabelle and get back to us *tout de suite*.

But my thoughts were, Clarabelle was AWOL and I had been on Tor's world for nearly two months. This meant we could be here that long, or longer. And who knew when or if we would find Clarabelle.

So, as far as I was concerned, I was moving forward, business as usual.

"Sweets?" Tor called and I looked from my list to him. "Put down your paper and come lie with me," he commanded.

I looked at the TV then back to him.

"I've got to do this and I'm not into baseball," I replied.

"I'll change it," he returned.

"I've got to do this," I told him, his eyes went to my knees then back to mine.

"You can do it later," he stated.

"No, I want to get it out of the way."

He turned to his side, gave me his full attention, and when he did I noticed the change in his eyes and I noticed it in three specific parts of my body.

"Put it aside," he said softly. "And we'll both go to your indoor waterfall."

Those three specific parts of my body twanged at the thought of a shower with Tor.

"Five minutes, honey," I replied just as softly. "I'll be done and we can shower."

He rested his head on his hand, elbow in the couch. "What are you doing?"

"Making lists," I answered, looking back down at my paper.

"Lists of what?" he asked and I looked back at him.

"Contingency plans."

His eyebrows rose so I explained.

"We don't know how long we're going to be here. So, if we're here awhile, like I was in your world awhile, there are things I have to do and things I don't want you to miss."

I looked back down at the paper and started enumerating.

"I have to go to the doctor, get the pregnancy confirmed medically, get some vitamins or whatever, start that whole gig. I want you, Mom, Dad and me to go to the seafood place where Dad asked Mom to marry him and where we go every year for all our birthdays. I want to take you for a drive down the coast so you can see all my world isn't dreary and some of it is actually really gorgeous. Since you're interested in baseball, I want to take you to a Seattle Mariners game before the season ends. And I want you to go over to Phoebe's so she can make you one of her dirty martinis, which are *divine*. And I forgot to buy you gum at the store so we have to get you some gum so you can try—"

"Cora,"Tor cut in and my head came up.

"What?"

"Put your list aside and come here," he ordered.

"Tor, I have to put this down on paper so I don't forget anything."

"Put it aside and come here," he semi-repeated.

"Honey, you took time out in your world to show me places and allow me to meet people and I want to give you what—"

"Love, put it down and *come here*." His voice was very firm and I'd been so intent on my list, I'd missed the look on his face.

But I wasn't missing it now.

I put the list down and went there.

When I was stretched out full on top of him, he lifted both sides of my hair and held it at the back of my head with one hand, his other arm closing around my waist.

"You can go back to your list in a second but when you do, you need to change it. You need to list all the things *you* want to do, people *you* want to see, in order of priority. Then we will do these things and see these people," he told me.

"But I want you—" I started but stopped when his head lifted and he brushed his lips against mine.

He dropped his head and whispered, "It is not me giving up everything for love, my sweet."

My heart clenched just as his arm tightened.

Tor kept talking and he did it with that tender look in his eyes and a low rumble in his voice.

"You must fill the time you have left here with the people you want to see and places you want to be and I'll experience your world through that. I want you to have that. You'll need it. And it will allow me to feel more at peace as our decades together pass in my world knowing that I was able to give that to you before you gave everything for me."

Tears suddenly and swiftly filled my eyes.

God but *God*, I loved this man.

"Baby," I whispered as one slid down my cheek, but it didn't make it very far before Tor let go of my hair and his thumb swept it away.

"Now, kiss me, my love, and then finish your list so we can shower together."

I stared down through my watery eyes at my gorgeous warrior prince.

Then I dropped my mouth to his and both of his arms closed around me tight. I tipped my head to the side, he slanted his the other way, my mouth opened but before his tongue slid inside and I could taste the gloriousness of him I felt myself flying through the air.

Yes, *flying through the air!*

I cried out in shock but my cry stopped abruptly when my back slammed painfully against the wall and blue sparks shot out around me.

Oh God.

I knew what that meant.

Oh God!

No!

"Tor!" I shouted after I slid down the wall, landed on my booty and lifted my head.

But the couch, the whole couch, was shrouded in blue mist. So shrouded, I couldn't see him, not even a little bit of him.

Nothing.

No!

"*Tor!*" I shrieked, jumping to my feet and taking one step toward him only to feel an invisible hand plant itself in my chest and I was shoved right back against the wall, violently, blue sparks flying again when I landed and that pressure at my chest did not go away.

I struggled against the invisible hold that held me pinned against the wall, pushing forward and screeching, "*Tor! No! Oh my God! Please, no!*"

Through my shrieks I heard an evil cackle I'd only heard once before. My blood turned to ice, the blue mist disappeared from my couch and the invisible hold that had me in its control melted away.

My couch was empty.

Tor was gone.

I collapsed to the floor not only in despair but in sudden pain. Excruciating, unbearable pain that made me curl my body automatically into a tight, protective ball.

And I knew what that pain was.

I knew exactly what it was.

Half my soul had just been torn away.

27

Get Your Shoes

~

Two weeks later…

"Nothing?" I asked, the cell phone pressed tight to my ear, my knees pressed tight to my chest, my tush on the tiled floor of the bathroom.

"I'm sorry, Cora. She's nowhere to be found. Harold and I asked all the people the other Circe talked to, went to all the places she told us she went and no one knows anything about Clarabelle," Marlene answered in my ear.

I closed my eyes tight and dropped my forehead to my knees.

"Remember, I have money," I whispered into the phone. "You can use all of it. I have seventy-five thousand dollars. Remember that."

"I remember, Cora. But there's no information, even information to pay for and you may need that money," Marlene said quietly back and I knew even through the phone she could hear my voice. She could hear the pain I lived with every day. The pain that got worse with every fucking *second*.

"And the other Circe, her power—?" I tried but Marlene cut me off.

"She says it's growing but she doesn't have enough, not near enough. She's asking around. She says there's a great deal of magic around New Orleans. She asked me to tell you if she finds someone she'll let us know immediately and you can fly there. But you need to save your money, Cora. She says if she can find someone, the amount of magic they'll need to use, it'll be expensive."

I lifted my head. "If there's anything I can do…" I trailed off because she knew, I'd said that a million times before.

Two weeks ago, Phoebe and I had been with Marlene and Circe's dad, Harold, every step of the way.

But with every dead end, every disappointment, the pain got worse and Harold and Phoebe seeing me endure that had put their proverbial foot down. When I ignored them, Phoebe told on me to my dad. I tried to ignore Dad but he told on me to Mom and well, that was that.

"Harold, Phoebe and I are doing it, Cora. I promise. And Brianna is asking around too, your folks, Harold's buddies, Circe's old friends. But if there is, I'll tell you. I promise, honey, okay?"

I sucked in breath and my voice trembled when I replied in a whisper, "Okay."

"We'll keep looking," she told me.

"Okay," I whispered.

"We won't give up."

I closed my eyes tight again.

I opened them and said, "Thanks."

"Hang in there, chin up. We'll get you home."

Home.

God. Yes, home.

Home was Tor.

I needed to get home.

"Okay," I said softly.

"'Bye, honey."

"'Bye, Marlene."

I disconnected and then called the private investigator I'd hired. He didn't pick up so I left a voicemail. It was my third message that day. I knew I was bugging him but I didn't care and he was ticking me off because he didn't seem to be doing anything and I knew this because the asshole never called and therefore nothing was getting done.

He was overweight, had bad teeth and stared at my breasts the whole time I sat in his office. He also demanded a five thousand dollar retainer that I thought was a little steep but I gave it to him. I'd heard from him once since and he said he was "working on it" though it sounded like he was at the racetrack.

I sat with my butt to the floor and stared at my bathroom cabinets thinking maybe I needed a different private investigator.

Then I sucked in breath in order to move.

It hurt to move. It hurt to sit. It hurt to lie down. It hurt to sleep. It hurt to *breathe*.

And every day, it hurt worse.

I wasn't bleeding. My skin wasn't ripping open. My hair wasn't falling out.

But I was dying. Dying inside, I could feel it.

Slowly, I walked through the bathroom, opened the door then walked out the door, through the bedroom and into my living room. I heard the murmuring voices and stopped, leaning against the wall to hold myself up and I listened.

"I'm worried," Mom whispered.

"Me too," Phoebe whispered back. "It gets worse every day."

"Is she taking her vitamins?" Dad asked as if vitamins would help with *this*.

"I don't know. She picked up the prescription the doctor gave her when he confirmed her pregnancy. I took her to get them myself. But I don't know if she's taking them," Mom said.

"One of us should stay with her all the time," Dad stated. "Make sure she's taking her vitamins. Make sure she's sleeping. Make sure she's eating."

"Agreed," Phoebe said instantly. "I can move in, sleep here at night."

"I can take the days," Mom added.

"We'll do weekends, Phoebe, give you a break," Dad told my friend and I closed my eyes again.

I couldn't endure another weekend without Tor. I didn't know if I could endure another second without him much less another whole week.

"She has that other Cora's money, Phoebe," Dad went on. "But Dara and I saved twenty-five grand for Cora's wedding. You, Harold and Marlene find someone who knows something, who can help and they won't do it without getting paid, you need it, you add that. You hear?"

I opened my eyes.

My dad.

God, he was such a great freaking guy.

And twenty-five grand for my wedding? That was way cool and that would have given me a kickass wedding, what he knew I'd always wanted.

Yeah, my dad was a great, freaking guy.

"Yeah, Forrest," Phoebe whispered.

There was silence then from Mom, her voice dripping with concern, "If she's going through this, what's Tor going through?"

I twisted my neck to press my cheek against the wall.

The very thought of that hurt too because I knew he was experiencing the same thing. My mighty warrior prince, struck low with this hideous pain. No one could endure this. No one. Not even him.

And certainly not me.

"She told me she holds half his soul and he's feeling the same as she is," Phoebe answered my mom.

"God, that man. I can't imagine—" Mom whispered.

"Don't," my father cut in. "Only imagine a solution to this problem. Phoebe and her friends will find a way. Negative thinking never helped anything."

"You're right, my love," Mom whispered.

"I know, my love," Dad whispered back.

My love.

I could take no more.

I forced myself forward and stopped in the kitchen doorway, seeing three pairs of startled eyes turn to me, eyes that were set in haggard, worried faces.

"You should be lying down," Mom ordered, bustling forward.

"I need some alone time," I told her.

"Sweetie, you can have it. Go to your room and—" Mom began.

"I need you guys to leave," I announced.

Her eyes got big and her torso shifted back.

"Cora, sweetie, that's not—"

"I know you're worried about me. I heard you talking, and even if I didn't it's impossible to miss. And okay, you want to watch over me. That's cool. But give me an hour. Just an hour. I just need to rest and clear my head and not think of you in here whispering or worrying. I just need to be alone and quiet for an hour. Then you can come back. Can you give me that?"

"We can be quiet here, sweetheart," Dad said softly.

"It's not the same, Dad," I replied.

"Cora, you're not too—" Phoebe began and that was when I lost it.

I'd been holding it together. Holding it by a thread. Holding on to that thread for two weeks, living for two long weeks with the constant feeling that thread was going to slip from my fingers. And, just then, I lost hold of that thread. It wasn't nice, it wasn't good but that was when I lost it.

"*I know what I am, all right?*" I shouted, shut my eyes against the worry on their faces and nodded my head sharply once. I opened my eyes and looked at them. "I'm hurting and I'm sorry and none of this is in anyone's control and you're all dragged into it and you're worried about me and you're giving up time and energy and it's making me feel guilty on top of everything else and I just need to be *free* of that. Just for an hour."

"You didn't do anything to feel guilty for, honey," Mom said quietly and I looked at her.

"I know that Mom but that doesn't make me feel any less guilty," I returned.

She bit her lip and I sucked in another painful breath and snatched back that thread, holding on to it for dear life.

Then I said gently, "I'm sorry. I love you guys. I loved you before you went all out to help me, to help Tor, worrying about me. I'll *always* love you, no matter what happens. But can I just have an hour to try to forget? Can I just have an hour alone? And then we can all go back to worrying."

And, for me, go back to the pain…though the pain never left.

Ever.

They all stared at me.

"Just an hour," I whispered. "Please?"

Mom looked at Dad. Dad looked at Mom. Phoebe studied me.

Finally Dad's eyes came to me. "Fine, sweetheart, one hour. Just one."

I slouched against the doorjamb such was my relief. "Thanks, Dad."

He came forward, wrapped a hand around the back of my head, pulled me to him and kissed my forehead. Mom came forward, squeezed my hand and kissed my cheek. Phoebe came forward and gave me a tight hug.

They left and they did this without me leaving the doorway to the kitchen.

After I heard the door close I stared for a long time at my kitchen, which was still full of Tor's food. I was taking my vitamins (of course I was, forcing them down for the baby) and I had been eating. I wasn't hungry but I was pregnant so I was eating for our child. But Tor bought so fucking much food…

I closed my eyes against the memory. Then I moved to the couch, lay down, grabbed the remote, turned on my stereo and did what I'd done what had to be a million times since he was torn away from me.

I played "Crash into Me," which was already queued up and ready to go.

When it was done, I played it again.

And when it was done, I played it again.

And again.

"Baby," I whispered to the ceiling, the tears streaming out the sides of my eyes, down my temples, drenching my hair. "Come back to me. Find some way to come back to me. I swear, swear, *swear*, if you come back to me, I won't ever vex you again. Never again. I won't be overly friendly to people who are common and I won't save half-dead birds and I won't sneak apples to Salem in the stables...or to *all* the horses in the stables, though I don't think you knew I did that. And I won't rumple children's hair. I'll be the perfect princess. I'll be your perfect princess. I'll live every second doing everything I can to make you feel nothing but happiness, to make you want to do nothing but smile your beautiful, beautiful smile. I swear. I *swear*," I forced through my blocked throat. "Just come back...honey, come back and crash into me."

My throat clogged, there came a loud banging at my door and I jumped.

Jeez, that couldn't have been an hour.

Heaving a sigh, I rolled off the couch, moved to the door and looked out the peephole.

Oh my God!

My heart flew into my throat. I unlocked the door, threw it open and flung myself in Tor's arms.

"Baby," I whispered, my arms around his shoulders, my face in his neck, my body pressing into his as I felt his hands, his long, strong fingers close around my hips. "Honey, oh God, I missed you. God, baby," I moaned in his throat.

"Cora?" his beautiful voice sounded.

I pulled my face from his neck, moved my hands to either side of his head and pulled him to me, pressing my mouth to his. I slid my tongue inside and I kissed him. Burrowing deep into his body, holding on to his head tight, I kissed him with everything I had.

His arms closed around me, he shuffled me into the apartment while still kissing me and I vaguely felt and heard him close the door with his foot.

I slid my hands to his neck and pulled away, looking into his gorgeous, light-blue eyes.

"Let's go to bed. Right now. Hurry, I need you, honey. Like our first time, just like then. I need you *now*," I whispered frantically, wanting him, *needing* to be connected to him, as close as I could get. I was moving backwards, trying to take him with me but his body locked and he held firm.

Then he spoke.

"Jesus, babe, what's got into you? Two weeks ago you blow me off and now you're all over me. What the fuck?"

I yanked out of his arms, took two steps back, my eyes scanning his face.

No scar.

Not Tor.

Noc.

I closed my eyes and dropped my head so my face was in my hands.

Not Tor.

Noc.

Bloody hell! I was going to start crying again.

I was right. I started crying again. The tears came back, the pain came back and my shoulders started heaving, wracked with my sobs.

"Cora, fuckin' hell, what—?" Noc asked softly, his arms sliding around me but I tore away from him, moving quickly back two more steps, lifting a hand.

"Stay away from me!" I yelled and his face switched instantly from concern to anger.

"What's with the multiple personalities, babe?" he asked, crossing his arms on his chest.

I stared at him.

God, except for the scar and the words he used, he was the same. The absolute same. Every inch of him, down to his voice.

Pain sliced anew, shredding me inside. I couldn't take it. I couldn't endure him being there.

"Get out," I whispered.

"See, that's not gonna happen," he told me. He dropped his arms and took a step toward me. I took a step back and he stopped and put his hands to his hips. "You got somethin' to tell me?" he asked.

"No," I replied honestly. "I don't have anything to tell you."

"Nothin' about an appointment with an obstetrician and fillin' a prescription for prenatal vitamins?" he prompted, his jaw hard, his eyes glittering angry.

Oh shit.

He went on, "Babe, I used protection but shit happens and I gotta know if the kid you're carrying is mine."

"It isn't," I said swiftly.

"That's interesting since I know you haven't been with anyone else but me."

Oh *shit*.

"Well, you're wrong. I have," I returned.

"Hard to do when I got your ass under surveillance," he told me and my mouth dropped open. "You're eight weeks pregnant and I know some other guy was around a couple weeks ago. But other than that, it was you, your shopping, your takeaway, your games, your crazy-assed driving that nearly killed pedestrians every time you got behind the fuckin' wheel…and *me*."

"You had me under surveillance?" I whispered.

"Clue in, Cora, I'm a cop. Jesus, fuck, are you that dumb?" he asked. "Christ, you found my fuckin' badge, looked right at it, held it in your hand for fuck's sake, lookin' at it like you'd never seen anything like that in your life. I was comin' out of the bathroom and I saw you. You put it right back where you found it, diggin' through my clothes, I might add, and after, you didn't change a thing. We were together for weeks after that and you didn't change one fuckin' thing. Freaked me out, didn't know your game, didn't expect to *be* at your place with my badge but you jumped me and I had no choice but to roll with it. And in the end it worked for me. No offense, babe, but you aren't too bright unless you're countin' cards so I figured, what the fuck?"

Oh boy.

Cora would do that because she'd actually never seen anything like a badge in her life.

My back went straight and I informed him. "I know you're a cop."

He jerked his chin up and his eyes went hard. "So, you actually *aren't* too bright and thought you were playin' me," he decided then leaned in, his face carved from stone. "Advice. You gotta get better at the game." I stared at him and he went on, "Like, say, that kiss you gave me before you booted my ass out, or better, the one you just gave me. *That's* bein' better at the game."

"Why are you telling me this?" I asked. "Doesn't this interfere with your investigation?"

"I brought down the games a week ago, babe. My guess is, you sensed that shit was goin' down since you packed my stuff and stopped goin' to the games.

I thought you were history and, sorry to say, I wasn't too broken up about it. That was until continued surveillance on you gave me the info you were goin' to an OB/GYN and gettin' pregnancy vitamins. Unfortunately that meant I had to come back."

"Why were you continuing to watch me?"

"Because you like the game, Cora. You like the money. You like the clothes and shoes and all that shit." He threw an arm out toward my bedroom. "You like it better, thinkin' you're fuckin' someone over, counting cards. You get off on it. In fact, I reckon it's the only thing you get off on. You got off on it so much, you didn't even care you were fuckin' a cop. You led me to one racket. It's in your blood. You need your fix, need it so much you made me and, still, you didn't stop so I knew you'd find another game so we stayed on you."

Oh.

That made sense. It was annoying but it made sense.

A thought hit me. "Is it normal operating procedure to sleep with people you're investigating?"

He crossed his arms on his chest and his eyes moved the length of me from top to toe and back again. "Babe, you were all over me. You're hot. I thought *it* would be hot. It was not. But it went that way, you thought you had me by the balls and I had to go the way it went."

"That's not very nice," I whispered, stung, though I didn't know why since he wasn't talking about me and his eyes narrowed as his head tipped to the side.

"Not very nice?" he asked back, his voice soft.

"To talk that way," I explained. "About, um…me."

He stared at me through narrowed eyes then he leaned back an inch. "Well, fuck me," he murmured. "She's got feelings under all that ice."

"No," I whispered. "*She* doesn't, but *I* do."

His head jerked then he asked, "Come again?"

I stared at him and as I did, it came to me.

I had a previous address and a first name, Clarabelle.

And he was a cop and cops had access to databases that had all sorts of information.

And it would kill me, being around someone who looked like Tor and sounded like Tor, but if I could convince him to help me find Clarabelle, I was going to do it.

The problem was I had no freaking clue how to convince him.

"I'm in love with another man," I said quietly.

"Well, congratulations," he replied, his mouth not quite but almost curling in a sneer.

My mind whirled and then I hit on it. A tactic that had worked before with my boss Dave.

Soap opera.

"And," I tried, "you knew Rosa, not Cora. I'm Cora and Rosa is my twin sister. Identical twins but she's the evil twin. She's a pain in my ass. She was watching my place when I was—"

"Jesus," he cut me off, his brows going up. "Seriously?"

I stared at him.

Okay, clearly Noc was not as bubbleheaded as Dave, my boss, who bought the amnesia story without a peep.

Shit.

"No, that was a lie," I admitted.

"No shit?" he asked sarcastically.

Shit!

I decided to stall in order to come up with a different strategy so I asked, "Do you want a beer?"

"No, I wanna talk about what you're gonna do about our kid," he answered.

"I think you need a beer," I told him.

"No, babe. I need to discuss this mess so I know what I'm dealin' with. What you gotta get is, I'm a cop. You have the kid, can't say that'll make me happy, but I'll take care of *my kid*. What I won't do is bust my ass payin' a shitload of child support so *you* can have fourteen hundred dollar shoes. And you'll also have to get off your lazy ass to do somethin' other than countin' cards and goin' shoppin' 'cause my kid's ma is not gonna be doin' that shit. *None* of it. You get me?"

Hmm.

Seemed he had Cora's ticket too.

Not good.

"I'm getting you a beer," I stated and started to the kitchen.

He caught my arm as I walked by him and I turned and tipped my head up as he exploded, "Fuck, Cora, I don't want a fuckin' beer!"

That was when I announced, "I'm in love with a man from an alternate universe. It isn't your child I'm carrying, it's his. He looks exactly like you except he has a scar on his face…"

I turned fully to him, reached up and touched his temple lightly. His face, I noted distractedly, was frozen with shock but my eyes moved to my finger against his perfect skin.

"Starting here," I whispered then curved my finger down his cheekbone. "And ending here."

"Fuckin' shit, you're insane," he whispered back. His eyes, when mine shifted to them, were moving over my face.

But I didn't really hear him. I was transfixed by his face, so like Tor's, so beloved, but not Tor's.

"He's a warrior," I whispered. "He has scars here," I moved my finger to touch his chest where Tor's scar was. "And here." I kept whispering, touching another place on his chest. "And…here." I finished with another touch and tipped my head back to look from his chest to his eyes. "He has your eyes, he has your voice and he has half my soul."

Noc didn't speak, just looked in my eyes.

So I kept going.

"I know you think it's crazy. It sounds crazy. It *is* crazy. But it's true. There are two worlds, the same people in each world. Cora from that world came here. You know her, not me. I'm not cold. I can't count cards. I don't even know how to play poker. And I'm nice. I make people laugh. They care about me. When I was there, I met you but the you of there. And I fell in love with the you of there and I'm having your baby…" I shook my head. "*His* baby. He was the man your people saw but I'm guessing they didn't get a good look at him or they would have told you he looks exactly like you."

His head jerked, his gaze grew intense, my heart leaped and I leaned closer to him.

"They did," I whispered. "They said he looked exactly like you."

"They thought he *was* me," Noc replied, his voice quiet.

"Did they get video? Pictures?" I asked hopefully, because if I never made it back to Tor, at least maybe I could convince Noc to give me the pictures.

"Only of the back of his head," Noc answered.

I closed my eyes and leaned back an inch.

"Babe," he called and I opened my eyes. When I did he said not a word, just stared into my eyes then his gaze moved over my face before it came back to me. "Jesus, fuck," he murmured. "You believe this shit."

"Only because it's true," I replied then I asked softly, "Standing here talking to you, am I anything at all like her? And looking around my place, is it anything at all like it was when she was here?"

His jaw clenched and he didn't even bother looking at my tidy apartment.

This was my answer.

It wasn't and *I* wasn't.

"At birth, in his world, half of his soul was separated from him and put in me. Now that we've met, our souls united so when he was pulled away, our souls were torn apart," I explained. "You won't ever be able to understand it, and I'm glad of that, but let me just say that the pain of having the other half of your soul ripped away doesn't feel all that nice as in..." I leaned in again and my voice carried the ache I felt inside when I finished, "*At all*."

He heard it. He may have even felt it and I knew that because it made him flinch.

Then he lifted his hand, curled it around my neck and whispered, "Cora."

I closed my eyes again and dropped my head. His touch, so strong, so warm... but not Tor's. His voice saying my name, so deep, so rough, the same...but not Tor's.

God, it fucking *hurt*.

His other hand came up. He caught me under my chin and gently pulled my head back up.

I opened my eyes and searched his face.

"You don't believe me," I stated.

"I believe *you* believe you."

I nodded and tried to move away but his hand at my neck held tighter and I stopped.

"Babe," he said gently, so gently that that one word and the way he said it proved...yes, he was sweet, probably *very* sweet. "You gotta get help."

"I know," I answered with feeling because I knew I did.

I just couldn't find her.

His hand left my chin and dropped so his arm could curve around my waist and pull me closer as he kept talking gently. "You got my kid inside you, baby, we gotta get your head sorted. After we do that, we sort out other shit, yeah?"

I sucked in breath.

He thought I was mental.

This was not going my way.

That was when I decided to bargain.

"All right, Noc. I'll make you a deal. I know someone who can get me back to Tor's world," I told him.

"Tor?"

"The other you."

His eyes flashed. "You called me that—"

"I know, the other week, when I got back and the other Cora left. Anyway, I promise to go…" I hesitated before saying, "*see* someone if you help me find the person that can help me get back to Tor. If she doesn't help me, then I'll go to someone else to help me, someone *you* pick."

"Babe—"

"It can't hurt and it won't take much. I have a first name and an address of where she used to live. If you can track her down—" I stopped speaking when his face started to get hard.

"Cora, I can't use department resources to track some random woman down. That shit isn't right."

"And sleeping with someone you're investigating is? You rolled with that, Noc. I get it but you kept rolling with it so much your clothes were in my closet." I returned and scored a point. I knew it when his eyes flashed again.

Still, he said, "Babe, I was undercover. Shit happens."

Damn.

He was right and I was getting desperate.

I tried something new.

"Okay, and the shit that happened is that you think you got me pregnant. That means you think we're connected. And that means, as the woman who you think is carrying your child, you being a cop and all, one of the good guys, you have to help me. Just look her up. You find her, you give me her address. I'll go to her."

"I'm not gonna provide you with an address so you can visit someone who's probably a whack job."

"She's not a whack job," I returned though I couldn't know that for sure. Maybe she was, but I couldn't worry about that now. "She can help."

"Babe, you got my kid inside you and this woman who might be a whack job also might be dangerous."

"I don't have your kid inside me, Noc."

His hand tightened on my neck. "Cora, you *do*."

"Noc, I *don't*," I retorted. "But okay, you think I do, then *you* can go with me to see Clarabelle."

"Clarabelle?"

"The lady I have to see."

"Cora—"

I lost patience. My hands lifted, I grabbed his shirt and fisted it in my fingers.

"All you have to do is look her up!" I cried. "That's it. Look her up, take me to her if you find her and if it doesn't work then I'll do whatever you want me to do *except*," I said sharply when he opened his mouth to speak, "get an abortion. If I can't get back to Tor and I live through this pain, I'm keeping his baby."

"Jesus," he muttered.

I twisted my fists in his shirt, got up on tiptoe and begged, "*Please*."

Noc stared down at me and he did this for a while as my heart beat hard in my chest.

Then he ordered, "Get your shoes."

My head jerked. "What?"

"Babe, get your shoes. You're comin' to the station with me. The state you're in, you aren't outta my sight."

I leaned back and his arm got tighter, his hand at my neck moving so his other arm could close around me but it did this up my back.

"Why are you taking me to the station?" I asked suspiciously.

"So we can look up this Clarabelle woman, I can take you to her then whatever you think is gonna go down is *not* gonna go down and then I can get you some *real* help."

Holy crap!

He was going to help me!

Hurrah!

I felt the pain shift, it lightened and I smiled at him the second before I let his shirt go and threw my arms around his wide shoulders.

"Thank you," I whispered into his neck.

"Fuckin' hell," he muttered but after a second, his arms gave me a squeeze.

Yep, totally a sweet guy.

Maybe, before I left this world, I should hook him up with Phoebe.

Um…no. That might be too weird.

Then again, I'd never feel it was weird because I'd be in my world with my Tor.

My Tor.

I'm coming home, baby, I sent my hope into the universe.

I pulled out of Noc's arms, gave him another bright smile and ran to get my shoes.

28

Crash into Me Part Two

~

"I cannot believe this!" Phoebe shouted in my ear.

I watched the headlights of Noc's SUV on the wet, winding coastal road, their light barely cutting through the dark night, the wispy fog and the drizzling mist, and replied, "Believe it and hurry. I've already called Mom and Dad. They're on their way."

"I'm already out the door," she told me then asked, "He's with you right now?"

My head turned to the left and I saw Noc's profile in the dashboard lights.

I looked forward again, "Yep."

"Holy shit. Is it weird? Are you okay?"

"Totally and totally not."

"Oh, honey," she whispered.

I loved my friend. I really loved her and her sweet understanding was one of the reasons I loved her but she had to get a freaking move on.

Therefore I cried loudly and bossily, "Would you quit talking and get your ass out here? I'll be all right but I'm not going to Tor's world without telling you good-bye so you have to hurry!"

"Right, I'm turning the key in the ignition now. I'll be there in a jiffy."

"Phoebe, it's an hour away. Be safe. It's drizzling, there's fog and the roads are slick," I warned.

"Right."

My voice dropped. "But hurry, honey. I don't want to miss saying good-bye."

"I'll hurry," she said back. "See you soon, babe."

"Later, babe."

"Later."

I disconnected and dropped my phone to my thigh.

Getting you up to date. Obviously Noc had found Clarabelle. After two weeks of searching he found her in ten minutes. When he told me he'd found her, I shouted, "Hurrah!" threw myself in his arms and kissed his cheek right in front of all his colleagues but I didn't care.

He found her. He *found* her.

And now I could go to Tor.

When my arms closed around him, Noc had hesitated then he'd given me a tight squeeze before he pulled his head back, looked down at me and studied my face with a weird intensity before he let me go, wrote down the address, grabbed my hand and pulled me through the station.

And now we were headed that way.

"Jesus, babe, I cannot believe you convinced your folks and your friend this shit is true," Noc said quietly and I looked at him.

"It *is* true," I stated. "And, by the way, they've also met Tor, the other Tor who is not you so they will so *totally* corroborate what I told you when you see them. That is, before you see me disappear to another realm."

And this was true. So true, I should have thought of it before. So true, I should have thought of it two weeks ago and tried contacting Noc then.

Alas, I didn't.

But now we were on our way. So, God willing, all's well that ends well.

He glanced at me. Then he glanced back at the road, shaking his head.

Then he muttered an unconvinced, "Unh-hunh."

Whatever. He'd see soon enough.

I hoped.

We fell into silence and I broke that silence because I was scared, nervous and excited so I had to do something.

"Thanks for doing this," I told him.

"We get this shit done then we get you to someone who can really do somethin' to help you. *Then* you can thank me," he muttered.

"I'm not crazy," I told him something I knew he'd never believe until seeing made him believe.

Again, I hoped.

"Yeah, babe." He was still muttering.

See.

He didn't believe me. He totally thought I was crazy.

Whatever.

"I'm sorry you're dragged into this," I said. "I've been cleaning up Cora's messes for a while and from everything I gather, she's unpleasant."

"Unh-hunh," he mumbled again. "*She's* unpleasant." The last he said like he was humoring a small child.

I ignored his tone and kept talking.

"So, well, it sucks you met her and you're caught up in all this mess. I mean, maybe not, seeing as she helped you bring down an illegal gambling racket, though, she kind of didn't know she was doing it. Still, you did it, but you know, sorry if she was cold or unpleasant or a bitch."

Noc was silent.

I was not.

"How *did* you meet her, can I ask?"

"Baby," he said gently. "You were there."

"No I wasn't."

"Right," he muttered.

Okay, I'd leave that alone.

Then, I blurted (mainly because I was stupid, curious and stupid curious), "Why'd you sleep with her?"

"You're hot," he answered immediately. "And there was the small fact you were all over me and not takin' no for an answer."

Well, it was nice to know he thought I was hot.

"Okay, then why'd you continue to sleep with her?"

His hand came out and curled around my thigh where he squeezed then let me go.

"Cora, babe, sorry, but at first, it served a purpose and you…" He shook his head. "You got somethin' about you. A promise. It just never was fulfilled and for some reason, signs you gave me or things I wanted to believe, I kept thinkin' it would be. I gotta tell you, there were times when I hoped it would be. When I thought maybe, no matter the fucked-up way we hooked up, we could sort our shit out. But then you would…" he paused, "be you. You tried, I could tell you tried, but you couldn't pull it off. But, if it helps, I know you tried."

God, he thought I was a mental case and was trying to make me feel better about Cora failing to be able to play him.

Totally a sweet guy.

I looked back out the front window and muttered to myself, "I wonder why she'd give it to you and not Tor, who's her husband. That's weird."

"You said you were into me," he answered my question and I looked back at him.

"I did? I mean, *she* did?"

"*You* did."

"I said I was into you?"

"Not in those words. When you're her, you don't talk like you do now."

"So, what did I say? Something like, 'You're my moon and my stars, my love?'"

He was silent and I got the message.

I turned back to facing forward. "Sorry. I shouldn't ask about—"

"Fuck," he muttered and I looked back at him.

"What?"

"Fuck," he repeated.

"What?" I asked louder.

He glanced at me then back at the road. "You said I was perfect. Completely perfect. You said exactly that. 'You're perfect. Completely perfect. As you should have come to me.'"

He *was* perfect, as far as I could tell (uh…mostly, when he wasn't angry and saying jerky things that was). Though not as perfect as Tor (who could also get angry and say jerky things, by the by, I just decided not to think about that).

"That was a nice thing to say, right?" I asked.

"It was nice and it was *weird*."

"Weird how?"

"You said it while touching my face, where you touched it earlier."

I sucked in breath.

Noc kept talking and now *he* was talking like it was to himself. "Later, when we were in bed, you kissed my chest and whispered, 'perfect, no scars, no bloody scars.'"

Oh my God!

"Cora didn't like Tor because he has scars?" I asked him a question he'd already inadvertently bloody answered.

"Babe—"

I twisted back to forward and snapped, "That *bitch*!"

"Cora—"

"Tor was only *scarred* while saving his *people* from King Baldur's tyrannical *rule*. He's a warrior. He had a kingdom to rebuild. Shit like that happens when you're at war!"

"Jesus," Noc breathed out on a sigh.

"Tor was right. She so *totally* is *not* the other half to his soul, I'll tell you that!" I clipped.

"Do me a favor," he said.

And I snapped, "What?"

"Calm down, yeah?"

I crossed my arms on my chest and grunted, "Yeah."

Cora, so…totally…*a bitch*.

I deep breathed and as I was deep breathing I realized what my outburst must have sounded like, not to mention all the other stuff I'd been saying, so I started to smile. Then I started to giggle. Then I started to giggle harder.

"Oh shit," Noc said. "You're not cracking up on me, are you?"

I shook my head and sucked in breath, trying to control the giggles and I forced out, "It just hit me what what I said must have sounded like."

Noc was silent.

"It's no wonder you think I'm crazy."

Noc remained silent.

I fought the giggles back and took a steadying breath.

"You all right?" he asked softly when my laughter died away.

"Yeah," I answered softly.

"You got a great laugh, babe." He was still talking softly.

"You've never heard me laugh?" I asked.

"Nope," he answered.

I'd heard *that* before.

I stared at the dark, slick road, the windshield wipers moving slowly to clean away the mist and I whispered, "You are, you know, as far as I can tell."

"I'm what?"

"Perfect."

I heard him pull in a breath.

I ignored that too.

"Do you want kids?" I asked quietly.

He hesitated before he answered quietly, "Yeah."

"How many?"

This time, he didn't hesitate. This time, he spoke like he knew exactly what he wanted.

"Don't care. As long as they're healthy, happy and I can provide a good life for them, I'll keep goin'."

I turned to him, looked at his beautiful profile and whispered, "I hope you find someone really fantastic, someone as beautiful as you who thinks you're perfect, has a great laugh and you want to keep going with her."

He glanced at me again and when he did he was smiling and his smile caught in my throat.

It was nearly as good as Tor's.

"Baby, you just described you."

"Shit," I whispered and turned back forward. "I kind of did."

He chuckled.

"Though I'm not fantastic. I'm cold and bad in bed," I reminded him and he burst out laughing.

That caught in my throat too because it was also nearly as good as Tor's.

He quit laughing but declared, "Babe, you made me laugh like that when we were together, I wouldn't have let you pack my bags."

Hmm.

"Good thing I did, considering I'm crazy," I reminded him.

"I could handle crazy, you make me laugh and you can kiss like you kissed me tonight."

I felt my eyes get wide and turned to look at him again. "Noc, are you *flirting* with a lunatic woman you think has multiple personalities, a gambling addiction and is pregnant with your child?"

He glanced at me before turning back to the road, his handsome face even more handsome with his smile. "Cora, if there's anyone I *can* flirt with, I can flirt with the woman who's pregnant with my child."

I faced back forward, muttering, "I can't argue with that."

Noc chuckled again.

I finally (and belatedly wisely) fell silent.

It was Noc who next spoke.

"Which one is you?"

I closed my eyes.

I opened them and replied, "I guess both are me, Noc, in a way."

"I prefer this you."

Poor Cora.

What an idiot.

"Everyone does," I whispered.

"I could work with this you," he muttered, again as if to himself.

Oh boy.

I turned to him. "Noc—"

I stopped talking when his eyes narrowed on the road and he started, "What's...?"

I turned back and saw what looked like—I leaned closer—*stars*. Little, glittering *stars*, hundreds, maybe thousands of them and they were dancing in a wide line perpendicular to the road.

"What the fuck?" Noc whispered as the stars started growing, glittering, increasing in number and Noc slowed his SUV but we still kept driving straight at them.

Oh shit.

"Noc," I breathed but said no more because the stars exploded.

Shooting out to the sides, they burst in a blinding light. I flinched against the sudden brightness, lifting a hand to shield my eyes, and when I recovered I saw that up their middle a black seam had split through.

"Fucking hell!" Noc shouted.

A black horse with rider surged through the seam.

Oh my God!

"Fucking hell!" Noc repeated as the horse's hooves hit the slick asphalt and came tearing straight at us. "Hold on!" Noc yelled and swerved his SUV, narrowly missing horse and rider.

I grabbed on to the dash but twisted my head to look back, seeing the rider pull the reins sharply to the side to round the horse and come back.

"Stop!" I cried.

"What the fuck is that?" Noc asked, looking in the rearview mirror.

"It's Tor! Stop! Stop. *Bloody stop!*"

Noc stood on the brakes, his SUV came to a sliding halt and I was out of my seatbelt and out of the car before Noc could finish shouting, "Cora!"

I took off on a run and cleared the back of the SUV seeing Salem galloping toward me, Tor on his back and I kept right on running but I did it faster.

At the sight of him, the pain that had ebbed with the promise of hope washed clean away.

Tor kept Salem coming at me and when he got close, he leaned down to the side. His arm hooking around my waist, he lifted me up and set me on the horse in front of him.

I didn't hesitate. I wrapped my arms around his shoulders, aimed my mouth at his and the minute our lips touched, they opened and his tongue slid in my mouth.

Oh yes. There it was.

I was home.

I didn't notice Salem slow to a halt under us because Tor's arms were around me, his mouth was on mine, his sandalwood scent filled my nostrils and his strength surrounded me. He kissed me hard and I kissed him back just as hard, pushing close, draining him dry.

His mouth tore from mine and his hands came to either side of my head where he held me still while his eyes searched my face, so I took that opportunity to allow mine to roam his.

Then he let my head go, his arms crushed me to him and he shoved his face in my neck.

"My love," he said there, his voice low and hoarse with unconcealed relief.

Feeling it, hearing it, my tears came instantly and started to fall.

"Honey," I whispered against his skin, holding him tight, but my arms still clenched in a futile effort to hold him tighter.

In return, his arms gave me a squeeze.

"I was dying without you," I told him, my voice trembling with tears.

"I know, sweets," he told me.

"You came to me," I breathed. "I prayed you would." I pulled my face out of his neck. His head came up and I smiled a tremulous smile into his beautiful face. "I prayed you'd crash into me, but, honey, I didn't mean it *literally*."

A slow smile spread across his face and he snatched me back into his arms. I shoved my face back into his neck and took him in with all my senses, opening them so I could suck everything I could from him.

Which was why I immediately felt it when his body went solid.

"Fuckin' hell," Noc muttered.

Uh-oh.

"By the gods, tell me you jest, Cora," Tor stated.

Uh-oh!

I pulled my face from his neck and looked up at him. He was looking down but beyond me. I followed his gaze and saw Noc standing in the drizzling rain with his arms crossed on his chest, his feet planted wide looking a lot like Tor.

Well, just like him, actually.

Oh shit.

"Uh…" I started and stopped when I felt the heat of Tor's gaze so I looked back at him.

"You were with this man."

"Tor, honey—"

"Jesus, Cora, babe, fuck me. You weren't lying." I heard Noc say, his voice heavy with shocked surprise and Tor's eyes narrowed.

"Cora *babe?*" he asked.

"Tor—"

"I thought I told you that you were not to be in the presence of this man."

"You did, but—"

"It appears to me, my sweet, that you're in the presence of this man."

"I am, but, you see, he was—"

"I was in my world, searching high and low for magic that would bring me back to you, and you were carrying on with this man," he ground out.

Now hang on a second.

My back went straight and I pulled away as best I could (seeing as we were on Salem), snapping, "I was not *carrying* on with Noc! He was—"

"You were in his transport with him," Tor interrupted me to point out.

"He was taking me to Clarabelle to find *you*, you jerk!" I shouted.

Tor's head jolted and I smacked his bicep before continuing.

"A Clarabelle who Harold, Marlene, Phoebe, Brianna, Dad, Mom and half of Seattle have been looking high and low for, but *Noc* found for me in, like, ten minutes. So you should be thanking him because we were on our way to her so I could get back to *you* before you came tearing through the sky on your mighty beast!"

At my mention of him, Salem threw his head back and whinnied, alerting me to his presence.

When he did, I instantly twisted and bent to pat his neck and coo, "Heya, Salem, missed you, boy."

He snorted, shook his head and stamped a foot.

"Thank you for coming to get me." I kept cooing and stroking.

Salem let out a soft, sweet whinny and I knew what that meant.

"I love you too, buddy," I whispered.

"This is not unusual," Tor announced. "Our souls are torn asunder. I move heaven and earth, tearing my kingdom apart to find magic that will bring me back to her. She spends approximately five minutes greeting me then she fawns over my horse." I twisted back to look at him to see he was addressing Noc. "It vexes me," he stated and his eyes cut to mine when he concluded, "*Greatly*."

"Jesus," Noc muttered.

I glared at my man. Then I stared at my man. Finally I put my hands to both sides of his face, pulled it down to mine and I kissed him.

He kissed me back.

The kiss started to get heated in a *good* way when I heard Noc say, "Kids, I can see this is a touching reunion but it's fuckin' wet and we're in the middle of the goddamned road."

Tor lifted his head and aimed his eyes to Noc. I kept my arms around him as I twisted to do the same.

"You have found the witch?" Tor asked and I saw Noc staring at him.

"Jesus, I don't know whether to be creeped out I'm starin' at another me, relieved I wasn't tagging a head case or pissed I didn't find this Cora before you," Noc muttered, not tearing his eyes from Tor.

I pressed my lips together to stop from giggling.

Tor, on the other hand, didn't find anything amusing.

"Have you found the witch?" Tor semi-repeated, his tone edging toward impatience.

"Yeah, man, I found the...*witch*," Noc answered, saying the words like he really wished he didn't have to say them.

"You must take us to her," Tor commanded.

Noc stared at Tor another second then mumbled, "Fuck me, this shit is whacked."

"Sir, you must take us to her," Tor ordered again, definitely losing patience.

Noc lifted a hand and nodded his head. "Yeah, yeah, I get that. Let Cora down so she can get in the SUV with me," he replied and Tor's body got tight.

Oh dear.

"She will ride with me. We will follow," Tor decreed.

"Uh...Tor, yeah?" Noc asked his name.

"That is me," Tor confirmed his name.

"I gotta point out, man, that it's raining and you're on a fuckin' horse," Noc noted.

"I'm aware of that," Tor retorted.

"And your babe is pregnant. She needs to be in a car where it's warm, dry and *safe*, not riding on the back of a horse in the rain," Noc remarked sensibly and logically, and I will add, sweetly.

I so totally had to hook him up with Phoebe.

Tor's arms convulsed around me and a low growl escaped his throat. He didn't want to let me go but he knew he should.

God, I loved my man.

Noc moved a step forward and continued in a quiet voice, "I understand that you two have been separated awhile and had your souls torn apart and shit. But I swear I won't let anything hurt her. She's safe with me. Yeah?"

Tor scowled at Noc but I watched his face gentle when his neck bent so he could look at me.

"You will ride with the other me," he said softly.

"Okay, honey," I whispered.

His arms gave me a squeeze and his lips brushed mine. Noc moved closer as Tor lowered me off of Salem, and Noc's hands caught my waist and steadied my descent. This made Tor's jaw get tight, and I had to admit it was a weird sensation to have the hands of two of the exact same, but entirely different, men on me.

When my feet were on the asphalt, Noc grabbed my hand and pulled me a couple of steps away from Tor and Salem.

"We cannot waste time," Tor announced, his eyes moving from Noc's hand in mine to Noc.

"I got a lot more horsepower under my hood than you're sittin' on," Noc pointed out.

"We will keep up, just proceed with haste," Tor commanded.

"Proceed with haste, gotcha," Noc muttered under his breath and his voice was shaking with laughter.

I squeezed his hand at the same time I shook it. "Tor's from another world," I hissed at him. "You know they talk differently."

Noc looked at me with amusement in his eyes.

It was a good look.

"Right," he muttered then the amusement fled from his eyes as they moved over my face. His hand got tight in mine as I watched it hit him that I was who I said I was, not some crazy head case he was tagging, and this was really happening. "Right," he muttered again, his tone soft, even tender, and he nodded before he whispered, "Let's get you two home."

Jeez.

Totally a sweet guy.

We started to the SUV, and as we did, Salem stamped a hoof and shook his neck. I looked toward the horse as I moved with Noc and saw Salem stamp his hoof again, throw his head back and whinny.

Then he started dancing with agitation.

Oh shit, I didn't get a good feeling about this.

I stopped, Noc stopped with me and we both looked at Salem.

"Salem, what do you feel?" Tor asked urgently. Salem danced, swung his head to Noc and me and whinnied more anxiously. That was when Tor shouted, "Get her to your transport!"

Noc looked from the horse to Tor. "What?"

"*Now!*" Tor roared, pulling the sword out of the scabbard in Salem's saddle and Noc got still at my side when we heard the steel hiss as it went. Tor's eyes were pointed into the dark distance but it was too late.

The air all around us turned blue.

I knew what that meant, my system flooded immediately with adrenaline but I had no time to react. The next instant the air surrounding us exploded in blue sparks that shot everywhere, filling the space, bouncing off our bodies.

"What the fuck?" Noc shouted, his hand grasping mine hard at the same time and he started dragging me to his truck.

But we didn't get there because the sky was swarming with vickrants and worse, what looked like an army of hunched beings with two arms, two legs, huge, deformed pointed ears, wrinkled faces, bald heads and bulging eyes were marching straight at us.

29

ASSISTANCE

~

"Head down!" Noc shouted.

I was tucked into his body as we moved in a near-crouch around his truck to the passenger side, the blue sparks of the vickrants Tor's sword was slicing through as he and Salem provided us cover bouncing off our bodies.

Noc pulled the door to the SUV open but it was rocking, those other…*things* were at the other side of it, pushing at it to turn it to its side, probably doing this so we couldn't use it to get away.

Keeping me tucked to him, Noc didn't delay. He reached in, pulled down the door to the glove box and grabbed a gun and two clips.

He extended the clips to me.

"Take these," he ordered.

I took them and shoved them in my back pockets as he pulled back the slide on the top of the gun and yanked us away from the shuddering SUV just as it teetered over and slammed on its side.

"Cora!" Tor shouted.

I peeked out from under Noc and looked at Tor. He was swinging his sword at vickrants one-handed at the same time pulling a dagger out of his belt.

I ducked out from under Noc, raced swiftly to Tor, took the dagger from him and he reached around his other side and pulled out another one. I took that one too.

"Rocks!" Noc yelled at Tor.

His arm snaking around me, he tucked me back into him and we raced off the road, through some scrub and into the sand toward some huge rocks. The whole time, Tor and Salem followed us, continuing to provide cover overhead as Noc aimed his gun at the legged creatures advancing on us from behind.

He pulled the trigger and one of the creatures howled, dropped to his back and exploded in blue sparks.

"Jesus fuckin' Christ," Noc muttered, but didn't hesitate, aimed again and pulled the trigger.

Another creature howled, collapsed and exploded in blue sparks.

The rest kept advancing as we kept going toward cover, not an easy thing to do through sand.

A vickrant flew low, sailing under Salem's neck. The horse whinnied but I swung my arm down across my body, yanked it back up and I sliced through the vickrant's chest, blue sparks shot into my face and the vickrant disappeared. Another instantly followed and I did the same with the other dagger. Catching the thing at its throat, it vanished in a shock of blue embers. I did all of this as Noc kept shooting and moving us, me in the middle, Salem and Tor close to my side.

I took down another vickrant before we made it around the tall rock the underneath of which the sea had eroded away, giving us an overhang and cover from the vickrants who, unable to get to us but coming just the same, flew straight into the top of the rock in their kamikaze mission, exploding *themselves*.

Whoa.

Tor dismounted and Salem stood vigil beside us, using his huge body to cut off access at the front of the rock and I watched in shock as Salem took out a low-flying vickrant with a nasty chomp of his horse teeth.

Uh…*whoa*!

Noc shouted at me, "Clip!"

I transferred one dagger to the other hand, pulled a clip out of my back pocket and handed it to him. He took it, instantly released the used clip, it fell with a thud into the sand and he shoved the next one in. Taking aim around the rock, he fired at the legged creatures, not missing. Though, it had to be said, they would be hard to miss seeing as there were so freaking many of them.

"Talk to me," he bit out to Tor who was standing, legs planted, just out from under the cover of the rock and striking vickrants down with every mighty swing.

"The winged creatures, vickrants, the legged monsters, toilroys," Tor explained and grunted through another swing that took out three vickrants at once. He went on, "The good, anything pierces their skin, they perish." Another swing, another grunt, another two vickrants exploding in blue. "The other good, they have no brain. They are programmed only with the mission so they aren't tactical and are unable to adjust their advance, for instance, if they are confronted with terrain that is difficult to maneuver."

"And the bad?" Noc asked, aiming and firing at toilroys as another vickrant flew low around Salem toward me, and I slashed out with my knife, catching it under its belly and blue flashes flew.

"There are *a lot* of them," Tor answered Noc.

"Fuckin' great," Noc muttered, aimed, fired and another toilroy bit the dust. "I'm almost out of ammunition, man, got a clip and a half left," Noc went on to inform Tor.

"Salem!" Tor bellowed.

The horse turned around and Tor stopped swinging just long enough to pull a lethal-looking axe out of a holder on the saddle. He turned and tossed it, head up, to Noc who caught it by the handle left-handed.

Well, the other good was, my man was a warrior and he came heavily armed.

"Terrific," Noc muttered, not feeling my positive vibe but keeping hold on the axe and turning back to aim and shoot, taking down another toilroy, "I run outta ammo, I gotta get close to those fuckers to take them out."

"It takes an extraordinary amount of magic for Minerva to conjure this many creatures and I would assume an incomparable amount to send them to another world," Tor stated as he kept swinging, the air rife with blue flashes where he connected.

Another vickrant came low, clawed feet first, aiming at me. I lunged forward and planted a dagger in his belly as another one came to the side and I swung wide with my other hand, catching it at its gullet.

"We have learned in the past that if we're able to reduce their number by half," Tor went on, grunted with another swing and concluded, "they've orders to retreat."

"That's good news, right?" I asked, plunging my dagger into another low-flying vickrant as two came flying in at my other side. I pivoted and swung wide again, catching them both with my other dagger.

"Babe, there's fuckin' *thousands* of these fuckin' things," Noc growled, aimed, fired then released the clip and it fell to the sand under our feet. "Clip!" I pulled it out of my back pocket, turned and tossed it to him. He caught it then shouted, "Cora!"

I felt them, talons in my shirt, starting to drag me back. I whirled quickly, the claws lost hold, I slashed out, my dagger tearing through the vickrant that had me and it exploded in blue just as another one came in and I threw out my other arm, catching it too.

"*Fuck!*" Noc thundered, shoving the new clip in his gun.

"*Bloody hell!*" Tor roared and both men moved closer to me.

We carried on swinging, stabbing and firing.

"You got any ideas?" Noc asked Tor as the creatures kept at us in an increasing wave.

"Don't give up," Tor answered Noc.

"Shit," Noc muttered, aimed, fired and another toilroy collapsed in a ball of sparks.

They kept coming at us. We kept fighting. My arms were getting tired but my body was singing from the adrenaline surging through my system.

Salem screamed and shook his massive body. Noc moved out from under cover, I saw his hand wielding the axe swoop up then down and blue flashes flew out. Salem shuffled further under the cover, closer to Tor and me.

"*Noc!*" I shrieked. "Get back here!"

He rounded the horse. A vickrant flew low, legs aimed at Noc's back. They connected, Noc started to fly back but Tor charged forward, and with a powerful upward swing, the vickrant exploded.

Both men moved back under cover, Noc finished his clip, dropped his gun and advanced. Both hands on the axe, he swung back and forth, tearing through the stream of advancing toilroys.

"This is not," he grunted on a swing, a toilroy disappeared. "Goin'." Another grunt, another swing, another toilroy vanishing. "Our way, man." Another grunt, another toilroy gone.

Then the vickrants stopped swooping but this was because the toilroys had surrounded us, closing in from all sides. Salem shifted, pressing me to the rock face as Noc and Tor moved around the horse, Tor at his head, Noc at his flank and they kept fighting. They did this without word and I was cut off from the action.

"Let me help!" I shouted over the horse as I watched them battle on.

"Stay safe!" Tor shouted back.

"Tor! I can help!"

"*Safe!*" he bellowed.

The toilroys pressed closer, blue sparks flew, dancing around, lighting the surface of the rock but where one evaporated, three more were there, pressing in.

"Gods!" Tor exploded on a mighty swing that took out four toilroys but four more were instantly in their place.

"God damn it!" Noc roared, slashing two toilroys with an axe but three surged in to fill their emptied space.

I watched the advance over Salem's back as my man, his horse and his twin were forced to close ranks as the toilroys relentlessly pressed in.

We were losing.

Losing.

Shit!

I closed my eyes and rested my forehead against Salem's glossy fur.

He pressed closer, pushing my back into the rock, and I whispered, "Please, please, please, please, please."

I heard Tor grunt and I heard Noc growl.

Then I heard an almighty shriek pierce the air, or I should say, what sounded like about thousands of simultaneous almighty shrieks. I automatically dropped the daggers so I could cover my ears against the loud, hideous, ear-splitting sound. My head snapping back, my eyes shooting open, and I saw a pink wave of light washing toward us, blue sparks blazing in its path. So many, the sky lit bright with blue and pink, illuminating everything all around us, saturating it with color so bright, I winced.

Suddenly, all went dark and there was nothing. No vickrants, no toilroys, no nothing but the sounds of the sea washing on the shore and our heavy breathing.

"By the Gods," Tor muttered.

"Holy fuck," Noc whispered.

I fought to catch my breath as the darkness and silence permeated my consciousness.

Then I ducked under Salem's neck and cautiously approached Tor. As I did, his body went alert (or, *more* alert), his arm shot out, caught me at the waist and he yanked me behind him.

"Who's there?" he called into the darkness.

For several seconds, there was no answer.

"Show yourself!" Tor commanded.

I put my hands to his hips and peered around his large frame.

My body froze as Tor's froze under my hands and I felt Noc and Salem go still when a soft, pink light illuminated the space in front of us. The light came from a glowing orb that hung suspended over a woman's upturned hand.

My mouth dropped open.

The woman aimed her sightless eyes in our direction.

"Harold tells me you need some assistance," Clarabelle remarked.

I stared.

Then I smiled.

Hur-fucking-*rah*!

30

Always

~

"We haven't much time," Clarabelle whispered to me urgently.

We were in her trailer, which was in the middle of no-fucking-where, having got there after Clarabelle righted Noc's seriously dented SUV using magic (which, let me tell you, was way freaking cool). She rode with Noc as Tor and I followed on Salem (drizzle or no, pregnant or no, after what happened there was no way in hell Tor was letting me out of his sight).

Her trailer was totally freaking cool. It was all witchy, illuminated solely by fairy lights and flickering, scented candles, these sending shafts of light from the varied-colored crystals and pretty stained-glass symbols hanging all around.

There was a big, crystal ball sitting on a fluffy, pink pillow on a table, cushiony, velvet-covered, plush furniture and scarves hanging over lamps, the purpose of which I didn't know seeing as none of them were lit and the old woman couldn't see. I could only guess that a witch had to decorate like a witch. Maybe it was a rule.

Clarabelle and I were standing at one end of her tiny living room, her hands holding mine, both of us were wet through. Noc and Tor, also both wet, both standing feet planted, arms crossed on their wide chests and both glowering identical glowers at us were at the other end. I could hear Salem snorting his impatience outside through the still open door.

I looked down at the woman whose face I knew but who was someone I didn't know but I knew I could trust and I would like if I'd had the chance to get to know her better. Her eyes were pointed at me, unseeing, but her fingers were working through mine as if she could read my thoughts through my skin.

"I want this," I assured her.

"You must be certain," she replied.

I looked at Tor. His glower intensified. He was getting impatient.

I looked back at Clarabelle and held her hands tighter. "I'm certain."

"There is no coming back," she warned me.

"I—" I began, starting to glance again at Tor.

"He explained he made a deal with the witch on the other side," she reminded me swiftly. "He gave her much gold. He had to, her power was depleted in casting the spell to bring him to you. It will take decades for her to replenish it. In the meantime, she will be vulnerable. And there are many powers at work in her world, not all of them good, and it is very dangerous for a witch to be vulnerable. For her efforts this night, she'll be a target. He has offered her his protection but in that world, as they are here, these powers can be insidious. She may end up needing his gold to buy safety."

Wow.

"Uh—" I started.

"What I'm telling you, Cora, is that she cannot bring you back," Clarabelle went on to explain. "I know of only four witches in his land who have this kind of power and your prince found the only good one. You do not want to strike bargains with the others. Not *any* of them."

"Minerva," I guessed.

"She is one," Clarabelle nodded. "But there are two others in Hawkvale. They plot, this I know. What they plot, I do not. But they keep their heads low and both are arguably worse than The Shrew."

Fantastic.

Plotting witches worse than The Shrew.

Brilliant.

Still, my mind was made up.

I moved closer to her. "I promise. I'm certain. I know what I'm doing."

Her unseeing eyes slid in the direction of Tor then back to me.

"Love," she whispered her accurate guess, her lips curving up.

"Yes...love," I whispered back, my lips doing the same. "And our family," I added, moving one of her hands to my belly.

"Ah..." she breathed, her lips fully forming a smile.

"Can we, just...wait a few minutes?" I requested. "My parents and my best friend are on their way—"

"We can, if you want to battle the hewcrows," she cut me off to reply. "The she-god is working to mount her next offense." Clarabelle moved closer to me too. "She's more powerful than me, my dear. It took great effort for me to vanquish her army. I have enough magic to send you both and his horse back. I do not have enough to beat back the creatures she'll send in her second wave *and* send you back. This magic would replenish faster than what it will take to move you between worlds, but it would still be years before I can build up enough to ensure you and your love's *safe* return."

Her emphasis was not lost on me and my eyes shot to Tor as my heart clenched.

"There isn't time to wait for Mom, Dad and Phoebe," I told him, though he had to have heard, he was only a few feet away.

Still, I watched his jaw clench.

"I'll explain it, tell them you wanted to wait, Cora," Noc said to me and my eyes moved to him. "Just get this done." I swallowed and bit my lip. "Go, baby," Noc urged gently.

I nodded at Noc, my eyes shifted to Tor and he lifted his chin in an "it'll be all right" that, for the first time seeing that from Tor, didn't make me feel all right.

Then I looked down at Clarabelle.

"If you expend all your magic, will that mean you're vulnerable?" I asked her.

She didn't answer but her face said it all.

"When my father comes, tell him I told him to give you the money...*all* of it," I told her.

She shook her head. "I am a certain kind of witch and this is about love. And the kind of witch I am is a protector of love, amongst other things. I have vowed this. It is my duty. This I do as my religion, Cora, dear. So, that's—" she started to refuse and I squeezed her hands and I did this gently but firmly, making my point.

"*All* of the money, Clarabelle," I stressed. "You must promise to take it all. I can't go unless I do my bit to keep you safe and maybe you can use that money to stay safe." She looked ready to protest again so I said, "I can't use it, honey. So you might as well, and trust me, my mom and dad are *so* not going to take no for an answer so you might as well save your energy."

She gazed at me seeing nothing for a long moment before she nodded.

"Let's get this done," I whispered, her hands grasped mine tightly and she nodded yet again.

Then she said softly, "Harold has told me, if you could find a way to tell his Circe that he is doing well, he misses her and she is always in his thoughts, he would appreciate this greatly."

"Absolutely, Clarabelle," I whispered. "Please tell Harold we'll do that as soon as we can."

Clarabelle nodded again, got ready for business and straightened her shoulders.

"You and the prince mount his horse," she ordered, let me go and Tor moved to me.

Hooking me with his arm around the waist, he guided me to the door and gently moved me in front of him down the trailer's rickety steps, joined me at my side when he'd descended and he walked us to Salem.

"Cora, I must know that you're sure," he whispered to me and I tipped my head back to look at him as he stopped us at Salem's side.

"What choice do we have?" I asked.

He turned me into his front and his arms curved around me.

"I stay here, in your world, with you."

I stared up at him.

"But the hewcrows—" I started.

"We'll fight them back," he stated firmly.

"And if she sends something else?" I asked.

"We'll beat it," he declared.

I kept staring but said no more.

"Cora, we will win."

"They almost beat us with the first wave," I reminded him.

"We will win," he repeated.

"You can't know that," I told him.

"I do," he replied.

"How?" I asked.

His hands lifted to frame my face and his head dipped so he was all I could see. "Because, after these last weeks, I know I will allow nothing to keep you from me. I will not go down fighting. I will stay standing until I taste victory."

I pressed into his strong body, my hand lifting to curl around his neck and I whispered, "Tor."

"Now, I must know, are you certain you choose my world?"

"You would stay here with me?" I asked.

Without hesitation, he replied, "Absolutely."

I smiled into his face, feeling the weird sensation of my heart singing just as it broke.

"Then that's good enough for me," I whispered, his hands grew tight, his face asked his question and I turned my head to Clarabelle who was standing outside the trailer next to Noc. Tor's hands dropped but his arms circled me again right before I called, "Send us back, please."

She nodded. Noc looked at his feet. Tor's arms grew tighter.

Then he let me go and moved us closer to Salem but I pulled slightly away, looked at his beautiful face and whispered, "One second."

I ran to Noc, threw myself in his arms and gave him a big hug. He immediately hugged me back.

"Cora," he whispered in my ear.

"Thanks, Noc," I whispered over his shoulder.

"Can't say it was fun, babe, but I *can* say it was an experience."

I smiled into the darkness.

"Sorry about your truck," I said softly.

"Shit happens," he replied and I held on tighter.

I hesitated only a moment before I whispered, "I was right, you *are* perfect."

I felt his face move to my neck.

"Be happy, baby," he said on a squeeze of his arms and I nodded.

That was when the tears filled my eyes.

"You'll tell them?" I asked on a broken breath.

Another squeeze then, "Absolutely." Another squeeze and a whispered, "Go to your man, Cora babe."

I nodded my head, held on tight for another second and let him go. Not looking back, I ran to Tor. The instant I got within arm's reach, he caught me up and planted me on Salem, swinging up behind me before my bottom even settled.

Tor's arm curled around me, he pulled my back tight to his front and I lifted my fingers to my cheeks to brush away the wetness.

"Do your magic, witch," Tor demanded.

I looked at Noc and Clarabelle and fresh tears came to my eyes.

Clarabelle lifted both hands to the sky.

I held my breath.

Then I shouted, "Noc! When Phoebe gets here, look her over. She's my best friend. She makes great dirty martinis. She's a little crazy and she *really* likes shoes but, trust me, no joke, she's loyal, she's funny and she's *awesome*!"

Tor's arm tightened around me as I watched Noc grin at me and shake his head.

"Seriously!" I yelled.

The air turned pink.

"Shut up and go home, babe," Noc shouted back.

"You be happy too, Noc," I yelled in return.

His face split into a smile and I heard his deep chuckle.

Clarabelle's hands started to glow and I looked at her.

"Thanks, Clarabelle!" I yelled.

"My love, be quiet and let the witch concentrate," Tor growled in my ear.

"We have to say thanks, Tor. She's—"

His arm squeezed the air out of me.

"Quiet," he grunted and his arm released.

"Bossy," I snapped when I had air in my lungs.

The pink mist started at Salem's hooves and moved up.

I pressed back further into Tor's strong body and tried to control my escalating breathing.

"We'll be fine," he whispered in my ear.

The headlights bumping down Clarabelle's muddy lane lit us from our other side. I turned my head and saw my dad's Volvo followed by Phoebe's Mazda.

Jeez, Dad drove the Volvo. It was a wonder they made it out of the city.

That thought made my throat burn and my nostrils sting. The pink mist had covered most of Salem and was at our waists when I lifted my hand to my mouth, touched it to my lips, curled back my fingers and blew my kiss.

Salem had disappeared and the pink mist was to our chests when the cars stopped, three doors opened and three beloved bodies urgently folded out.

"I love you!" I yelled, raising my hand high to wave over the advancing mist. "Always!" I yelled before my throat closed and the mist masked them from view.

"Always!" I heard Phoebe yell.

"Always, my funny girl!" Mom shouted.

"Always, sweetheart!" Dad bellowed.

The sob tore out of my throat and I closed my eyes. Tor buried his face in my neck as his arms squeezed tight and Salem threw back his head and snorted.

One tear slid down my cheek and I opened my eyes.

The soft light from colorful lanterns all around and coming up from the city illuminated Tor's courtyard where Salem was standing. I saw the ships bobbing at sea, their lanterns slanting long reflections across the glassy water. I heard the gentle water of Tor's big, beautiful, circular fountain tinkling. Above us, billions of stars blinked brightly, a glittering curtain of night sky.

Tor's mouth moved to my ear.

"We're home, my love."

"Home," I whispered.

Salem stamped a hoof.

I sucked in breath.

Then I twisted in my man's arms, threw mine around his wide shoulders and held on tight as I stuffed my face in his neck and burst into tears.

One of Tor's arms held me close while his other hand slid up my back to play with the ends of my hair.

He did this for a long time as I cried.

31

Compassion

~

Six weeks later…

I could hear the city of Bellebryn bustling with activity and see the white garlands of fresh blooms adorning the shops and houses. There were so many of them, the very air smelled like a blossom. All the lanterns had been changed, even the ones on the boats that rocked at anchor on the emerald green sea. They were all now white. The huge wrought iron, silver-crested gates to Tor's castle were festooned with draping sheets of ivory held up at the sides in massive rosettes decorated with flowers. And in the fountain in the courtyard, blossoms drifted as the water sprinkled down, twinkling like diamonds in the sun's rays.

Today was a day of celebration.

But first, there was some unpleasant business to attend to and I wasn't looking forward to it.

To say the least.

The fingers holding my hand squeezed.

"Tell me again about our parents in your world, Cora," Rosa whispered from my side and I turned to my sister and smiled.

She asked me to do that a lot and I figured she did it because she thought it helped the ache in my heart.

And she was right.

"They're funny and crazy and they would love you," I told her what I always told her which also happened to be the truth. Rosa, I had discovered what I thought to be true when I first met her, was *very* lovable.

Her head tipped to the side and her pretty blue eyes lit. "Do you think our mother has talked our father into getting rid of his…" She hesitated then finished, "Car?"

I shook my head, looked back to the amazing view and whispered, "Probably not."

And this was probably true.

Rosa moved closer to me and I let her hand go so I could slide my arm around her waist. She reciprocated the gesture.

Aggie, on my shoulder, hopped gently and gave a soft, "Chirpy, chirp?" which meant, "All right, Cora?"

"I'm all right, Aggie," I whispered.

Aggie gave my neck a soft peck and that made me smile a soft smile.

Rosa was doing well after the loving care Dash and her parents had showered on her once she'd been rescued from the clutches of Minerva. She hadn't talked to me about it. Rather she seemed intent on learning more about me. This was likely in an attempt to create a replacement for the sister who had betrayed her, a sister she loved, a sister she could never again trust.

I was letting her have that play because Rosa *was* delicate and she needed it but it wasn't entirely altruistic.

I liked having a sister.

I let the happy vibe in the air fill me as I gave her a squeeze and let out a sigh at the same time I heard the beat of boots on the marble floors behind us.

I let Rosa go and turned to see Tor striding purposefully our way.

God, he was hot.

Tor stopped at us, swept me with his eyes then he looked at his soon-to-be sister-in-law.

"You'll stay in these rooms, no matter what. Yes, Rosa?" he asked gently.

She nodded. "No matter what, Tor."

He watched her a second then his eyes came to me. He reached in, took my hand and I sighed again.

"Come, my love," he murmured, clearly looking forward to this as much I was. "Leave the bird," he ordered and I nodded.

Rosa's hand came up and Aggie hopped from me to her.

Without delay, Tor pulled me away from my sister.

Well, might as well get it over with.

As Tor pulled me along, I looked back at Rosa.

"I'll be back in time to help you get ready," I promised.

"I'll be here," she replied on a smile that was half bright, half sad.

She knew where we were going.

Poor thing.

As I hustled after Tor, I gave her what I hoped was a reassuring smile then turned away to follow him through the bedroom, and I saw Perdita rushing in carrying a ring of needlework.

"She doesn't leave these rooms," Tor ordered.

"Yes, your grace," Perdita said on a quick curtsy.

I smiled at her and gave her a wink. Perdita smiled and winked back. She did not curtsy to me because I told her not to. I didn't like people curtsying to me. It weirded me out and enough people curtsied to me everywhere in town, in the courtyard and around most of the castle, I didn't need my closest servants curtsying to me (in other words, Perdita, all the girls in the kitchens and all the maids who cleaned the castle). So, I asked them to stop doing it.

Tor led me out of our rooms and when we were through the doors and walking down the wide hall, his head bent to me and he caught my eye.

His face was disapproving.

He'd seen me wink at Perdita and he'd noticed the absent curtsy.

I looked away, biting my lip.

Okay, so, I promised never to vex him and be the perfect princess. And I was breaking that promise.

Hmm.

I gave this a moment of reflection then I mentally shrugged.

Oh well, whatever. He'd get over it.

He always did.

"You understand what you have confessed, Cora?" Tor's dad, King Ludlum, was sitting in Tor's uh…prince chair (or whatever you call it) in Tor's throne room. It wasn't exactly a throne, as such, but it was a freaking big chair, the seat and a big panel at the back covered in royal-blue velvet, the intricately carved wood painted a gleaming black and it had a lot of silver accents on it that looked real.

I didn't know what Tor's mom looked like. But, now knowing his dad, I knew Tor took after him. And hopefully Tor would age like him. His dad definitely still had it. He even looked not stupid wearing a big, gold crown with lots of brilliant sapphires on it and seriously, anyone who could pull that off *definitely* still had it.

Tor was standing to his father's right side, Orlando to his father's left. Dash was on his way to Bellebryn having spent the night in a village miles away.

They were taking *no* chances that day.

I was standing next to Tor. There were four sentries across the room, standing two and two on both sides of the door.

The Forrest and Dara Goode of this world were down the steps to the right, holding hands and looking like they were doing exactly what I was certain they were doing.

Fretting.

Seeing Rosa's parents didn't hurt me like I thought it would. This was mainly because I knew them both now and I was getting to know them pretty well. They might look like my mom and dad but they were not one thing like them. Forrest of this world would be a staunch conservative Republican in mine and Dara wasn't all that bright (albeit sweet and kind).

I knew they were worried about their daughter but they were already treating me like one, even though I could tell it startled them to look at me (still). Then again, I was now a dab hand at this business and they were not.

They'd get used to it.

The Cora Goode of this world was bowed in a curtsy before us. This was the first time I'd seen her. She had been sequestered the minute Tor returned to his world (the time he returned without me, of course) and she had not been allowed to talk to anyone but Orlando and members of his trusted guard.

Seeing her freaked me out. Definitely ten pounds lighter than me, at least, even with all that takeaway and junk food she ate when she was away.

But other than that, all me.

Creepy weird.

Tor had the annulment drawn up the evening we arrived back in his world, waking some official dude to do it. He signed the paper before the ink was dry.

Then he took me to bed.

I would have preferred it the other way around but in the end I got what I wanted (three times) so who was I to quibble?

Four days later, Rosa, Dara, Forrest, the king, Orlando and Dash all descended on the castle and Tor and I were wed in this very room.

I wore a new kickass gown made of ivory silk.

Tor wore his usual black but he added a brocade vest for the occasion.

I wanted to invite all the servants in the castle to the festivities but I wasn't allowed. The information that I was not of this world would be held only by the inner sanctum (the inner sanctum being whoever Tor decided to let in, I might add). This was Tor's decree, but at least, even being bossy in giving it, he took the time to explain it to me.

He made sense so I gave in.

We had one more guest. Aggie attended the ceremony and he did this perched on the pastor's shoulder.

Salem, although the throne room was big enough to accommodate him, was not invited (Tor put his foot down, saying, "I've already given in on the bird. I'm not having a horse at my bloody wedding.").

Just to be safe, I didn't see Tor the day of our wedding until Rosa and I walked hand in hand into the throne room.

We got married at seven o'clock in the morning.

This was another Tor edict. He didn't want to wait to take me as his bride, he said. And after two weeks of enduring the same pain as I had *while* he was searching the kingdom high and low for a witch who could magic him back to my world, he wasn't all that hip on spending even half a day without me.

I got where he was coming from.

It was a bitch getting up way early to prepare for my wedding. But I did it.

And, in the days prior to the wedding, I thought it kind of sucked I wasn't going to have a big do to celebrate my nuptials, nuptials that bound me to a handsome prince from a fairytale land.

All the heroines in animated movies got their big do.

But Dara and Rosa had arranged for me to have a beautiful bouquet made of peach roses and white lilies. Tor had arranged for us all to have a delicious wedding breakfast after the ceremony. And Perdita and the girls went all out on a sumptuous spread (Perdita and the girls obviously being in Tor's inner sanctum since they were there to see us disappear, and they were sworn to secrecy, and thus they knew the important occasion they were preparing for so they went all out).

Then Tor took me straight to our rooms and neither of us left them for twenty-four hours.

So, in the end, it wasn't a wedding extravaganza but it was still sweet and it meant I was Tor's *real* wife and a *true* princess so I certainly wasn't complaining.

I watched Cora lift her head and she started, "Your grace—"

King Ludlum cut her off, "You sought the company of witches for reprehensible purposes, to find the means to keep your sister, who you should cherish and do all in your power to keep from harm, and her intended, who, incidentally, is my son and a prince of this realm, from being wed. You discovered the existence of another world and conspired with The Shrew to transport yourself from this world to that. You schemed to place your sister in harm's way. And all of your plots succeeded, causing your sister to be held by the she-god putting her, your prince, your other self and your world at great risk."

This was all true. She'd copped to it. Tor told me.

It was all about Dash.

Stupid cow.

Cora came back to this world, Tor guessed, because Minerva had double-crossed her, not meaning to send her to my world for all her natural born days as Cora said Minerva had promised she would. When we went back, Tor had come along for the ride, again a guess, because he held me in his arms—a mistake Minerva rectified with all due haste, taking Tor away from me but separating us before she did.

Since no one had (or wanted) a direct line to the evil Minerva, we would never know. Except, of course, Cora, and since Minerva couldn't get to her on sacred land, she couldn't ask either.

What was certain was that Tor and I shared a soul. That we knew (*boy* did we know). And from the battle on the coast, Minerva was willing to throw everything at keeping us apart, which one could assume meant that was her plan all along, to bring us together then tear us apart…forever.

And the Cora of this world had fed into her scheme beautifully.

Luckily, however, her plot didn't succeed.

"But, your grace, in doing this, Prince Noctorno found the true half to his soul—" Cora started.

"A lucky coincidence," King Ludlum cut her off tersely and Dara Goode started visibly trembling.

Her daughter's lip curled. Tor shifted at my side and I looked up at him to see his jaw was hard. He'd seen the lip curl and it pissed him off.

I looked back at Cora when she kept talking and saw she'd managed to control her expression.

"They are happy...*your son* is happy...does this count for nothing?"

"You did not hatch your schemes with the intent to make my son happy, Cora," King Ludlum said quietly and she lost control of her expression and her face twisted.

Then she cried out, "This is not fair! This is not just! *He* was not destined for *me*!" She tipped her head to Tor. "*He* was *never* destined for me! Don't you see? This was why I had feelings for Prince Dashiell. This was why I found my mate in that other world! Doesn't anyone care about me?"

"Oh boy," I muttered and Tor's hand moved, his fingers curling around my own.

"You found your mate in the other world?" King Ludlum asked, his brows rising.

"Yes! *She*," she pointed at me, "is the destiny of Prince Noctorno but *I* am destined for the Noctorno of the other world!" she announced.

"Oh boy," I repeated and Tor squeezed my fingers.

"*My* Noctorno is perfect!" She kept going. "*My* Noctorno is beautiful. He suits me!"

My body locked and I whispered, "Um...*hell no*."

"Still, love," Tor ordered and I did as he asked.

It was hard but I did it.

"Send me back to the other world so I can be with my mate!" she demanded. "*That* is fair! *That* is just! And in the end, all will be well for *everybody*!"

This was a mistake. I knew it when I felt the air in the room get heavy. I felt Tor's body tense and peered around Tor to see King Ludlum's face was hard as granite.

"I believe, my dear, that *I* am your king and *I* decide what is fair and just," he said quietly.

I looked back to Cora to see her grinding her teeth to keep her mouth shut but her eyes were flashing.

"It pains me," King Ludlum went on, "to see you do not struggle with the consequences of your actions. That you do not wish to atone for the decisions you made which caused harm to others. That you do not understand that conspiring with Minerva..." he shook his head, "Cora, that *alone* is an act of high treason."

"And I do not, your grace, because Prince Noctorno is bound to his true mate and my sister weds hers this very day. If not for me, the former would never have happened and everything, in the end, is as it should be," she retorted.

Tor's fingers squeezed mine and I drew in breath. I did this because, it sucked, but this was true.

"It also pains me," King Ludlum stated, "to agree that this is true."

My head snapped around to look at the king again but I didn't miss Cora's face brightening with hope.

King Ludlum looked at me. "Cora, the Gracious," jeez, I totally loved that, "it is my understanding you came to know my son of the other world."

"Yes, your grace," I replied.

"Is it his wish to be bound to this Cora?" he asked, tipping his head at Cora.

Oh dear.

"Um..." I avoided looking at the other Cora's parents and then said honestly, "No. He's not that into her."

I felt Tor move and I looked up to see his head tilted slightly back but I could also see him fighting a smile.

"Not that that into her?" King Ludlum asked, taking my attention back to him.

"He doesn't like her much," I explained.

"He loves me!" Cora exclaimed. "He's devoted to me! *Totally* devoted to me."

I looked at her.

"Uh...not so much," I muttered and I heard Orlando stifle a chuckle.

"She lies!" Cora shrieked, my body got tight but not as tight as Tor's.

"Careful, Cora," he warned low.

She wasn't careful. "*She* does not know and *you* do not know what we shared."

"I'm afraid we do. He was a member of their city guard. He was investigating illegal gaming and using you to do it," Tor told her and she gasped. "When my Cora returned and broke things off with the other me, he said nary a word and explained later to my Cora that he was relieved to walk away. He said you were not very bright, you were lazy and he held disdain for your incessant gaming..." Tor's eyes swept her pointedly. "Amongst other things."

Her face had paled before she whispered, "That cannot be."

Oh dear.

She *was* into Noc. She *did* try. And she failed.

Poor Cora.

Tor didn't reply.

"That can't be," she repeated softly, her eyes searching Tor's face.

She saw the truth, dropped her head and her shoulders slumped as she looked to the floor.

"Cora, your king demands your eyes," King Ludlum commanded and, slowly, she looked at him. "You will be sequestered in solitude, except for your guard, at Merrygate for the rest of your days."

The air in the room changed again. Both of the Goodes, I noted, looked relieved at this announcement. Orlando sent a dark look to Tor who was also glancing at his brother so I couldn't see his reaction. After I caught Orlando's look, I turned to Cora to see she was about as happy as Orlando.

"Merrygate?" she whispered.

"It is a lovely property with vast gardens. You will be happy there."

"It's a five day ride from anything!" she cried.

"Indeed, and also surrounded by sacred land which means it will be difficult for you to find trouble," King Ludlum replied.

"But—"

"I could give you a choice," King Ludlum interrupted. "You can live your days in Merrygate or you can live them in the dungeons of Castle Tristrom. Your choice."

She snapped her mouth shut.

Well, with that reaction, I guessed Castle Tristrom wasn't Club Med.

"Merrygate, your grace," she forced out.

"Excellent, it is decided," King Ludlum started to stand but Cora spoke again.

"Will I be allowed to see my parents and Rosa?"

King Ludlum settled back in his seat. "They have a new daughter and sister now."

My body jerked at this announcement, Cora's face froze and he went on.

"But they care about their old one. Although it still astounds me my future daughter-in-law holds any regard for you after your heinous deeds. Nevertheless, Rosa did no wrong, nor did your parents so I do not see any reason to punish *them*.

They will visit you, but as your existence will be held in deepest secret, these visits will be rare so I will advise you to make the most of them when you have them."

Her mouth thinned but she said not a word.

King Ludlum continued and he did it with quiet warning, "And I will remind you, Cora, that your existence is to be held in deepest secret. If you connive in any way to reveal that secret to anyone, it will be considered treason against the crown. Your second such offense. And that one will *not* be handled with the generosity I am bestowing on you today. Is that understood?"

She stared at him, fear plain on her face.

I figured treason didn't buy her a trip to Castle Tristrom but something a lot less fun.

Oh dear.

"Cora, is that understood?" the king prompted.

She stared at him some more before she gave in with a soft, "Yes, your grace."

He nodded, then, pushing to standing, he declared, "We're done here."

Once he was on his feet, he flicked a wrist at the four guards standing at the opposite end of the room. They advanced forward and the king's attention went to the Goodes.

"Say your farewells, my good people, then we will move on from this sad business to the celebration."

The Goodes nodded. Forrest bowed. Dara bobbed a quick curtsy. Then they rushed to their daughter and crowded her as she was led out of the room.

Cora didn't look back. Cora had no words for Tor or for me. Cora had no words for Orlando, who put his neck out and expended considerable energy saving her sister. Cora was thinking about Cora.

Stupid cow.

Sliding an arm around my waist, Tor turned me to face him and I looked up into his eyes.

"It is done, my love," he murmured. "Go to your sister, share this news. It will bring her relief so she can put it aside and focus on her wedding day."

"Your dad made a compassionate decision, I gather," I murmured back.

"It is his way."

Yeah, I was noticing that. King Ludlum was a decent guy.

I nodded and remarked, "Orlando didn't seem happy about it."

"Orlando rescued a drawn, terrified Rosa from Minerva's clutches. Orlando was also called upon by Algernon to assume my rule while I was in your world, making it so those who witnessed our disappearance did not speak of it, taking on all my responsibilities while I was away at the same time trying to discover the powers that were at work that took me away. Orlando cannot call up much compassion for Cora, the Exquisite."

Hmm.

Understandable.

His head dipped down and he brushed his mouth against mine.

Jeez, I liked it when he did that.

"Go to your sister," he urged quietly when he'd pulled away an inch.

"Okay," I whispered, smiled at him and realized it was over.

Done.

The bad shit was behind us and all we had to look forward to was the good.

That was why my smile got brighter. Tor's arms got tighter when he witnessed it, I got up on tiptoe and touched my mouth to his then moved away.

"See you guys at the wedding," I called, starting to descend the steps that led up to the dais we were on and waving at Orlando and King Ludlum as I went.

"My sweet," Tor called.

I kept walking but looked at him, raising my brows. He pressed his lips together but his eyes lit with humor.

Then he reminded me, "Cora, my love, you're leaving the presence of your king and *two* of your princes."

I stopped, whirled to face them and cried, "Oh shit! Right." Then I dropped into a low curtsy to my king and *two* of my princes.

"Rise, my dear," King Ludlum commanded, his voice shaking with laughter and I rose. "How about we leave such formalities for formal proceedings," he suggested and smiled at me. "We will just be…*us* when it's family."

When it was family.

That felt nice.

"That's cool with me," I told him on a grin and heard Orlando stifle another chuckle.

The king and his handsome son didn't stifle theirs.

"Later," I called, turned and hurried through the throne room.

"Until then, my dear." I heard the king say to my back.

"Erm…later, Cora." I heard Orlando say.

Tor didn't reply but at the door, I turned and saw him huddled with his family. He must have felt my gaze for he looked my way. I caught his eyes and blew him a kiss.

With that, I rushed through the door and through the castle to go help my sister prepare for her wedding.

"My prince," I gasped.

"Eyes," Tor growled and I tipped my head down to look at him, our gazes locked then my body fell forward, my hand landing in the bed by his shoulder as I came.

I was still coming when he flipped me to my back and continued to drive into me, his lips so close to mine, their touch was a whisper and I felt his groan against them when he climaxed.

I rounded his body with all my limbs and the fingers of one hand slid into his hair. His face went into my neck and I felt him kiss me there.

I loved his soft bed. I loved his lush sheets. I loved the room filled with candlelight. I loved the gentle breeze drifting in through the doors opened to an emerald sea. I loved the weight of him on me. I loved the feel of him inside me. I loved his scent in my nostrils. I loved the thickness of his hair.

I loved everything that had anything to do with my fairytale prince.

Therefore, I turned my head and whispered in his ear, "I love you, honey."

He lifted his head and looked down at me through the flickering candlelight, his eyes tender, his face soft.

"And I you, my sweet," he replied quietly.

I bent my neck until my forehead was against his and I smiled.

Then I dropped my head to the bed and noted, "We had a lovely day."

"Indeed," he agreed.

"It's just you and me now," I told him.

"For a time," he replied, his body shifting, his hand sliding so it was resting on my belly that now had the barest hint of a hard, beloved bump. "Then it will be you and me and our son."

"Or daughter."

Without hesitation and without indication of a shred of preference, he repeated, "Or daughter."

I grinned at him. "It's good being a princess."

His hand left my belly and came to my face, his thumb sweeping my cheekbone when he remarked, "This I find surprising."

I tilted my head to the side on the pillow, "You do?"

"Yes, for my princess doesn't *act* like a princess."

I let out a small giggle then informed him, "I'm the new and improved kind of princess."

"Right," he muttered, his mouth twitching.

God, he looked hot when his mouth twitched like that. Then again, he always looked hot.

I wondered if I'd ever think differently and decided I would not.

Not ever.

Not *ever*.

I sighed happily and when I did, I realized I was exhausted.

So I asked, "Are you going to let your princess sleep? I had a long day, danced all night and this kid is beginning to take it all out of me. Yesterday, I fell asleep right in the middle of reading to Clarabelle. Aggie had to peck my hand to wake me up."

"No, I'll not be letting my princess sleep," he answered and I blinked at him.

"You'll not?"

"No, love, you're a princess. You can sleep all day." His head dipped, his face disappearing in my neck. "Your prince gets your nights."

"Tor—"

He nipped my earlobe and commanded, "Quiet."

"Tor!" I snapped.

His lips moved to mine, he kissed me hard, deep and sweet and I was quiet.

Oh well, whatever.

He was right, I was a princess. I could sleep all day.

So I rolled him to his back and then *I* kissed *him*.

My prince's strong arms got tight around me and he kissed me right back.

Epilogue

~

Commotion

Nine months later...

I heard the commotion outside, my head came up from the book I was reading and I saw Clarabelle holding my sleeping, dark-headed three month old son, Hayden Noctorno Hawthorne of the House of Hawthorne, heir to the Kingdom of Hawkvale and the city-state of Bellebryn.

I totally *dug* my son's title as any proud mother of a future king was wont to do.

I saw Clarabelle's head tipped to the side and her sightless eyes were aimed at the window facing the sea. My eyes went there too, but I could see nothing but emerald-green waters and large galleons floating.

The commotion was coming from the street, which was on the opposite side of the house, a location we could not see.

Aggie hopped excitedly on my knee and I looked down at him.

"Chirpity, chirp, chirp," he said, which meant, "Something's happening, Cora."

"I know, Aggie," I whispered then I looked at Clarabelle who instinctively had pulled my son protectively closer to her chest and her head had turned to me. "Is something happening today, Clarabelle?" I asked.

"You are princess of our city, my dear," she reminded me with a kind smile. "Do you know of something happening?"

I shook my head and since she couldn't see me doing it, I said, "No. I—"

I stopped speaking abruptly when I heard the door downstairs fly open, crash back on its hinges and loud, heavy footsteps intermingled with light, clumsy ones were running up the stairs.

Standing as I gave Aggie my finger and he jumped on it, I turned alertly to the door while positioning myself between it, Clarabelle and my son all the while adrenaline flooded my frame.

Since my return, we'd had good times—no *great* times, months of them. Sunny days, family, friends, the safe delivery of the next heir to the throne, which heralded parties and revelry all through Bellebryn and Hawkvale (of which I didn't partake, seeing as I'd just had a kid and was exhausted) but it was all good stuff.

The only pall was that I didn't get to share it with Mom, Dad and Phoebe but the rest was so good, I could live with even that.

Still, whatever that commotion was that led to someone racing up the stairs didn't bode good things and I hoped I didn't have to assume warrior princess mode considering I had no weapon, limited experience, some time had elapsed since I'd wielded daggers, and therefore I was a little rusty.

On this thought, Blanche (fortunately not a threat) suddenly filled the door, her much bigger now toddler at her hip (in fact, the kid should be on his feet, he could walk, just not steadily which was why I figured she was hauling him around, due to her haste), her five-year-old's hand clutched in hers. Such was her dash, he was swinging in her grip, unable to stop himself as his mother came to a dead halt.

"The sergeant-at-arms is heading this way, my princess. You're needed at the castle," she announced.

My heart clenched because I was never "needed at the castle." My son needed me, my husband needed me and Perdita, every once in a while, needed me.

I had a good life, a beautiful life. My time was my own. I was a princess who did my princess gig the way I saw fit (which was the way Tor had finally quit bitching about and just let me be and that was to say friendly and open and often out amongst "my people").

I highly doubted Perdita needing to discuss the week's menus (which we'd agreed two days ago) was what sent Algernon off to get me. If Perdita needed me, she usually waited until I got home if I wasn't home already.

Therefore, I wasted no time, turned instantly to take my son from Clarabelle, lifting my hand so Aggie could perch on my shoulder.

Confirming Blanche's announcement, a loud banging could be heard from downstairs with a shouted, "Princess Cora! Your prince requires you at the castle immediately!"

Algernon.

And it was Tor who needed me.

Hells bells.

What was happening?

Clarabelle lifted Hayden to me, I took him from her and he fussed in his sleep for about two seconds as the transfer was made before he settled.

My baby was a good baby. Quiet and content most of the time, he let it be known in a weirdly commanding way when he was hungry or wanted to be changed (he got this from his father, I decided). But mostly he was happy to take in his surroundings, although that said, there was a weirdness about that too considering, since birth, not kidding, he was alert, almost watchful. As if he could see, sense and process all that was going on around him.

Like I said, it was weird but still, it was cool.

I tucked him close to me, bent quickly to kiss Clarabelle's cheek, murmuring words of farewell, and then straightened and hustled toward Blanche to whom I did the same thing.

Then Hayden, Aggie and I shuffled around Blanche and her son who were moving out of our way so we could quickly leave the room. I headed down the stairs, seeing my personal guard, Geraint, standing at the side of the open door with Algernon in its frame.

Since before Hayden was born, my prince, taking no chances, decreed that if I left the castle and Tor wasn't available, then Geraint went with me.

Geraint was one of Tor's warriors.

No, strike that, according to Tor, he was *the best* of Tor's warriors, tall, broad, muscled, dark-blond hair, light-brown eyes and entirely forbidding. When I met him, he looked so ferocious, so *capable* of being all things warrior, I was thinking he would not like his new duties of looking after a woman and child.

I was wrong.

Sure, he wasn't talkative. He also wasn't friendly (at all). He was broody and intense.

But he took his responsibilities seriously. He was guarding the future queen and the future (future) king of the realm. This was serious business and he communicated that in every action, every move, every tilt of his head or glide of his gaze. I never saw him when he was not fully armed (that was to say, sword at his back, daggers at both sides of his waist and another knife shoved into the side of his right boot). And I never saw him looking tired, distracted or bored.

Never.

Including now.

"Is anything wrong?" I asked when I was halfway down the stairs.

"We need to get you to your prince," Algernon answered, his eyes glued to me and mine went to Geraint.

"Geraint?" I called when I got to the bottom of the steps.

"Swift," he growled.

Geraint, by the way, didn't do anything but growl and when he did it was usually monosyllabic words. Sometimes he'd string two or three monosyllabic words together but this was rare.

I did not know why he wasn't very communicative but, considering the amount of time I spent with him, I had attempted to coax this information out of him. And when that didn't work, pry it out of him. That also didn't work so I gave up on him and asked Tor.

Tor's response was slightly more informative, but not by much.

"War is war, sweets, and most things that need to be done during war for any soldier are not enjoyable," he explained but his eyes held mine and I saw his were somber when he went on. "And then there are things that need to be done during war by some soldiers that are even *less* enjoyable. Geraint was my warrior who did *those* things."

I decided, after getting this explanation, that I didn't need further information.

Therefore, as I did whenever Geraint deigned to speak (or, more accurately, growl), I did what I was told.

I hastened out the door and saw that Algernon was not alone. There was a small guard (if twenty could be considered small) and this did not give me a good feeling since I had never, not once, had a guard of any number except one (Geraint). My feeling got worse when they moved instantly to flank me all around, Geraint taking point, Algernon walking close to my side.

I did not quibble. Instead, with the guard, my son and I moved swiftly up the cobbled streets to the castle, through the gates and I sucked in breath and pulled my sleeping son even closer to my chest as I saw what I saw filling the vast courtyard of my home.

Soldiers…

No.

Warriors.

Hundreds of them. All on horses. All with long, black hair plaited or bunched down their backs, wearing pants made of hides, shirts made of hides, swords at a slant at their backs, knives at their belts, boots on their feet, their dark eyes, fierce brown-skinned faces and immensely huge and muscular bodies all on obvious alert.

They looked like a tribe of giant Native Americans without the feathers and such.

And I knew instantly they were Korwahk.

What the heck?

We had, of course, sent several missives to Circe but we had also not had any communication in return. And nothing we said in our letters would lead to a squadron of gorgeous but frightening warriors taking up the courtyard.

As my gaze moved from the Korwahk, I saw standing on the steps to the castle a motley crew of about a dozen men wearing shirts, breeches, boots, and they were also armed. Motley they might have been but they were also all handsome and well-built, just rough around the edges. They, too, were obviously on alert.

And lastly, there was a phalanx of about fifty soldiers opposite the Korwahk. These men were mounted and looked to be from Hawkvale except the colors of the Vale (as well as Bellebryn) were blue and green and those soldiers were wearing red and gold, which meant they were from somewhere else.

I quit looking around as Geraint led the way to the steps. I held Hayden close, my guard peeled off and Algernon guided me up the steps to the top where Tor was striding out the front door.

My heart settled at seeing him then skipped at the look on his handsome face.

Yes, if the guard didn't say it and the courtyard filled with warriors didn't say it, Tor's face said it.

Something was wrong.

"Your grace," Algernon muttered, being far more formal than usual, likely due to the huge audience he had, before he dipped his chin respectfully, lifted his hand silently for Aggie to hop on (and Aggie, clearly feeling the vibe, did this without even a chirp) and then Algernon fell back soundlessly.

Without a word, Tor expertly pulled Hayden out of my arms, tucked him to the side of his chest in the curve of his own arm and wrapped his other arm around my shoulders, quickly escorting us into the castle.

It was safe to say Tor adored his son. Considering his days were filled doing prince things and mine were filled doing princess things (which was to say, whatever the hell I wanted to do and what I wanted to do was be a mom so I spent all my time doing that even when I was doing other things too), Tor had decreed in the nights he got Hayden.

This, of course, came with me being around as well (which was also a Tor edict but I didn't quibble about that either seeing as being with my husband and son was where I wanted to be anyway). But if Hayden was awake, Tor was holding him and playing with him. When Hayden needed to be put down to sleep, Tor took him to his crib. Even if Hayden needed to be changed, Tor did that too.

He was totally a hands-on dad.

Something which I liked, like, *a lot*.

I could definitely say that my hot husband went off-the-charts hot when he was with his son.

Definitely.

It was also safe to say that Tor was relieved my pregnancy was over. Although I had an easy one, some morning sickness just after we arrived back from my world, but that was it, my labor and delivery was not Tor's happiest memory even if the end result was spectacular (what could I say?—our son was gorgeous).

Actually, it wasn't that bad, although the labor lasted for eight hours which definitely sucked. But the midwife explained that amount of time was not unusual and the delivery didn't take long at all (though it felt, at the time, like it took freaking *years*).

My prince, however, did not like to see me in pain, and since he didn't leave my side from start to finish, he had hours of it, just like me. Furthermore, his father had lost three wives, his mother had died while having him, my mother nearly died while having my sister and my sister *did* die.

Therefore, my cries, moans, whimpers, and eventually shouts were pure torture to him and he did not hide it.

Through it, I did my best to make him understand it was all natural but considering I was going through labor and having a baby without fun stuff like drugs, I wasn't very successful in these endeavors.

I didn't like that he so clearly suffered right along with me (maybe, if it could be believed, he'd suffered more).

But still, I loved him all the more for it.

And although relieved my pregnancy was over, that didn't mean at his earliest opportunity after Hayden made his entrance into this world Tor didn't go about another attempt, or, I should say, spectacularly going about a *number* of *regular* attempts (as usual) to get me that way again.

When we were out of earshot and up the first four of the curving, marble stairs, I whispered, "Honey, what's—?"

He cut me off, eyes forward, arms still engaged in cradling his son and holding me close, "We've had disturbing news, my love."

Damn.

"What's that?" I asked and Tor didn't answer until we were at the top of the stairs and several feet down the wide hall.

There, he stopped me and curled me into his front so my son, my prince and me were all in a close huddle.

This, normally, would make me feel great. At the troubled look in Tor's beautiful blue eyes, I didn't feel great.

I lifted a hand and rested it on the wall of his hard chest just as I slid my other arm around his waist in a successful effort to make our huddle closer.

"Frey Drakkar and Apollo Ulfr of Lunwyn and King Lahn of Korwahk are all here," he told me and I blinked.

I knew of Lunwyn and I knew of Korwahk. In fact, I knew quite a bit about both considering much had happened in Lunwyn (the icy country to the far north of the continent where Hawkvale was), the former Middleland (which had been its own country until a recent war meant it reverted back to Lunwyn) and, obviously, Korwahk. Tales had spread widely of what had gone down in Lunwyn, Middleland and Korwahk and all of this had something directly or indirectly to do with the now deposed and really not well-liked King Baldur of the former Middleland, who was currently in exile on some island somewhere.

I also knew of these places because, obviously, Circe of my world was the Korwahk Queen.

"Why are they here?" I asked.

He took in breath through his nose but didn't lose eye contact before he started, "Firstly, I have just received the news that Frey, who is a long-time friend of mine, is wed to the Ice Princess of Lunwyn."

I nodded, knowing this including the fact that Frey Drakkar was a friend of Tor's and also knowing he sounded like one seriously cool dude considering he commanded dragons (awesome!) and elves (also awesome!) and he was like a Viking or something to boot.

Further, everyone had heard of him and the Princess of Lunwyn considering their love match was a tale told far and wide seeing as their marriage was arranged and yet, within months, they were clearly, obviously and unguardedly head over heels in love.

Tor went on, "That isn't the news, Cora. The news is, I learned from Frey that Princess Sjofn, he calls her Finnie," his arm gave me a squeeze and his voice dipped low, "she is of your world."

I blinked and felt my lips part.

Then I whispered, "No joke?"

Some of the intensity in his eyes shifted as his lips twitched and he whispered back, "No joke, love."

"Wow," I breathed.

Cool!

He gave me another squeeze and the intensity came back into his eyes as he continued, "You will meet her very soon. As you will meet Circe, who came with Dax Lahn. They're all in my study."

This time, my mouth dropped open.

Cool!

Tor kept talking, "They do not come with good tidings, Cora."

My mouth snapped shut and my heart squeezed.

Then I whispered, "What?"

His head dipped closer as his arm held me and our son closer and he said gently, "Those who hold magic in Korwahk, and Lavinia of Lunwyn, a very powerful witch, received word from the gods. These were promptly communicated to Dax Lahn and Frey with all due haste."

Word from the gods?

The gods of this world talked to people?

I had no chance to ask this but Tor answered it anyway. "This is highly unusual, in fact, I have never heard of this happening before, my love, not ever."

Oh boy.

Tor kept going.

"Not knowing the others had received like communications, due to what was communicated, they all immediately moved to come here to meet with me to form an alliance at the same time sending out several scouts to ascertain if the information the gods communicated is correct."

"What information?"

Tor did not hesitate to reply.

"The information that Baldur has escaped his island and aligned with Minerva and two malevolent witches of Hawkvale. They have seized Cora, the Exquisite for reasons we do not currently know and they are very close to instigating some nefarious plan, the results of which they hope to achieve, we also do not know."

I stared at him as my body got tight.

"Was the information correct?" I asked.

He held my gaze and said carefully, "The one scout who returned, a Korwahk warrior, confirmed it was."

The *one* scout?

Oh my God.

"Tor," I whispered, pressing closer to him and our still sleeping son.

"These witches are known, Cora," he told me softly. "They are not good women. They have been watched and it is known they have been amassing power for decades. We are not unaware of this situation."

"That's good, isn't it?"

"Yes, love, it is. What is not good is that we *have* been taken unaware by their recent movements, which were entirely covert. Further, we have no idea what they intend to do. We have no idea why they have taken Cora. The allegiances they have made are more than a little concerning, including Baldur, who was not a good man before by any stretch of the imagination but who now more than likely has vengeance on his mind. And, lastly, they hold massive power."

I closed my eyes.

"Sweets, eyes," Tor whispered so I opened them. "Lavinia of Lunwyn is also very powerful. So is Frey, the power at his command is beyond anything consider-ing he controls the dragons and commands the elves. And lastly, Lavinia has called to a witch of your world, a woman named Valentine. A woman Lavinia says is the most powerful witch she's ever seen. She is also a woman who has agreed, for payment, to help."

"Well that's good too, isn't it?" I semi-repeated.

Tor nodded.

I slightly relaxed.

Tor kept going.

"Over the months since our return from your world, I have also received many reports that Minerva is weakened, significantly. The power it takes to move beings between the different worlds as well as the armies of vickrants and toilroys she was forced to create when she was playing with us has reduced her to her weakest in centuries."

I relaxed a bit more and whispered, "Good."

"Further," Tor continued, "my warriors have had years of peace but they are warriors. Even in peace, they train and keep sharp. And they know battle. They also know triumph. They, too, are formidable."

I relaxed more and nodded.

Tor wasn't done. "And Frey's men are also highly trained in a variety of ways, including using daggers, bows and swords but also cunning and stealth."

I sighed, relaxed even more and nodded yet again.

Tor still wasn't done. "And Frey's cousin, Apollo, is a revered strategist."

"So we're good," I whispered and I felt him still so I instantly went back to not relaxed.

"I fear, sweets, we face war and in war, until victory is achieved, you never make the mistake of thinking you are..." He hesitated then finished, "Good."

Damn.

His head dipped so his forehead was touching mine and he murmured, "I do not wish to concern you but I do need to prepare you."

I sucked in my lips and nodded again, my forehead rolling against his. His arm gave me a squeeze and he lifted his head an inch but held my eyes.

"It does not escape me, Cora, or the men in my study, that we are all married to women from your world, our feelings for our mates run unusually deep and the loss of any one of you would be devastating not only to us, your husbands, but also to each of our countries. For the gods of the countries of Korwahk and Lunwyn to speak to the witches of these places and warn them of what is happening in Hawkvale, instruct them to come to our aid…" he trailed off.

I held my breath.

Tor finished, "Frey, Lahn and I, as well as Apollo and Lavinia, feel this is not a coincidence."

I let my breath out on the guess, "Minerva isn't done with us."

He confirmed my guess. "Minerva isn't done with us. In fact, sweets, I would assume our victory over her and her carefully laid plans, the amount of power she had to use and still not win, is sticking in her throat. And Baldur is not done with Frey, Finnie, Circe and Lahn, all of whom he holds deep antipathy for for a variety of reasons. But there is more. This is larger than both Minerva and Baldur. We just do not know how large it is or what, if anything, it has to do with you, Circe and Finnie."

Great.

Just great.

"So, what now?" I asked.

He studied me a moment.

Then he said, "Now, you meet your compatriots, their husbands, their children and then you amuse the women, as only you can do, while the men prepare for war."

Great.

Just *great.*

Still, on the bright side, I was looking forward to meeting Circe and this new chick, Finnie. Spending time with folks from home would be awesome.

And anyway, I was a princess, and someday I would be queen. I was also a warrior's wife (and a part-time warrior princess not too long ago) so I had to suck it up.

Not every minute could be a fairytale even in a fantasyland. I'd learned that the hard way.

So, I sucked in breath, pulled slightly away from my husband, bent to kiss my (still! he was such a good baby) sleeping son's forehead, squared my shoulders and through this, I held his gaze.

"All right, baby," I said, "let's go do this. I'll amuse the girls so you boys can plan to kick some bad guy ass."

Tor stared at me a moment before his eyes warmed with a light that could only be described as proud right before he started to chuckle.

Then he leaned in, brushed his lips against mine, turned and guided me to his study.

The double doors were opened and we walked right through, took two steps in and we stopped.

And, for my part, I stared.

I did this because there were three men in that room that were hotter than hot. Tor, of course, beat them all in the hot department (mostly because he was my husband) but not by much.

Lahn was huge, dark, fierce and, I will repeat, h-u-g-e *huge*.

Frey was only slightly less huge and fierce, dark-haired, brown-green-eyed (or green-brown-eyed, I couldn't say which exactly, but I could say I could happily spend some time trying to figure it out, up close, if I already didn't have my own hot guy who ruled a city-state and would eventually rule a nation) and g-o-r-g-e-o-u-s *gorgeous*.

And Apollo was also slightly less huge, but no less fierce looking than Lahn, green-eyed (definitely green, gorgeous green, *unbelievable* green) and h-a-n-d-s-o-m-e *handsome*.

And there were also three women, and considering their men held two of them closely, protectively, the same as Tor was right then holding me, I knew which ones were Finnie (white-blonde hair, ice-blue eyes, stunning, wearing breeches, boots and an old-fashioned shirt, her husband cradling a baby just like mine was doing with ours) and Circe (gold hair, gold eyes, beautiful, wearing a kickass sarong (a sarong!) sandals, a thin-knit, short-sleeved sweater type thing, really cool jewelry and she *and* her big husband were cradling babies, his swaddled baby had blonde hair, hers had black).

And after taking them all in, including Lavinia of Lunwyn who wasn't claimed in a close cinch by a hot guy, it was Circe whose eyes I caught.

And when I did, I smiled and whispered, "Harold says hi."

I watched her remarkable eyes get bright and her big, badass, hide-shirted, hide-pants-wearing, sword-bearing, knife-belt-sporting husband pulled her even more protectively closer as she smiled back.

Valentine

"You are here," she heard the deep, appealing male voice say, her body turned and her eyes went from the beautiful vista of the glassy dark sea and its tall-masted ships to the beautiful vision of the tall, dark man who formed out of the shadows of the castle beyond him.

"I am here," she agreed to the obvious.

He stopped on the balcony six feet from her.

"I have waited some time," he informed her and the witch Valentine Rousseau knew by the tone of his voice he did not like waiting.

"I know you have," she said softly.

"And I have heard no word," he told her something else she knew and something else it was clear he did not like.

"Ulfr," she whispered, not believing she was going to do this but she was going to do this. So before she could stop herself from doing it, she said quickly, "I will return your payment."

He stared at her, his green eyes gleaming even in the dark night illuminated only by the soft lanterns of the city.

Finally, he guessed, "She is dead in your world too."

Valentine shook her head.

Ulfr's brows rose. "Then you have not found her?"

"I have found her," Valentine said carefully and she watched his big, heavenly body grow taut, which made it even more heavenly.

"Then, what—?" he started.

"In my world," she quickly interrupted him, "Ilsa is married."

It must be said, as she watched his heavenly body grow *more* taut, Valentine found it a fascinating show.

He remained silent and it wasn't until he spoke again that she understood he did this to consider his options.

Then he declared the one he'd chosen. "This matters not."

It was a surprising, dictatorial choice but Valentine couldn't help but think he was right. It didn't matter. With her eyes beholding the specimen of man before her, Valentine knew a woman could love a man in her world and be taken from him and offered to this man and she'd eventually forget her other man existed. She knew this even though she knew very little about Apollo Ulfr. What she did know was the depth of his capacity for love and her experience was that only three men had its equal and they were all of this parallel world and they were all currently residing in this castle.

Unfortunately for him, the one woman he wanted, it was Valentine's considered opinion, was the one woman in both their worlds he had no hope of winning.

"It does," Valentine told him cautiously.

"It does not," he returned immediately.

"Ulfr—" she started.

"Bring her to me," he ordered.

"Ulfr, it's my understanding you are at the cusp of war," she reminded him.

"This is my concern, not yours."

Valentine took in a delicate breath.

Then she told him what he needed to know.

"Ulfr, Ilsa of my world is married—"

He cut her off, "You have already told me that and—"

She interrupted him in turn, "To *you*."

Ulfr's body again grew tight and she heard him pull in a sharp breath.

Then he whispered, "To me?"

"To the you of my world," Valentine explained.

Ulfr made no response.

Valentine continued, "This is not unusual. In fact, it's highly usual."

Ulfr's eyes moved to study the sea but she knew he didn't see it.

They came back to her. "This also matters not."

Love.

Goddess, but this man could love.

Blinded by it.

"Ulfr—"

"It matters not," he repeated.

"Ulfr," Valentine leaned in, "it *does*. And it does *not* because she is deeply in love with her husband as you are with your dead wife. It does because the you of my world is *not* a good man. He is a *bad* man. A *very* bad man. Foul. Selfish. Criminal. Cruel. And the reason I had trouble finding her was because she is on the run from him. She will not want you, Ulfr. She will not want anything to do with you. If you bring her here to spend time with you, she'll—"

"Bring her to me," he demanded again.

She took a step toward him and, uncharacteristically losing control in defense of a fellow female (or at all), she hissed, "You must allow me to explain. He, the other you, who *looks* just like you and *sounds* just like you has *not* been good to her and when I say that, Ulfr, I mean in every way a man cannot be good to a woman. She fears him and she hates him with an intensity it will be impossible for her to grow to—"

"Bring her to me."

"Ulfr!" she snapped and he leaned in threateningly, so threateningly, even Valentine reared back.

She might be a witch, a powerful one, but he was a man, a large one *and* a powerful one. And she was human, not immune to being hurt, and he was a man who knew what he wanted and would do anything to get it.

"This is *my* concern, not *yours*," he growled. "Bring…her…*to me*."

Valentine held his jade eyes.

Then she leaned back.

"So be it," she whispered.

Apollo Ulfr leaned back too, his body relaxed, and he stated, "Tomorrow. I will tell you the time and the place."

Valentine nodded.

Ulfr did not nod back. He turned on his boot and walked away.

It was a good show, and even after that scene, Valentine enjoyed it.

When she lost sight of him, she sighed delicately and turned back to the sea. Moving to the balustrade, she rested her hands on it and felt rather than saw the other presence who had been hiding in the shadows move out of them and come to her side.

"He will not succeed," Valentine informed the sea.

"Love is powerful," Lavinia of Lunwyn whispered in return.

"Indeed, love is everything but hate is the other side to that coin and it holds equal power."

"Mm," Lavinia murmured then asked softly, "But the distance around that coin is not far, is it, Valentine?"

This was true. The coin of love and hate flipped and it did so regularly.

Still.

Valentine stared at the sea and, again uncharacteristically, she felt unease therefore she shared quietly, "Ilsa is broken."

"As is our Apollo," Lavinia replied and that was the truth.

"But he does not love the Ilsa of my world. He loves a dead Ilsa," Valentine reminded her friend.

Valentine knew Lavinia turned her head to look at her when she spoke again.

"Three times, Valentine, *three*, love has spanned universes. You've seen it happen once and you know of the other two times. He loves a dead woman, he mourns her, unabated. But that does not mean he cannot find love again, a different love with a different woman who is yet the same. He has known beauty but his full story is untold. And she has not known beauty. Who is to say that he cannot guide her to beauty? A man such as him is capable of many feats, even those that seem impossible." She paused and whispered, "Love has its own magic, Valentine, you know that too."

Valentine looked to the other witch.

"You don't know how bad it is. I don't see good things. He pines for a dead woman. The Ilsa of my world will not thank him for tearing her from her world, no matter that that world holds nothing but terror and flight, and forcing her to live with a man who physically is, even though he is not, a man she fears and detests all the while he wants nothing but his dead wife back, not *her*. She is not the Ilsa he loves and that is all he will see. Until he comes to understand she is not the woman he so desperately wants returned and then what? Disappointment, if she is lucky. Anger, if she is not."

"There are other possible outcomes," Lavinia returned.

"Indeed, but there are also those two."

Lavinia held her eyes before she smiled and whispered, "We shall see."

That was the truth too.

Valentine sighed and wondered why she cared.

She came to no conclusions. It was simply that, unfortunately, she did.

She looked back to the sea.

"I have work to do," she said softly.

"You do, indeed," Lavinia agreed. "As do I."

She did. Troubled times lay ahead and if Valentine was not taking back trunks of jewels and gold, she would have nothing to do with it.

Valentine did not have a good feeling about what was to come for this universe.

Not at all.

And she'd been trapped in that universe during war and she had not enjoyed it even a little bit.

That said, the work she had to do at that moment didn't have to do with the troubles this world faced. It also didn't have to do with Apollo Ulfr and his blind devotion to a dead woman.

It had to do with something else.

Something she was not doing for payment.

Something she was doing just for fun.

And also, since she seemed to be growing soft of heart recently (also unfortunately), something she was doing for love.

Then again, love was everything so she forgave herself her soft heart…this time.

Valentine turned back to her friend. "Until tomorrow."

Lavinia lifted her chin and smiled.

Valentine lifted both hands then, moments later, in a mist of green, she disappeared.

She reappeared not in New Orleans, her home.

No, she reappeared in a living room in Seattle.

"Jesus, fuck! What the fuck? Who the fuck are you?" the man walking out of his kitchen carrying a bottle of beer and spying her in his living room burst out.

Valentine allowed herself an indulgent moment to study the extremely handsome Noctorno Hawthorne of her world.

Then she said words he would undoubtedly understand immediately.

"Cora needs you."

His powerful body went statue-still and he glared at her but behind his blue eyes he was alert and he didn't even attempt to veil his concern.

He transferred his glare to the ceiling.

Then he muttered, "Fuck."

At that, finally, Valentine smiled her cat's smile.

*The next tale from Fantasyland, **Broken Dove**, is available now.*

Glossary of Parallel Universe

~

Places, seas, regions in the Kristen Ashley's Fantasyland Series

Bellebryn—(place) Small, peaceful, city-sized princedom located in the Northlands and fully within the boundaries of Hawkvale and the Green Sea (west)

Fleuridia—(place) Somewhat advanced, peaceful nation located in the Northlands; boundaries to Hawkvale (north and west) and the Marhac Sea (south)

Green Sea—(body of water) Ocean-like body of water with coastlines abutting Bellebryn, Hawkvale, Lunwyn and Middleland

Hawkvale—(place) Somewhat advanced, peaceful nation located in the Northlands; boundaries with Middleland (north), Fleuridia (south and east) and the Green Sea (west) and Marhac Sea (south)

Keenhak—(place) Primitive, warring nation located in the Southlands; boundaries with Korwahk (north) and Maroo (west)

Korwahk—(place) Primitive, warring nation located in the Southlands; boundaries with the Marhac Sea (north) and the nations of Keenhak (southeast) and Maroo (southwest)

Korwahn—(place) Large capital city of Korwahk

Lunwyn—(place) Somewhat advanced, peaceful nation in the farthest reaches of the Northlands; boundaries to Middleland (south), the Green Sea (west) and the Winter Sea (north)

Marhac Sea—(large body of water) Separates Korwahk and Hawkvale and Fleuridia

Maroo—(place) Primitive, warring nation located in the Southlands; boundaries to Korwahk (north) and Keenhak (east)

Middleland—(place) Somewhat advanced nation with tyrant king located in the Northlands; boundaries to Hawkvale (south), Fleuridia (south), Lunwyn (north) and the Green Sea (west)

[The] Northlands—(region) The region north of the equator on the alternate earth

[The] Southlands—(region) The region south of the equator on the alternate earth

Winter Sea—(large body of water) Arctic body of water that forms the northern coast of Lunwyn, filled with large glaciers

Made in the USA
Las Vegas, NV
10 May 2022